WRATH

THE FAITH TRILOGY
BOOK 2

NICK NIELSEN

Edited by
LESLIE WATTS

LUMINIS PRESS

PROLOGUE

HELLO.

You're back.

It didn't put you off?

It did, me … at least at the start.

Well, we're going to pick up twelve weeks after the last.

Buckle up. Get ready.

1

I TURN down the last road. Old brick houses line both sides, with the occasional two-storey apartment building wedged in between. Most have tattered white trim and balconies so rusted they look set to fall off.

The rambling suburban area lies several miles to the east of the city centre and close to London's inner ring road – the perfect place for a pickup.

My eyes take in the T-junction at the end of the block, the target address on the far side, while time counts down in my head. Only fifteen minutes left. Still, I risk slowing my steps.

I scan the street. A guy wanders the pavement, sipping from a can. A couple of mothers push battered strollers. No one is eyeing me or the destination, and I make sure not to glance at it.

A group of kids round the corner. All male, all torn jeans, baggy tops, and attitude, and all swaggering in my direction. I fix my eyes on the leader. The guy narrows his gaze at me and then turns to prattle at the others. One gives another a shove. I sidle to the edge of the pavement and continue on.

When they're a foot away, I see a blur of movement in my peripheral vision, and my gaze shoots to the side as a grey figure dashes out of sight around the opposite corner. I stumble to a halt, that sense of having been watched prickling up my spine.

A stalker? Or worse … a thing*?*

The testosterone display shuffles past, and I sniff the air, my eyes locked on the end of the block. No grey-clothed figure reappears, and the T-junction remains clear up ahead.

With shoulders tense, I force myself toward it, break into a run for the final fifty feet, and then spin around the corner.

More battered houses. More apartment buildings. And a couple of shops line both sides of the street. I search the pavements. No sign of grey, no one hanging around. Only a few mopeds whizzing by, the traffic still heavy for the evening commute.

My eyes find the building opposite. The pickup address. It resembles a few of the other blocks – multiple flats abandoned with several of the windows scarred by soot – aside from one nasty difference. A mouth-like entrance descends into a garage beneath, gaping and dark, and broken bricks lie scattered across the opening like crooked teeth.

My breathing speeds up. I hate cramped spaces. I feel as if I'm already deep underground, the walls squeezing in on me and the ceilings pressing down. And *there*. A thin shaft of metal pokes out from one side of the garage entrance, glinting in the dying sunlight.

My insides plunge, and I don't even check the road before I just barrel across it, my pulse thumping. A car horn blares, but I keep going, hurrying to the garage opening and into shadow.

The sentry steps directly out into my path, the entire gun visible now, slung across him.

"Runner," I say, chest heaving.

"You're late," he snaps. "Package has already been here twenty minutes. You were expected two fucking hours ago."

"Can't do that," I mutter.

"*What?*" He grips the gun tighter.

"I mean, sure," I say, fake a smile, and then take a half step toward the guy.

But he doesn't move out of the way, just squares his shoulders.

My rage sparks, my thoughts still, and my internal count starts up, the veil pulling back automatically from my senses. Energy builds at my core. My fists clench tighter—

I scrunch my eyes shut, forcing my thoughts on and the veil back into place. The energy diminishes.

My head turns. The shadows on the street are already lengthening with less than a bloody hour till night falls. And the sentry continues to stand firm in front of me, blocking my path.

Leaning further out of the garage, I fix my gaze on a point across the road. "Wait, is that ..." I start, keeping the guy in my peripheral vision.

The sentry's eyes automatically follow mine. He edges forward to see. I tense my stomach and spin around him.

"Hey!" he yells and grabs for me with his free hand.

I duck under the swinging arm, and the barrel of his gun clunks me on the temple. My head reels, causing me to stumble, and I barely keep my feet.

The guard lunges again, but I dodge and then scurry beyond his grasp. My vision remains blurry as I head down the spiralling ramp. After a moments, his thumping footsteps cease behind, and I continue into darkness.

First level. Second level. The scent of fumes gradually replaces the smell of damp and piss. And along with my heavy breathing, the familiar sense of constriction builds in my chest the deeper I go. A low voice pricks my ears.

"We're providing a key service. Corporate moles and hackers make online encryption insufficient nowadays."

The company sales-speak echoes around the concrete walls.

I try to focus on it, but my concentration keeps slipping, my head starting to pound.

"For sensitive packages – legal papers, prototype designs, secret patents – physical delivery with decryption devices is becoming the prime choice."

I hurry faster down to the base of the garage. An armoured car sits parked between concrete pillars, the interior bulbs the only source of light. Two more sentries stand poised on either side of it while four people are grouped around the bonnet, one guy talking.

"The packages have already been six hours on the road," the boss says. "We've taken them as far as is safe by car. Now you're the last leg. It's a high-value delivery, which means a high rate."

Two of the four shuffle excitedly. I pad forward and listen again, trying to place the boss's voice. The guy goes quiet and swivels in my direction. They all do.

The silence and darkness envelop me, images of the growing dusk outside needling at my mind, and the ache grows behind my temples. I try to get my breathing under control.

"Well?" the boss says to me, his voice dangerous and low.

I've not met him before – thin, balding, and intense-looking with an expensive suit hanging from gangly limbs. Nor the other runners to his sides. Two of them are older, stocky, with matching shaved heads and cruel smiles. The third runner avoids my gaze. He has long hair, a hooded top, and is younger – probably his first or second run. Poor bastard.

Still, the boss stares at me. Prickling disquiet climbs my body, and words of apology rush to my lips. But I silence them, keeping my mouth shut as I stride toward him. I take up position next to Tweedledee and Tweedledum and just hold the boss's gaze.

Eventually, the guy shakes his head and turns away. "As I was saying," he continues, "speed and delivery rate determine your standing and your pay. And of course, who ends up delivering the real package."

The twins mutter with anticipation. The boss raises a finger, and one of the guards strides to the armoured car and grabs something from the back.

Four sets of envelopes – a lot of misdirection.

The sentry lines them up side by side on the bonnet of the car, and the twins eye them expectantly. I keep my gaze on the boss.

"Now for the specifics," he says. "Stalkers."

Both older runners grimace.

"Our client has some big competitors, and we've collected intelligence about a potential hit," the boss continues. "They'll be coming after you, probably with an entire team: coordinators, spotters, grabbers. And we know they're hacking CCTV, pulling headshots of runners from previous deliveries. You have to be prepared."

The image comes of the grey figure outside, but concentrating on it, my head pounds harder.

"If you're taken, you know the protocol," the boss says. His gaze lingers on the younger runner. "Keep quiet. Say nothing."

"And no one's coming to get you," I mutter.

The boss glares at me and then raises his voice to the others. "Your meet point in the city centre will be in here," he says and indicates the smaller envelopes attached to the larger packages. "Memorise and destroy it. Delivery window ..." He checks his watch. "Fifty-six minutes."

There are quick intakes of breath. "No way, man," Tweedledee says. "It's four miles. That means taking major routes. It's too dicey."

The boss gives a faint shrug and then points at me. "We have our late friend to thank for that," he says.

He turns to the packages on the bonnet. Tweedledum ripples his biceps, leans in, and goes to barge me out of the way.

The fire burns inside. My thoughts still automatically, and again the veil peels back, energy building in my feet and my torso. I tense my shoulder, and when the guy hits me, he bounces off, the impact hardly registering.

I spin and shoot my arms up to shove him backward. Then I stop as familiar images form from my dreams, and I scour the darkness at the rear of the garage.

Nothing there.

I force a slow breath. The veil slides back into place.

The boss turns back to us, packages in hand. Tweedledum fixes me with a glare and steps closer to the boss along with his twin. I squeeze my fingers together and then force myself up beside them.

The boss distributes the envelopes to the other three runners. "Get to your destination, find your contact," he says. "And be quick. We're already behind schedule."

Packages in hand, the others turn and bolt for the up-ramp. I go to grab my package, but the boss yanks it out of my grasp, avoiding my eye.

"Lateness, a bad habit," he says, his voice all patronising. Then, after a pause, he turns to me. "I've examined your track record. You used to be good … no doubt, but your times have been slipping. And this isn't the first instance you've been late. Is it?" He makes a clicking sound with his tongue.

I just stare back, embers sparking in my chest.

"You're on two warnings. A third is suspension … or maybe even termination, and we *will* do it," he says and cracks a thin smile. "We simply can't have the lack of respect. It sets a poor example." He heaves a sigh and continues in a relaxed tone. "So, I think we'll be hanging around here for a little while longer."

He places my envelopes back on the bonnet, in easy reach.

Fucker.

Then he pulls out his phone and makes a call. "Runners departed, delivery window started," he says, then disconnects.

I eye the package.

"Termination," he says again, his voice soft, "and with

your lack of prior employment record, we'll make sure no other company hires you." He shrugs. "No job, no future."

My teeth grind, and the pledge I gave Natasha sounds in my head … *never thieve again.*

The bastard smirks and starts scrolling through messages on his phone while I just stand there like an idiot, my fingers tapping against my sides. Time ticks by. Every minute, the guy checks his watch, and I sniff the air. Still no smell of sulphur. No heat. My insides churn.

After an age – a full ten minutes standing there – he finally nods at me.

"Forty-six minutes," he says. "You may go."

I grab the package from the bonnet and scramble up the ramp. The larger envelope goes into my shoulder bag, and with a pounding head, I try to memorise the contents of the smaller one, the address of the meet point – a street beyond Billingsgate Park, a large public space by London's Docklands. Quite a distance away.

I climb faster and rip up the paper, scattering it in my wake.

Finally, daylight glints through the garage entrance. The sentry's gone as I sprint the rest of the incline and stand blinking in the sudden brightness. The sense of constriction eases a fraction, and I scan the surrounding streets.

More souped-up mopeds speed past, half a dozen cars also – traffic still heavy. A homeless guy shouts from the pavement opposite. And *there* … Another flash of grey clothing – some kind of business suit – disappearing around a corner, two blocks away.

My heart thumps against my ribs. *A stalker?* That makes no sense. If they know the pickup location, why not hit it earlier?

I shake myself and dart across the road, turning toward the city centre. The network of residential streets follows a rough grid pattern, and I choose a smaller side street and start to run.

No one gives chase.

Out in the open again, my chest eases further, the sky above me once more, and the familiar rows of houses and tower blocks stretch out on either side. The usual haze hangs in the air – dust from crumbling brickwork along with the smog from rusted engines – heavy in my lungs. Sweat trickles down my sides. Temperature records being broken every day, and it's still only June.

With my shoulder bag bumping against my back, I leave the residential area behind and hurry down wide streets, past lines of shops with garish LED displays and security-grated windows. I consult the mental map I've built of the city, the routes ahead larger, more direct, but busier and hence a lot more damn risky.

Still, I press on and barrel across another junction, heading for one of the main roads. The skyscrapers of the Docklands area dot the horizon ahead. Curving forms of glass and steel tower unfeasibly high – the domain of gods among men – and still miles away. With the delivery window ticking down, ten minutes gone, the evening slinks in as shadows creep across my shoulders like fingers tapping at the nape of my neck.

I find myself angling toward a row of five-storey apartment buildings on one side of the road, their rooftops covered with shacks of scavenged wood and metal built by migrants flocking to the city. Many of the structures link the rooftops together, and sometimes it's hard to see where the buildings begin and the shelters end.

My head turns toward an alleyway that runs between two of the buildings, the tang of rubbish so familiar in my nose. And *there* – the metal ladder, halfway down. An old fire escape. It scales the entire block, rusty but solid, and I find my legs slowing as memories swirl.

All those evenings up there. Peeling back the veil, engaging in the priest's many drills. Free-running. I remember leaping between rooftops, the shimmering world spread out in all its majestic detail, the air viscous around my body. It used to save so much time. Out of sight of stalkers, of everyone. As a runner, it made me unequalled.

My jaw clenches with my gaze still on the ladder.

What the hell am I doing?

I turn my head and scan the street for any sign of the *things*. Are they sent by Gabriel?

Time continues to dwindle as I hasten away from the alleyway and then stop. Another image forms – the three of us up there practising under the sky, Father Thomas, me, and … Natasha. Sadness pulls at my chest like a weight. Then an instant later, the flames build, and the weight crumbles to ash. I shake my head at the memory.

So fucking naïve.

I push myself fast down the road, continuing to run across interchanges and focusing instead on every face, every passing vehicle. It's almost three miles and a full thirty minutes before it starts to ring – my internal alarm.

2

I'M BEING SWEPT along a wide pedestrianised street, my gut twisting – my early warning system – while the skin tightens up my back. I force myself not to look around, to keep moving with the flowing crowd.

An army of night servants rushes toward the city centre down one side of the road while the day workers trundle in the opposite direction on the other. They're like lanes of traffic but without the central barrier, and the highway's bounded by office buildings that loom over me like cliffs.

I glance ahead. A major intersection approaches. The pedestrian road crosses a real three-lane highway pounded by the armoured cars of the rich. It links the tunnels underneath the Docklands area with their islands of green beyond the city's stink – the perfect location for stalkers. And fucking avoidable. My eyes dart automatically toward the tops of the buildings, and the internal count starts in my head, my thoughts slowing and the veil peeling back—

No. I wrench my gaze away and hide myself among the surrounding masses. The current speeds up, the interchange fifty yards away, and my target address is only several roads beyond. I lick my lips, though my internal warning system keeps on ringing.

I peer between heads, scan the pavements for stationary people or anyone surveying the crowd.

A large SUV with black-tinted windows stands parked on the far corner of the crossroads, hazard lights flashing. Two guys hover by the driver's door, one gazing across the throng, both in grey business suits.

My feet automatically slow. Suits. SUV. Better resourced than your standard stalker crew.

One of them swivels in my direction. I duck my head and start to creep away across the flow toward the buildings that border my side of the street. No one yells. No one shoves in my direction. And the current pulls me ever closer to the interchange. All the while, my gut twists further, my internal alarm getting louder.

I risk craning my neck again and peer toward the crossroads ahead.

The place is teeming, people swarming everywhere. And I'm being pushed this way and that by the crowd. I can't get a proper look. Plus, I see several black-market hawkers, half my sight blocked by a damn table with a high mesh backboard that some guy's parked right in the centre of our flow. The current pulls to either side of it while a few people stand in the quiet beyond, speaking on phones.

I press my way toward the table, my body jostled constantly, the odour of sweat, of toil, pungent in my nose. I keep shoving, and finally the current eases to calmer waters a few feet from the stall.

My breath comes a little easier while the minions continue to rush around me toward the interchange only fifty feet ahead. One guy beyond the stall pockets his phone and follows along.

I sniff the air and peer at the crossroads through the mesh backboard. No sign of hunched figures or more grey suits; just pedestrians poised on both sides of the highway and brave workers darting between the barrelling cars like fish fleeing crocodiles.

My eyes find the stationary SUV again. The hazard lights continue to flash on the opposite corner of the crossroads, but the two suits have disappeared. The car is now deserted, with other grand carriages rocketing past.

I blink. Have they hitched a ride? Businesspeople scooped up in some plush courtesy car?

An itch climbs my scalp. Have I got this all wrong?

Standing on tiptoes, I risk scanning my surroundings again as the itch becomes shivers lancing my neck. My gaze flicks back to the stall, to the man still waiting beyond the mesh backing, only a few feet from me.

I freeze and force my gaze down again, bringing my feet right up to the table. Then I stare at the seller's merchandise, looking without seeing. The guy beyond the stall stands peering across the flow of people toward the other side of the pedestrianised street, scanning faces. Well built, scarred lip, he's wearing combat trousers and a ripped coat despite the heat. And he's got his finger pressed to an earpiece.

Stalker.

My hand grips the satchel tighter while my thoughts whir. Do I try to sneak past? They're ruthless fuckers. Often ex-gang members. And the boss's warning rings in my head … *they may have headshots.*

The stall owner sidles up to me on my side of the stall. Wiry, pale skin with a threadbare shirt. "Interested, friend?" he asks all too loudly while motioning to his wares.

I wince and swivel away from the backboard. I pick up a glass paperweight from the table while shooting the occasional glance at the stalker.

Still, the guy stares across the flow, his eyes wide with dilated pupils. High on something. And still time advances, my delivery window steadily vanishing. Fifteen minutes left. Plus, the night's coming on fast, and I'm standing fucking still again. My shoulders knit up while my internal alarm clamours, and perspiration coats my legs. The temperature – is it getting hotter? I'm sniffing the air when the stalker slips a shaking hand into the side pocket of his coat. He pulls out a gun, a silencer already attached.

My throat constricts. The guy's only six feet away with nothing but mesh between us. I crouch, preparing to bolt. Then the guy sets off from behind the stall and begins traversing the heavily populated street toward the opposite side. He winds his way across the flow, his arms down by his side, drawing ever further away.

Relief laps inside me like cool waters, and I exhale slowly, closing my eyes for an instant. When they open, I don't turn. Instead, I'm following the stalker's gaze.

And there he is. Another man, shorter, squatter, weaving through the crowd with his eyes on his colleague, wearing a similar tatty coat and undoubtedly the same earpiece. And he's halfway across the busy road already.

My mind hollers for me to get out of there.

The stall owner's voice comes from behind me. "If you touch, you buy."

I nod without thinking and drop the paperweight back onto the table, but my feet don't move as I just stare on at the stalkers. They're moving closer together, like a net across a river, the flow of night servants passing in between them.

Pincer movement.

My head turns, and I scan the crowd further down the street. Office clerks, cleaners, waiters, and waitresses – all with eyes glazed and heads bowed. All heading for the cross-roads. And amid them, a guy with a satchel slung over his shoulder, familiar clothes, and his hood over his head, making him even more bloody conspicuous.

A new weight grips my insides, and I sense my hand reaching down toward the stall. My fingers tighten around something. I yank the oval paperweight to my stomach, swivel away to hide it from the owner, and dive into the crowd after the stalkers.

What the fuck am I doing?

I keep going, shoving my way forward. Both stalkers halt

in the crowd, only twenty feet from each other, the nearest one directly in front of the young runner. And there they turn their faces away and wait, the throng flowing between them.

I scramble in their direction, banging and jostling my way through the moving crowd, still forty feet from the nearer stalker. The young runner keeps coming, the current drawing him on. I keep willing the guy to look up.

The taller stalker rotates his head to align the runner in the corner of his eye, his gun still at his side and earpiece still in place. Someone is probably radioing him the runner's position. Probably mine as well.

I thrust my way harder through the flow but keep getting bounced backward with the crowd moving so damn quickly across me.

Automatically, the count starts in my head, and my thoughts still with a strange ease. The veil peels back, time slows, and spaces appear in the crowd, just like in the priest's training. And then, before I can stop it, the darkness rears up inside – as it always does now behind the veil – a burgeoning abyss of pain and despair. My chest shakes.

Too much.

I force my mind into action … *paperweight, hit the first stalker, alert the younger runner, I can make that throw, years of practice …* and with the cascading thoughts, the shimmering world dissolves, the veil slips back into place, and the despair recedes to a dull ache.

Yet doubts about the plan plague my mind. My pace slows, and I peer through the hustling bodies. The young runner's now only twenty-five feet from the stalkers, and the idiot shows no signs of stopping.

I grit my teeth, take another step, and plant myself amid the rushing crowd. People whisper angrily and shoot me annoyed glances. I fix my gaze on the first stalker, raise the paperweight to my ear, and then let fly …

And miss.

Some fuckwit bumps my arm, and the paperweight careens off into the throng.

The runner's only fifteen feet away from the net. I plunge once again through the tightening crowd, pushing ever harder toward the first stalker while thrusting and wrenching with my hands. But the pedestrians shove my arms out of the way, racing past me for the interchange. The runner continues to draw nearer, the stalker still well out of my reach.

I take a deep breath and bellow into the chaos. *"Hey!"*

A dozen heads turn – eleven plus the first stalker. The taller guy's eyes widen even further at me, and his pupils are like black discs. He spins all the way around and raises his arm.

I leap forward, trample some poor office worker, and dive for the gun in his hand. The stalker expects the tug and pulls back. But I grip the barrel and yank it downward, trapping the bastard's finger behind the trigger guard, and then I twist. The guy yells in pain, opening his hand to retract his finger, and I wrench the gun free.

The guy stumbles backward into the throng and cradles his hand. I glance over his shoulder. The shorter stalker's already shoving his way faster through the masses toward me. Only ten feet away. The young runner's somehow still oblivious, still approaching with the flowing crowd.

I grip the silencer and unscrew it. Jabbing the gun in the air, I squeeze the trigger.

The shot's so loud it's like the bullet's ricocheting inside my skull. I flinch, and the torrent seizes around me. A hundred people drop to the ground and stare about them in panic. But not the second stalker. The guy glares at me with a sneering smile, his pupils just as massive as his colleague's and his shaking arms poised by his sides.

I lower the gun, the grip hot and sweaty in my hand, and glance to my right. The young runner is on his knees, his face pale, gazing between us like some newborn babe. And I'm standing exposed, a hundred more sets of eyes fixed on me, probably spotters and grabbers alike.

The runner swivels and bolts between those crouched at his sides. The second stalker's hand darts to the weapon in his pocket. I yank back my arm, shift my grip around the gun, and hurl it directly at the shorter guy's head.

The stalker's forced to duck. He raises both hands to shield himself, and it's as if someone's pressed the play button on a music video. The hordes careen about us, pushing, shoving, trampling to get away.

I spin and dash in among them, flinging myself toward the crossroads, just waiting for a bullet in the back, the sting of hot pain.

3

No one shoots. I hurry along with the fleeing crowd, bodies all around me, the interchange up ahead. I can't help glancing to the sides and scanning faces for other stalkers as well as the younger runner. No sign at all. And time continues to count down in my head – so much fucking wasted – only twelve minutes to deadline, now.

I scramble across the crossroads. Royal carriages wait backed up behind the escaping crowds, horns blaring at the impertinence. And the SUV flashing the hazard lights remains parked beyond the interchange.

My feet almost skid to a stop. One of the grey-suited guys is still there, now standing on the opposite side of the car. He probably never bloody left. Our eyes meet. Then he spins and jumps into the passenger seat and, as I stare, the SUV accelerates off into the flow of cars and buses.

I throw myself across the highway and into the thronging crowd beyond. I yank multiple times at the zipper of my jacket before finally managing to rip it off. Then I flip it inside out to reveal the smart-looking side and a white shirt underneath.

I barrel down narrow roads, past higher buildings, toward

New Poplar – the area around London's Docklands – my delivery address still a few blocks away.

My feet take me past flashier shops, more expensive bars. Fewer people here means less cover. I choose the busier streets wherever possible, the sound of distant shouting in my ears. And at every corner, I check for the SUV while my mind plots mental maps of the neighbouring roads, charting routes they could take to block me off.

I dash across an intersection and spy a street full of pedestrians, the shouting louder up ahead. I dive down it, plunging into the cover of the crowd, and then glance behind me. Still no sign of the car.

I keep snaking forward, making good progress, till the throng grows thicker. People block all sides of me, unable to move further themselves. I hear more yelling ahead, the sounds of rumbling disquiet. I crane my neck to spy over the flood of heads in front of me, and the breath catches in my throat.

The street's cut off by a huge demonstration – a deluge of grey-clad men and women, twenty people across, making its way along one of the major arterial roads that spans the north of Docklands.

They move arm in arm in their near-identical robes while people stand packed together on the banks of the flow. Several businessmen shout, hands gesticulating, trying to find their way across the murky tide. The Puritans ignore them, placards held above them like flags borne into battle.

They're just one of many Christian denominations, but their movement's spreading like wildfire, society angry and desperate. And with the election approaching, their political party's growing every day, their leader promising to empower the disenfranchised, irrespective of background or religion. I shake my head. Such delusion. The rich will fight ever harder to hang on to what they have.

I fix my gaze on the banks of the grey tide, the din loud in my ears. Workers shout encouragement while the rich yell outrage. No one's getting through. The Puritans walk in tight formation, hand in hand, unstoppable, blocking off the entirety of the Docklands area. The air thrums, and my fingers tighten. Only eight minutes till my window ends.

My head starts to swivel away but something catches my eye – a businessman on the near bank of the demonstration with three guys around him. His security detail. And the man is screaming at them, jabbing a fat finger over the deluge and bouncing up and down, red-faced with fury in his shiny silk suit.

My eyes widen.

Is he really going to try?

I thrust toward him through the crowd, pressing myself forward with elbows, knees, and hands. The throng grows steadily denser, and more people push me back, trying to get through as well. After a while, it becomes impossible to move any further, the bank of the demonstration still thirty yards away.

Again, the count starts up automatically, my thoughts stilling to access the shimmering world. And again, I banish it, all too aware of dusk descending, of the last rays of sunlight glinting off the mirrored high-rises ahead. My pulse starts to beat faster.

I push and strain harder, grabbing shoulders to heave myself on. A guy plants himself directly into my path. He's huge – at least four inches taller than me – with flared nostrils and bulging veins in his trunk-like neck. I go to dart around him when the hulk blocks me off with one arm before raising his other hand behind his head, a massive fist aimed at my face.

In that instant, my thoughts calm, the count starts up, and the veil peels back from my senses automatically. This time I don't banish it. I feel the hulk's punch as it approaches, every vector clear in my awareness, and cinders spark amid the stillness. I duck out of the way, raise my arm, and smash my palm into the back of his fist just as it passes his head, crashing the guy's meathook knuckles into his own temple.

The hulk sways, off-balance. I leap beyond him and beyond the next person, too.

Time continues to slow, the shimmering world erupting around me. Surfaces glimmer, and the sensation comes of being connected to every surface, every person. I can *feel* it all. As I gaze out at the surrounding crowd, it moves as one in my mind – a synchronised dance to be read and understood – and my body flows into gaps the instant they appear.

I weave forward, springing into spaces left and right. The demonstration edge still looms twenty yards away … ten … five. And all the while the darkness grows again at my core, a fathomless void opening up inside me. I clench my stomach and wait for the blessed release … And there it is, a moment later – the fire, the rage. It blazes in my chest, pushes out of darkness, the pain, flaming breath shooting down my arms and legs.

Shut it down. Shut it down.

I spy movement ahead, between the bodies before me. The businessman and his security guards are already cutting a swathe through the grey tide, bulldozing through the demonstrators. The Puritans push back at them, but the guards are big *and* strong. The three of them muscle their way in, creating a tight circle for their boss, and incrementally, they move across the current.

The Puritans at the demonstration's edge surge around the back of the circle, blocking anyone else from leaving the bank. And I'm still ten feet from the front.

I breathe deeply and squash the panic, focusing harder on the shimmering world. I let the red-hot fire take me.

Power rushes through my limbs, the awful strength. I claw at arms, at bodies, yanking myself forward easily. People tumble to the ground, and the crowd scrambles away from me. My vision hazes, spots of black appearing at the edges as my awareness begins shutting down.

Still, I keep fighting, all the way to the frothing edge. The circle of guards remains a few feet from me, and I plunge my hand between the Puritans to grasp one of the security guys by the shoulder. Then I pull, flattening two Puritans in the process and almost dragging the security guy over.

Finally, I manage to haul myself into the manmade circle. It's like a raft on a grey river, the Puritans on all sides of us, and we battle forward with the torrent.

The Puritans yell, "Shame! Shame! Shame!" many of them jabbing their fingers at the businessman and at me.

The three guards fight to create space among them. They surround their boss as a human circle, only six feet across, facing inward with their massive arms spread. The three of them force their way through the grey tide, the businessman and me shuffling forward in the midst of it all.

"Who the fuck are you?" the businessman demands, turning on me.

I peer around, my vision strangely dreamlike. The straining bodies resemble the swells in a shifting sea. The fire still burns inside me, the darkness just underneath. And even though I tense my limbs to keep it in check, the flames aren't receding.

My head snaps up, and I scan the horizon for one of the strange figures while sniffing the air, but the surrounding hordes block my view on every side, and multiple odours fight in my nose – sweat, fumes, and the scents from neighbouring shops.

The human raft plunges on through the demonstrators, and I drive my mind into action, forcing my thoughts on. Gradually, the veil slips back before my senses, the darkness receding from my chest, though an icy chill takes its place, my nerves stretching.

We're still twenty feet from the far side, moving so fucking slowly. And the Puritans are thickening around us, yelling louder at the businessman and me, many of them ramming the backs of the guards. The three grit their teeth against it as sweat drips from their foreheads, their arms shaking more wildly with each impact.

My gaze flashes around the circle. The guards' utility belts are packed – mace, stun grenades, electric batons, and more bloody guns. And all pointless. All out of their reach, their hands pinned.

The Puritans continue to ram even harder now. Several of them shout biblical verses while the businessman screams back at them, his face beet red. Then he turns his ire on the guards while their limbs tremble, their arms and legs starting to give.

I retreat toward the rear of the manmade circle and face the guard who's furthest forward, the far bank beyond him. Then I lean back against the joined hands of the guards to either side of me and push myself into the Puritans behind.

The inevitable shove sends me staggering across the circle toward the furthermost guard. I feign a stumble and thrust out my hands to prevent my fall, aiming for the guard's belt, for the holster of his gun. With arms pinned, he can only watch. I tumble into him, flip open the holster clasp with my thumb, and then knock the gun free with my other hand. My shoulder bounces off the guy's chest while the gun clatters to the ground at my feet.

It's like a boulder plunged into foaming waters.

The guard roars, "Get *back!*"

He shoves even harder at the Puritans behind him, his arms wide, thrusting to clear a bigger space as his fingers twitch to reclaim his gun.

The Puritans don't hear him. The shouting is too loud. And after the grey waves flow out, they prepare to surge straight back in again, the Puritans rallying. I fall back a step, ready.

The demonstrators yell and barge even harder toward us. And with the extra momentum, they break through the guard's grip. He drops one arm, and several Puritans stagger forward into the circle, creating a gap just behind.

I leap into it, slip beyond the furthermost guard, and dash past two more layers of people before they can regroup. Then I swivel and use my shoulder as a battering ram to drive myself through, leaving boiling chaos in my wake, a gun hidden somewhere in its midst.

4

I BREAK free of the demonstration and stumble forward through gawkers on the far side, clawing breath into my starved lungs. The shouts of anger carry as far as the next interchange. In my head, I can't help picturing them all swivelled toward me, all yelling vitriol at my back.

I hurry on. The crowd gradually thins out as the Docklands area draws nearer. The shadows continue to lengthen with night falling. And then, finally, Billingsgate Park – the domain of the super-rich.

The space is at least a hundred and fifty yards across, and green grass gives way to tessellated areas around the paths – intersecting zones of lawns, of ponds, of pebbles, with scattered benches – like some stupid Zen garden. Occasional wide hollows dot the park, where escalators lead to subterranean levels of glittering shops and restaurants. And beneath these, tunnels feed underground car parks that transport society's kings and queens into the heart of their dominion.

My delivery address is just on the far side of the park. Only a few minutes left to the end of the window.

I scan the space. Numerous guards patrol the paths in their polished suits with weapon belts at the ready. I press on down one of the main avenues, keeping the nearest pair at the edge of my vision.

A man in slacks and a turtleneck frowns at me from three paths over. I pat down my rumpled clothes, trying to smooth them out, but my hands shake, and memories from the demonstration gouge their way into my mind – the crowd scrambling to get out of my way, me dragging people to the ground.

Using the veil. *Fucking idiot.* After two months of training with the priest to peel back the veil, I've spent half that time trying to unlearn it.

What the hell were you thinking?

Again, flames rise inside me and bile bites at my throat.

Further down the path, a couple glower at me with screwed-up faces, like they've swallowed something bitter. They're living sculptures in skirts and capes. Pristine makeup and coiffed hair. The truly wealthy, the gilded.

Still the fire burns inside, and I see myself stepping over and slapping the guy, pummelling his perfect face into—

My chest goes cold. I tilt my head down and hurry past them. Then I scan the far reaches of the dimming space for any sign of the *things*.

The figures appear mostly at night but never approach. And no one else ever seems to bloody see them.

My head swims, the fatigue a constant thumping behind my temples, and I force my gaze toward my target location. It's only forty yards away now, on the edge of the park between two neighbouring skyscrapers.

I peer around for my contact, scour the sides of the buildings, the narrow road between them. No one's there.

As I slow to a halt, sweat trickles down my back, and my eyes find a flowered sculpture with benches below and a clock above. Less than a minute before my delivery window closes.

I try to picture the bit of paper again, the typed address,

but my head's properly pounding once more, and the image refuses to resolve itself.

Fire sweeps up my insides, and I grip my knuckles and squeeze. *Where the fuck's my contact? Is this my termination?* The embers burn hotter in my chest, and flames flash down my legs. *No way*. My security box is almost empty. *I need this job*.

A couple of guards stare suspiciously from the corner of the park.

I sidle over to the clock sculpture, plant myself down on the bench, and grip the wood to keep my hands still. It doesn't stop my heels bouncing up and down.

A few solitary stars glint in the growing black while the network of hanging lights above casts an ethereal glow on an emptying garden. I breathe deeply and focus on finding some calm. When my sight hazes again, and the fathomless void swells in my chest, memories arising from my recurring dreams …

My mother, lying lifeless before me, her golden hair splayed out like scythed corn. Then the scent of sulphur's in my nose, and my mind conjures the familiar image of the *things*, staring at me out of the darkness. The shiny black eyes, the hunched posture, the varying clothes, the arms hanging down, the head rotating – almost animal-like.

I blink hard and try to peer around the park to banish the visions. As they fade, another familiar image takes their place – three parallel slashes, all equal height, like vertical tears in my perception. They're superimposed on the green grass in front of me, on the skyscrapers that fringe the road. Everywhere I fucking look.

My teeth clench, and again I scour the space for the *things*.

One of the two security guards starts toward me, his hands on his belt. My shoulders tense, and I glance back toward the rambling city and my squat beyond.

A low voice comes from behind me. "Hey, you."

I spin.

A man stands there, ten feet away, the skyscrapers at his back. He's in his sixties, lean, with styled white hair, an immaculately cut suit, and no tie. He wears a tiny earpiece.

My contact.

"Come here," he says and motions to me like I'm some kind of pet.

I stand and pad toward him, yanking the package out of my satchel.

The man ignores it. "What happened?" he asks.

I blink at him.

"En route, you observed likely aggressors," he says, his blue eyes cold. "Correct?"

I pause and then nod.

"So, *tell me,*" he says. "What did you see?"

Again, I try to shove the satchel into the man's hand. He doesn't take it.

"What … did … you … see?" he repeats, his voice raised.

My internal warning's ringing louder now. And a new smell hits my nose – layers of sulphur and an acrid stink like burning rubbish. I swivel and scan the edges of the darkening space again. The gloom creeps in between the hanging lights. A bulb above my head buzzes. And again, the void opens in my chest as if I'm sinking into a chasm with every painful memory lurking down there in the darkness, amplified a hundred times. My muscles clench, and in the next instant, relief comes in its fiery blaze. I breathe it in, letting the flames fill me, and energy flashes down my arms. The buzzing sound above me grows into a shrill whine.

The man pulls out an envelope from his inside pocket. "Tell me, and you receive your pay," he says.

I glare back at him. "Why d'you want to know?"

"Only one other runner reached his contact," he says.

My insides tighten. "Who?"

The man shakes his head. "That's immaterial," he says.

"No—"

"It's immaterial!" the man snaps. "What matters is intelligence. Stalker numbers, routes, tactics. Start talking."

The fire continues to build, my chest burning now as more images spin in my mind – the boss from earlier sneering at me as he held back my package, the gangs that took over my childhood home and got my mother addicted to drugs, the enforcers who forced me to work as a thief – all fusing together. Power surges through my limbs, and I see myself grabbing the man by his pristine lapels, tearing him apart.

I leap toward him, my fists balled. The guy stumbles backward. My jaw clenches, and my teeth grind. It takes every ounce of my concentration not to strangle the fucker.

Then the breath freezes in my lungs. The man's face has grown white as his shirt, his mouth a cavern, his eyes wide. And he's not looking at me. He's staring just over my shoulder.

A caustic smell rakes my throat, and superimposed on the man's chest burns the familiar vision of the three slashes.

I lurch forward and grab my contact's arm, preparing to haul him away. Just then light flares around us, and the bulb above explodes with a colossal bang. An inhuman screech erupts from right behind me. It stabs at my eardrums, the blood rampages in my veins, and every muscle in my body tenses like rock.

Still, I make sure not to turn. Instead, I yank at the man's arm while he anchors his feet and grips my wrists, continuing to stare over my shoulder with his skin ever paler. Saliva trickles from one side of his trembling lips.

The smell of sulphur intensifies, and the heat scorches my back through my jacket. My mind rages to leave him. Yet I tighten my grip on his arm and try to drag him to the side. Still he resists, his face contorting in terror. He locks eyes with me and takes one hand off my arm to claw at the centre of his chest. His legs shake. He's not breathing.

Heart attack.

I feel myself rooted to the spot, a strange jabbering in my

head. The void veers up inside me again, and again the fire blazes so quickly at my core. I grit my teeth, feeling the power building in my arms, and set my feet to wrench even harder.

The man's legs buckle. He drops to one shaking knee and continues to stare directly up at me, his eyes like plates. His mouth opens and closes soundlessly.

I can only gaze back. The man's wild terror throbs inside me as if it's beating my heart. The jabbering sound intensifies in my head, and I shake myself, tense my hips, and rip my arm from the man's grasp. Then I throw myself to the side and scramble away across the grass. Twenty feet along, I steel myself and glance over my shoulder, searching the space for my first proper glimpse of a *thing*.

But there's no sign. No fucking sign at all. Just one of the security guards barrelling toward me while the other hurries toward the dying man.

And ... *wait*. Beyond the security guards, further along the edge of the park – an SUV is parked up on the kerb. Two figures in grey suits hover poised by its open doors, their gaze fixed on me. As I stare, both disappear into the front seats, and the car accelerates down a side road.

I spin back around and stumble away into the night.

5

Something pulls at my awareness – an incessant banging like a drill at the centre of my mind. I open my eyes and roll onto my front. A familiar mattress comes into view, slick with sweat, while the rest of my room's a haze. The banging continues and reality dawns. My body goes rigid.

Shit.

I strain to rise, tiredness like concrete around my limbs. Then I glance down. I'm fully dressed, my shoes still on, and my blanket and sheet are nowhere to be seen.

Memories of the evening before rush in … that acrid smell, the burning heat. The closest a *thing* has *ever* come. It took me two hours to escape the city centre, making sure I never stopped, that they had no chance to locate me. Because the fuckers always seem able to. It started six weeks ago – these *things* appearing on the horizon and staring at me with that strange interest, invisible to everyone else.

Till last night.

My breath hitches, a growing weight in my gut.

The banging stops, and I close my eyes to shut it all out – both sounds and memories. And behind my lids, the dream waits. Not a few but dozens of hunched figures, numerous black eyes gazing on as I'm plunged into a cavernous void, an echo chamber of agonising memory, abandonment after betrayal.

My head pounds, and the banging starts again, the door to my squat shaking on its hinges – the squat I've done bloody everything to keep a secret, told absolutely no one about.

Then realisation hits, and my groggy brain rings like a bell. I scramble from the mattress to stand, swaying as my vision coalesces. And the sight almost knocks me back down.

My single-room squat looks as though a bomb has gone off. Chairs lie splintered, items of clothing torn to shreds. The door I use as a table, balanced on bricks, has been split in two. And my rudimentary cupboard – someone's gouged three parallel lines down its scavenged-wood front.

The three vertical slashes. I suddenly see them everywhere – hovering over the floor, the ceiling, the walls – shifting every time I move my head, like gashes torn out of my vision and bigger than ever.

The dream washes back in. New images bubble. Scenes of ash and lava, of destruction. Buildings reduced to rubble, bodies strewn. Flashes of individual figures – my delivery contact with those haunting eyes, my mother with three slashes hewn into her torso. Then the perspective changes … I see myself standing above her, holding a knife, no longer human size but much larger. And the fire surges down my arm, into my hand …

My eyes scrunch shut, my breathing speeding up, and I grip the wall to steady myself. The banging continues. Like chisels carving out my skull.

"Fuck … off," I mutter.

I stumble through my squat, scanning the wreckage. Nothing seems to be missing. My blanket and sheet lie crumpled by the far wall, well out of reach of the mattress. And both the door and the solitary window are intact, locked from the inside.

An icy hand squeezes my ribs.

The banging stops again. I put my eye up to the peephole

and squint. There they are. Natasha and the priest. I close my eyes and breathe, picturing the wreckage behind me. Natasha bangs on the door even louder.

"Coming!" I yell, my head thumping with each impact.

I twist the upper and lower locking mechanisms before heaving the door open.

"Jacob!" Father Thomas says, his eyes shining. His grey hair sprouts wildly from the top of his head, as is the norm, and the creases from his smile merge with the well-worn lines around his cheeks and temples.

"My friend, it's good to see you," he says, not a hint of annoyance in his tone.

I sigh, my anger boiling off like mist.

He clasps my shoulder, and I quickly scan the alleyway beyond them, the makeshift set of steps up from the dumping ground below.

There's no one.

The priest faces me the entire time. He's in his decrepit mode – shabby black habit, crooked posture, leaning on a walking stick. He reaches his hand to my face and feels the contours of my cheeks.

"You're sweating," he says, and his forehead furrows. "Is everything okay?"

I can only nod, and Father Thomas rests his hand there for a moment. Then he pats me on the shoulder again and hobbles past through the doorway, still limping slightly. Which leaves me facing …

Natasha. She stands there, her arms folded, mouth a tight-lipped line. With the fire diminished, a dull ache throbs in my chest, one that's both painful and sweet.

"Are you not going to let me in?" she says and leans to the side to peer around me.

I step across to block off her line of sight. She raises an eyebrow and remains standing, her hips tilted. She's dressed in fitted jeans and a shirt, quite a contrast to the stiffness when we met three or so months ago. A half smile pulls at her mouth.

Eventually, I sigh and shift out of the way. She reaches up with her hand, cradling my cheek, and my chest buzzes.

"You look awful," she says and steps past me.

I swivel and glimpse the three slashes hovering in the middle of her back. I feel a sudden pressure on my palm – the same sensation of holding the knife from my dream. I shake myself. The vision fades, and I kick the door closed behind them.

Natasha pads to the centre of the floor and freezes. Her hand goes to her mouth as her eyes comb the rectangular room – the destroyed furniture, the shredded clothes.

"What happened?" she asks, concern and anticipation mingled in her tone.

I keep my mouth shut and shuffle over to the pile of bricks that used to be the legs of my table. I start piling them up again, and the priest comes over to help.

She swivels toward me. "This is not the first time. Is it?" she asks, her eyes gleaming.

The weight builds at my core, and I straighten. "Nat, why are you here?"

She frowns. "We came to see you," she says, her tone hurt. "Is that not enough?"

I hold her gaze. Her fingers fumble together.

"And we discovered something," she says.

"About?" I question.

"The angels, about Gabriel," she says.

I can't help the jolt that passes through me.

"We thought you should know," she goes on and then gazes determinedly at the destruction again. "And this *has* to be connected. It's the dreams. Isn't it?" Her voice strengthens, and she finds my eyes again. "They're still happening. I thought you said they had stopped?"

I glance away. *Yeah, right.* And my own speculations start to whir. Gabriel. Is this all really his revenge? Or is this a result of me using the veil? Am I becoming a fucking angel? My fingers squeeze together, and I close my eyes. The sense of tiredness is bone deep.

"Are you okay, Jacob?" Father Thomas's voice is soft.

He's found a crate and sits against the side wall, looking up at me, his eyebrows knitted.

"I'm doing fine," I say, heading over to lean against the opposite wall.

"You had another dream?" he says.

I find myself nodding.

"What do you remember?" he asks softly.

Natasha's gaze burns my cheek, and I clench my jaw, keeping my eyes on the priest's. He smiles, and I feel the warmth in his gaze. The pressure in my chest releases a fraction further.

"Still the same figures?" he says.

I sigh and my shoulders drop. "Mostly," I admit. "But I only remember flashes. I see them surrounded by scenes of destruction. There's this crushing pain. Then rage. Dead bodies all over the ground – my mother, my contact from last night …"

The weight doubles in my stomach. *Did I kill him? Was it me?*

"Jake, I know this is hard," Natasha says, "but you have to tell us what's happening."

I shake my head, the sensation of the knife in my hand again. "No way, Nat."

"But, Jake, you must," she insists. "You have to realise this is bigger than you." She spreads her palms. "There have been happenings all around the world – a vast increase in religious attacks, in political instability, in people suffering sudden psychosis …"

I frown back at her.

"It's not just that," she says and glances across at the priest.

He gazes up at me and takes a deep breath.

"We've been tracking Gabriel as well," he says. "Via networks that trade information about the supernatural. And it's rumoured that he's involving himself *less* in our world, not more—"

"But it is not just happening in our world. Is it?" Natasha presses. She stares intently at me. "That's what is crazy. Apparently there have been attacks on angels, too."

6

I KEEP my gaze impassive and stare from Natasha to the priest. "So?"

Natasha gapes back at me from the middle of the room. "Jake, this is Gabriel," she says. "We destroyed his disease. He will be *furious*. You think he will sit idly by?" Her tone hardens. "He has always defied the wider pantheon. Qetesh told us that."

"Qetesh is dead," I say.

"Qetesh sacrificed herself so we could *live*," Natasha retorts. "And there is no *way* that what is happening to you can be a coincidence. It *has* to be linked with the angel attacks."

"You can't be sure of that," I say, embers sparking in my chest. "You can't be sure of anything. We've no idea *what* he's planning."

Natasha opens her mouth, but Father Thomas cuts in.

"We have *some* idea, because we know Gabriel," he says, glancing between us from his crate opposite. "Gabriel is a master at one of the most powerful forces in history, and he *will* use it."

"What force?" I ask.

"Story," he says.

I can't help snorting.

The priest holds my gaze. "Jacob, reflect on what you already know," he says, his voice moving from intense to calm. "Gabriel created the Bible. Its canons have controlled humanity's beliefs more powerfully than the scientific paradigm or any other force since. Stories are an aspect of our faith at the deepest level. From the beginning, tribes told stories to enshrine their values and guide their actions. And today, every one of society's norms and morals can be traced to a story or myth."

I find myself frowning.

"And think of the disease Gabriel tried to fabricate," the priest continues. "We know it would have first affected the rich, the modernists, the unbelievers – just like the ten plagues of Egypt – leaving the faithful comparatively safe. So if his disease had been able to spread, the religious would have seen it in these terms, as some kind of divine flood. They'd have turned it into a biblical event. Think of the devotional power it would have generated."

He pauses, and I meet his gaze, my eyebrow raised.

"Yet I believe his plague was as much a whim for him as it was a pursuit of his aims – turning modernity's tools against itself," the priest says. "But his rage will now push him down more familiar paths, and you can be sure they'll align with a story – one with great power. With roots so deep that new seeds of belief will sprout readily when he sends it forth."

"So, if we find this story," Natasha says, "we will understand what he's doing."

My eyes track back to the priest. "Father, this is crazy," I say. "Last time we went up against him, we got lucky. There's no chance Gabriel will let it happen again."

The priest merely smiles. "There was no *last time*, Jacob," he says. "It's simply one weave in a bigger tapestry, in a much larger story that continues to unfold. And we remain its strands."

"A bigger story?" I ask, scepticism thick in my tone.

The priest nods. "The biggest," he says. "God's will. The golden thread in every strand, in each one of us, the foundation of the entire weaving."

My chest tightens, and the fire builds inside me again. "Bullshit," I say. "There's no God's will. Just the dumb choices we make, day in and day out."

The corners of the priest's mouth curl upward. "Jacob," he says. "God's will … your will. How could they be different?" He raises his hands at his sides. "You're one of God's children. You simply need to be open to the story he's trying to weave through you."

I grit my teeth and clamp my mouth shut.

The priest clears his throat. "Jacob, you're involved. I have no doubt about it. It's not just these strange dreams. It's your practices, your abilities. I've not heard of that speed of progress in the history of my lineage. In weeks, you've made advances that would normally take years."

I shake my head.

Natasha motions around my wrecked squat. "This new strength you have," she says. "Who else could have done this?"

I glance between them, feeling the weight of their stares, the air more stifling with every passing moment.

"This is all happening for a reason, Jake," she says. "You have to help us discover *why*."

The fire blazes inside, and I scrunch my eyes closed, pressing my palms to my forehead and pushing.

The priest's voice cuts through the darkness. "Yet we have to trust you," he says.

I stare at him.

"With everything that's happened, if you're still sure you don't want to get involved, Jacob, your reticence is itself an aspect of God's will," he says. "Hence it's important that we honour it."

He rests his head against the wall. "Often we can only

focus on the next step," he says. "That's all that God shows us. And right now, we need to wait."

He nods, and silence steals over the room. An engine revs outside. My flames abate, and the sound of my heartbeat steadies in my chest. I lean back, too.

"No," says Natasha.

I blink. Father Thomas swivels to face her as well.

"No," she says again, her voice prickly. "We do not have time for this. Gabriel is mobilising *now*. I'm sure of it. Chaos is building everywhere. Just look at the rising temperatures, the famines, the storms. It could be related. *We don't yet know*. This is not about Jake feeling it's not the right time." She pauses for a moment and swallows. "He's scared."

The priest raises a hand. "Natalia."

Natasha motions to me and turns to the priest. "It's true —" she starts.

"I'm trying to keep you *alive!*" I shout, my fist clenched to my chest.

Natasha shakes her head, and her mouth twists in pain. "You're not, you're avoiding," she says, more softly. "We need to work out what is happening, and more specifically, what is happening with *you*. It is the only avenue we have." Her voice drops to a whisper. "I believe *she* is at the heart of this …"

My mouth opens, a million words crowding my throat.

"Your mother," Natasha says, staring back at me. "She is in your dreams, again and again. There has to be a reason. They are trying to tell you something."

I shake my head again, more violently this time.

Natasha swivels to the priest. "His mother was an orphan, never knew her parents. She grew up at the whim of these wild forces inside her," she says.

I just stand there, fire rising, as memories flood in of confidences I shared with Natasha on the rooftops.

I'd not told another soul.

"Jake inherited his potential from her," Natasha says. "Not

from his father – he never knew him – and not from anyone else." She swivels back to face me. "The sense of timelessness you describe in your shimmering world is a reflection of the experiences you had with *her*."

I grind my teeth as memories whirl, my mother's presence like liquid sunshine. The experience of losing her feels akin to death. It echoes in my dreams most nights, my heart being lashed raw over and over.

"Whether you want to admit it or not, your angelic experiences did not start with Gabriel. They started long before," Natasha continues. "And so, she *has* to be connected with why you're involved in all this, why you cannot escape it, no matter how hard you try."

Natasha keeps her arms crossed while tears well in her eyes. My mouth just opens and closes, the void, the fathomless darkness, plunging away inside me.

"And you need to face it. Not turn away," she says, gripping her arms ever tighter. "You are worried that *you* abandoned your mother all those years ago, not the other way round. You are furious at the gangs for taking her away from you ... but you are angrier at yourself."

A tear rolls down her cheek. And I find my gaze fixed on it as if nothing else exists in the world. I feel my awareness drifting out of my body.

Natasha keeps going. "That is why you have not tried to track her down," she says. "You blame yourself for failing to protect her from the gang, and you will not let yourself imagine that she could still be out there somewhere, vulnerable ... alone," she says, motioning toward the world beyond the door. "But by staying away, in your heart, you are still abandoning her."

I scrunch my eyes shut again.

"Your mother might still be alive," Natasha says, speaking more quickly. "I know it is painful, but you have to face it. There is a chance you could find her ... perhaps find some peace."

I hear her turn toward the priest, her feet shifting on the bare floorboards.

"We may discover what his role is in all this," she continues. "What is behind his powers, what his purpose is."

My eyes open. She's staring at me again.

"Who knows where it will lead?" she says. "But this way you will be able to finally move on, to embrace your fate, wherever it takes you." She swallows and her shoulders drop. "Otherwise, you will be running from it your entire life."

Running.

My whole body vibrates. My hands clench and unclench. Gazing down at them, the centre of my attention reels up through the ceiling. It's as if I'm staring down at myself from somewhere in the sky, somehow disconnected.

Then my awareness slams back into my body, into an ocean of pain – the void, deeper than I could imagine, the fire blazing ever brighter on top. The heat climbs my chest, tightens the muscles in my shoulders, my arms, curls my fingers, jerks me into action. I push off from the wall and scramble for the door.

Natasha steps in front of me and raises a hand. "We can do this, work out what is happening," she says. "Together."

I shove past her and grab the handle. Hauling the door open, I lurch through it.

7

"JAKE!"

My legs drive me on, Natasha's words still echoing in my head while blind heat flashes through my body. It forces my feet on faster, faster, the world a blur around me – streets, buildings – it hardly registers. Instead, images come from the dreams – scenes of destruction, the dark eyes watching, my mother dead. The void opens up inside me, and fresh memories churn – me leaving her on the doorstep of my childhood home, my mother's vacant stare, her drug-addled indifference … and me walking away, never returning. So quickly, the fire sweeps over me like a maelstrom. I'm vaguely aware of passing a corner, of stalking across a junction.

"Jake, stop!"

A hand touches my arm. I spin around, my teeth bared and my fists clenched like steel.

Natasha stands before me, her hand still on my arm. "I'm sorry!" she says and bends over, breathing hard.

My chest heaves and sweat coats the backs of my arms. A gust of wind chills my neck as I shake my head, and my gaze shifts down the road behind.

I find myself staring at rows of three-storey buildings on

both sides of a residential street. A couple of shop fronts glint beyond layers of security grating while a gang-tagged apartment building stands opposite. Next to it stands an abandoned community centre turned homeless shelter. All familiar. And all seven or so blocks from my squat.

I blink.

Seven blocks?

Natasha gazes up at me. "I'm so sorry," she says. "I had to."

I swivel to face her.

"What's happening," she continues, "is too important." She raises her hand to cradle my cheek again.

I retreat a step, the flames licking up my throat.

She nods and lowers her eyes, folding her arms. "Look—"

"Nat, you've got to let this *go*," I say. "Someone *died* last night!"

She opens her mouth but says nothing, just looks up at me.

A few rubberneckers stare as they pass, the pavements filling up with handfuls of pedestrians scurrying back and forth. The sun's peeking above the buildings in a budding blue sky. Still early morning.

I edge toward a shop to avoid the passersby and try to settle my breathing. "My contact ..." I say and then pause. "He saw one of these *things* ... and had a heart attack." My voice descends with the growing weight.

Natasha blinks. "You think that should *stop* us?" she demands, incredulity spiking her tone. "What will it take to wake you up, Jake? So many more people are going to die! We have to do *something*."

The fire flares again. I clench my jaw. "But *what?*" I press. "What are you hoping to *find?* There are no easy clues out there, Nat." I sweep a hand over the cracked pavement. "No simple answers that you're going to stumble across."

"But think what you have seen," she says, and the gleam

returns to her hazel eyes. "These figures you have talked about, these *things*. And your squat, the destruction."

I tilt my head down and avert my gaze.

"And the dreams—"

"They're just *dreams*, visions ..." I snap back. And so quickly the void grows inside me again, the pain. I scrunch my eyes shut and turn away. The thumping in my head has returned, and I squeeze my temples.

"I'm hardly sleeping, Nat. My brain is *wired*. It's probably just me seeing stuff. They could be anything."

"I know this is hard, Jake, but your pain, your anger ... they are a part of *you*," she says. "There is a reason this is all coming up now. You must not ignore it."

I open my eyes and stare back, the heat still simmering in my body. I take a deep breath to try and calm the flames.

"I'm dangerous, Nat." My voice falters. "How can you not see that?" I clear my throat and finally say it. "You're safer away from me."

She shakes her head. "Jake, we are here *with* you," she says, and squeezes her fist. She steps toward me. "This is all connected – your dreams, the figures you see, our experience with Gabriel, what he is planning now." Her voice rises again. "You have to trust me, to trust it. Tell us what has been happening, *please*. Together, we can work out what is going on, what his plan is."

"Trust it?" I splutter, my shoulders tightening. Then I take another deep breath and quieten my voice. "You say all these happenings are linked, that they're some part of Gabriel's master plan. But if that's right, why would he send these *things* after *me?"* I press a finger to my chest. "I'm a nobody, an *insect*. I'm not part of any global conspiracy. Why would I be?" I shake my head. "No, if this is Gabriel, it's just his twisted revenge. These *things* stalk but don't kill me. They want me alive to feel the pain and fury, to lose control ..."

My lips press together.

To kill those I'm closest to.

Natasha opens her mouth but then shuts it. I inhale deeply and let it out, staring down the street again.

The sun reflects off the windows, and the light hurts my eyes like a million tiny spears. It's still the early-morning rush, people hurrying along the main road to the black markets to work.

I feel a sudden twist in my gut. My internal alarm.

I swivel and grasp Natasha's arm. "Walk. Don't look back."

She pulls against me as she turns to glance behind, but I drive her harder on down the road.

"What is it?" she asks.

"We've got a tail," I say.

It was only a glimpse – a figure vanishing around a corner – but the image acts like money in a slot machine. Dozens of other images tumble into my mind, glimpses in reflective surfaces, at the edge of my vision. People trailing us. The same profiles, the same gaits, disappearing and reappearing in the streets far behind. All buried in my subconscious as I fled, hidden somewhere amid the fog of my anger.

My fingers squeeze around Natasha's arm. I go to run, but then I stop and force myself to breathe. I continue walking up the main road, focusing on maintaining my stride length, my pace. I lean my head toward Natasha's.

"Keep talking," I hiss.

She frowns up at me.

"We've got to look like we're still arguing," I say.

Natasha stays silent and stares forward again. She bites her lip, her eyes contemplative.

"Oh sure, *now* you go quiet," I grumble.

She grabs my arm. "Jake, this is an opportunity," she says, tugging me backward. "It might be connected to what's happening, to the angels. We can face them, find out who—"

The heat tightens my calves, my thighs, and I yank her along faster. "We've got no idea who these figures *are*, Nat, or what they want," I say. "Is it to follow us somewhere? Confront us? Kill us?"

We pass a corner, and I glance covertly down the side street. No sign of anyone suspicious. Just a few people walking past dilapidated houses, a few higher apartment blocks at the end – the start of the Grange estate. I stare ahead and scan the coming junctions. *There.* A shop on the far side of the next crossroads, its window intact, slivers of the facing building reflected between its metal bars.

I pull Natasha toward it and around the corner, keeping tight to the wall with my eyes trained on the shop window opposite. I hold the gaze as long as possible, scouring the street behind us in its reflective surface …

I almost stop in my tracks. Gooseflesh breaks out across the back of my neck. Figures in grey business suits loom three blocks behind, at least one on each side of the road. And still, my internal alarm clamours on.

"What did you see?" Natasha asks, glancing over her shoulder.

"Not sure," I say through gritted teeth. "A couple of them, I reckon."

"Who are they?" she says.

"No bloody idea," I say. "They're too far away."

I picture them ducking down a parallel road, making sure they can follow from behind. The heat flares in my chest, and I break out into a sprint toward the next crossroads. *Fucking stupid.* Still, I drive my legs faster and burst around the corner, poised to run back to where the two figures might emerge to get a closer look.

My feet screech to a halt as a new suited figure darts out of sight around a nearer corner, only sixty yards away. My chest tightens, and I gaze about me, my mind conjuring images of numerous followers out there, ready to surround us. Memories flood in from a lifetime ago. The gang stalking me as I fled my home; finding me, beating me, and forcing me on errands. They always got me in the end. And standing there, the darkness yawns deep inside me, the flames rearing up so quickly. I clench my jaw.

Natasha arrives, panting at my side.

I keep my voice level. "These people. They were there on my delivery run yesterday. They're after me. You go." I jab my finger back the way we came.

"What?" she says, her expression taut with shock and anger.

"They're all around us, Nat. Playing some kind of fucking game," I say. "I'll lead them away. You head back to my place. Father Thomas may still be there."

I push Natasha down the street. But she refuses to budge, simply staring up at me.

"No," she says. "We are in this together. How do you know they will not just follow me as well? You said there is more than one."

Her words are like a slap. I blink. She's right. And again, the void opens inside me, more memories revolving around in the darkness: my mother, the gangs, all those times I tried to get rid of them, all the times I failed.

Heat rages through my body once more. I spin away from her and hurry on down the residential street. Striding past more houses and apartment buildings, I feel my legs burning, my fingers clenching and unclenching.

"Where are we going?" Natasha says, hurrying to catch up.

"No idea," I say, my insides tight. "They hold all the fucking cards, Nat. Roaming all around us, keeping their distance. We can't run. We wouldn't be fast enough. And if we go to ground, hole up, they'll just wait till we surface again. They're clearly in no rush. They'll happily hang back till we tire."

The fire builds in my veins, and I stomp faster down the road.

Ahead of us, the Grange tower blocks catch my eye. The apartment buildings are of varying heights and, with space at such a premium, they stand right next to each other. A thought sparks, and I hurry toward them, the broiling energy driving me on.

"What are you doing?" Natasha asks, just behind me.

A smile crosses my lips as I stride. "Changing the rules."

8

I PACE down the street toward the next crossroads, my gaze fixed on its far corner – one of the Grange tower blocks rising into the sky. Ten floors of flats while both neighbouring buildings are only three storeys high, with flat roofs, and only a few feet away from the corners of the taller building. The block's entrance has a few gang tags on either side, and the door stands ajar.

"We're going … in there?" Natasha asks, catching up to my shoulder.

"Oh, yes," I say, striding on toward the block's entrance. "Tailing someone with a crew is easy *if* they're out in the open. But in a building, they're hidden from sight. One entrance. One exit. Numbers count for nothing."

"But won't they just come in after us?" Natasha says.

The embers continue to spark in my chest. A part of me *yearns* for it, but I shake my head.

"They've kept their distance so far," I say and nod toward the gang tags around the entrance. "And what group's going to want to stumble into another's turf? No. They'll surely keep outside."

"So, what will we do?" Natasha asks from behind.

My smile widens, and I quicken my steps across the interchange while taking in the building opposite the block's entrance. Some kind of office. Five storeys rise above a metal awning, and a ramp leads down to a car park beneath the building. I peer into the darkness of the garage.

That's where I'd wait.

I swivel and head up the concrete path to the tower block, passing straight through the open door. Then my feet skid on broken plaster.

The entrance hall resembles a war zone, with its lift front smashed in and the stairwell door to its side ripped off its hinges. Bullet holes pepper three of the walls, a few of them still smeared with blood, all pretty recent. A chill settles at the base of my back.

"What—" she starts.

I dart a finger to my lips.

"Gang fight," I breathe. "Likely over territory, protection rackets."

I pad into the stairwell and listen hard. Natasha steps carefully to my side.

"Are they still here?" she asks.

"Not likely," I whisper. "The gangs control plenty of buildings, but sometimes their top people do take the plush flats, the upper ones."

I peer up the stairs. There's no movement, no sound. The place seems deserted. The sense of cold climbs my spine, the flames continuing to ebb in my chest.

"Just stay behind me," I whisper to Natasha.

I begin the climb, two steps at a time, placing my feet as gently as possible. One storey and then another, Natasha following. The stairwell's been stripped of its rubber flooring, and the walls are all bare concrete, all covered in more gang tags. Third storey. I lean over the railing and listen again. Nothing. The stairwell below is still entirely silent.

"They are not coming in," Natasha whispers.

I grin and head up one more floor, above the level of the neighbouring rooftop, and push through the doorway into a narrow corridor. It extends to both sides and behind me, forming a square with our stairwell and the lift shafts in the middle, the apartments around the outside. A faint light filters down from an emergency green bulb embedded in the ceiling, and all remains quiet.

Two doors face us, each opening into apartments that overlook the street below. One's shut, while the other's smashed in with gang tags all over the dented surface.

My breath held, I push the beaten apartment door open. A short hallway leads to what looks like a bare living room. And there's no response. No sound at all. I usher Natasha inside and close the door behind me. The flat's empty. Two tiny bedrooms, a kitchen, all stripped. Natasha gazes about the living room, her hands on her hips.

"Someone who couldn't make good on their protection money," I say with a shudder.

"Wouldn't an empty flat be taken in a flash in this city?" Natasha asks.

I can't help nodding.

Unless it's guarded.

Natasha steps past me and heads toward a cracked window overlooking the street. "You want to spot them from up here?" she says.

I grab her arm and haul her back and out of sight of the window. "Wait," I tell her. "Not yet."

She turns on me, her brow furrowed.

"You've got to pretend to be me," I say. "Tie back your hair, stand in the corner and peep out of the window now and then. Make yourself taller."

"*What?*" she asks, her frown deepening.

"I'm going to get down to a neighbouring roof. Try to get behind wherever they're hiding and then find out who they are, and how I can get us out of this," I say.

She just stares back at me.

"And you're staying here," I say.

"No, no, no," she protests and shakes her head vigorously.

The embers spark hot in my chest again. "You want to learn who they are to discover more?" I snap back. Then I grip the wall to my side and close my eyes for an instant. "If they don't come closer, this is the only way."

Her frown diminishes a fraction, but her lips remain tightly pressed together.

"Please," I say and raise a hand, my palm toward her. "Stay here. I'll discover what I can. I promise."

After what feels like an age, she nods. "Okay," she says.

"Okay," I echo and nod back.

I half turn for the door and then stop, the weight building in my throat and a sliver of the darkness inside. I swallow and force the words out.

"If I can't make it back," I say, my gaze averted, "don't stay too long. Get out of here. Go find Father Thomas."

Not waiting for her reaction, I stride back into the entrance hall and check the corridor. Still empty.

I make sure the door's closed behind me and then turn toward the neighbouring building that's hidden from the street, its flat rooftop three storeys high. My gaze finds the closed door to the nearest apartment. Its windows should directly overlook the lower rooftop, a jump of only five or six feet.

I pace over, grab the handle, and find it locked. I tap the door with my knuckle. Plywood. My eyes flick to the ceiling above and whoever might be up there. I bite my cheek, raise my foot, and – like an idiot – kick hard under the handle.

A clanking noise rings out. The door vibrates with a dull thud, and pain shoots up my knee. *Fuck*. Metal-plated.

My ears strain. Still no sound.

I spin around and dart back into the stairwell to head up another storey and peer into another dully lit square corridor. No one is there, the two doors straight ahead both smashed in. More empty flats. More lost revenue. The doubts squawk louder at the back of my brain.

I hurry toward the same corner apartment on this floor

and push the door open. Again, I see no sign of anyone, all furniture stripped. I head into the living room and stop dead. The windows facing toward the neighbouring rooftop are covered in corrugated iron. Of course they are. As protection. To stop people climbing in from the nearby roof.

The fire blazes inside me as wild energy tears down my arms and legs. The veil's so palpable in front of my senses, so easy to peel back. The heat pulls at my forearms, my fingers, and I clench my jaw along with my fists, only just stopping myself from kicking out at one of the living-room walls.

I wheel around to face the door, trying desperately to breathe. The anger ... *Is it mine?* I sniff the air. An acrid scent hits my nose.

I scurry back through the apartment and into the barren stairwell again. Climbing the steps, I keep my focus on my breathing, on calming the storm inside, on keeping my thoughts running ... Another storey means a twenty-foot drop to the neighbouring rooftop. Memories come of training with the priest, of using the veil to try and defy gravity. So fucking hard. And I'd risk the void, the anger.

Again, my insides squeeze. And, turning the corner in the stairwell, I scrunch my eyes shut for a moment, my mind still whirling. A new smell invades my nose – engine oil and stale sweat. My head shoots upward, and I spy the figure hovering above me.

9

A MAN STANDS POISED at the top of the next flight of steps. Puffer jacket, jeans, and heavy build, with a tattoo under his right eye – two tiny stars. Gang enforcer. His face is lined and scarred; he's probably only thirty years of age but looks a hell of a lot older. The guy's hardly breathing. He's entirely still, staring down at me, eyebrows raised, the idiocy of my presence there furrowing his worn features.

I drop my gaze, avoid glancing toward Natasha, and start up the stairs again, my insides clenched.

When we're six steps from each other, the enforcer starts down the stairs in my direction. He says nothing, just moves to the railing side of the stairwell, giving me plenty of room to pass.

My heart thumps, and I make sure not to react, not to turn toward him. He slows down as he gets within a foot, the scent of cheap aftershave mingling with those of oil and sweat. I tense my shoulders, my chest, ready—

The guy lunges toward me, slams both his hands into my shoulder, and shoves me hard into the stairwell wall. Pain flares up my back and the impact scatters my breath.

"Little *bitch*," he hisses and holds me in place with one hand, my arm pinned across my chest. "What've you got?"

He keeps his voice low and uses his other hand to pat my pockets. He presses hard on my arm to compress my lungs and make it hard for me to cry out and attract anyone else.

So, he's not alone but doesn't want to share me with a fellow enforcer.

Bastard.

The embers flare again, and my mind slows automatically. The veil starts to peel back from my senses, time slowing ... *No.* I tense my stomach and banish the shimmering world. *Think.*

My back's to the wall, the remaining stairwell climbing up to the guy's left. He's using that hand to pin my arm to my chest while he pats me down with his right.

I set myself, raise my knee, and stamp down hard on the arch of his foot. The guy growls in pain, and the pressure on my pinned arm loosens for an instant. All in one motion, I grab his right wrist with both of my hands and twist it inward and down. I go to yank him off-balance and down the stairwell.

He's too strong. The enforcer pivots and drives hard toward me again with his shoulder, slamming me back against the wall. This time, the guy grits his teeth and thrusts his neck forward, going for the headbutt.

I release his wrist and duck. The enforcer's forehead flashes past my ear, missing me by inches. I squeeze my body under his arm and dart up a step.

The guy grasps for me with both hands as the flames blaze in my chest, unstoppable. I raise my leg and knee him hard in the side, under his armpit. He grunts, teeters on the step, and spins to face me. The energy sweeps down my legs, and I kick out at the guy's stomach, sending him stumbling down the rest of the stairs.

The enforcer pirouettes on the steps, barely keeping his feet. He hits the facing wall with a thud and flashes around, his shoulders raised and teeth bared. And the flames continue to rise inside me, hot blood racing through every vein. I stalk down a step toward the fucker, my jaw clenched.

"Want some more?" I yell.

The enforcer glares back, his eyes like slits, and worries filter through the haze of my rage. I can't help glancing toward the ceiling.

The guy spins and stalks further down the stairwell. I'm about to turn away but then stop.

A fleeting image appears across the guy's back as he vanishes from view: the three slashes. I find myself staring down the stairwell at nothing in his wake. Only bare concrete walls and dust remain.

I shake myself and leap up the remaining steps two at a time to the fifth floor – another square corridor with smashed locks on almost all the doors and gang tags covering every surface. As before, I head toward the door of the corner apartment. This one's as empty as the others with the living-room windows boarded up. But not with metal – *with wood*. Two wide, solid-looking boards cover the corner window frame, shutting out much of the light. I hurry forward through the gloom and peer through the horizontal gap between them.

There it is – the neighbouring rooftop, a spread of makeshift shacks on top, and twenty-five feet down, far too high for a normal jump. This requires the leap of faith, which makes my stomach churn.

I shut down the thoughts, squeeze my fingers through the gap, and grip the top edge of the bottom board. I pull hard, but it doesn't move. Anchoring my feet against the wall, I yank harder, my teeth clenched and arms shaking. But the wood's nailed down too well.

Suddenly, it's as if the room's shrinking, the shadows deepening around me, the walls moving in, the ceiling descending. My heart beats faster, and the void opens up inside. Memories surface in my mind. The gang members locking me in my mother's chest or cupboards for hours. I grasp the board again, the darkness growing, my fire building, and this time, I let the flames come. Power rushes up my insides, down my arms, and into my hands as the veil flies back from my senses.

In that instant, every surface glimmers and I can *feel* it all – the walls, the floor, the window frame, the boards, and the wisp-like clouds beyond – as if I'm linked to everything via invisible threads.

I grip the board tighter, sensing the nails connecting it to the frame, and tug again. The board creaks but holds firm. I picture the fuckers down on the street still lying in wait for us, and the flames burn hotter. Power floods me. I focus it into my hands, grit my teeth, and squeeze my eyes shut, preparing to pull … And amid the maelstrom, a sound creeps through.

"Hey, *bitch*." The words slightly slurred in the slowed time. "There be no way out now."

My head turns. The enforcer stands in the doorway's gloom – twenty feet away – a butcher knife in his hand.

"You made a big mistake," he says, his fingers tight around the handle. "And now, I'm gonna fuck you up."

He stalks across the room, his footsteps light, lips pressed together, and muscles tense.

I swivel back to the window, my hands still clasped around the board. Behind the veil, I can still feel every inch of space in the room – the guy's striding legs, the hand with the knife lifting, his breathing high in his chest. And still the fire burns at my core, the flames continuing to build. More power races through my body, and I roar, yanking again with my hands as I heave with everything I have.

With a crack, the nails pop and the board comes free in my hand – four feet of solid wood. I stagger backward with the force of the pull. My arms ache, though the sensation hardly registers. The pain is a mere whimper against the burning fire, my niggling worries engulfed by flames. I continue to rotate, the power driving me on, and yank the board around me in a wide spin.

The enforcer's there … only ten feet away, a knife held out in front of him. The blade gleams in the light from the uncovered window.

Facing him, I release the board. The guy only has time to close his eyes before the wooden plank smashes into his chest. The force slams him halfway across the room, a full five feet. He crashes onto the floor, bounces, and ends up lying flat on his back.

My mouth gapes. The flames recede in my core, and a frigid cold takes their place. I fix my eyes on the enforcer's chest and spy it moving subtly up and down.

With a trickle of relief, my thoughts jabber, and the heat continues to diminish as the veil reasserts itself. My felt connection to everything starts to fade.

No! I need it!

I spin back toward the window, trying again to still my thoughts and regain the shimmering world. But my head's pounding and my mind's a wreck.

Grinding my teeth, I grab the window frame and picture my followers below, the *things* that stalk me, and Gabriel – the archangel who's ruining my fucking life … The flames burn even hotter in my chest. And as I focus on the growing power inside, the veil now peels back so easily from my senses.

I place a foot on the ledge, lean forward, and thrust myself up through the gap and out through the window. The sky and neighbouring rooftops stretch out on all sides, and my weight teeters. I don't have enough space to stand – the overhang is too broad.

I concentrate more intently on the fire, channelling the energy down my limbs. The shimmering world spreads out wider, the sense of physical connection to everything around me strengthening – to the outside of the building, to the rooftop below. The power invigorates every muscle of my body, every sinew.

It feels so fucking good.

Not bothering to keep my balance, I focus on the solidity of the wind, plant both feet on the ledge, and let myself tip forward into the open air.

10

With the veil pulled back, I take a foot off the window ledge and lean out into space.

The city stretches out before me – tower blocks and houses, the neighbouring rooftop twenty-five feet below. The fire still blazes inside, the energy pulsing around my body, and gravity takes its hold.

I keep one foot on the ledge, my knee bent as my gaze tilts downward and my body starts to fall, so gradually in slowed time. I focus on the feeling of the surrounding air, on it suspending my body and pushing me up. My eyes centre on the roof below, and in the shimmering world, every detail's so clear – the makeshift shacks of interlaced wood and metal, the creases in the clothes drying from fashioned wire racks, the five-foot band of rooftop covered in boards with slivers of cut glass and vertical nails right below me.

My mind screams warnings, the thoughts a distant echo behind the veil. And with one foot still on the window ledge, I focus hard on the flames at my core. Instead of zeroing in on the memories, I just concentrate fiercely on the sensation of my rage, remove all constraint, and let the bonfire in my chest burn higher and wilder.

As I topple down, power floods my legs. I kick out with

that foot, thrust at the ledge with every ounce of force, and feel myself fly upward and further away from the tower block wall.

Beyond the veil, I can sense every surface around me – the thin gap between the buildings, the boards with nails, and then a bare space followed by a dozen shacks spread across the rest of the rooftop. I aim for that open space and concentrate on the rushing wind against my body, imagining the air cradling me, holding me up. Just like the priest taught me.

Come on, believe …

And then the ground comes. My feet slam down inches in front of the glass and nails, and the burning fire dulls any pain. My knees crumple and my body automatically goes into a forward roll.

I spring back up and find myself face to face with a man and woman. They've taken up defensive positions before their shack of boards and torn canvas, fists clenched. Hostility flares in their narrowed eyes, and still the flames burn hot in my chest.

The man shouts and raises both arms to push me back. In slowed time, it's as if the image flashes through my mind before it happens. I sweep his hands aside with one arm and slam my other palm into his chest. The man careens backward, his arms windmilling as he crashes through the thin wooden wall of his shack. It splinters with a crack and he tumbles to the ground, landing on a dirty mattress.

Right next to a young kid.

And in that moment, it's like water's been poured onto the burning embers. The fire sputters out in my chest, and shame grips me. I duck my head and hurry past the woman between the rows of shacks, toward the far edge of the roof.

A dozen other men and women emerge from their dwellings to stand defiantly in scavenged doorways. I pass by without raising my eyes, seize the metal ladder that extends over the edge, and shuffle down it, angry stares on me the entire way.

I jump down the final few feet and land in a thin alleyway behind the tower block, clasping the ladder and squeezing. *Get a grip.*

I sniff the air. No sign of the sulphur. Nor the strange heat. The fire continues to ebb from my body, and I take a deep breath. Then I hurry down the alleyway, my mind circling back through my plan: skirt around the buildings, get behind our followers, and discover who they are.

My steps slow, an additional weight growing in my limbs, and my thoughts clear with the banished rage.

And then what?

With a pounding head, I hasten on around the block all the way back to the main street. Then I peer beyond the corner and scan the tower block's bullet-ridden entrance, plus the metal awning of the office building opposite, fifty yards away.

A couple of cars pass, but no one's hanging about. And my eyes track up to the fourth floor, images forming of Natasha behind the far window, waiting with the same deep frown on her expression.

I tear my gaze away, dart across the street, and then hurry faster down the alleyway on the far side. I skirt around the back of the office building before turning the last corner toward the tower block and the street that runs in front of it.

There, I force myself to slow and to tread silently along the office building's wall. A rectangular opening appears in the middle of it, three feet across and two high, a few inches above the pavement – an air circulation hole for the garage below. I hunker down by its side.

The scent of old fires wafts up through the opening, the garage some kind of haven for the homeless. All is silent now as I peer through the hole into the gloom and wait for my eyes to adjust.

The floor's six feet below me and the garage is large, over a hundred feet square. My rectangular hole is in its side wall, near the back corner. Staring into the dark, shadows swim across my vision.

No visible figures.

But most of the garage is out of sight from my angle.

My heel bounces up and down, tension building in my calves. I wait for the sound of a large van passing and then grab the edge of the opening, scissor my legs through, and drop into darkness. My knees take the impact of the garage floor. And I crouch down and hold my breath.

A shiver slinks up my spine.

Three figures, all wearing suits, stand in a line between me and the garage entrance along the same side wall where I'm crouched. The nearest one's fifty feet away while the far one's positioned just before the pool of light that spills down through the ramp with a clear view of the tower block opposite. And they're all facing it.

Beyond the figures, the entrance ramp spans the first thirty feet of the far wall while the remaining seventy is solid concrete, the opposite corner of the garage ensconced in shadow. A fourth figure hovers there, to the side of the ramp, fidgeting slightly. The boss? The other three remain completely still.

Professionals.

I straighten slowly and pad into the deeper shadow of the side wall. The smell of soot is heavy in my nose, and my pulse pounds behind my ears as I scan the figures. No radiant outline, no cordite smell – the signs of angels. And no hunched postures, either.

Each has a long thin object strapped to his back.

My eyes flick to the garage ramp beyond, and the image comes of me sprinting past them. Could I draw them away?

Or would they leave a couple behind to deal with Natasha?

The fire burns again, the heat flaring down my arms, and my gaze darts to the nearest guy along the wall. My jaw tightens. I picture myself smashing his head into the concrete and then incapacitating the others, forcing one to tell me what he knows.

The prospect prickles my fingertips.

My sight starts to dim, and again, memories whirl: the enforcer's crumpled body in the tower block, the father sprawled on the mattress, and my delivery contact dead the night before. I see glimpses of my dreams – scenes of destruction, bodies strewn among rubble. The heat's suddenly overpowering, my breath burning hot in my throat. A new stench in my nose. Sulphur. And the void yawns inside me, the sense of plummeting through an endless dark …

I scrunch my eyes shut and stumble backward. My mind spins images of Gabriel, trying to infect me with his serum, his crazed eyes staring straight into mine. I shake my head and focus on the feeling of my soles on the ground, of my chest moving in and out.

"Sir." A low voice in the silence.

My eyes fly open. Blink. The garage space. Still wide and dim. And the nearest guy's facing me now. The other three figures spin in my direction.

"Careful," the boss man says from beside the ramp.

The nearest guard stalks along the side wall toward me while his two colleagues spread out in a fan. The nearest guy raises a hand behind his head and draws the thin object from behind his back. It glints in the low light.

A sword.

He levels it at me, his legs spread in some kind of fencing position. I glance past his shoulder, toward the garage ramp beyond, his two colleagues having blocked it.

A fiery wind fills my chest, my feet, my calves. Each of my limbs vibrates with the growing power. My shoulders tingle and it's as if someone's whispering sweet words in my ear – *attack, strike, maul, fight* – the fire coming so wild and fast.

I tense my legs and focus on staving off the intensifying flames.

The nearest guard takes another step forward – only thirty

feet from me now – his two colleagues behind. He pads away from the concrete wall to force me back against it, his sword still levelled at my chest.

I notice movement in the corner of my eye, and I find my gaze drawn beyond him, beyond the boss, toward the far side of the underground space.

A fifth figure. Right in the corner of the garage, barely visible in the darkness. My gut twists while gooseflesh forms across my entire back. It's a posture I recognise – hunched over, leaning forward, arms hanging down. Human-sized but not human-looking.

It stands there, unmoving, its eyes fixed on me.

More memories infiltrate my mind, other scenes from my dreams – my mother dead, the knife in my hand – and then her face morphs and changes … into Natasha's. I try to blink the visions away. The three slashes suddenly appear, superimposed on the *thing*, on the guard, on everything my eyes fall upon.

The boss is standing only ten feet from the figure. He turns his head to follow my gaze and then whirls around completely and stumbles away from it toward the ramp behind.

"Oh god," he says, his voice shaking. "What have you done?"

Me?

I stare from the boss to the *thing*, the flames rising again in my core. And again, those sweet whispers sound in my head – *attack, charge, strike …*

Tensing every muscle, I concentrate harder on keeping control, on peering through the growing haze in my vision, on shutting out the throbbing behind my temples. The *thing* shuffles across the far wall of the garage, toward the boss, toward the ramp.

Just where a new figure appears outlined against the light of the entrance. Human. Slim. Long hair.

My heart creeps up my throat.

Natasha hurries down the ramp into the murk of the garage while darkness fights with blazing fire inside me. And still, I focus hard to dam the rage and maintain control. It's like my body's become a volcano, my concentration the thinnest sliver of rock on top.

The two guards further from me train their swords on the *thing* while the nearest one remains where he is, his sword pointed at my chest, his eyes wide. And there he stands, between Natasha and me, and I find myself moving toward him … running … The lava seethes inside, ready to explode.

Over the guy's shoulder, I spy the boss retreating across the garage entrance from the *thing*. The two other guards scurry toward the ramp to get in between. And the *thing* scuttles sideways for the ramp, an awful crab-like movement. Its four limbs propel it toward the guards, the boss, toward Natasha, all in a line …

I abandon my concentration, and the fire erupts from my depths. The veil rips free of my senses, and I can feel everything – the guards, the concrete walls, floor, and ceiling, and the air in between. The fire within becomes a river of flame, and it carries me, sweeping me on, every inch of me burning. My legs thrash faster. My gaze falls on the nearer guard, still standing in between Natasha and me. Dark spots appear at the corners of my vision, and I can barely make out the guard's terror blossoming white across his face.

His feet remain rooted as I fly toward him. He thrusts with his sword. And I can *feel* his movement. Can *feel* the blade slice the air. I dart out of the way of the strike, swivel my body to face him, and slap the blade away as if it's an extension of my hand. The guard spins himself as I careen past, chest to chest, and he twists the sword, cutting my palm with the edge.

The pain evaporates in the blazing fire.

The guard pulls back his sword, and I whip both forearms up, pinning his arm between them – one in front of his elbow and the other behind his wrist. And as the guard straightens his arm to withdraw it, the power burns through my body. I snap my forearms past each other and jerk his arm in between.

So easy.

He lets out a harrowing scream as the crunch of ligament resounds in my ears. I shove the guard to the ground, the river of fire frothing ever wilder. And I sprint onward, my feet pounding on the garage floor.

The hotter the fire becomes, the more my sight clouds. The image of the garage mists and larger spots of black appear in my vision. I try to pick out the *thing*. It's on all fours, scuttling toward the ramp's pool of light, now only ten feet from the two remaining guards, from the boss, and then from … Natasha.

My mind conjures images of her body splayed out, her eyes blank, and three slashes carved into her torso.

My legs churn, and my arms flail. I throw myself onward. And amid my burning rage, the realisation hits that I'm floating out of my body, impassively watching myself scrabbling forward among a growing haze. And the more the fire builds, the further I find myself drifting away, my awareness shutting down. I'm passing out.

No, no, no!

I thrust myself faster and strain toward her, the river of flame a torrent through every part of me …

And then darkness comes.

"Jake … *Jake*."

Sounds. Remote. They echo around my head.

"It's okay. Everything's okay."

The voice again. Someone's holding my hand.

I open my eyes and squint.

Natasha's there, crouched by my side, staring down at me.

Her hair hangs down over her shoulder, the garage ceiling high above her head.

It feels as if a great weight is pressing every part of me down onto the concrete ground. I feel hollow, spent, exhausted, as if the fire has gutted me entirely.

"What the hell was that thing?"

Another voice. A man, his tone accusatory.

My eyes close, and memories flash behind their lids … The wild rage. Me breaking the guard's arm, scrambling to get to Natasha. And then darkness.

A full-on episode.

I could've killed her.

I grind the back of my head into the concrete and focus on the pain.

"What did he do?" The man's voice again. The boss is standing to my side, gazing at Natasha but pointing at me.

Natasha rises to her feet. "This was not him," she says. "Was not us."

Scuffed footsteps sound from somewhere behind, and I rotate my neck. A guard stands there, eyeing me with obvious fear, his face pale.

My insides go cold.

The boss turns to stare at me as well, clearing his throat.

"That creature," he says and jabs his finger toward the garage ramp. "You're going to tell me what you know."

11

The boss keeps up his steady stride as he leads us down a busy high road, past cafes and shops, with Natasha a few paces behind. I can barely keep up, though. It's only been a twenty-minute walk from the garage, but I'm already exhausted, breathing hard, my back wet with sweat. It's like my insides have been gouged out, the flaming anger only a memory.

I grit my teeth and force my trembling legs on faster, the tissue Natasha gave me still pressed to my bleeding palm. I stumble up to her shoulder. "Let's get out of here," I say, my voice barely a croak.

She keeps her gaze fixed on the boss. "No way," she says and follows him down a particular side road. "He clearly recognised that creature. Did you not notice?"

Again, I glance around to scan the shadows along the edges of the narrow street. I sniff the air. The acrid smell of refuse remains strong in my nose.

The boss halts in front of what looks like an all-day-breakfast place. His guard clocks both ends of the street before opening the door for us. I keep my distance. My head swims, and I prop myself against the window security bars for support.

"Come on, Jake," Natasha says, leaning in, the glint back in her eyes. "The guy might have answers."

My shoulders tense. "That's the fucking problem," I grumble.

But Natasha's already heading through the diner door. The boss and his protector continue staring at me, the guard's jaw hard. The boss guy goes to follow Natasha, but I cut him off and lurch through the doorway after her. The boss trails me, and the guard starts to walk behind. Then he stops, the boss guy shaking his head.

"Sir?" the guard says, glancing at me, his frown deepening. He grips his sports bag tighter, one of those shiny swords inside.

The boss turns to Natasha by the diner counter while angling his head in my direction. "It'll be okay. Won't it?" he says.

I just stare between them, my mouth slack.

Natasha glances at me and then nods back.

The boss smiles grudgingly, and the guard complies, heading back out the door. He situates himself to one side of it, his back to the diner, and watches the street.

The boss strides past the diner counter toward the booths. Dozens of them line both walls, and several groups of customers sit at scattered tables in between, talking in hushed tones. A young waitress approaches, and boss guy flashes a smile as he passes. She grins back and steps out of the way.

The boss chooses a secluded booth at the far end, the table a network of scratches and the seats covered in more silver repair tape than the original red plastic.

Natasha slips in first, and I slump down beside her, letting my head fall back against the wall behind. I've got a full view of the place and can hardly keep my eyes open.

The boss guy sits down opposite and scoots back in his chair.

The waitress appears at his side. The guy doesn't ask us but simply orders three coffees. She hurries away.

I blink hard and glance around me. Lights hang down from the ceiling, but every other bulb is missing. Shadows hang between the booths, creating a shroud-like effect – well designed for privacy.

My gaze falls on the guy. He's younger than he appeared in the darkness, his face hardly lined at all. Maybe late twenties, light blue eyes, and foppish good looks with stubble and unkempt brown hair. His suit and shirt are crumpled but fit him perfectly. And he's staring right back at me.

"So, who are you?" he says.

I keep my mouth shut.

Natasha edges toward him. "You first," she says. "Why were you following us?"

The guy doesn't reply but just glances between us. The quiet deepens in our dome of light. And I grab a napkin out of the dispenser to replace the tissue against my palm. The bleeding's finally stopped.

"I'm Ben," he says eventually. "Ben Whittaker."

Still I hold the silence and continue cleaning my hand.

"Special adviser to a prime ministerial candidate," he goes on. "Paul Hawcross."

Natasha takes in a sharp breath.

"You may have heard of him?" Ben says.

Who hasn't? The leader of the Puritan party in the upcoming election.

"One of my jobs is to identify threats," Ben goes on.

The word escapes my lips before I can stop myself. *"Me?"*

His eyes fix on mine. "I have two guards in the hospital," he says.

"Wait ... two?" I say, a weight growing in my chest.

Ben nods. "One by you, and the other by ..." He trails off and clears his throat. "Wilson tried to stop the creature, but it tossed him against the garage wall, broke his leg like a twig."

"You chased after it," Natasha says, admiration in her tone.

"I tried to," Ben says. He sighs, slips a hand into his jacket, and brings out a pack of cigarettes – paper not electronic. He places one between his lips, in front of two rows of perfect teeth. "But it ran away down the street. Bounced from door to door like it was trying to escape into some other building." He lights up and takes a long drag. The smoke bites at the back of my throat. "It disappeared out of sight, inhumanly fast."

Then he fixes me with another stare. "Inhumanly fast *and* strong," he says.

Among the ash of tiredness, embers spark. "You think *I'm* one of these *things*?" I snap, my insides tightening at the ridiculousness.

But images swirl from my dreams – scenes of destruction, bodies strewn, the three slashes everywhere.

"I don't know *what* you are," the guy says. "That's why I'm here." He taps his knuckle on the tabletop. "It's why we've had you followed and what I need to find out. We've been monitoring a spate of strange sightings, unprovoked attacks, local electrical systems crashing, odd-looking figures—"

"You have seen them before?" Natasha says.

Ben's mouth forms a single line before he continues. "We think so, but we've only been able to catch glimpses." He takes another drag. "The CCTV footage ends up hazy at each sighting. Some kind of surge fries the systems."

He points his cigarette at me, smoke curling from the tip. "But we've spotted *him* in several of them. Yesterday evening, financial district, Emerald Gardens. A male in his sixties, found dead at the scene. Sound familiar?"

I let out a slow breath, and the table goes quiet. The waitress brings the coffee, depositing the three cups on the table with a momentary glance at Ben. Then she's gone.

"Wait," Natasha says, glancing between us. "How does this relate to Paul Hawcross?"

"Because I need to get him elected, and he's in danger," Ben says.

"He's a politician," I say with a frown.

"Yes." Ben nods. "And the masses love him, the poor. And given the chance, he's going to win." He balances the burning cigarette on the ashtray.

I shrug. "So?"

Ben pauses. "The risk to Paul isn't from the opposition," he says. "His popularity's huge. He's going to overthrow our rulers, empower the ordinary man with what's been denied for so long." His voice rises and his eyes shine.

Natasha sits up in her seat while I raise my gaze skyward. It's like listening to Father Thomas.

"Paul Hawcross is a danger to some, and it goes back much further than the last few decades or even the last few hundred years," he says, facing Natasha. "And I think you know who I mean."

Natasha's mouth drops open, and she clutches the table.

"Angels," she says, her voice breathy.

"Indeed," he says, his gaze lingering.

Heat prickles my cheeks, and I clasp my hands together in my lap.

Ben turns on me. "We've been compiling footage, tracked your movements, seen you do some pretty incredible things," he says, his tone hard. "Melting through crowds, running over rooftops." He peers at me through narrowed eyes. "So, I'm going to ask again ... what *are* you?"

From nothing, fire flares across my chest and down my arms. "I'm no fucking angel," I growl.

Natasha extends her hand toward the guy. "Ben, we are on the same side. I promise you," she says. "We went up against an archangel ... went up against Gabriel."

Ben's eyes widen while my heartbeat rises. I swivel toward her. "Nat—"

But she keeps going, her words quickening with the familiar excitement in her tone. She recounts our story, the idiocy of insects foiling an archangel, destroying his disease. Ben remains still the entire time, the gloom deepening between the surrounding booths. He hardly blinks as he listens. Faint lines appear across his perfect brow. In the end, he just nods.

"I have my networks," he says. "I'd heard rumours."

"So you see?" Natasha nods. "We are against the angels as you are."

Ben smiles grimly. "With all due respect," he says, "you challenged a single archangel, while we're trying to bring down the entire *pantheon*."

"With politics?" I ask, unable to keep the scepticism from my voice.

"With emancipation," he says evenly. "This is the angels' ultimate fear. What they undermine at every stage of civilisation. That humankind might take back its power, that eventually we'll all be united without need for our rulers."

"And that's what your leader's going to do? Give his power away?" I ask, with an eyebrow raised.

Ben smiles wryly and sits back in his chair. "It's hard to believe. I appreciate that. But it's genuinely true," he says without a hint of defence in his tone. "He's that kind of person. Our corrupt leaders have thrown *everything* at him." He flicks his hand. "Nonstop media, TV and online ads. But they've failed. He's a Puritan, and that's key, as the movement won't trust anyone else. But he's a genuine unifier, able to reach out to all sides. That's why he's going to win the election."

I just stare at him. There's no aggrandisement in his tone, no obvious exaggeration. So either it's all true or he's an idiot.

"And this is going to end angelic rule?" I say.

Ben nods. "The only sustainable way."

"But if you know about the angels, why not dethrone them?" I say. "Tell everyone the truth, strip the angels of the devotion they need?"

Ben eyes me like I'm simple. "Who would believe us?" he says. "They'd think we're mad. No" – he wags a finger – "the only way to erode their power is to stop people looking outside of themselves for salvation. That's what my mentor believed. And that's the duty he passed on to me."

He sits there, his eyes still bright and his cigarette slowly burning down in the tray. "This is a key moment." His voice becomes low but keen. "We have our leader, and the world needs him more than ever. It's been *centuries* getting to this point again, and don't think the angels will stand idly by. They want chaos, another Dark Ages, so people will look to the heavens to be saved."

We keep quiet.

"So, you can see the danger," he goes on more quickly. "We only have days until the election, and we've worked *so* hard to get him here. I hope Paul's too popular now to assassinate, out of risk of creating a martyr, but you can never be sure." The guy smiles grimly. "An attack will come, and we need to be ready."

He glances between us. "So … these *things*, these demonic-looking creatures, I need to understand if they're a threat," he says. "What do you know about them?"

Natasha opens her mouth, and my whole body stiffens. I jump forward. "Nothing," I blurt. "I tell you, we don't … know … *anything*."

Ben stares at me. "Look," he says and places both hands on the table. "Whatever you are, they're clearly attracted to you. They have to be. Two sightings in two days?" He rotates his hands, palms up. "That's too much of a coincidence. Something must be going on. What *do* you know?"

Again, I'm about to retort when Natasha touches my arm.

"It is true," she says. "Sadly, we know very little. Just that these figures turned up a few weeks ago, started following Jake, and that sometimes his strength coincides with their appearance. But we do not understand *why*. That's what we've been trying to discover …"

She trails off, and the pressure in my chest releases a fraction. Ben stares from Natasha to me. The silence deepens within our curtain of shadow.

"But we believe Gabriel is behind it," she says eventually. "And that whatever he's doing, he will be recreating an ancient story, maybe something biblical, to stimulate devotion. If we can find out which one, we will be able to understand the coming threat."

Ben nods slowly. "Okay," he says.

Natasha leans toward him. "And so really, we need *your* help," she says.

I shift in my seat, the prickly heat shifting down my back. Then an idea stirs. I blink.

"Yeah," I splutter. "With all your … resources, you guys could take this on, you could—"

"No," Ben says, his tone stern.

Natasha goes to retort.

"I can't help directly," Ben says quickly, gazing back at her, his features softening. "My job is to keep Paul safe, and that's everything right now. Without more evidence of these *things* being a direct risk, I can't commit more resources. I *have* to keep doing my job." He smiles sadly at her. "It's our best hope."

Natasha's hands form fists. "But this is Gabriel, the *real* danger," she says.

"And there is something I *can* do," Ben says, tilting forward and sliding his hand toward hers across the table.

Natasha remains there, bent forward, poised, her fingers only inches away. My teeth clench.

"If you say Gabriel's following an old myth, there's someone who might know," he says. "He's the foremost expert on that kind of thing. He used to be part of my network, and he knows about the angels. But be aware, he is a little … strange." Ben raises a shapely eyebrow. "A total recluse nowadays. He lives underground, in a labyrinth of tunnels. There's a community down there that knows him."

Natasha stares back at him, nodding along with his words while my ribs constrict. The void's deepening inside me, the darkness pressing in like the sides of a crumbling well.

"These people are a sorry lot," Ben continues. "The whole thing's a tragedy. First, they were victimised on the surface and then persecuted for their choice to go below. But the netherfolk know where this expert lives." He looks between us. "*If* you can find them. And *if* you can get them to help you."

Ben raises a hand above his head, and the waitress reacts immediately. She heads behind the counter to fetch the bill.

Images of the tunnels continue to bombard me, the limited escape routes, the confined spaces.

Ben smiles at Natasha. "Do keep me informed," he says. "And if you find out anything more, if the threat to Paul proves real, we will commit, we *will* act." He nods. "I promise."

"Okay," says Natasha, nodding back.

And I just stare at her.

Ben lifts a single finger in warning. "But you mustn't reveal who told you about all this," he says. "My network is everything. It's how I do my job."

"That is all fine," Natasha says.

"No, it isn't," I counter.

Natasha swivels to face me. "Of course it is," she says.

I lean toward her. "Nat … us … underground …" I whisper. "It's too risky." I feel again an echo of the void and my anger like wildfire. "That guard in the garage, I put him in the *hospital*." His scream echoes in my ears. "What if I do that again …"

She meets my gaze.

"You won't," she says.

12

I TRUDGE along the side tunnel after Natasha and Father Thomas, the occasional lights of the working Tube line lost behind us like some distant sun. The ground between the rails lies thick with dust, and the darkness that hangs in front of me resembles an endless set of heavy curtains, barely penetrated by the beam from my headlamp. And we've already been walking these tunnels for bloody hours.

"Nat, nothing's down here," I call forward.

My voice echoes against the concrete surfaces, the tunnel only ten feet by ten. And I force myself to breathe, to ignore the growing feeling of constriction while a prickling sensation forms in my lower back.

Natasha doesn't turn. She simply keeps on scouring the darkness ahead of her with her headlamp. The priest pads behind her. He's abandoned his doddery persona, his walking stick, and – despite his limp – stalks forward between the rails with amazing agility.

We went straight to see him after meeting Ben. Natasha insisted, and of course he was up for following the lead. Total faith, as always.

"Nat—" I shout.

"Ben said it should be just up ahead," Natasha calls as she stalks onward.

I clench my teeth, roll my eyes, and mutter, "Ben said—"

"Wait!" she says. "*There ...*"

I squint into the black. The beam from her headlamp rests on a faint horizontal plane jutting out of the side of the tunnel – a station platform.

Natasha jogs forward, and I lengthen my stride to keep up. The tunnel broadens out around us, the ceiling higher above our heads with the walls further out on both sides – the familiar space of a Tube station.

I shine my headlamp along the walls, along the platform. There's no one. No movement at all. Nothing except silence, darkness, and the sense of being lost in time. Even the ancient notices have all been ripped off the curving walls, leaving bent frames and the scraps of grimy paper hanging limply down.

Natasha's already up on the platform, staring intently down at its surface.

"Oh, wow ..." she says.

Gooseflesh breaks out across my neck, and I scramble up after the priest.

"Footprints," Natasha says softly and points downward.

I take a few steps along the platform, my headlamp aimed at the marks in the dust. Hundreds of them head in every direction.

No, thousands.

Natasha holds her breath and aims her headlamp along the length of the concrete platform. And there she waits, poised, her beam of light swallowed so quickly by the darkness.

No one walks out of it.

The prickling sensation climbs my spine, and I sniff the air. The scent of dust and age is strong in my nose. Natasha continues to stare into the gloom.

"We're in their turf, Nat, and they don't want to be

found." I keep my voice low. "Isn't that what Ben said? This is why they came down here. To get away from the surface world."

Natasha angles her headlamp back at the concrete platform, and the darkness creeps closer around us.

"So we need to follow them," she says and uses her beam to trace a set of marks in the direction of an arch in the centre of the platform wall. "See where they lead."

She pads toward the arch, illuminating footprint trails as she goes. I keep my mouth shut and follow behind while sweeping my beam over the crisscrossing patterns in the dust.

We end up in a central hallway between the platforms that's thirty feet wide and blocked at one end. A disused set of steps climbs from the other. All's dark. All's quiet.

Natasha continues to trace the many trails with the beam from her headlamp. And after ten minutes, she ends up returning to the same spot in the middle of the concrete floor, her hands on her hips.

I shrug at her. "Impossible, right?"

She stares at me, the light from her headlamp almost blinding. "So *you* track them," she says. "This is *your* expertise."

I raise my arm, avert my eyes, and then ponder.

"Okay," I say.

She frowns, and I train my headlamp on the ground. Then I shuffle toward the very edge of the central hall. The thoroughfare becomes a little easier to follow here, hundreds of footprints heading to and from the stairs. I amble in their direction, keeping my pace slow.

"This way," I say.

I lead them gradually up the steps and along a passageway above the tracks. We reach a four-way junction and then another set of stairs down to another platform. With the blackness filling every tunnel, it's seriously disorientating, difficult to get a sense of their layout. And with each passageway we navigate, I have to concentrate hard to build up a mental map of the space.

I keep us following more passageways, more stairs. Some straight, some curving. And a myriad of footprints covers every section of the floor. Only the very sides enable us to find trails to follow.

We descend another set of steps and pass through an arch onto a train platform. I pad right to the far end, my headlamp beam glued to the trail I'm following. Natasha keeps behind me, her beam only a few feet from mine. I angle us toward another archway when Natasha stops dead.

"Wait," she says and reaches out to touch my arm.

I swivel. The priest comes to a halt at her side. Natasha shines her headlamp at the blank noticeboards on the opposite side of the tracks, at the bent frames and the few bits of paper hanging down.

She whirls on me. "This is where we started," she snaps. "We have gone in a loop."

I force my mouth into an O shape and then go to ogle the billboards. But her eyes pin mine, and I can only meet her gaze, a thin smile on my lips.

"This search has been pointless. Hasn't it?" she says, and jabs a finger at me. "You have already got it all worked out, the footprints. I *know* you have."

Her accusation hangs like the motes of dust in our averted beams, and I feel the strange prickling sensation across my back again, an itchy heat.

I clear my throat. "Maybe."

The priest laughs. The noise echoes out into the gloom.

Natasha inhales deeply and then lets it out. "Jake, we are *with* you," she says, her tone thin. "Painful or not, you have to face what's happening. It will *not* go away on its own."

The embers spark, and I shake my head. "I've told you, Nat, it's *dangerous*," I hiss. "What about those *things*? What if one's down here?"

"We will know we're on the right track," she says.

I scoff and turn away.

"What makes you think they are not connected with Gabriel's plan?" Natasha asks.

Suddenly, the flames scorch my insides. "What makes you think they *are*?" I snap back at her, and the sound of my shout reverberates around the station.

I take a breath to settle myself. "If they're real, they're drawn to *me*. No one else," I say. "And making my life a living hell doesn't advance Gabriel's plan, doesn't spark devotion in the world. It's got *nothing* to do with it."

Natasha stares back at me. Tilts her hips. "Prove it," she says.

"What?" I say.

"Find Ben's expert and prove it," she says and gestures along the platform. "If you are so sure."

I try to make out Father Thomas's expression in the darkness. Is he smiling?

"And if we don't find anything, any connection, I promise I will abandon it all," she says.

My mouth falls open. *"Really?"* I say.

She nods. "Anyway," she says and lifts her chin. "I'm not leaving until we have found the community, the netherfolk."

And again, she holds my gaze. I fidget, my fingers twitching. She crosses her arms and raises an eyebrow. I grunt and tilt my eyes down, focusing once more on the concrete platform.

I pad back toward the arch, tracing my beam across the many trails, but instead of trying to make out the visible ones, I search for the bits of floor with *no* observable marks, the well-used areas where the dust has been packed down to evenness by countless footsteps. It requires following a few dead ends, but eventually the uniform areas lead me to a side tunnel off the hallway between the first two platforms, to a particular manhole set in the floor.

I crouch down and run my fingers along the sides of its

circular cover. Numerous scrapes mar the edges – crowbar marks or something similar.

"What do you think?" Natasha asks, stepping to my side.

I gaze up at her. "And if we find no link, you'll give this up?"

After a while, she nods.

The priest squats down next to me and grips the cover handles. "We have to try," he says, his eyes finding mine. "Surely, this is why we're here."

I breathe and stare downward. "And there's always that darling Ben if we *do* find something," I mutter.

"What was that?" Natasha asks, leaning in, her tone sharp.

"Nothing!" I say, tensing my arms.

Father Thomas and I haul the cover open together, sliding it to the side. The metal disc moves easily, well greased and well used.

The manhole shaft descends straight down, far narrower than the tunnels so far at only a few feet across. Staring at the hole, my vision hazes, and the sense of constriction builds in my chest, like massive hands squeezing my ribs. My body scrabbles backward while Natasha paces right to the manhole entrance and stares down into the shaft.

A stale warmth wafts up from the darkness. Water pipes or simply the Earth's natural heat? And a dank smell. Stagnant water and rotting things. Again, I sniff the air. Some kind of acrid scent lies beneath it all. My gut twists – my early warning system – as Natasha reaches for the sides of the manhole.

"Wait!" I say and dart forward, flinging my arm out to stop her.

Too fucking slow. She's already lowered herself over the edge of the opening. I grip the manhole, only able to watch, my heart pounding, as she descends a set of metal rungs driven into the wall of the shaft. The whole thing's fifteen feet deep, and eventually there's a splash of water as she hits the bottom.

I lean my head down into the narrow space, and the sense of constriction is enough to set my ears abuzz. The clashing desires seize me. Should I follow her down or simply run?

I hold myself steady.

"You okay?" I yell down to her.

"There's another tunnel," she says, her soft voice echoing upward. "Wait." Sudden tension fills her tone, and she shines her headlamp in both directions.

I lean further over to see, that acrid scent in my nose again … Definitely sulphur. My heart beats like hammers on anvils.

"I think someone is down here," she says, her voice wavering.

I hold my breath, tense every muscle, and jump into the shaft. I clamber down two rungs at a time, my feet repeatedly sliding off the slick metal.

The confined space presses in on me on all sides. Closer. Tighter. I push myself on downward. Sweat beads on my temples. And I leap the final five feet. Water splashes up my calves and I'm forced to crouch, the tunnel much narrower, its ceiling only a few inches above my head.

It continues in both directions, and Natasha trains her headlamp one way and then the other, illuminating stained and rusted walls. The black swallows the beam after a dozen or so feet.

It's like some kind of ancient crypt – dripping concrete, stale air, a fusty smell.

Natasha faces one direction and stares on.

"You okay?" I ask again, my voice hardly a whisper.

"Fine," she says with a nod, getting her voice under control. "I thought I saw …"

She trails off. A new sound in the silence. A distant pattering. I strain to listen over my racing pulse. The noise of hands or feet moving on concrete surfaces, one over the other, the speed unnaturally fast – animal, not human. And then more sounds come. An occasional jabbering, unintelligible – the strange language I remember from my dreams, but sharper, more guttural.

My skin crawls. And the void plunges so deeply inside me. The same images flash – my childhood home, the gang selling drugs, locking me in the chest – but coming faster, now. The memories inundate me while the tunnel walls press ever more tightly from all sides, wringing the air from my lungs. I'm struggling to breathe.

And *wait*. There, in the tunnel's blackness. The outline of a crooked figure – front limbs hanging down, animal-like. Just standing there, barely visible, and staring forward. Natasha continues to gaze in its direction, no change to her expression.

No change at all.

There's a sudden splash at my side.

I whirl around. Shoot my arms up. When a hand grips my shoulder.

The priest stares into my eyes. "Jacob, what's wrong?" he asks.

Natasha's gazing at me as well.

I spin back to stare down the tunnel. The crooked outline of the figure, the flash of dark eyes … *gone*. The smell of sulphur is gone, too. I blink into the darkness.

The old man tightens his fingers, and warmth spreads down my chest. My lungs relax a fraction, my breath coming easier.

Natasha swivels back and directs her headlamp toward where I glimpsed the *thing*. "I think it's this way," she says.

My whole body tenses. "Nat, please!" I beg.

She spins to face me, the gleam in her eyes visible again in the reflected beam.

"It's too dangerous," I say. "We've got no idea what's down here."

"The netherfolk, Jake, at the very least," she says. "You found the trail."

She starts down the narrow tunnel.

I grit my teeth. "*Wait*," I say.

She stops. And I sweep my headlamp along the tunnel walls to both sides of us, peering closely at the water marks. It's marginal, but the residue reaches a little higher up the walls in the opposite direction to Natasha.

"This way," I say and point.

She arches an eyebrow at me, and I indicate the raised water marks.

"Splashing feet," I say.

She nods and falls in behind as I stumble on into the darkness. Even hunched over, my head still bumps on the low ceiling and exposed pipes while images of the *things* circle my mind.

It takes an age, traipsing down endless tunnels and navigating junctions based on the level of corrosion on the walls. There's no more sulphur smell, no more prickling heat. And the silence presses in at my ears.

The higher splash marks take us down another narrow passageway, and I swing my headlamp from side to side. Then suddenly the end of the beam becomes lost in darkness.

My stomach flips, and I lurch to a halt.

The walls ahead of us have vanished on either side. I step over a threshold into what feels like a larger space – a *much* larger space. Dust hangs heavier in the air, and my headlamp beam doesn't reach the far wall. I angle it up and illuminate the start of a flat ceiling far higher above my head, but the rest of it's quickly lost in the gloom.

A deeper silence descends. Natasha steps to my shoulder, and my gut twists again, my internal warning ringing loudly.

13

I EDGE FORWARD into the open space and probe the darkness with my headlamp.

The outline of shapes emerges, the faintest lines of grey on black – tents, tarpaulins, mats – stretching out across a sprawling floor ahead of me. Natasha takes another step and searches the space with her beam. A makeshift altar appears to one side. Items hang down on bits of twine from the ceiling – religious paraphernalia, crosses – a couple shifting fractionally in the air. I hold up my fingertips and feel, but there's no wind down here.

A shudder runs up my spine.

I peer forward, straining to pick out whatever's moving in the darkness.

The priest's voice splits the quiet. "Greetings, friends," he says. "Please come into the light."

More silence.

"My children, we're not here to hurt you," Father Thomas tries again. "I'm a priest, a shepherd in these dark times."

The sound echoes off hidden walls and resounds back with ever-greater power. It vibrates my chest, pulling at my solar plexus.

His command voice.

Still there's no reply, and I picture movements in the darkness. A few of the hanging crosses swing a little further, like the gears of some gigantic waking mechanical monster. I'm about to probe the shadows again when an authoritative female voice rings out.

"Your flashlights!"

Natasha glances at me and removes her headlamp, averting its beam toward the floor. I keep mine focused straight ahead. Natasha narrows her eyes, and eventually, I follow suit.

Still nothing happens.

"Turn them off!" a male voice shouts.

My eyes find Natasha's. "Too risky," I hiss.

She holds my gaze for a moment and then switches off her headlamp.

I gape back at her. "There's most likely an army out there," I say. "This is their territory. They know it too well."

The silence deepens.

Natasha nods urgently at me. "*Jake*," she says.

The air prickles with charge, the tension building. My fingers flex.

Natasha softens her voice. "It will be okay."

I mutter and grip my headlamp hard, but then I extinguish it.

Absolute blackness reigns. It grips my chest, my throat, and it's like the walls are rushing in again, the ceiling pressing down. My heart pumps ever faster.

I hear the faint sound of scuffing feet coming from both sides. First just a few, but then more. And then many more, all padding to form some kind of arc around us, the edges getting ever closer. I tense my arms, lower myself, and prepare for an onslaught. And then lines of small lights turn on along the borders of the space – LEDs. They illuminate the entire room. Everything.

My mouth falls open.

The space – *it's huge* – is probably seventy yards deep and fifty wide, rectangularly shaped with both a flat ceiling and floor. Primitive wooden structures and tents litter the ground, canvas mats in between. The room could sleep hundreds. And in the centre lies a large, clear, circular area with boxes and crates around its edge. A section of tarpaulin stretches down half the length of one wall, with several mats spread underneath it. A hundred people stand in a semicircle facing us. Some hold makeshift weapons: metal poles, knotted lengths of rope, wooden clubs. And they all eye us with taut features.

A solitary figure steps forward from the crowd. A woman. She has long grey hair that reaches her waist and a simple staff in one hand, her fingers tight around it. And though she's short, only up to Natasha's shoulders, she holds herself upright with real poise. Clearly some kind of leader.

Father Thomas bows low, his hands held in prayer. "Apologies for the intrusion, friends," he says softly. No command voice this time. "We're simply here to beg for some help. We're not with any agency and will tell no one of your location. We don't want to cause you any trouble."

A man stalks forward to stand behind the female leader. Unlike her, he's stooped in posture, with an unkempt beard and blazing eyes. "You *are* trouble," he says, his voice shaking with anger. He jabs his finger at us. "Leave!"

The leader doesn't admonish him, and a hundred pairs of eyes stare at us intently. A couple of figures holding weapons step up to the side of the man.

"We are looking for someone!" Natasha calls out over the crowd.

"People come here not wanting to be found," the female leader says.

"He is an expert on scripture," Natasha says, speaking quickly. She motions at the makeshift altar with the religious symbols hanging down. "Apparently, he lives down here?"

More silence. Yet colder. The entire room goes still.

I lean in toward Natasha and whisper, "They're not going

to help." I put my forearm across her and tense my shoulder to nudge her backward.

Bearded guy growls, "Leave now—"

A new noise cuts him off. A pitter-patter sound in the passageway at my back. Bare feet on stone?

Goosebumps prickle across my forearms. I spin. The tunnel entrance looms before me, and a jabbering sound starts up out of the darkness. The same strange language from my dreams, like taunts this time.

I swivel and scan the crowd. They react too. People scramble around the cavernous space, staring in all directions and conversing in urgent whispers, all the focus on us gone.

Natasha grasps my arm while my heart pounds harder. A biting scent in the air – acrid, sulphurous – and the void surges inside me. Images flash through my mind. My mother dead again, Natasha, the three slashes carved into them … And in an instant, fire erupts up out of the black. I grip Natasha's hand and thrust myself between her and the tunnel entrance. Then I search the darkness with my headlamp, my mind conjuring images of the *thing*. The flames rage at my core – blissful release from the void inside – power surges down my legs, the veil starts to peel back …

With Natasha only feet from me.

I breathe and bite down on the rising flames, keeping my thoughts going to force the veil back into place.

An inhuman shriek rebounds around the space behind me. The sound came from everywhere. And now people are backing away from the walls, huddling together in the middle of the room. Some fall to their knees, clasping their hands in prayer, while others scream. The female leader raises her arms and shouts vainly for calm. And I stare over the agitated masses.

It's clear panic … but not confusion. They *know* this threat.

My eyes land on the bearded guy while people rush madly around him. He's standing stock-still, his mouth open in shock.

I scramble toward him, grab his arm, and shout into the growing turmoil, "What's out there?"

The words are like a switch. He whirls in my direction, his eyes wide, and throws himself at me, flailing with wild punches.

I raise a hand to protect myself, my own fire rising to meet his. The heat sears across my shoulders and down my arms. I grab one of his wrists and squeeze, trying hard not to throttle the guy.

"Let me *go!*" he yells and tries to wrench himself free.

I hold on tightly and shout louder this time, "What ... *is* ... it?"

He flies at me with his free hand, clawing at my chest. "It's you!" he shrieks, spittle flying. "You've brought it here!"

I grab both his arms, which makes him thrash more wildly in my grip.

"You're fucking devils!" he screams. "Witches!"

Natasha appears at my side and says, "Devils?"

She holds the guy's shoulders and tries to soothe him, but he bucks ever harder against me. And all the while, the man's accusations echo in my mind.

I clasp his wrists tighter while the void swells inside me, a growing weight choking the flames.

Bearded guy shoves at me again. "Let me go!" he wails, and then he starts to moan. "I must protect them ... protect them ..." The guy strains toward the rear corner of the cavern, toward the tented area.

"Your family?" Natasha says and leans closer to hear amid the bedlam.

The guy suddenly sags in my grip, and I let him go. He crumples to the floor and wails, repeating the same name over and over. "Gemma ... Gemma ... it took Gemma."

And standing there amid the tumult, more memories form in my mind. I glimpse the *things* I've seen, their different sizes and shapes, but always the same posture, always that same haunting stare.

I blink, a new question whirring.

The *thing* shrieks again, and I jump before spinning around.

The sound's louder this time, closer, its source a tunnel entrance two-thirds of the way down the side wall. A group of women sobs hysterically in the centre of the space. Several netherfolk cling to each other while a handful scramble in our direction, prodding and poking at us with their rudimentary weapons. They push us back toward the tunnel behind.

"Get out, get out, get out!" they yell, as I ward them off.

Chaos reigns. The *thing* shrieks louder, and the netherfolk are screaming, crying, and scrabbling all over the place. The cavern has become a bubbling cauldron with more frenzy ladled in every moment. And the more the turmoil grows, the hotter the fire burns inside me. The energy squeezes my ribs, power building in every cell of my body.

And all the while, the same question nags at me.

I tense my fingers, hands, arms, shoulders, chest as I force the energy up my throat.

"Stop!" I scream.

The sound detonates in the underground space, far louder than I imagined.

A sudden stillness descends, a pregnant pause. And all eyes turn toward me.

14

The yelling's stopped. The *thing* is quiet as well, no more shrieking or jabbering. And while some netherfolk continue to moan and whimper, a hundred sets of eyes are trained on me.

I stare back at them all, my heart thumping hard, the embers smouldering in my chest. I clench my fists and channel the energy up my throat again.

"Listen!" I shout, and the sound echoes out around us. "I'll go out there. Find this *thing*. And drive it away."

The quiet deepens, and the netherfolk's expressions morph from shock to incredulity in the low light. Countless mouths gape at me while doubts needle my brain …

Bearded guy continues to mumble at my feet – "Gemma … Gemma …" – and I search out the female leader amid the rows of disbelieving stares. She stands among the netherfolk huddled in the middle, staff in hand, frozen in the act of organising them.

"But I need maps of the tunnels," I call out to her. "I need to know the layout."

She appraises me for a moment, her features hard. Then she swivels and whispers a hushed command to a group of people standing at her back. A boy breaks from the group and scampers toward one of the dark corners behind us. Everyone else remains still, most of them continuing to stare at me.

My heel bounces up and down.

The boy returns a few moments later with a leather satchel, holding it reverently in front of him. Hesitantly, he offers it to me when an inhuman shriek splits the silence from behind. The boy jumps and spins in terror, clutching the satchel to his torso. The sound makes me start also, sending my adrenaline racing. I gaze over the boy's shoulder at one of the tunnel entranceways, further down the side wall.

The jabbering starts up again – hissed syllables that run over each other. The netherfolk huddle closer together, their whimpering growing louder as the sense of frenzy builds once more.

"The maps!" I bark out at all of them.

The boy swivels, his eyes like moons in the dull light. And many other netherfolk gaze back at me, too. The noise settles.

"Hand them over," I say, and hold out my palm.

Eventually, the boy opens the satchel and pulls out sheets of grease-stained transparent paper. Handmade maps of the tunnels, drawn with incredible detail, all taped together. He clutches them in trembling fingers and lays them on the ground at my feet. The surrounding netherfolk back away while the female leader brings over an electric lamp and holds it aloft.

I scrutinise the sprawling maps. They display multiple levels of endless tunnels, scrawled in different hands, covering a massive area, undoubtedly built over decades. And so hellishly complicated that I can't even find this cavern's location.

All the while, the jabbering continues. The *thing* shrieks intermittently from the nearby passageway. While the community huddles ever closer, their terrified whispers building again, the various sounds pull at my concentration.

Father Thomas leans over my shoulder, and I shake myself. Then I ask the female leader questions about our location on the maps as well as their scale and orientation. I cram the details of the neighbouring tunnels into my head, building the kind of mental model I have of the city streets above. Through it all, the pressure builds, all those eyes staring down at me while my pulse beats harder behind my ears.

When my brain starts to hurt, I straighten up. Some of the nearby netherfolk stumble backward, and I spin to face the left wall of the cavern. The boy collects the maps from the floor.

The priest faces me. "I'll go with you," he says.

Natasha steps to my side. "Me too."

"Nat, I—"

"Don't even think about it," she says, cutting me off with a raised hand. "You are not leaving me behind again."

The heat builds once more, embers blazing at my core. I jab my finger at the nearby entranceway.

"In there?" I say, my voice rising. "Into the tunnels?"

As if on cue, the sound of the *thing* shrieking echoes around the dark cavern.

Natasha simply folds her arms across her body and nods.

I take a breath. "You think I'm going to go into a confined space with you, with one of these creatures nearby?" I say, trying and failing to keep my voice low. "D'you think I'm *crazy*?"

"Jake, you—" Natasha starts.

"It's not safe! I could lose control!" I say, my jaw clenched. "I told you before, that's *exactly* what Gabriel wants."

My shout echoes away in the growing quiet. I swallow as the netherfolk look on around us. Natasha simply stares back at me.

"Nat, *please*," I say, lifting my hand.

She steps closer. "Jake, you cannot protect me, or anyone else, in every instance," she says softly. "You understand that, right? You are going to have to let go."

The sense of void's there at my core, the darkness below

me like an abyss, and the noise of the distant jabbering starts up again in my ears. Images form from my dreams – Natasha's dead body, me standing above her with a knife.

I squeeze my fingers together. The flames spark inside.

"*Please*," I say again, my voice barely a whisper. "Let me try to help these people, to drive this *thing* away."

I pause and meet her gaze.

"I may even find out more about it," I go on.

Natasha stares back and eventually sighs.

"Okay," she says and touches my arm. "I will stay." She turns to the side. "I'm sure I can do something." She faces the length of stretched tarpaulin that runs down one half of the wall, the community's sick and injured sprawled on mats underneath.

With a deep breath, I calm the fire. Then I swivel toward the cavern's edge, my mind running through the mental map of the underground tunnels. I lope off toward the sound of the *thing's* jabbering – also the direction of one of the branching passageways. Father Thomas falls in beside me. The netherfolk break the circle and line up silently to watch us stride past, their expressions ranging from disbelief to shock.

"Father!" yells Natasha.

I swivel, my tongue poised, but she simply throws a headlamp through the air. The priest catches it with a mere glimpse behind, and she holds my gaze, her expression unreadable. Anxious? Sad?

I leave her there and pace on across the cavern, the sensation of tonnes of earth gradually lifting from my shoulders. We reach the tunnel entrance halfway down the side wall. From the maps, it's a hundred yards long with several diverging passageways, probably for water, sewage, electricity lines. All built to support the Tube stations and the city above. I step over the line of LEDs and switch on my headlamp, directing it into the tunnel opening as I probe the darkness.

Nothing.

Nothing except for the *thing's* strange jabbers echoing from somewhere up ahead. I force myself through the opening. Father Thomas follows just behind. We walk at a measured pace, the air dank, and my tiny beam illuminates mere slivers in the blackness – patches of tunnel, dripping brickwork, empty wire brackets – before it moves on and the darkness rushes in to fill them. The *thing's* inhuman shrieks echo back to us, acting as some kind of beacon to follow, and we press on, reaching junction after junction and following winding tunnels in the black.

We walk for what feels like an eternity, but the *thing's* jabbering grows no louder. It doesn't approach me for a glimpse as they do above ground, instead keeping its distance while retreating further into the maze we're walking into.

My eyes find the priest, walking only feet away.

Is that why?

In the next instant, the sounds stop. The priest and I halt as well. An eerie silence descends, darkness looming on all sides. The raging fire at the heart of me … gone. Replaced by a sense of cold that prickles my skin.

I traipse onward. More slowly now. And the sound doesn't start up again. Instead, after ten more yards, we find a manhole in the middle of the tunnel floor, its lid hinged open in the vertical position. I hold my breath and shine my headlamp on the opening, peering closer at the hinge. Some kind of fabric is caught there, a tattered purple cotton, old and faded. Again, bearded guy's words come back to me.

Gemma, Gemma … it took Gemma.

"Do you think it went down there?" the priest says, his voice low.

"It's possible," I say. "The sounds might not travel well between levels."

My fingers trace the rim of the lid. Its edge is as corroded as its top.

I hold up the piece of purple cotton. "This could've been there for days or weeks," I say.

The priest nods.

I straighten. "Let's split up," I say.

He holds my gaze in the averted headlamp.

"I'll stay here and yell if I see anything," I say. "You go down and do the same." I direct my beam into the manhole. "There's another tunnel below." I picture the map of the multiple levels and trace the direction of the lower tunnel with my headlamp. "It continues on and then branches to the left."

"I remember," the priest says.

"Just before the branch, you'll see a loop, a narrower passage that leaves and then bends back to the main tunnel," I say. "The *thing* could've gone that way. We might hear nothing up here."

Again, the priest gazes back at me, his brow furrowed. "Are you certain you want to do this?" he says.

I take a deep breath and peer out into the tunnel, images of a hunched figure forming in the black. Then the vision morphs, and I see Natasha safe with the netherfolk, busy nursing the injured.

And like an idiot, I nod. "I want to see if we can get a proper look at this *thing*," I say. "Then we drive it further away if we can."

The priest says nothing. And for a moment, we stand together in the silence, shoulder to shoulder, our eyes fixed in the enveloping dark. Then, without a word, he steps over to the manhole and lowers himself into the open shaft, peering back up at me.

"The tunnel down below, then the loop," he says.

I nod again, my hands on my knees.

"I'll yell if I catch a glimpse," he says, then he clambers down the metal ladder and disappears from view.

I glance both ways. The quiet stretches around me. Like pads over my ears, patches over my eyes. It draws the darkness in closer. The surface world could be a thousand metres away, or a hundred thousand bloody miles.

Entirely alone. Yet not.

I breathe and shake myself, forcing my legs further on down the passageway. After thirty yards, a T-junction appears out of the dark. Still no jabbering. No sound at all. I take a left and pad onward, guessing when I'd be out of earshot of the priest, and stop just before. I shine my headlamp down the tunnel in both directions. The beam disappears quickly in the black.

And I wait, biting my lip.

All those times the fuckers found me above ground if I stayed in the same place for too long.

Yet still, there's no sound. The holes on both sides resemble vast mouths, gaping and hungry. No sound from the priest, either.

I turn, traipse back to the junction, and then continue another twenty yards in the same direction. The darkness seems thicker here, my flashlight beam weaker. I shake the headlamp. Its bulb glows no brighter.

Batteries?

An icy chill trickles down my spine, like the moisture dripping from the walls, and I lean forward. I scour the blackness with the remaining light. Still nothing. And the beam's becoming increasingly dim, the shadow's edge creeping closer to my feet.

The chill spreads up my neck, and I swivel around before hurrying back toward the T-junction. My mind spins; every fucking tunnel looks the same. I reach the open shaft and shine the headlamp in the direction we came from. Still no sound or sign of the *thing*. It must have been over half an hour now. And the image comes of the netherfolk's cavern beyond, far away through the maze of tunnels, Natasha with them, a half-hour journey from here.

The realisation dawns, and I stand there motionless, the ice coating my entire insides.

What have I done?

In the depths of the earth, the abyss opens up at my core again. So big. So fucking wide. And without thinking, I search for the sparking anger, for relief. The fire builds, energy firing down my legs. I throw myself across the open shaft, back toward the cavern. Then I skid to a halt.

The smell's sharpened, the scent of sulphur now stinging my nose. And the strange jabbering language echoes out of darkness from behind. I whirl around, my pulse racing, and probe the black with my headlamp.

There it is, just beyond the edge of the dome of light: the barest outline of a standing figure. Hunched posture, head extended forward, arms hanging down. The hint of a misshapen face, its features contorting horribly in the shifting darkness. More bitter memories invade my brain – enforcers hunting me, beating me – while the fire burns hotter with every second, the flames tightening the muscles of my legs, my shoulders, my arms …

Too much. Too much.

Still the *thing* stares on. Practically invisible except for those shiny coal-black eyes, the same curious gaze. A part of me is desperate to step forward, to get a closer look. Yet the void's already so deep, the heat like a bonfire inside my chest, and my body starts to shake.

I try to breathe, my pulse a living drum, and focus on the open shaft in between us. It's two feet from me, five from the *thing*, and Father Thomas is somewhere below us. The *thing* jabbers and hisses louder, words almost intelligible in its madness. And the river of fire burns ever wilder inside me. My hands twitch with the urge to leap forward, to punch, to tear, to fight …

With gritted teeth, I concentrate even harder on the manhole, clenching every muscle in my body, and fling myself toward the circular gap. Just as the *thing* lets out an almighty shriek.

15

I JUMP for the open shaft, for the rungs down the far side. My feet hit the slick metal strips and slip, causing me to tumble down the manhole. My elbows slam against the rim. The impact vibrates my teeth, and pain screams up my arms. But the fire roars louder, engulfing everything, as energy surges through my body. I fling myself down the remaining rungs and drop to the ground.

Water splashes, and I stagger forward a step. The smell of rot is strong in my nose. Sulphur, too. The jabbering language intensifies above my head but then dies. The heat inside me diminishes a fraction, and a growing chill takes its place.

I tense my legs and hurl myself down the new tunnel, the beam from my headlamp bouncing from floor to wall, floor to wall. The further I travel, the less the void grips my insides. The desire seizes me to just keep on running, to follow the passageway as far as it'll go.

Still, I force my attention back to the priest.

"Father!" I yell and slow my steps to illuminate every passing side tunnel.

No sign. Of the *thing* either. No splash behind me. No sound aside from my running footsteps, the galloping of my heart.

I direct my beam up ahead. The tunnel branches and, to its side, the narrower loop – a semicircular passageway that heads off this main one before rejoining it. I'm only ten yards from its entrance when the jabbering starts again. The sound of scrabbling hands and feet grows louder behind me.

The void opens up my core, and for an instant, my vision swims. Memories come of me being chased by the gang – sprinting down the entrance hall at home, fumbling the door open, my pulse wild, and then being grabbed by powerful hands and yanked back …

I blink hard and shove the thoughts aside, throwing myself faster onward. I focus intently on the approaching loop entrance. It's a perfect circle, only six feet in diameter, cut into the side wall of the main corridor, a foot and a bit off the ground. I grip its slick walls and scramble up onto it on my knees before thrusting myself into the hole, imagining the priest up ahead somewhere …

My forehead smacks against something, and my body crumples. Pain throbs behind my temples, and I find myself blinking up at a low pipe that runs across the tunnel, two-thirds of the way up. My sense of time is scattered, and the void yawns far wider inside me, a crushing aloneness, while the icy chill steals up the back of my skull.

I fling myself under the pipe and dive down the narrower tunnel, shoving myself faster onward. Despite that, the darkness grips my entire body, the void deepening with every lurching step. I pass a junction on the inside wall and drive myself on down the curving passageway, back toward the main tunnel up ahead. The jabbering continues to grow louder, to draw closer behind no matter how fast I go, the strange heat scorching the back of my neck.

My heartbeat gallops and, with the abyss so deep inside me, it takes everything to force myself to come to a halt. To spin back around.

My body shakes as I stand there, plumbing the dark with my headlamp while searching the walls. My brain reels. The tunnel's symmetrically shaped – a perfect circle – with no other features to prove up or down. And the same sulphuric smell stings at my nose, getting stronger.

Head pounding, I feel my vision fog once more, and pictures form in the blackness, the jabbering language ever louder in my brain. Again, it's memories of my home, of the gang. The rage that seized my twelve-year-old self. Yelling. Crying. Trying to shove grown men out the door. Their laughter. And then rough fingers over my mouth. Being hauled to my mother's wooden chest. Her in another room. On another planet.

Then the outline of a hunched figure appears at the tip of my headlamp beam and morphs into a vision of my mother. It's as if I'm back on the doorstep of my childhood home, ready to leave, and she's turning away, unresponsive. The memory plays over and over, the jabbering intensifying as the pain tears at my heart, the void like a bottomless well. And I'm falling, falling ...

No, no, no ...

The fire blazes in my chest and catapults me out of the darkness. The inferno spreads down my legs and across my shoulders. My body throbs, the rage taking me over. The void feels cavernous underneath.

Nevertheless, I take a trembling step forward.

The image shifts in front of me, the vision of my mother fading piece by piece ... Her cream dress morphs into one that's faded purple. Her golden hair becomes matted brown. Her posture twists. Her expression contorts. And I find myself staring at a woman with clothes ripped and stained beyond recognition.

Gemma. Bearded guy's wife. I'd bet on it.

She hovers by the junction in that same awful posture – hunched forward, her arms hanging down, her head held at an angle – and her black eyes give me a knowing look. Three slashes hover over her crooked body. She opens her mouth and staggers half a step toward me, sounds burbling.

"You," she says, the word barely intelligible.

Flames scorch my insides, the fire surging ever wilder through my veins. My vision hazes again ... and she becomes one of the gang members from my home. In that instant, I see myself leaping forward, grabbing the guy's neck and smashing his head into the tunnel wall. The same sweet words from the garage whisper in my ears ... *maul, fight, kill.*

My body coils, every muscle tense. While it's as if a growing part of my awareness is watching this all from on high. I bend my knees, lean toward the figure, and prepare to launch myself ...

With a sudden flash of movement, the entire world lurches. Something shoots out of the junction in the side wall.

Father Thomas crashes into the *thing,* and the tunnel somehow flips upside down. Gravity reversed. The woman's sent flying up, bounces off the roof of the passageway, and hovers there in the light of my headlamp, horizontally suspended a few inches under the ceiling.

I feel myself pulled upward as well and cast my hands out to grab at the curving walls, trying to keep my feet.

The priest jumps and clasps the *thing* by the shoulders at the very instant gravity rights itself. Then he drops to his knees and slams the woman's body into the ground.

She's on her back, unmoving, rasping for breath. Father Thomas jumps astride her. And in the next moment, the *thing* twists and writhes, arms and legs flailing. The priest grasps one of its wrists and then another, pushing them down hard. He trains his headlamp beam on the woman's face.

The jabbering screams louder in my head as I grip my ears. And the *thing* bucks and thrashes at the priest like a crazed bull. It shrieks, brings both knees up, and thrusts them desperately at Father Thomas. Somehow he hangs on.

I can only stare. The *thing's* movements grow faster and faster, its flailing limbs almost too quick to see. With the fire raging inside, my thoughts cease automatically, and the veil peels back so easily from my senses. The void intensifies, almost taking my breath away, and time slows.

The *thing* shrieks and bucks again while Father Thomas levers himself up and slams its body back down again. And then the *thing* stops writhing. A moment of calm. It swivels its head in my direction, giving me a leering smile.

My mouth drops open.

With the veil pulled back an inch, I glimpse something inside her. A small black figure – two feet long, with arms and legs of equal length and a bulbous skull. It's as if I'm seeing the images superimposed – the black form inside the woman, hovering within the top of her chest, its head within hers, their eyes lined up so perfectly that its black irises stare out of her face.

With an enormous crack like a gunshot, the woman's limbs flail upward, and a wall of energy rolls through me. It shakes my sternum as the smell of sulphur assails my nose.

The black form slips free, leaves the woman, and scuttles away down the tunnel on its four limbs, fleeing the shimmering flashlight beam. And with the creature gone, the woman's body collapses lifeless to the ground.

I suck in dank air, and realise I've been holding my breath. Exhaustion claims my body. My legs sway and buckle, all fire spent, the veil back in place, and I slump down to the floor.

My head pounds again, all thought suspended. The priest steps off the woman's body, stands over her a moment, and then slides down the side of the passageway himself, breathing hard.

I grasp my headlamp from my head and, with shaking hands, direct the beam back down the tunnel after the black creature.

No sign.

My headlamp beam falls on the woman lying there. Her chest moves faintly up and down. Breathing. Relief sweeps through me. I blink, and her image morphs into one of my mother splayed out on the ground, the three slashes superimposed onto her torso.

I sit up, my body tense, and blink again.

The form has changed once more. Now it's Natasha, also lying still, the image morphing so quickly it's like I'm thumbing through the pages of a flip-book.

I stagger to my feet and lurch over. The previous face returns. Caked in grime. And still breathing. Her shoes and purple dress are ripped. Two of her fingers broken. The vision of the three tears continues to hover over her torso. I glance over at the priest.

He's staring at me, not the slashes.

I avert my gaze and scrunch my eyes shut, working on blanking my mind. And the fucking slashes remain – three vertical tears – carved on the insides of my eyelids.

I try to blink them away, and Father Thomas pushes himself to his feet.

"Come," he says.

Then, silently and gently, we bend down on either side of the woman and pick her up.

ALMOST AN HOUR LATER, the priest and I step over the LEDs and into the netherfolk's cavern, the woman's body held in our arms. The community stands in a long line, silently, their eyes fixed on us. While a few voices rise above the quiet – one of them Natasha's – somewhere beyond, discussing instructions for care and medication to get hold of.

We stalk past tents and shacks. Some people come closer to peer at the woman we're carrying. There are inhalations of shock, murmurs of surprise, excitement. We enter the clear, circular space in the centre of the cavern. A figure rushes forward, hands grasping.

"Gemma, Gemma, oh my god, oh my god," bearded guy says.

He sinks to his knees and reaches up. Father Thomas and I pass the woman over, and he cradles her as if he's handling a porcelain doll.

The group presses in tightly around us, and scuffing sounds come from the back. My body turns.

Natasha breaks through the crowd and bounds forward to throw her arms around me. She squeezes tightly, and I find my face pressed into her neck, the warm smell of her hair in my nose. And then she pulls away, moves over to the priest, and hugs him tightly as well.

"Thank god," she says, glancing back at me, her features softer. The gleam of excitement's in her eyes again, and she grips my fingers. "You—"

I shake my head and make a shushing sound as I tug her away from the crowd. We retreat several steps, and she holds my gaze the entire way.

"You know what this means, don't you?" she whispers and clasps her hands together.

I open my mouth, all kinds of ripostes forming on my lips.

"The creature was terrorising this community *long* before we got here," she goes on.

My jaw clenches.

"Which means they're *not* just targeting you," she says, speaking faster. "They have to be part of something bigger."

I hear more shuffling to our side, and we swivel.

The female leader steps out of the surrounding ring of people, her staff gripped in both hands.

"Thank you," she says, her voice trembling, all hardness gone. Her eyes sparkle with tears. "Thank you *so* much."

The priest bows deeply toward her from within the circle.

"We can tell you where to find the man you're looking for," she says with a glance behind her. "Someone here knows."

16

"One hundred and five," Natasha says, her eyes on the ground, counting her steps along the tunnel floor.

It's been over a bloody hour since we left the netherfolk, and she continues to plod laboriously down yet another darkened service passage. The priest and I shuffle behind her. We're parallel to a train tunnel, dusty cables running between brackets down the right-hand wall, and the acrid smell's growing stronger in my nose.

For the thousandth time, I glance over my shoulder and probe the darkness in both directions with my flashlight. The beam continues to weaken steadily.

"One hundred and ten," Natasha says.

Embers spark, and my shoulders tighten. "Nat, can you let me lead?" I say. "*Please?*"

She stops walking. Straightens up to face me. "Like you did around the Tube station?" she asks, an eyebrow raised. "That worked brilliantly."

She gives me an empty smile and turns to shuffle onward while the familiar prickly heat forms in the middle of my spine.

"Will you at least hurry, then?" I plead.

She stops once more. "The netherfolk's directions were

very precise," she says. "Do you want to mess this up and have to start again?"

My gaze automatically flicks behind me. And when I turn, Natasha's craning her neck, peering over my shoulder.

"Do you think one of those *things* is here?" she says, excited.

I can't help glancing down at my chest, picturing the creature inside me, its arms in my shoulders, its legs in my stomach. The void grows, and the fire sweeps in so quickly to banish it. My hands squeeze with the surging energy.

Natasha swivels and begins padding away while I keep myself rooted in place, body tight, and wait till she's a good distance from me. Then I shake myself and follow behind, the priest in between us.

Natasha reaches the next junction and glances up.

"Two hundred and ten," she says with a satisfied breath. "We turn here."

And she then lumbers on down yet another fucking service tunnel, her endless numbers echoing back to me.

"Twenty … Forty … Sixty …"

The darkness presses in at my ears and my eyes while my mind swirls. I bite my cheek as we walk.

"Eighty … One hundred … One hundred and twenty …"

Eventually, the words just spew. "This can't be some global conspiracy," I call out.

She spins. The priest as well.

"Even if people are seeing these *things*, what's Gabriel trying to do? Scare people toward God?" I say and lift my arms. "It'd take thousands, maybe hundreds of thousands of them to impact the whole world. We've not heard of *any* sightings on the news or anywhere else."

The priest grins back at me. "You could be right, but who knows what we'll discover?" he says. "You may be surprised."

His smile remains. And the three slashes form in my mind, hovering over his chest. I glance away.

"We're clearly here for a reason," he goes on.

"And Ben *knows* people," Natasha says. "He would not have sent us to him if he did not think it was truly worth it."

My insides tighten, and I glance to the heavens. Natasha's already gazing down the tunnel.

"We may get clues as to what's going on," she says. "And what these creatures want."

She pads off into the blackness. And the memory returns of the *thing* staring at me in the passageway. And its garbled word … *You.*

"One hundred and fifty-five," Natasha says triumphantly. "This should be it!"

I blink up at her. She and the priest are twenty paces further up the tunnel. The section looks identical to all the others – curving walls, grime-covered floor. I hurry to catch up. The priest approaches one side wall, raises a hand, and runs his fingers along it.

"Well, would you look at that," he says and steps back, his gaze still fixed on its arched surface.

Natasha's flashlight beam follows the outline of a door cut into the side wall, barely visible, even with the light shining directly on it.

"Do we knock?" she asks.

I fold my arms. "I'm not sure they'll be too happy to know we're here."

Natasha leans closer to the door's outline, and my muscles stiffen. The prickling heat's back – stronger and gripping my whole spine.

"There is no handle or lock," she says.

I sniff the air, and the acrid scent of the tunnels is pungent in my nose. Natasha opens her mouth, and I raise my foot and kick out hard at the concrete surface, right in the middle of the outline. The impact sends shooting pains up my knee, and the section of tunnel swings inward.

I stare through the opening into some kind of inner passage, seven or eight feet long, lined with wooden slats and low-voltage LEDs at floor level. The scent of fresh air wafts out to merge with the caustic smell of the tunnels. A door stands ajar at the far end, and light filters around the edges.

I throw myself into the inner passage, my mind conjuring images of a door slamming in my face and a lock turning. I sprint faster, reach for the solid wooden door, and shove it open. I stumble into a bright room and then swivel on the spot, my hands raised and eyes searching for an attacker.

There's no one.

And my mouth falls open.

The room's bright, large, and airy with wood-panelled walls, an oval glass table, and carved dining chairs around it. Leather armchairs sit in front of a sculpted fireplace on the opposite side of the room, an embroidered rug in between. And there are plants … *plants*. A few stand in pots by ornate lamps in the corners, while a creeper meanders up the far wall.

But the books rule here. They're everywhere. Thousands of them. Bookcases line almost all the walls, each one crammed with volumes of different widths and heights. And most of them are old. Battered leather spines, inlays of gold leaf, and a few with titles written in strange languages.

And everything's immaculate – all the surfaces clear, the chairs perfectly aligned – museum-like. I sniff the air. It's pure, the grime-filled tunnels a dream.

Natasha stumbles into the room and stands there, her eyes wide. The priest follows just after.

"No one here?" she says.

"Not that I can see," I reply.

She strides toward the far corner of the room and a corridor beyond while I swivel back to face the door, the echo of the strange heat still there, just beneath my skin. I examine the handle. It's black iron, solid and ancient-looking, with a large keyhole. But having scoured the nearby walls and shelves, I see no sign of a damn key.

Natasha strides back toward us. "Bedroom, bathroom. Both beautiful. And both empty," she says.

I ignore her and grab the nearest bookcase. I try to haul it across the door, but the thing's bolted to the wall. Next, I try the table. It's far too heavy. My eyes find Natasha. She's staring at me with a frown.

"Should we wait?" she says. "Do you think they have stepped out?"

I gaze around at the lit room and then at the unlocked door. "Unlikely," I say.

A search of the place doesn't reveal much. It's full of furniture and plants – hardly a square foot of floor free – and aside from a few cupboards, there's nothing anyone could hide inside.

Having explored everywhere else, my gaze lands on the long bookcase. It lines the entire wall of the main room, opposite the passageway door, and is the only area of the room clear of stuff. I wet my hand with spit and pace along it, running my fingers across the spines of the books. Having traversed the whole bookcase, there's nothing. Not the slightest chill. I head back the other way.

"What are you doing?" Natasha asks.

I raise my other hand and concentrate harder on the sensations in my palm. After one more pass, I feel it – a fractional change in temperature, the faintest of air currents against my fingers, halfway down the wall. I stand back and gaze up at the bookcase.

"A secret door?" the priest says.

"Maybe," I say.

My eyes scan the case up and down, searching for a common edge between the volumes. There isn't one. Father Thomas steps up to examine the shelves to my side.

"One of the books?" he says.

I shrug and start pulling them at random, high and low, and they all come away fine. No obvious unlocking mechanism. There's hardly any dust, either. No easy way to spot sections of frequent use. Natasha and the priest do the same, Natasha working a door's width to my right. And thirty seconds later, I hear a click. She's holding a book that sticks out halfway, red binding with silver leaf. We grip the volume and pull. A door of books appears inside the bookcase. It swings open toward us on smooth hinges.

"That's a lot of effort to hide something already buried in the bowels of the earth," the priest says.

My pulse speeds up. I peer around the door and glimpse a wall beyond. Covered in shelves, glass cabinets, and …

My heart sinks.

More fucking books?

Some of these volumes are larger, and the glass cases hold bound manuscripts, the paper far older – aged creams and yellows. Plus, the air that filters through is cool. Temperature control.

I yank the door fully open, and the whole of the room comes into view. It's even more sprawling than the first. Yet more books, more cabinets – shelves and shelves of them, stretching away for a hundred feet – along with a table and chair on the right side of the space.

And behind the chair stands a figure.

17

The man holds himself so still, it takes me an instant to notice him. And when I do, it's the strangest sight. Upright, lean, maybe in his sixties, he's dressed in a white starched shirt, pleated trousers, and a green velour dressing gown complete with golden trim. Like his rooms, the man's outfit is immaculate. Not a crease. Not a speck of dust. And his features are aristocratic – razor-sharp cheekbones, piercing green eyes along with enamel-white skin that probably means he's been decades without the sun. Decades without leaving this place.

"What is the meaning of this?" he demands and lifts his chin to gaze down his nose at us, his tone ringing with indignation. "Out, out!" He flaps his hands to shepherd us back beyond the bookcase door.

I can only stare back.

"You are covered in dirt," he says, going to prod my shoulder with a fingertip. Then he pulls back, unable even to touch me.

I just stand there. And the more the man waves his hands in my face, the more strongly I anchor my feet. My arms tighten, my fingers clench—

Natasha nudges my back. "Come on," she whispers.

I stare at the flapping man and the endless rows of bloody

bookshelves at his back. Then I let out a sigh and allow myself to be herded into the main room with the others.

The man pulls the bookcase door closed behind him and locks it with a click. Then he pivots and looks hotly at each of us.

"I don't know why you are here or what you are looking for," he says in his superior voice, "but I truly have nothing of value."

He parades imperiously to stand at the head of the table while we line up at the opposite end, Natasha and the priest to both sides of me.

"We're here because we need your help," Father Thomas says, using a hint of command in his voice. "Someone told us of your expertise."

The man says nothing but just stares back doubtfully at the priest from across the table.

"Concerning the angels," Natasha says.

His eyes narrow instantly, a look of disdain covering any shocked reaction.

"*Who* informed you of my … *expertise*?" he asks, his words slow, his voice soft with irritation.

Natasha presses her lips together, and I picture wonderful Ben, his foppish hair, his wide smile.

"I am sorry, we cannot say," Natasha says.

The man stares between us, his face flushed and nostrils flaring.

I can't help shaking my head.

"The angels – we need your help," the priest tries again.

Still the man remains quiet, his breath held and hands clasped behind his back.

The priest nods his head toward the hidden door. "I know the real power you're keeping safe beyond that wall," he says.

I turn toward Father Thomas and lean in. "There's only books in there," I whisper.

The man makes a rasping sound, like he's trying to keep an eruption in his chest. His cheeks grow redder with every moment that passes. I glance back at the priest. The hint of a smile forms on the old man's lips, just for an instant.

Then the fine-featured man explodes. *"Only books?"* he yells. Despite his anger, he pronounces both words perfectly. "Those are among the best-preserved ancient scriptural texts you will encounter anywhere in the *world!"* He balls his fists. "The narratives they chronicle are the very foundation of our civilisation!"

"And the archangel Gabriel knows this better than anyone," Father Thomas says calmly.

This time, the man has to work harder to hide the reaction. And almost manages it. His right eye twitches, and his skin grows paler. He goes quiet again.

"We have encountered the archangel before," Natasha says. "We think he is planning something, and we are trying to work out what it is."

"We believe it will align with a particular story or myth," the priest adds. "Something described in the scriptures."

The man takes a slow breath and glares at the priest. "A great deal is recorded in the scriptures, sir," he says, with not just a bit of sarcasm in his voice.

"And so we have something that may help," the priest says, his tone still upbeat, ever friendly. "Information about current happenings that'll hopefully be of interest, that may provide clues as to the particular narrative he's aligning with."

The man's expression sharpens at the priest's bait; into suspicion or curiosity, I can't tell. My gaze flicks to Father Thomas, who keeps his smiling eyes on the man.

"Come, please," the priest says and motions the man to sit. "I'm Father Thomas. What do they call you?"

"No one calls me *anything,"* the man snaps. "No one knows I'm even here!"

The priest maintains his smile. "Your name?" he says.

The man stares back with a pinched brow. The priest holds his gaze.

"Capell," the man says eventually. "Dr Andrew Capell."

"This is Natalia and Jacob," the priest says, gesturing to us.

Natasha smiles. I barely nod. Then Father Thomas shifts over to one of the chairs placed perfectly around the table. He pulls it out and sits down, facing the man. Natasha does the same. I remain standing and lean against the wall to Natasha's side.

Capell glares back a while before nodding curtly. He sits at the head of the table and takes a moment to settle himself, his hands in his lap.

"What do you have that might be of interest?" he asks and turns his gaze on the priest.

"Sightings of short, black, four-limbed creatures," Natasha says and glances across at Father Thomas. "With oval heads and dark eyes."

Capell frowns.

"They possess people, control them," Natasha continues. "More seem to reside underground and come out at night."

She goes on to describe their posture, their movement, their strength and speed – everything she's learned from the priest and me. And Capell stares at her the entire time, his features fixed.

"Are you aware of how many texts were written in ancient times?" he says. "More than you can imagine." Then his tone hardens. "And a great many of the older scriptures contain tales of possession, and of demons and angels too, of course." He sweeps his gaze between the three of us. "But the descriptions of demons, for example, are often very general, with a great deal of overlap between the writings."

Standing there, listening to him, memories come of the *things* staring curiously at me out of the darkness.

"To pinpoint a particular text, a particular narrative, you will need to be more specific," Capell continues, zeroing his gaze on Natasha again. "Names used, phrases uttered, for example. Precise details that single them out." He taps his fingers on the table and glances at the priest. "But if you have something, and there *is* an occurrence of it in the scriptures, I *will* know about it."

The image morphs till I'm seeing Gemma's body lying on the ground.

Natasha leans forward. "There is this feeling of flatness when they are around, along with a dry heat and the smell of sulphur," she says.

My eyes close, and three slashes appear hewn into Gemma's chest, like three vertical rips in my vision.

"Sulphur? Flatness? Heat?" Capell says. "You are describing hell, of course. Or something similar. There is some consistency in the writings, but less than you might expect."

"But—" Natasha starts.

"There is speculation that the realms – earth, heaven, hell, purgatory – do not exist in different locations, but are all superimposed over each other," Capell says. "*If* real" – he raises a finger – "these sensations may indicate the barrier between the realms is thinning, and that one might feel despair, the anguish of hell seeping through."

I can't help leaning forward, my neck and shoulders tingling.

"But it all remains speculation at this point," he says, shaking his head. "Hell, demons … there are so many writings, but without more detail, something else to triangulate with, I can tell you very little definitively, I'm afraid." He glances back at her, and the merest of shrugs becomes the weakest of smiles.

Natasha opens her mouth, but nothing comes out. Her shoulders dip and her hands fall flat on the table. Capell remains quiet. My mouth goes dry, and though Natasha and the priest merely stare back at him, I feel as if I'm seeing the priest in the tunnel again, his knowing eyes fixed on mine.

Capell grips the arms of his chair and starts to rise, to dismiss us.

I push off the wall. "What about three slashes?" I say.

Capell stops mid-movement and stares at me as if he hasn't heard. Natasha and the priest both turn, Natasha's eyes wide.

I take a deep breath. "Three vertical slashes."

Capell's green eyes twinkle, and his frown becomes a smile, or possibly a scowl with lips pressed together and nostrils flared. He lowers himself back down in his seat.

"Three … slashes …" he says.

"Yes." I nod. "With jagged edges, like a knife has made three parallel tears in something. I see them in dreams, visions. Often they come before seeing the …" *things*. "I glimpse them etched onto everything."

My voice ebbs into silence, and again the image forms of my mother's lifeless body, then Natasha's, the sensation of the knife in my hand.

Natasha spins to face Capell. "Are they to do with …"

Capell raises an eyebrow. "Demons?" He shakes his head. "Well, no … not really. This is different. It narrows your search down considerably," he says, a new intensity in his tone. "It is an ancient symbol, only present in texts from well over two thousand years ago. Very few of those are left. Most were systematically destroyed."

Natasha shifts in her chair. "What are the slashes a symbol for?" she asks.

Capell fixes me with a stare and holds it a while.

"The devil," he says eventually.

I blink, and Natasha flinches with the word.

The priest breaks the silence. "Can you tell us more?"

Capell brings his hands together. "Only a little," he says. "And much of it is speculation as only fragments of the original texts remain."

He leans forward, places his elbows on the table, and steeples his fingers. "While the biblical scriptures you are familiar with describe angels, demons, and other mythical creatures, all of them part of God's pantheon …" He trails off before resuming. "These older texts describe an altogether different world … the devil and his demons roaming the earth, the forces of darkness so immense that they were powerful enough to equal the light, to equal the angels, despite being dwarfed by their numbers. And so, the forces of light and dark were balanced, directly intervening, actively fighting for the heart of man using miracles, visitations, possessions, whatever weapon they had. It meant populations lived at the whim of supernatural forces every single day, the world a battlefield."

He glances between us again. No hint of any smile. "This is the world the Gospels saved us from, the darkness that the light of Christ was said to have purified," he says. "These older references ceased at that very time."

Natasha frowns yet sits very still. "So why might Gabriel be scaring people with an ancient symbol that no one recognises?" she asks. "What story could this align with?"

"I do not know," Capell says, and then he stares directly at me again. "But he is not scaring *everybody* with that symbol. Is he?"

The weight builds on my chest again, as if the ceiling's pressing down on me.

"So, if none of the surviving scriptures reference this symbol," the priest says, "how do we find out what it really means?"

Capell retreats into his statuesque pose, his hands in his lap. He waits a long while before speaking, and I work on steadying my breathing.

"There *is* something you could try," he says eventually, his voice soft. "Someone quite different."

Natasha stares back at him. "They better have a long memory," she says.

Capell almost smiles again. "Among the longest," he says. "More than two thousand years."

Natasha's eyes go wide.

Capell glances at each of us, his features stern. "But whatever you do, tell no one about this," he says. "No one."

18

The closer we get, the more the crowd swells around us, Natasha and I almost the only ones not in robes or grey. Reaching the final corner, I try to usher her behind me – supposedly a fucking angel up ahead – but she shoves right past, and we gain our first glimpse.

All Saints' church.

One of the largest in London's East End, it's situated at the edge of Stepney Green Park. A towering stained-glass window adorns its front with rows of stone arches all around it, statues of Jesus and other heavenly figures in some of the higher niches, while someone's pulled many of the lower ones down.

And the place bloody teems with Puritans. An army of grey worshippers is trooping up the tarmac path toward the entrance, the chattering noises already loud from here.

I pull Natasha to a halt on the pavement opposite. "This can't be it."

"Apparently, it is," Natasha says, staring at the entrance, the priest on her arm. Father Thomas is in his decrepit mode again, armed with his walking stick, bowed posture, and wild grey hair.

"We're supposed to find an angel in *there?*" I say and

gesture toward the masses. "What d'you think they're doing, worshipping it?"

Several Puritans glance over. I dip my head but keep them in the corner of my eye, scanning for faces that would recognise me from the demonstration – those crazies that screamed and jabbed their fingers in my face.

I steer Natasha further along the pavement.

"Not exactly," she answers.

"Right," I say and keep going, putting more distance between us and the group, the path … and the church itself. "Capell was wrong—"

"Not necessarily," Natasha says and veers away from me, leading the priest across the road.

"Nat!" I call.

More Puritans stare, and I clamp my mouth shut as she bustles on in the direction of the entrance, the priest at her side.

I set off after them and push through the churchgoers at the back of the path. Several of them stare at me, and their eyes take in my non-Puritan clothes before glancing up at my face. I keep my gaze averted, though it gets harder as the crowd grows denser toward the church.

I grab Natasha's shoulder and pull alongside. "What if he was just spinning that stuff to get rid of us?"

She whirls on me as she walks. "You don't buy what he said?" she asks. "Forces of darkness and light actively fighting for man's hearts, the world a battlefield. You don't think that is the kind of thing Gabriel would want?"

"It is," I agree, barely keeping parallel with her and the priest. "But Qetesh said there was no God. She was clear on that. D'you really think there's a devil?"

Natasha shivers. "I hope not."

Several nearby Puritans shoot me alarmed glances, and I urge us beyond them, the crowd continuing to thicken. The babbling prayers grow more intense, the entrance only ten yards away.

"And the only proof we've got for this fiction is the three slashes," I say. "And only *I* see them. They can't be used to drive global devotion. The symbol's unknown."

Natasha glances across at me. Her lips arc upward in a sly smile, and she lets herself be carried on with the sea of Puritans, right till she's only a few feet from the church entrance. Their excited chattering's loud in my ears.

"Maybe the angel will know," she says.

My mouth opens, and Natasha nudges me on through the doors.

All sounds of conversation die, replaced by ardent murmurings.

I snap my mouth closed, embers sparking inside. The hush deepens around us as we're bustled further down the central aisle, further into the religious domain.

My head darts up, my body tight, and I scan the vast interior.

Chandeliers hang from high vaulted ceilings. Stained-glass windows run the length of the top of the walls, along with rows of defaced statues. Some spluttering cleric presides over a conversion ritual from the pulpit – a line of people donning grey robes near the front. Every pew's full. A great many pray fixedly, while others rock forward and back in their seats. And there's no sign of an angel anywhere. No radiant glow. No obvious cordite smell. Just the scent of oiled wood, dust, and age.

The tension eases at my core. Natasha takes my arm and tugs me out of the flow toward the rear of the church. The priest hobbles behind us, his walking stick clicking on the stone floor. We come to a halt at the side of the main doors.

Father Thomas faces the front and presses his hands together in prayer, his back to the wall and his eyes shut tightly. Natasha does the same on my other side. They both bow their heads, and the priest begins whispering a silent prayer while I just stand there, muttering.

A couple of robed Puritans glance over as they pass along

the rear aisle in front of us. Their gazes narrow in suspicion. I retreat and squeeze my hands together before my face, bowing my head and feeling like a complete idiot.

Natasha shuffles closer to me. “The angel. Where do you think we’re supposed to look?” she whispers.

“No idea,” I say.

“You are sure?” she asks. “Not like underground?”

I swivel to find her gazing up at me with an eyebrow raised.

“I’m positive!” I snap, my hands dropping.

A few Puritans on the rear pews turn to glare at us. I clamp my fingers back together, my jaw clenched.

“I told you, the guy was having a laugh. You want angels?” I say and tilt my head toward the upper walls.

She lifts her chin and takes in the paintings of radiant sunshine, golden clouds, and haloed angels gazing down from up high – all divine and perfect. No sign of darkness, devils, or demons.

“Whatever we’re supposed to find, we’ll find it,” the priest says from my other side. The old man’s eyes remain closed, his lips somehow still mumbling out the same unintelligible prayer. “We’re the right people in the right place,” he goes on. “Remember the bigger picture that’s being weaved.”

I swivel back to face the church interior with its packed congregation. Several Puritans continue to stare over their shoulders at us.

“Well, we’re not going to find it here,” I say and dip my head again.

The priest nods. “I agree.” And with that, he pivots around and begins studying a statue carved into the rear wall. “There has to be some kind of hidden door,” he whispers. “It’ll be ancient. We need to find the oldest bits of the church.”

And I realise the priest’s not examining the statue. He’s scrutinising the stone behind it.

I turn and lift my eyes a fraction. The sun shines directly in through the stained-glass windows that circle the top of the walls, colours staining the pale limestone bricks. Two rows of massive columns run the entire length of the church, from front to back, splitting the larger central area and two wide aisles on either side. The four corners of the church have square recesses that extend further out. I find my gaze falling on the nearer rear one, the stone walls darker there.

Natasha's gazing in the same direction. She points discreetly and glances back at the priest. "Over there?" she says.

The old man nods and sets off more quietly now, his stick entirely silent on the hard floor. Natasha follows right behind. I sigh, turn my face away from the masses, and lumber after them toward the square recess.

The recess is twenty feet by twenty and extends ten feet beyond the rear and side walls, like one of the four turrets of a castle, the space strangely set apart from the main body of the church. And while it's empty, several Puritans at the end of the rear pew turn to stare as we approach.

The priest reaches the near corner of the square and swivels to face the rest of the church. He stands there as some kind of shield while resuming his whispered prayer.

Natasha slinks past the old man and begins to search the recess. I do the same, keeping my back firmly turned to the congregation.

Not much is here – no statues, no artwork. Just a patchwork of different-coloured stone bricks and circular pools of water set into the middle of the floor. I run a wet hand over the walls, the darker bricks more dappled in texture, some of the mortar crumbling in between. But I feel no obvious airflows from hidden compartments, and every brick is firmly wedged in. The ancient flagstones at my feet as well.

After five minutes, my efforts have found absolutely nothing.

Facing the front and the priest, I shake my head while a vague notion niggles at my brain.

I turn. Natasha's stopped examining the walls. She's

gazing at one of the pools instead, each of them three feet in diameter and surrounded by a thin circular stone lip with water just below the surface of the floor. Some kind of drainage system. She stares intently down into the pool and moves her head from side to side, adjusting her gaze.

The niggling sensation grows in my head.

I pad to Natasha's side and try to follow her gaze. I find myself staring at the reflected image of a stained-glass window, the one atop the opposite wall of the church. Natasha continues to adjust her gaze, making tiny movements. Nevertheless, I see nothing. Only bright outlines of Christ, knights, dragons, and saints, all shining through the glass in the sunlight with identical images in the window and its reflection.

I go to walk away when Natasha grasps my arm.

"Here, *look,*" she says.

She steps behind me and gently places a hand on either side of my head to direct my gaze at the water, then moves my head slightly to the side, toward the edge of the pool, toward the edge of the stained-glass image, where the window meets the wall …

The breath stops in my throat.

At the edge of the window, there's no brick as there is above me. There's blue fucking sky. I blink down at the image and then up at the window on the opposite church wall. It's the same design, but the glass is bordered by stone, not sky.

The connection forms … Qetesh's door of water between realms. And her pool we jumped into.

I stare at Natasha, my ribs tightening.

She grins back at me. "The alignment has to be perfect," she says and points at the water. "Look to the edge. You can only catch a glimmer."

"Well done."

Natasha and I both start.

The priest stands hunched at her side. "This is it," he says, his voice low.

I turn to him. "But we've got no idea what's on the other side," I say, my voice hushing. "Angels, *things*, Gabriel … What do we do?"

The priest holds my gaze. "We get the angle right, fix our attention hard on the image, and believe," he says. "Then we just jump."

I stare back at him and then at Natasha. She nudges me out of the way.

My insides squeeze further, and the void unfurls at my core, the fire filling my veins. I reach out to grab her by the waist but stop.

Some Puritans at the rear of the church are staring at us again. And Natasha places her hand on my arm.

"It will be okay, Jake," she whispers, the smile still on her lips. "We can do this."

I just stand there, and eventually the Puritans turn back to face the front. Natasha fixes her gaze on the pool, takes a deep breath, and bends her knees.

My mouth opens.

Natasha leaps. Her feet hit the water, and her body disappears and hovers there simultaneously … frozen in time. Then it's as if the liquid reaches up to consume her.

And she's gone.

19

I CLENCH MY JAW, close out the sounds of the sermon behind us, and train my gaze on the drainage pool, on the reflection of the stained-glass window and the bordering blue sky. And with the priest's stare burning my cheek, I leap for the water.

The liquid envelops me, climbing my body. I shut my eyes and feel myself spat upward, not down. I feel a sensation of weightlessness, of soaring. Rainbow colours play before the backs of my eyelids while celestial bells ring in my ears. Time loses all meaning. Still, I keep the image of the blue sky fixed in my mind – the cloudless azure, the replicated stained-glass window.

Finally, I land … upward. The top of my head hits the ground and then my shoulder. I curl over, settle gently on my back, and just lie there, my body cradled by softness while the smell of fresh grass steals into my nose along with the faint scent of cordite.

Unmistakable.

My eyes shoot open, and the world lurches. The ground is now below me, while above there's a hazy blue. In fact, nothing's distinct, the scene around me full of diffuse and radiant shapes. The very air seems to glow.

Propping myself up, I blink hard, and gradually my

immediate surroundings come into focus. I'm lying on a grassy bank by the side of a large oval pool, thirty yards across. And in the water I see the same image of the reflected stained-glass window, but bordered by grey stone as it is in the church, the likeness so far away.

I lurch to my feet. Two figures stand on the opposite bank, the haze of imagery coalescing – Natasha and Father Thomas. I sigh with relief. Both begin climbing the gentle slope toward a low ridge that runs all the way around the pool. They stare out at the fuzzy landscape beyond. The scent of cordite's faint but still present in my nose.

I stumble up the bank myself, my eyes scanning for points of radiance, for any sign of the angels.

More distant features swim into focus, and at the top of the slope, the resulting scenery brings me to a careening halt.

The ridge that encircles the pool flows down into a gentle valley and then back up into smoothly sloping hills, interspersed in the distance with perfect visions of rivers, bridges, waterfalls. And across this meadowland lie many islands of stone, each one maybe thirty yards wide, covered with a jumble of walls, columns, arches, and fountains, all open to the air. It's like cathedrals have been broken into their constituent pieces and scattered across the land. Every island has stained-glass windows bordering the blue sky, the same image that was visible through the drainage pool.

The haze continues to retreat. My gaze lifts, and new features come into focus.

Somehow, the land's not whole.

Immense lakes border the grassland on both sides, as bright blue as the sky. In fact, they *are* sky. I turn a full circle at the top of the bank and stare, mesmerised.

We're standing on a narrow strip of land. The grassy hills continue forward and back as far as one can see, but they're only a couple of hundred yards wide. And to their sides are chasms of blue – the sky above *and* below. I stare down into the open space and make out another strip of land running vertically, many miles away, with the same features of hilly grassland and intermittent islands of stone.

My eyes rove about, up and down, left and right … and these strips of land are everywhere, above us and below, intersecting and splitting apart, continuing in all directions, like we're part of a massive geometric maze, all contained in blue sky. Each strip is only paper-thin and seemingly identical, all ending in snowy peaks that rise far in the distance.

I gaze out at the nearest stone island on our strip of land. One of its stone walls forms the floor of another strip that rises perpendicularly upward into the sky with the same meadows and stone islands, the furthest reaches of it still a shimmering haze.

My eyes continue to rove the landscape, searching every surface for any sign of an angel. There's nothing. No visible movement. Though staring out at the absolute perfection, the obvious thought strikes me, and a creeping chill forms across my lower back.

If this is heaven, we don't belong here.

And the veil's so insubstantial over my senses, as if the merest wish could peel it back …

I scrunch my eyes shut and keep my thoughts running and the veil in place while I sense into my body and search for void or fire. But I only find a growing feeling of expansiveness, of peace, a lightness in my core that I've not felt in such a long time.

I inhale deeply and let the air out.

The priest has already descended the other side of the bank and crossed the grass plains of our strip to the nearest stone island. He steps up onto it and up to the wall that forms the junction with the vertical strip. Then he places a foot on the bricks, at waist height, and somehow takes his trailing foot off the earth, his body now parallel to the ground we're standing on.

I can only stare.

Father Thomas begins to walk *up* the wall, which has

become the floor of a stone island on the perpendicular strip of land that extends vertically up into the sky above me. Somehow, he's shifted gravity by ninety degrees, and just watching him makes it start to shift for me as well. My vision lurches and my stomach heaves. I have to focus on my feet to keep them anchored to the strip beneath me.

The priest glances back at us, his smile wide with glee.

"How are you doing that?" Natasha asks with excitement.

I can sense my pulse speeding up, my body itching to try it out.

"Remember, these realms are much more pliable than the world you know. The power of belief is augmented here," the priest shouts. "In fact, it may be that the magnificence is, in part, based on our expectations." Then his tone turns playful. "Come, explore!"

The thrill grows inside. I experiment with jumping down the slope on the opposite side of the ridge, focusing on the belief of being able to leap far and fly. And while making sure not to peel back the veil, I still find the air thicker than normal as it holds me up. Incredibly, I can cover several metres in a single bound, the void a memory, a sense of peace and timelessness permeating my body.

Memories come of my mother, of basking in her glow, those times before her moods, before the gang came. I see her smiling down at me – those instants felt like an age, a sensation of total completeness at my core.

I bound away across the grassland beyond the priest and reach the next of the stone islands on our strip of land in mere moments.

It's a stone platform, walled on two sides, with no ceiling and church-like columns that rise twenty feet into the air. There are open windows on both the walls and the ground, too.

A tree stands in the middle of the island, extending above the strip of land and below, its roots visible through the window in the floor as they entangle and hang down into space. Its limbs bear no leaves, and its trunk comprises the same tightly packed branches as the roots, making it impossible to tell which direction is which.

Tiny yellow flowers dot every branch, each one vibrating. I step closer. They're not flowers but butterflies. Minute butterflies. Luminescent. And everywhere. Thousands of them, flitting through the skies, perched on every surface. How did I not see them before?

I swivel on the spot and take it all in. The island has carved sculptures of cherubs, the details exquisite. And around the columns, enormous bunches of grapes hang down. I do a double take. Grapes that, surely, weren't there a moment before.

Closing my eyes, I picture the other stone islands I've seen across the landscape. Focus on their common features – walls, windows, arches …

Fountains.

There's not one here that I've noticed. I fix the image in my head and glance behind me. Sure enough … there it is: a fountain bubbling on the edge of the grey platform.

I gaze further down the strip of land – more meadows, more sky, and many more stone areas with varying combinations of the beautiful trees, fountains, sculptures, and benches. They exist on the perpendicular strips of land as well, entire worlds to explore, and only a flip of gravity away. The excitement sends tingling energy across my skin, my pulse quickening further.

"Over here!"

The call splinters my thoughts. Natasha's voice sounds agitated, echoing from a long way off.

I whirl around and give a start.

She stands on the green crest we arrived by, her figure tiny. Somehow, a vast strip of land lies in between us.

The purpose of our visit comes back to me, and the static turns to chill beneath my skin. My eagerness drains away in an instant.

I throw myself back the way I came, bounding toward Natasha and pushing myself harder, faster, the sense of cold deepening inside my ribs.

Eventually, I reach the initial pool. The priest's already standing at Natasha's side atop the crest on the far side of the water. My eyes widen. The grassy bank below them is littered with huge chunks of hewn stone that I somehow missed before, and Natasha's pointing beyond the crest.

I leap around the bank, my feet flying more than running, hardly touching the ground. The butterflies sparkling in the air make way for me, keeping a distance from my body, and I weave between the scattered rocks. I skid to a halt beside her at the top of the crest.

"What is it?" I ask between snatched breaths.

"I am not sure," she says, staring down the gentle slope toward another grey platform.

I lean forward, breathing hard, and follow her gaze.

It's another stone island, sixty yards away, in a small dip beyond our ridge – invisible from the other side of the pool. And as with the other islands, it's composed of a stone floor, arches, trees, a fountain, benches …

"Oh, shit," I say.

Most of it's in ruins. The arch stands split in half. Fragments of stone wall cover the ground, clearly flung as far as the pool behind us, and two sculptures lie toppled. There are even giant gashes in the earth beyond it, like some monster has taken huge bites out of the landscape.

A strange sense of wrongness permeates me. The site resembles the centre of a detonation, the epicentre of an earthquake. Or some kind of fight …

I glance across at Natasha. She's staring back at me, her brow pinched and nervous excitement in her eyes.

The priest's gaze remains fixed on the destruction. "This way," he says and sets off down the slope toward the platform.

Natasha follows behind. While I don't move, my eyes are

drawn to our heavenly surroundings again. The chill's growing along my entire spine.

Natasha reaches the stone island, and I jog down the slope after her. The air's almost empty of butterflies. Just a handful flit here and there. None of them cover the remaining walls, the fountain base, the debris on the ground.

Then I stop in my tracks, several paces from the stone platform. Among the rubble lies a large mound, probably ten feet by eight, right in the centre of the island. It's entirely yellow – not thousands of butterflies but millions. All in one place. A number of the glowing insects lift off the mound, hover, and land again in a constantly rippling yellow sheet.

All covering something.

I pad toward it, and the sense of wrongness grows with every step. I can't look away, my heart pounding and my gut starting to twist.

Natasha steps onto the stone platform and draws closer to the yellow mound as well. And when she gets a few feet away, the edge of the yellow sheet lifts, the nearer butterflies rising into the air as one, the little creatures maintaining their distance from the interloper.

I hold my breath.

The sheet peels back to reveal … feet, then legs. Slender but powerful. Huge, chiselled muscle. Calves clad in some kind of flowing metal, intricately decorated with gold leaf, like strands of shining hair.

And unmoving.

I blink once. Twice.

"Incredible." The priest's voice at my side, barely a whisper.

My internal alarm rings ever louder while sweat breaks out across my neck. Natasha continues forward. I open my mouth, a yell of warning on my lips. Yet no sound comes, my gaze transfixed by the yellow mound, a vision gradually forming of what's underneath, as if I can already see …

The butterflies peel back further to reveal a waist, a lower back … the image flawless, beautiful. A woman, a female angel – it has to be – her glow diminishing with every second. She lies on her stomach, one of her arms bent at an impossible angle. And there, on her back …

My lungs seize.

Three large vertical slashes carved into her skin.

My vision hazes. The sense of wrongness coalesces into the void inside me, the crushing darkness. The image morphs, and I see my mother, sprawled there on the stone island, golden hair like a halo, the three slashes etched into her back. And the sensation returns of holding the knife in my hand. The horror's like claws around my throat. And my internal alarm starts to clamour.

My eyes find Natasha. I see anticipation in her gaze, her eyes fixed on the dead angel.

I dart toward her and grasp her arm. "We've got to go!"

She whirls to face me. "But the slashes! This is it!" she says, and strains against my grip. "This is—"

I swallow. "*A trap,*" I say.

And there, in the distance: a whistling noise, its pitch augmenting every second. Something approaching fast.

20

We back away across the stone island, my eyes scanning the horizon – the rolling hills ahead of us, the other strips of land that crisscross the azure blue. And the sound continues to grow louder … louder … Like a jet aircraft, a high keening in my ears. My entire body shakes, and I feel as if my skull might split apart.

"Get ready!" the priest yells.

I haul Natasha back onto the grass. The yellow sheet of butterflies descends back over the angel, and the three of us hurry up the gentle slope toward the crest around the pool.

There's a tremendous detonation, like a sonic boom. The blast wave smacks me across the back. I lose my grip on Natasha and fling out my arms, stumbling several more steps and barely keeping my feet. Then I spin.

Two figures – one on either side of the stone island, each one forty yards away, their radiance blinding. I raise an arm to protect my eyes while the smell of cordite, of burnt metal, stings my nose.

The figures uncoil to their full heights, their radiance ebbing. A man and a woman, not colossus-sized like Gabriel, but the woman at least my height and the man a foot taller. They're impossibly muscled. Perfect human specimens. Sporting high boots, pleated robes, and golden armour. Their legs and arms are bare, and capes hang around their necks, fastened with clasps – a crucifix with angel wings.

The same symbol as on Gabriel's building.

My shoulders tighten, and I edge toward Natasha. Thousands of butterflies flit around the two figures, and neither of them draws closer. And neither's noticed the yellow mound. I keep my gaze focused ahead.

"Mortals, *here?*" the man says, his voice like clashing cymbals.

The woman merely stands there, her blue eyes shining, her cheekbones as sharp as knives. She's semi-naked with bare arms, thighs, stomach, and upper chest, without a hint of self-consciousness. A braid of black hair coils down over the flawless dark skin of her shoulders, and her appraising gaze shifts from the priest to Natasha and then to me, where it lingers.

My heartbeat accelerates.

"Why are you here?" she asks, her voice somehow in my mind, the words searching, probing …

And before I know it, my head's turning and I'm gazing toward the yellow mound. I tense my neck but too damn late. The woman follows my gaze, and my pulse thumps even faster behind my ear.

The man reaches a massive hand over his head and pulls something out – a sword almost as tall as Natasha. He wields it before him.

"Explain yourselves!" he says and leans forward, eyes blazing, his voice trembling with anger.

I lift my arm across Natasha and urge her backward toward the crest of the rise again, twenty yards behind us.

The priest tracks rearward at our side. "Are you angels?" he yells, using his command voice, the words hurled out across the space.

The male's face darkens. He grips his sword tighter, and I

can feel his rage, the embers sparking in my chest. I keep my thoughts running. The veil in place.

"Emissaries," the male hisses. "Nakir … and Eleth. Guardians of the seraphim, of the divine pantheon, of the most holy Malakh. And *you* are mortals, children, *invaders* here."

He takes a gigantic step toward us, and I quicken our retreat. My gaze finds the woman again – Eleth – striding steadily toward the stone island now, toward the yellow mound. And my stomach tightens with each step she takes.

"You will *not* corrupt the Malakh with your presence!" the male emissary – Nakir – bellows and begins stalking forward as we retreat, every one of his strides almost double ours, only thirty yards away now.

Natasha resists my pull. She shuffles backward on tiptoes, craning her neck to peer forward, her gaze fixed on Eleth. And this time, I slow with her. Can't help staring, too.

Eleth has reached the yellow mound. She pads slowly toward it, almost reverently, and the blanket of butterflies begins to lift.

Nakir follows our gaze and stumbles to a halt. Natasha, the priest, and I stop entirely as well. And my gaze remains fixed on the yellow butterflies as they rise further. Revealing the feet, then the legs, and then the waist of the dead angel, the dark splatters covering her lower back. My heart's hammering now, the tips of my fingers buzzing.

And there they are, the three ragged gouges.

My eyes dart to Eleth. She's frozen in mid-step, her hand halfway to her mouth. The butterflies cease whirling in the sky. All wind dies. And it's as if the entire realm's holding its breath.

Then the emissary's beautiful features morph, lines etching themselves across her forehead. She swivels toward us.

"What is it?" Natasha shouts, anticipation in her voice. "The slashes! What do they *mean?"*

Eleth keeps her gaze on me, and the pressure builds in my skull. I tighten my jaw, start the count, and still my mind.

"You've seen these before," Eleth says, the words in my head again.

And images from my dreams bombard me – the hunched figures, the three slashes.

I can't help nodding.

Eleth's eyes go wide, and her perfect brow creases further; with intrigue or fear, I'm not sure.

"Who are *you?"* she says, the words still spoken in my mind.

My gaze finds Nakir again. He's swivelled back toward me, his sword held loosely in his hand.

"What have you *done?"* he demands, his voice soft.

More memories come. My destroyed apartment. The scenes of ruin I remember on waking. The sensation of my fingers around the knife. I stare between the dead angel and Nakir, his question spinning through my brain. The void blooms at my core. My mouth opens, and Eleth stares on at me, her eyes burning into mine.

"I didn't kill her!" I yell and cast my hand toward the dead angel.

Nakir's entire face goes red. He tenses his gigantic muscles, raises his sword high, only thirty yards away, and utters a blood-curdling roar. My hands fly to my ears. Then he throws himself toward us, Eleth only ten yards behind.

"To the water!" the priest bellows with his command voice, the sound pulling at my legs.

I whirl around and begin sprinting up the hill, Natasha and the priest at my side. My feet pound at the ground, my breathing fast and shallow – though with every stride, I can feel the heat rising in my chest, Nakir's thumping footsteps growing ever closer.

I push myself faster. We reach the crest, the grassy bank before us, the pool at the bottom, and the blocks of stone and half-cut arches scattered in between. Plus, a reflection in the water. The church – stained-glass windows, dark limestone walls, and still twenty-five yards away.

Nakir's breath is hot on the back of my neck as I run. His footsteps shake the ground beneath my feet, his shadow looming over me. The void plunges inside, the fire burning fucking wild as a result. My muscles tense. The veil so easy to pull back.

Natasha is sprinting hard at my side, only feet away.

I bite down on the veil, keep my thoughts going, and shove her hard away from me. She stumbles off toward the priest. Just as something smashes into my back and sends me flying.

I soar, hit the ground hard, and roll over several times down the slope, my back alive with pain. I lie there blinking and then lurch to my feet again, my head woozy as I try to focus.

Nakir's bearing down on me, his sword held behind his shoulder and his fingers clenched tightly around the hilt. Fury radiates off the guy, and my anger rises to meet his, energy swirling inside. The veil's so thin over my senses, and then it starts to peel back.

My eyes find Natasha and Father Thomas traversing the slope diagonally away from me yet still only thirty feet distant. I kick-start my thoughts, my head pounding now.

"Watch out!" the priest yells.

I throw myself to one side, and the emissary's stabbing blade shoots just past me. It's impossibly long, the blade so sharp it cleaves the air with a snap.

I right myself and scramble away while Nakir's already drawn his sword back and is swinging it at me, two-handed, in a wide flat arc, his entire upper body a blur.

My legs give out. I plummet to my knees, lean back as far as possible, and find myself staring up at the sky. The blade sweeps an inch over my head, and the smell of burning metal sears my nostrils.

"Jake!" Natasha yells.

I stagger upward. Nakir's already darting forward. He crashes his knee into my side. And again, I'm sent sprawling to the ground. My ribs scream, and my head barely misses one of the broken archways.

Nakir leaps over me as I struggle back to my feet. And there he stands, between me and the water's edge, his sword held in front of him, his teeth clenched in a smile, and his eyes alight.

Again, I can *feel* his rage. It makes my heart beat faster and tightens my muscles.

The priest and Natasha have reached the bottom of the slope now, fifty feet away.

"Go!" I yell.

Natasha doesn't move, but Father Thomas steps toward Nakir along the water's edge.

"Over here!" he yells and waves his arms.

But of course, Nakir keeps his focus on me, his mammoth blade pointed at my chest with the pool behind him, while my head's thumping harder. My vision swirls for a moment.

"There's no way out!"

I spin. It's Eleth, standing atop the crest behind me. And while I'm staring at her, Nakir's rage continues to make mine build.

And this time, I let my internal resistance go.

Energy surges around my body, and I whirl back to face him. The pain in my head and ribs recedes to a dull ache, and my mind goes blank, the veil peeling back in an instant. Time slows and the shimmering world expands, the physical connection forming again to everything around me. While concentrating hard on containing the growing fire, I take it all in ...

The grass, the massive stones scattered behind and to my sides, Nakir, the pool at his back, the sloping hills beyond, and several strips of land crisscrossing the sky in the distance, one of them rising straight up into the azure above my head. It's miles away and joins our plane way beyond the rolling hills. Staring at it, my eyes find the tiny features of stone islands, curving rivers, lakes of blue, all visible from on top.

A crazy idea starts to form.

I reach out with my senses and feel the broken archway I almost crashed into, several feet up the slope behind me, and shuffle backward toward it, away from the pool.

Nakir lifts his sword in the air, his arm muscles like boulders. I lower my stance and concentrate on feeling the emissary's fury. Power courses up my arms and down my legs while the veil peels back further, the shimmering world intensifying.

Eleth's voice chimes in my head again. *"Wait!"*

I keep my eyes on Nakir. He leans toward me and bares his teeth while I focus the energy in my legs and spring backward and up, pushing hard with every muscle and yelling with the effort. My feet catapult off the ground. The memory of weightlessness still lives in me, and with the shimmering world all around, I concentrate intently on the air's solidity, on it cradling my body, as I leap for the broken arch.

Nakir darts toward me as I spring upward through the air – four feet high, six feet – away from the pool. Already my foot extends behind me, toward where I sense the arch is. My sole connects with the bricks, eight feet above the ground, and I push off again, thrusting myself even higher into the air while pitching forward toward the water. My mind remains blank the entire time.

Nakir hurtles up the bank and swings his sword toward me from below. It takes every effort to tear my gaze from him to focus on the perpendicular plane beyond his head, rising vertically into the sky, many miles in the distance. I fix my attention on its tiny features – the stone islands, the meadows, the rivers – and imagine it as the ground below me. My body elongates as if I'm diving toward it, the viscous air holding me up, and I focus hard on flipping gravity.

All the while, I can feel Nakir's sword arcing closer, its blade cleaving the air, ready for me to fall back down and spear myself. I concentrate even more fiercely on the perpendicular plane. And in slowed time, the world lurches, gravity flipping by ninety degrees. The grassy bank below loses its hold on me, and I begin falling toward the distant strip of land, up and over Nakir's sword.

The emissary jumps and stretches his blade toward me. I rotate out of the way, but its tip still slices at my upper arm, the impact sending me spinning. The fresh pain claws at my concentration, and my body plummets wildly past him and toward the strip of land so far below.

The surface of the pool shoots past me like a cliff face, the church reflected in its mirror-like surface. I focus hard on it, trying to recover my foaming attention, and concentrate on shifting gravity again, on believing the pool is downward once more, on falling toward it.

Nothing happens. The water remains a cliff face I'm falling down, the far bank approaching all too quickly. Doubts wail, the veil slipping back into place, my head, arm, and ribs all aching.

I hear a furious yell behind. Nakir. And instead of tuning it out, I focus on the sensation of the rage, feel it building the flames up inside me. With the extra energy, I concentrate every ounce of my attention on the pool and bring back the memory of gravity shifting. I work to believe I can, but my head throbs with the effort.

And finally, the world lurches again. Gravity rights itself. And the water becomes down once more. I start to fall toward it, toward the reflected image of the church.

My eyes search out Natasha and the priest. He's pulling her into the pool at the same time as the water reaches up and grabs me.

21

Streatham Park, South London. Natasha and I are padding down a residential road with dilapidated houses on both sides of the street, their yards full of rubbish and many of the windows cracked.

The heavenly realm's already a distant memory. Somehow it was late afternoon when we arrived back in the church, hours having passed.

And we came straight here.

I keep my eyes trained ahead, the final junction looming, and for the hundredth time, my fingers reach to adjust the homemade bandage on my arm.

"It's fine, just leave it alone," Natasha says and swats my hand away before smoothing out the bandage.

"I must've been injured in the head to let you talk me into this," I say.

The edge of nausea remains in my stomach, the ache still there behind my temples since Nakir sent me sprawling. And again, my vision clouds. I shut my eyes, and the three slashes appear for an instant on my closed lids.

I shake my head, and the memory of Eleth returns – her shock at seeing the symbol, and the words spoken in my mind. *Who* are *you?*

"This is the right call, Jake," Natasha says, striding on at my side. "It all started with her. Who knows what we will find."

"I've not been here in ten years," I say, approaching the final corner. "The house might've been bulldozed, for all I know—"

My feet stumble to a halt.

There it is across the street: my childhood home. The same two storeys, bay windows, and alleyway running along its side. But the front stands more grey than white now, with peeling paint and each of the windows boarded up. It's like a face that's aged horribly, its surface covered in dirt and rotted wood. Plus, gang tags cover the flaking paintwork on either side of the door.

Staring at the front porch, the darkness grips my insides, and all of a sudden, I'm bloody fourteen again, standing on the threshold with a rucksack on my shoulder, gazing back down the hall to catch a last glance of her.

"Come on," Natasha says, gripping my arm. She hauls me on. "Let's go see."

I anchor my feet, and the memory continues to unfold. My mother in her drug-induced fog – glazed eyes, vacant expression, turning away – the last time I ever saw her. Again, the steel band squeezes my heart.

"It will not take long. I promise," Natasha says.

She shakes my arm. I glance over.

"I'm with you," she says. "And remember what Father Thomas said. Sometimes we can only focus on the next step."

She tugs again, and this time, I let her pull me across the road toward the house.

With evening approaching, the sky's dimming, and my eyes scan the boarded windows for chinks of light from the rooms beyond. There's nothing. And no other signs that the house's inhabited.

Visible ones, anyway.

Natasha slips through a smashed gate and across a front

yard that was once a wild thicket of bushes and flowers, now concreted over. The sides have become a dumping ground for piles of rubbish and broken building materials. The smell of rotting food's heavy in my nose.

I follow her to the front door. She knocks hard, the raps resonating through the solid wood. No response. Natasha knocks again. Waits.

"If someone's in there, they're not coming," I say.

She ignores me and steps toward the boarded window at the side of the door. She tries to peer around the slats.

The front door of the next house opens, and an elderly neighbour shuffles out – grey wispy hair, wrinkled mouth, and dressed in a frayed dressing gown. I search my memory but don't recognise the guy. He narrows his eyes at us over the remains of a cracked fence.

Natasha steps toward him. "Sir, do you know who lives here?" she says. "Or have a key?" She motions at me. "This is ..."

The neighbour's already swivelled away. He hobbles back inside his house and slams the front door.

Natasha continues to stare for a moment and then spins around. "Okay," she says, and her eyes dart up and down the street. "Who else can we ask?"

I heave a sigh and then pat down my left pocket, feeling for the familiar rectangular pouch. My set of lock picks.

Not there.

"Shit."

"What is it?" Natasha says.

"Nothing," I say and amble toward the larger mound of rubbish on one side of the yard. "Just need to find something." And I use my foot to rake through the crumbling bricks, ripped tarpaulin, and piles of splintered wood. I find a pile of rags and some crushed aluminium cans.

"Er, Jake?" Natasha says from behind me, her voice tight and low.

I go still.

"Someone is watching," she says.

My gut twists, my head darts up, and my gaze falls on a young guy standing fifty yards down the pavement, his eyes fixed on us.

My chest loosens, my breathing coming a little easier. No tilted head, no hunched posture. Plus, there's no sulphur on the wind, no prickling heat. The guy's maybe fifteen or sixteen years old, skinny, with a denim jacket and black bandana tied around his upper arm.

I turn my head back to the rubbish. "Spotter for a local gang," I say and go back to rooting through the pile with my foot. "This must be one of their houses."

I kick aside a bit of burnt carpet. And *there* … An old bike tyre, mangled, a few spokes hanging free. I rip a couple of them off and approach the door.

"And so?" Natasha says, arms folded across her chest.

"He's here to make sure no one seizes or squats in the place," I say and push the first spoke into the lock. I apply a little pressure and then start delicately raking the pins with the tiny hook at the end of the second spoke, trying to set each pin.

Natasha touches my shoulder. "He's pulling something from his pocket," she says, the tension still in her voice.

"Probably a phone," I say, keeping my attention on raking the lock. I've got three of the pins to set. Only two to go. "He'll call the enforcers if he thinks we're serious about breaking in."

Natasha goes quiet. I keep wiggling the spoke and finally set all the pins. The lock clicks open.

She stares at me. "I'd say we look pretty serious."

I glance between her and the gang spotter. His eyes are still trained on us, the phone fixed to his ear.

"But you said we'd be quick. Right?" I say and then shove the door open and step into the entrance hall.

Natasha follows and closes the door behind us.

I stand there, barely breathing. A thin shaft of light shines down the staircase from the floor above, dust floating in the beam.

"Hello?" Natasha calls.

We're met with only silence.

"Let's take a look around," Natasha says and heads down the hall toward the kitchen.

The words hardly register. My vision's clouded again, and new memories push forward from the back of my mind – streams of textured images as if I'm in some kind of dream. I stare to my side into the living room and see myself there at five or six years old, playing games at my mother's feet. And she's just sitting, watching me as she would, smiling the entire time.

Then the image morphs. The void grows as I glimpse the gang slouched on the sofas ... a row of stoners jeering at me, ash on every surface, the pungent smoke heavy in the air.

Natasha marches back toward me from the rear of the house, shaking her head. "Nothing there," she says, her tone still hopeful. "But maybe upstairs?"

I follow her absently upward, my body drawn on in the dreamlike state, the darkness expanding inside with every step.

My old bedroom. It's empty. Stripped of furniture. In the bathroom, the scuffed outline still remains on the floorboards where her chest once stood. And just staring at it, my pulse quickens and my throat narrows, the breath strained in my lungs. I shake myself and turn away to plod further along the hall.

My mother's bedroom. Also stripped. No bed, no mattress, the soft carpet and bright wallpaper gone. I hover on the threshold, concentrating on containing the darkness at my core. It doesn't spread. Instead, it's supplemented by a budding warmth, the ache diminished behind my temples. Staring into the empty room, more memories flit at the edge of my mind.

I venture inside and get flashes of weekend mornings –

me toddling across the landing in huge pyjamas, crawling into her bed and lying there for hours. Her warm scent on the pillows, the sensation of her fingers in my hair, the lilting sound of her voice.

My breathing softens, and for the first time in a long while, along with the void, I feel an echo of her presence – the joy, the bliss, the *love* – still so faint.

At the sound of footsteps on the landing, I swivel. Natasha's in the doorway, her brow furrowed.

"I searched everything. Drawers, cupboards. There's nothing," she says. "But maybe we can ask around?"

And before I know it, I find myself nodding back.

Natasha blinks at me. Then her face brightens, and she smiles before hurrying down the stairs.

"We should get out of here!" she calls.

My shoulders tighten, and my eyes shoot toward the front door into the street beyond. I hasten down the steps after her and out of the house, scanning the far pavement.

The spotter's still there, his phone gripped at his side. But no enforcers. Yet.

"Sir?" Natasha calls.

She's standing by the alleyway between the houses, staring over the cracked fence through a window into the elderly neighbour's house. The window's been boarded up from the inside, a vertical gap between the wooden slats.

"Sir, we only want to ask you a few questions," she calls.

I follow her gaze, and the outline of a figure appears in the gloom beyond the boards. Bent, wiry. The same elderly man. He says nothing but remains ensconced in shadow, wearing the darkness like a protective cloak.

My eyes search the street again. Still almost empty. And the spotter's taken a step toward us, his features tight, his phone tapping against his leg.

"I am so sorry for the intrusion," Natasha says.

"What do you want?" the elderly neighbour barks, his voice raspy.

"We are looking for someone, and I wonder if you could help us?" Natasha says.

She starts to describe my mother, the likely time she lived here, all the snippets she's gleaned from our prior conversations.

Eventually, the old man takes a step forward, appearing between the boards. "Yes, I remember her," he says, his eyes shining for a moment. Then they cloud. "It was a while ago now." He stares down at the floor. "She moved to Browns Wood."

He trails off before remembering the address – a housing estate, relatively close by.

"I went to visit a few times," he continues. "But then she moved again." He shrugs. "It was difficult to keep track."

His chest heaves, and he continues to gaze downward, motionless.

Natasha smiles sadly. "Thank you, sir," she says. "Thank you very much."

She bows to him, and we hurry away from the house together, the spotter glaring at us the entire way.

22

THE LIGHT'S dying as we leave Oaklands Estate. A collection of tower blocks, a mile or so from my childhood home, the last two hours spent following fucking breadcrumbs. Four addresses. None of them quite right. And at each one, no one wanted to talk. Natasha kept searching, kept asking till eventually we found someone who remembered my mother. Their expressions would open, faces gleaming, and they'd smile, all too willing to help before sending us to the next place. And then the next. And then the next.

Natasha glances down the street. "It is not too far from here," she says.

I'm staring the other way, scouring distant pavements and the shadows around high-rise buildings in the direction we came from. My vision clouds again, and I blink it back into focus, the ache that bit less behind my temples, the nausea finally ebbing as well.

"What is it?" she asks.

"He's not there," I say.

"Who?" she says.

"The spotter," I say. "He's been trailing us since we left the house."

Natasha tightens, and her gaze trails mine. "Why?" she says.

"Probably to track us down for his enforcers, trying to avoid a beating for bothering them for no reason," I say. "And he's good, too. Always keeps a few roads behind us, barely visible."

"But now he's gone?" she says.

I nod. "It makes sense," I say. "I've not seen him since leaving that last place, and we're most likely a fair distance away from their territory now." I turn. "Come on."

And we traipse off down the street toward our new destination. It's another residential road with rows of apartment blocks and dirty green spaces in between. The given address is about as vague as they come – a building with four floors, external balconies, and grimy yellow brick. I scan each one as we trudge along the street, the putrid smell of rubbish pulling at my attention. It lies piled against the walls, having clearly laid there for weeks.

Eventually, I stop in front of a three-storey place. It's the wrong height, but all the other features match. The stench is particularly bad, and my eyes find bunches of withered flowers that someone's laid by the front door.

I peer closer.

There's an assortment of photos among the petals, like some kind of offering or shrine. My mind flicks back to my mother's timeless presence, the effect she had on people. My pulse accelerates. I take a breath and force myself on toward the building's front door.

It's open, and as I step inside, the acrid smell's worse again, biting at my nose. I spy food and more flowers on the stairs. Perhaps two or three weeks old. Nothing newer. My heart sags, and the nausea grows alongside the darkness at my core, the memory spinning of me abandoning her ten years ago, never returning.

I clamber up the stairs while images flash from my dreams: scenes of destruction, bodies strewn, my mother dead. I climb faster. First floor. Second. A pile of wilted flowers lies around the edge of a doorway. I try the handle, my hands shaking. The lock clicks and the door opens.

I stand in the entrance hall, skin tight all over my body. Natasha pushes past me and hurries toward an open door at the end. My eyes find a tiny bedroom on one side with a mattress on the floor and a single blanket.

"Jake!" Natasha yells excitedly.

My stomach's in my throat, and I swivel. She's poised in a doorway at the far end of the hall.

"Over here!" she says.

I start to run. Down the hall and through the doorway, into a joint kitchen and diner. The room's thirty feet square and split in half by a worktop. Cupboards line the walls on the kitchen side along with a sink and a flat work area. Everything's filthy. Mould creeps down the walls like infiltrating hordes. The wallpaper's torn, and the two windows on the diner side have been blackened over, the shadows deep around the corners of the room.

Yet nothing can dent her radiance. She shines like a source of light herself, an island of beauty among the blight. She sits unmoving in an armchair, facing away from us, by one of the blacked-out windows. Her golden hair a wild threaded tangle. And she's so gaunt, almost a skeleton, as if she's not eaten in weeks.

The sense of weight builds inside, thoughts of self-blame shouting louder in my head ...

Though they quickly die, my mind stilling automatically, the weight replaced by a sense of peace, of warmth in my chest. Every surface begins to shimmer – the worktop, the floor, the walls – and there's a fullness, a timelessness in each moment, the veil so thin before my senses. An echo of the world that Gabriel showed me all those months ago. And so familiar from my childhood. I shake my head. It's like I'd forgotten.

My mother's mumbling something while staring forward,

her eyes blank, locked in her own world. And my gut clenches, slivers of darkness infiltrating the fullness at my core.

Natasha approaches her, crouches down beside the chair, and gently takes her hand. She gazes up into the brightness of her face, and I can only watch as Natasha's eyes widen, her lips part, and a tear trickles down her cheek.

My mother turns slowly to Natasha, as if noticing her for the first time. She stops mumbling and reaches out with an emaciated hand to brush Natasha's chin.

"There you are, darling," she says, her voice a dry whisper. And she smiles as if the sight's entirely expected, as if Natasha's been gone only a matter of hours.

"There you are," she says again and gently runs her fingers down Natasha's cheek.

I feel myself stuck to the floor.

Natasha touches my mother's shoulder and nudges her in my direction. My mother turns her head. Focuses on me. And her smile grows. She beams at me with her eyes, her mouth, and her cheeks, her smile so wide it's almost the width of the room.

Natasha moves toward me and reaches out. She grasps my hand, squeezes, and pulls me forward to squat at my mother's side. Then she backs slowly away.

I stare into my mother's eyes. And the tears come. My heart, the sense of love in my chest … it's all as wide and deep as an ocean. Gazing at her, more memories bubble to the surface. Times before and after the gang came, a stream of images and sensation – joy and pain, relief and anguish. I start to shake, the emotions too vast for my body, flows of love and regret cascading through me, the pressure splitting me apart.

My cheeks are wet, my throat raw. "I'm so sorry," I croak out.

She smiles again and shakes her head. The golden threads

waft in the air. "It's okay, my angel," she says and reaches for my hand. "Everything is okay."

The ocean swells. I shut my eyes to fight the tears. A wave of heat moves through me, a fire in the depths, as more memories seize my mind, so damn real …

The gang enforcers, lounging on chairs in our kitchen. My mother shuffling in to see them, having drugs passed into her trembling hands. And there, in the deepest parts of the ocean, I feel again the crushing aloneness. All those times, no matter how hard I tried – the screaming, the fighting, the pleading – I could never persuade her to throw them out, never make them leave.

Fingers stroke my cheek, and I blink. My mother's gazing down at me from her armchair.

"It's not your fault, angel," she says. "You were just a boy. You did the best you could." She smiles her wide smile again. "Always remember that."

Another wave of bliss passes through me, though the void's so strong beneath it. And the memories pull like deep currents, yanking me down …

I scrunch my eyes shut, breathe, and focus on blocking out the images, the sensations—

"No, no!" My mother's call splits my concentration. She shakes her head vigorously. "No, my angel." She leans in closer, her eyes so bright. "It's your *gift*," she says.

She places a hand over my chest, and love fills the depths within. It plunges more deeply than I'd ever imagined possible, the veil peeling back in an instant. Bliss and anguish intermingle inside, leaving me breathless. It's pain and longing, amplified beyond reckoning.

I freeze. My mind stops. And staring into her eyes, I can sense her pain along with my own … the immensity of holding such joy, and then having it vanish without warning, to be swept into vortexes of despair.

The sensations continue to build – so fucking intense –

every cell of my insides flayed raw. It's as if my heart might crack.

I go to back away when she grabs my other hand and tugs it to her, pulling me close to stare into my eyes.

I feel a sudden heat on the back of my neck. An acrid smell. Again, I go to move, but she squeezes my fingers with enormous strength, a new intensity in her gaze.

"Only by knowing pain can we truly know love," she says, speaking quickly. "*Always* remember that."

The scent grows stronger, and then I hear the creak of a floorboard behind me.

My gut screws tight, and I spin.

23

Swivelling around, my body tenses, and my eyes scan the room for the gang spotter, for the enforcers he brought. And focusing on the figure before me, my lungs seize and my brain crashes.

The elderly neighbour. Frayed dressing gown, wisps of grey hair, and hardly recognisable. Black eyes. Twisted features. The familiar hunched posture. His neck extends straight ahead while his arms hang down in front.

Natasha spins as well and goes rigid with shock.

And still beyond the veil, I see it all – the small black creature hovering inside the top of the old man's chest, its bulbous head superimposed over the neighbour's, the shiny black eyes that gaze out through the man's sockets. Foot-long arms and legs shift inside him.

And, shit, the *heat*. My forehead's wet with sweat. The air stinks of putrefaction. The room decays before me, shadows creeping in from the corners like rot. And inside me, the sense of bliss crumbles, every happiness deconstructed, the void growing with every second. I steel myself against the coming fire.

It doesn't come.

Instead, I feel myself still anchored by the fullness, the calming nature of my mother's presence.

The *thing* simply stands there, animal-like, staring straight at me with the same strange look in its eyes – a kind of curiosity. Then it shifts its gaze, stretches its neck, and peers to my side. My pulse fires, and I whirl.

My mother's armchair's empty.

The shock's like a punch to my sternum. My gut tightens further, and I swivel slowly back around. Praying … praying …

And there she is, somehow standing in between the *thing* and me. So insubstantial – her nightie resembles a tent over her skeletal form. She raises a hand. Tilts her chin up.

"So, vile one, can your master hear me?"

Her words resound with such power it's as if she's a different person, her radiance no longer tranquil but fiery. The darkness creeps back toward the corners of the room. I just stand there, stunned.

The *thing* dashes to the side to get a clear view of me, but my mother steps in its way. Then it darts in the other direction. And again, my mother blocks its path. Behind the veil, I glimpse the black creature tremble inside the elderly neighbour, and I can feel its rage, the heat growing in my chest.

I tense my stomach as the *thing* smashes both hands down onto the worktop to its side. The counter cracks, and a wave of power sweeps over my body like I've been shaken by a giant hand. I barely keep my balance.

My mother stands taller. Shines brighter. Beyond the veil, her radiance is like burning fire, such potency channelled through such a frail frame. When the *thing* takes a step closer and the darkness plummets inside me again, bliss and despair combine, joy and terror, my emotions a swirling maelstrom. So much, I can't move and can barely breathe.

"The Alpha and Omega is to come. Your master can't stop it," my mother continues, loud and strong, the tone split like she's speaking with two voices, octaves apart. "Hear the roars of rushing water, the peals of thunder."

And with every word, the *thing's* shaking increases – not just the black creature now, but its puppet too – the elderly neighbour's entire body shuddering. Again, the *thing* tries to lurch around my mother. And again, she steps in its way.

"Your lake of fire, of burning sulphur, your false prophet," she says and raises both her hands, palms out. "The torment will be forever and ever."

The currents careen through me, my legs quivering. And still, I feel myself rooted to the spot, the sensations overwhelming.

Natasha gasps at my side. The *thing* stops vibrating. In slowed time, I can read the signs of what's coming – a tensing of the old man's chest, a tightening in his neck, and his jaw gaping wide. The *thing* screams. The sound's deafening, a butcher's hook in my eardrums. It shatters the sense of radiance, and the dread reaches up and grabs me by the throat. My lungs constrict.

In the next instant, the *thing* darts forward and grasps my mother's nightdress. I feel my own mouth open, but I've no breath, no sound. Then she doesn't resist as the *thing* heaves her up effortlessly and smashes her head into the worktop. Her body collapses to the floor, limbs lax, like a sawdust doll.

And lies there unmoving.

I just stare. Her radiance diminishes, as if someone's drawing the shades in the room. Shadows slink closer, the veil slips back into place, and the void grows as never before. The abyss is no longer just below, but all fucking around me, like I'm trapped at the bottom of the ocean in the deepest of trenches.

The *thing* jabbers, conjuring memories in the depths. I recognise some visions, but others I don't. Just pain … *pain.* My legs start to crumple, and I see again the vision of my mother's strewn body from the dream, the three slashes carved into her back, the knife in my hand. For I finally did it.

Brought a *thing* here and killed her. My heart's squeezed like it's being crushed by weights.

Her light dies entirely. Darkness reigns inside and out. And with her calming presence gone, the pain's too much. My body convulses. I can't handle it.

My eyes rise to the *thing*, and I force my thoughts back to the moment of her death. I picture its hands around her night-dress, her head smashed into the worktop … and down in the depths of me, a volcano builds, a burning eruption in my chest. The sense of power – again, it's like nothing I've ever known. The veil peels completely away once more, and I let the flames lift me up … up … up out of the darkness, out of the pain. Such relief.

"Jake, no!"

Natasha's voice. But distant. The fire's untouchable inside me. Flames rage at my core, course down my legs and across my shoulders. I bend my knees, tense my arms, and leap toward the kitchen counter, throwing myself at the *thing*.

It scurries out of the way with its strange shuffling gait and jumps toward the side wall. So quick.

Natasha dives for the other side of the room as I wheel around and kick the armchair across the floor, watching myself do it, the river of fire wild inside, the images coming in spurts. The *thing* vaults the chair and springs unnaturally high to land on all fours by the blackened window.

And we face each other. Only six or seven feet apart. It's as if I'm staring at myself from above. Dilated pupils, flared nostrils, bull-like. Images overlapping in my mind – past, present and future. I glimpse myself lunging forward an instant before my body does it.

The *thing* throws itself at the blackened window and smashes straight through.

"Stop!" Natasha yells, the shout extended in slowed time.

And I tear after the *thing*. Natasha's fingers grasp at me, her nails scratching my skin, the sensation a mere stroke in the raging fire. Two strides, and I fling myself through the broken window.

Daylight. Blinding. Beyond the veil, the air caresses my body as the fire pulses every nerve, every part of me alive. I imagine my limbs like lead and will myself to fall faster.

Two storeys. Twenty feet. My body rotates in mid-air. Feet down, I land right on the *thing* just as it's ready to bolt. I crush it into the ground, into a concrete patio behind the building.

The impact barely registers, the pain in my legs a distant echo. I grab at the *thing's* neck, and it wriggles against my hold, bucking and writhing till it squirms free. Yet the fight's only fuel to my fire. Laughter bubbles up my throat as I scramble to my feet and careen after the fleeing form. Blackness creeps across my vision.

The *thing* runs, smashing through the rows of garden fences as it barrels along the backs of the neighbouring apartments. It makes darting changes of direction – sometimes running on two legs, sometimes four. It throws itself at door after door, straining to get inside the buildings.

I'm seeing only glimpses now as I run, the bonfire ever larger within. The spots of black grow as my awareness shuts down.

Then darkness.

THE HAZE of an alleyway appears before me, seen entirely through my own eyes again. And a dull noise sounds in my ears.

"Jake!"

The noise resolves itself into a shout. My heart hammers in my chest.

"Jake, please!"

A hand on my shoulder. I whirl around, fists raised, the fire still blazing inside my ribs. I'm about to lash out when her image comes into focus, and I stop dead, my lungs choked.

She stares at me wide-eyed, breathing hard. My fingers loosen, and my head shakes from side to side. The fire starts to abate, the episode fading. And in its place, the void grows, the last few minutes a blank in my mind.

I fight to maintain my focus on Natasha and keep the darkness at bay.

"What happened?" I ask, my voice barely a croak.

Then images come ... the *thing* running, crashing through fences, trying to break down doors. The void builds inside me, the fathomless dark waters. The vision of a broken window, of me lunging out from on high, of a head smashed against the worktop.

"Oh god," I say, merely a whisper.

My legs tremble. And then the tremble becomes a quake. The immensity of the black ocean rises up and prepares to smother me.

My legs give out at the same moment as arms grab me and then grapple with me as I fall. My body slumps to the ground while the arms hold on.

"It will be okay," Natasha says, gripping my hand. "Let it come ... let it come."

I let go. My focus breaks, and the ocean rushes in like thundering waves, every inch of me flooded. And I cry.

24

"ARE you sure you'll be fine?" Natasha asks.

I nod blindly and lumber up the final stairs to stumble out onto the dark corridor of my mother's floor. Peeling paint covers the walls, most of the hanging bulbs broken, and all the doors stand closed.

Except for the one to my mother's apartment.

I just keep breathing and then swivel away from it and slump down against the cracked plaster, landing hard on the floorboards.

"I will find someone to help," Natasha says, leaning over me. "I won't go far, and it will only be a moment. Then we can get out of here."

The acrid smell still hovers around us, my palms sweaty with the heat, and when I gaze up, her expression's tight and easy to read.

The *thing* could return.

But my eyes don't probe the corridor shadows. My body's completely numb, gutted by fire and flood. And I simply nod again.

Natasha squeezes my hand, tears pricking her eyes. "I am so sorry, Jake," she says, and her voice fails. "This was all my idea."

I try to force a smile. She straightens and draws a quick breath before hurrying off banging on doors and calling out for help. I just sit there.

Eventually, a door opens on a chain at the end of the hall.

"Who is it?" a woman says, her tone croaky.

"Oh, thank you," Natasha says. "Something terrible has happened." And she describes a burglary gone wrong.

"Dear God," the neighbour says. "I knew that woman, and she's dead?" Her voice wobbles. "In the apartment?"

The image sears itself into my brain – my mother, lying on her side, golden hair spread out, body broken. The darkness plunges away inside me. I can't stop it, the abyss immense, far greater than before. Like my mother blasted open my heart, every emotion amplified a hundredfold. I take a slow breath and unfocus my gaze, trying to return to the dazed state, but it doesn't work. New thoughts creep in.

Gabriel. It's his perfect revenge – create joy and then destroy it entirely. Wait till I'd found my mother and then separate us forever. *That's* why the creature ran. I'm not supposed to die. My anguish is better. Again, the darkness veers up inside me, my heart like a gaping wound with the scab ripped off. I scrunch my eyes shut.

"Her son discovered her and he is in real shock. We need to get him out of here," Natasha says. "Would you mind helping out? Contacting the authorities?"

The void maintains its grip, and I focus hard on my thoughts. I bring back my mother's words to the *thing* – *Alpha and Omega, roars of water, peals of thunder* – somewhat familiar.

"I'm so sorry for your loss," the neighbour calls toward me down the corridor. "She was a kind lady."

I tune out the words and squeeze my eyes tighter shut.

So, vile one, can your master hear me?

Master. Was she speaking to a real being? I hear again Capell's claim about the three slashes representing the devil. My jaw tightens. That makes no fucking sense. Capell said the devil and demons are long gone, and so how could my mother be speaking to the devil now? And why would he be sending his minions after *me?*

The embers spark inside but are quickly swallowed by the blackness. Again, I breathe and try to keep my thoughts moving. But they're in a spiral now. The void growing.

"They're always hanging around," the neighbour says.

I concentrate on her voice this time, my mind gripping tightly onto each word as a distraction.

"These thieves, these criminals," the neighbour goes on.

Thieves. Troublemakers. I keep the words spinning. *Always hanging around.* Something niggles the back of my brain.

Always around.

The revelation hits me like a slap.

My breathing stops. My eyes go wide. And gooseflesh rises across my neck. For what feels like an age, I sit there blinking while the neighbour blathers on at Natasha.

Then energy builds at my core, coursing into my legs and hands. My toes tap the floor, and suddenly, it's too much to sit still. I jump to my feet.

Natasha swivels away from the neighbour.

"Nat … the words …" I say, connections forming.

For an instant, she just stares back at me. Then she frowns and takes a few steps in my direction.

"The words my mother spoke," I say. "The thunder, the lakes of fire. You recognise them, right?"

Natasha glances over her shoulder. The neighbour's standing in the corridor now, peering strangely at me. I stare back at Natasha.

Her expression's hard. "Jake!" she hisses and strides toward me. She grabs my arm and tugs me out of sight into the stairwell.

"You recognise them. Don't you?" I say again.

Natasha makes a shushing motion with her hand.

"Don't you," I press again.

She meets my gaze, her lips pursed, and then nods. "The book of Revelation," she says, with a hushed voice.

I shake my head, a laugh bubbling up my throat. "We've been so blind," I say and pivot to jump down the stairs, the new energy surging around my body.

Natasha grips my arm. "Wait!" she says.

I glance back. And for a second, she holds my gaze, her brow knitted.

"Jake … your mother just *died,*" she says with weight in her voice and expression.

The void threatens to take me again. And I swallow it down, the energy still buzzing through me. "We've got to get out of here, you said so yourself," I say. "The *thing* could come back."

She glances over my shoulder down the stairwell, and I leap down several steps.

She heaves a sigh. "Give me a moment," she says.

I pause. And she darts back into the corridor. Her muffled voice starts up in conversation with the neighbour. I stand there, heart beating fast, my fingers gripping the banister.

Eventually, her footsteps approach. "And we will ring you later," she calls before reappearing around the corner.

I bound down the stairwell, two steps at a time. Then I push through the apartment block door and out onto the street, the darkening sky above me.

Wind gusts, and I take a deep breath and face the way we came, toward the local high road. Shadowed buildings line both sides of the street, and I start to pace, my hands twitching as a plan begins to crystallise.

"Hold up!" Natasha calls and jogs to my side. And we tramp past the mounds of rubbish, the shuttered garages, and the few working streetlights. "Those words, why … why are they important?"

"Because I know who my mother was talking to," I say, maintaining a swift pace. My eyes find the high road ahead and the direction that leads to the city centre.

"Lakes of fire, burning sulphur … The devil?" Natasha

says, worry creeping into her tone. "You think the devil is real?"

"Oh, he's real alright," I say. "You heard Capell, his rundown of the devil and his demons walking the earth, fighting for the heart of man."

"But Capell says texts about that have not been seen for over two thousand years," Natasha says.

"Exactly," I say with a nod, "because the devil was supposedly bound. Right? Revelation says it. I remember your bloody lectures. It's the biblical story we've been looking for."

I head on fast toward the end of the street, the main road ahead of us. A smattering of shops jostle around the crossroads, most of them closed now, and the ones that aren't still have their security gratings pulled down. A bus stop stands off to one side.

Natasha slows her walk behind me, and I turn my head while continuing to pad onward toward the crossroads.

"You said supposedly," she says.

"Yeah, because we've seen his demons walking the earth right now," I say, my jaw tight. "Causing chaos and wreaking havoc."

The fire burns inside me … intense but no longer uncomfortable. Welcome. *Desired*, even. It drives my steps.

Natasha's face pales under the flared streetlights.

"It doesn't make sense. Does it?" I say, now pacing backward toward the crossroads, my arms held out at my sides. "After two thousand years of exile, why would the mighty devil send his black creatures, his minions, after *me*, a mere mortal? It makes no sense."

Natasha's mouth forms a tight-lipped line.

She won't say it, but there's only one explanation.

25

A DIESEL ENGINE growls behind me. I twist and spot a bus travelling at speed up the main road toward us. Number sixty-seven. Heading in the direction of the city centre. Only twenty yards away and closing fast.

I throw myself toward the crossroads and the bus stop on the far side, two roads in between. Energy courses down my legs, and I dart across the first street, dodging around a gunning car, its horn blasting in my ear. My feet push on faster, the bus stop still thirty feet away.

The bus driver sees me reach the kerb and accelerates to get away. I lurch out onto the road, directly into his path. Brakes screech, and the bus skids to a halt, its front bumper ending up a foot from my shins.

The driver stares down at me, his nostrils flared and fingers throttling his steering wheel. He doesn't open the door, and I don't step back, his anger driving my own.

Natasha arrives panting at my side and puts a hand on my shoulder. The heat diminishes inside, and I breathe as I manage to form a smile at the driver.

Eventually, the hiss of compressed air sounds to my side. The front doors on the bus swing open, and we climb aboard. As we're tramping up the steps, Natasha swivels to face me.

"Wait, where are we going?" she asks.

I don't reply. Just root around my pocket for the correct change.

Natasha glances in the direction the bus is heading. "Back to the church?" she guesses.

"Eventually, yes," I mutter and deposit the coins on the driver's counter. Then I usher her down the central aisle while scanning a scratched map of the bus route on the wall, plotting it against my mental map of the city.

The bus lurches off, and I grab a pole. Natasha's already standing in the square open space opposite a middle set of doors, rows of metal seats in front and behind.

The bus is half-full, most people in ragged clothing, carrying fraying shopping bags. And pretty much everyone's avoiding my eye. Except for two guys in the back row. They're staring all too intently – one in jeans and a jeans jacket, the other in a hooded top. No gang colours, no caps at an angle, though they don't look away when I meet their gaze.

Averting my eyes, I continue toward Natasha. She's leaning against the side wall of the bus, ignoring the fold-up seats behind her legs. Each is covered in gum and grime. The bus continues to wind through the neighbourhood as I slide beside her, and she leans in.

"You think it's *Gabriel?*" she asks. "That *Gabriel* is disguising himself as the *devil?*"

"No, it's the other way around. The archangel is the disguise. Has to be," I say, my shoulders tightening. "It's too much of a coincidence that the devil was bound at the same time as the Gospels were written. Instead, the devil changed form. Whether he pretended to be bound and became an archangel, or whether he killed one to take its place, it makes little difference. He then simply wrote the Gospels to create devotion in his new role. It's bloody genius."

A male passenger shuffles to the middle doors right in front of us.

I lower my voice. "These *things*, they must be some kind of demon. Under his control."

The bus stops at a junction, and the passenger thumps the emergency button above the doors. They open immediately, and he steps through, slapping the button to close them again. The bus speeds up once more as I turn back to Natasha.

"They're Gabriel's army, and now he's seeking to return to his prior form," I say.

Natasha shakes her head at my side.

My jaw clenches. "Nat, this makes sense!" I say, my voice rising. "God doesn't mess with people's lives. Right? That's the *devil's* role." Images come of the *thing* killing my mother. "He torments, influences, and schemes. That's what he *does!*"

Natasha keeps her gaze averted and continues to stare ahead through the doors at the passing streets.

"And who enjoys that?" I prompt and beat my fist against a side panel. "Who's been doing it since forever, since the dawn of time? Who, according to Qetesh, has pissed off every other angel by continuing to involve himself? Who's created each of man's dark ages since the Gospels, just as the devil did before?"

I hear a rustling sound at the back of the bus. Passengers shrink toward the windows and pull shopping bags from the aisle as the two guys stalk between the seats in our direction. Hoodie guy is around my size, while jeans guy is a good few inches taller, with a thick neck and rounded shoulders. They stop only a foot away, standing side by side to block us in.

The heat turns to flame, and my ribs tighten, the energy building at my core.

Jeans guy looms over us. And I step right up into his face. Natasha shoots an arm out in front of my chest and pulls me backward. Jeans guy grins. And the fire blazes hotter, my mind forming visions of me pummelling the guy, but I take a breath and force myself to calm. I push both Natasha and myself down onto the folding chairs.

Jeans guy leans in, his head between Natasha's and mine. The smell of aftershave is pungent in my nose.

"It's your lucky night, friends," he says and leers at Natasha. "We're going to have some fun. But first we'll be taking a little ride."

Her eyes burn, but she still shivers under his gaze. And again, I steady my breathing to keep the flames in check, to keep them merely simmering inside. I lower my head and hunch my shoulders to look small. Then I feel around underneath the folded seat for bits of discarded gum. Each time the bus slows, I glance up, but neither guy faces the doors. My search continues, and pretty soon, I'm out of soft gum to find.

Hoodie guy starts checking Natasha out from every angle. He lifts her chin with one finger and stares down at her chest. Curbing the fire with even deeper breaths, I lift myself slowly and sidle over her lap while urging her onto my seat and out of hoodie guy's reach.

His top lip rises in a snarl, and I bow my head even further while searching the underside of her seat for more soft gum. Eventually, I find enough and then sneak coins out of my pocket. I use the gum to stick them together.

A movement catches my eye, and my head shoots up. Jeans guy's staring out the front of the bus, the fingers of his free hand drumming against his thigh. I glance through the middle doors. The bus is making all kinds of narrow turns, the two guys hanging on tightly to their poles. I squeeze the gummed coins in one palm and bite my cheek to keep my legs still.

Finally, the bus straightens out and accelerates. I risk a quick glance above the seats. The bus is on a long straight now, traffic lights green up ahead. My thoughts urge the driver on faster as my attention flicks to the guys in front of me. Both have relaxed their grips on the poles, the bus no longer weaving around, and jeans guy is clenching his free hand with excitement, still staring intently out the front window.

The bus holds its speed, and fire grows at my core, the energy building. I lean in toward Natasha.

"Hold tight," I say, my voice barely audible over the howling engine.

She frowns but does so, and I channel the energy into my legs and leap up from the seat. I thrust my head right next to hoodie guy's ear.

"Hey!" I shout and stare out over his shoulder, through the middle doors.

Both guys swivel their heads automatically.

And with the flames simmering inside, I still my thoughts, peel back the veil a fraction, and focus hard on the emergency button above the centre doors. It's ten feet away and only a few inches wide. I yank back the ball of gummed coins and send it flying. Over the guys' heads, across the bus, till it clatters into the side of the emergency button.

Immediately, the doors fly open and the air roars since the bus is still racing along. Both men spin fully around now. I clutch the handrail above my head and hold on with both hands.

The driver brakes hard. The bus lurches and throws both men forward while I grip the handrail tighter. Jeans guy smashes straight into the seat in front. Hoodie guy tumbles into him, makes a grab for me, and almost hits Natasha. I release a hand to shove his arm away, almost losing my grip.

Hoodie guy rights himself, fury burning in his eyes, and scrambles toward me. Power surges through my limbs, his rage propelling my own. I grit my teeth and yank on the handrail, lifting my legs from the ground to drive a kick at the guy's chest. I miss but hit his arm. And because he's off-balance, the impact sends him spinning, and he goes down hard.

Natasha's upright at my side, and we dash for the open doors. The bus is still going quickly – well over ten miles an hour. And Natasha wobbles at the edge. She throws her arms outward to keep her balance.

Jeans guy is back on his feet, and he lunges.

"Jump!" I yell while focusing again on the fire in my chest.

With one hand, I slap the emergency button while with the other, I grab Natasha's arm and yank her behind me.

We leap through the closing doors. The pavement flies past beneath me, energy rushing through my body. Still partly behind the veil, I focus hard on the air holding me up, but the ground comes so quickly, slams into my feet, and sends pain shooting up my calves. I stumble forward several steps and use the veil to keep myself from falling. Then I spin.

Natasha barrels into me. I get my arms around her and barely bring us to a stop.

The bus continues on, the doors closed again, picking up speed down the tree-lined avenue. I clock jeans guy, with one hand on the side window, staring daggers at me. A smile pulls at my cheeks, and then the fire starts to ebb. The veil slips back into place, and I watch the bus disappear down the road.

Natasha touches my arm.

"Let's go," she says.

"You okay?" I ask.

"Fine," she confirms, though her brow's furrowed, her expression a little uneasy.

And my ankle's throbbing from the fall.

"Okay," I say. "Let's go."

And I march off into the darkness of a side road, making sure we get out of sight.

Despite the pain in my ankles, I still keep up a fast pace. And Natasha stalks along at my side. We pass rows of houses, crosses in many of the windows. Almost all of the lights are off now that night has taken hold, the pavements deserted.

A Puritan area.

Natasha glances both ways. "Wait – this is not the way to the church," she says. "Where are we going?"

"You'll see," I tell her and stride on, my mind calling up the layout of the surrounding streets. Clapham Town ahead.

Our destination still a fair distance away. "There's something we need to do."

She opens her mouth and shuts it again, taking in the roads before us, and it's as if I can hear the cogs whirring in her brain. She brought me here the first time.

After a good fifteen minutes of walking, Natasha breaks the silence.

"Jake, your idea," she says, keeping her voice low. "I've been thinking about it."

I swivel to meet her gaze.

"And you have to admit," she goes on, "it is pretty far-fetched."

"So let me *prove* it," I say. My walk's become a hobble now, my ankles sore, though they're not getting any worse. "You asked me that underground."

"But that's just it. I cannot see how we can?" she says, her fingers playing with the crucifix around her neck. "Capell cannot help. He said any real writing about the devil and the three slashes no longer exists."

"Of course," I agree. "Gabriel would've destroyed every mention."

"So, we are stuck," she says with a shrug. "The angels won't tell us."

"And do they even know?" I ask. "You saw Eleth's reaction to the three slashes. She recognised them, no doubt. But Nakir accused *us* of killing the angel, not Gabriel. Which makes sense." I nod. "Much easier to pull off this transformation if most of your fellow angels don't know about it. It'd help with his and their faith."

Natasha shakes her head. "It doesn't matter anyway," she says. "The emissaries will not let us past them."

"Aha," I say, my pulse beating faster and my gait lengthening. "But the angels weren't the only ones around two thousand years ago."

And with that, we reach a T-junction with another main road – Clapham High Street. It's busy with cars speeding along. And fifty yards down the street, I find myself gazing at a familiar rectangular two-storey building with its grimy front and barred windows.

Natasha's stopped dead, staring at me instead. "Jake, that's crazy," she says.

"Probably," I say, nodding, "but I know they can speak."

I hear again the garbled word one spat at me underground ... *You*.

Her eyes widen. "You've been running from these *things* for weeks, and now you want to interrogate one?"

"Why not?" I snap, the embers flaring at my core. I fling my hand toward my mother's apartment. "Those I care about remain in danger no matter *what* I do."

Natasha blinks at me, her lips parted.

The fire settles back into the buzzing energy, and I take a breath. "You said it yourself. I can't protect everyone all the time. Remember?"

After a moment, she nods. "But how ..."

I smile. "Don't worry," I say and spin to face the morgue. "That's why we're here. I have a plan."

26

My back shifts against the crumbling warehouse wall, my crossed legs numb beneath me, the smeared grime itching my cheeks and forehead. And I glance down the alleyway for the millionth time.

It's a pretty good view – fifty yards in one direction, right the way to the main road – and ten yards in the other, toward Neal Street Market, the sprawling expanse of market stalls and tables.

And there's still no bloody sign.

Just the gang-tagged warehouse walls on both sides, the open roller doors, and the last dozen or so black-market traders marching between them along with the stink of chemicals and rotting produce.

My knees bounce up and down, my fingers tapping out endless rhythms on my thighs. It's been hours. Plus all the prep since leaving the morgue the night before. All fucking pointless. My fists clench while the sense of void still swamps my chest, ocean-like, right beneath the surface.

The traders continue packing up their stalls, bustling about with their remaining produce. And a few gang enforcers rove between them, extracting their cuts at the end of a day's business.

My gaze flicks upward. Slivers of sky filter through the corrugated sheeting between the warehouse buildings, the colour an increasingly inky blue. Getting damn late.

I risk pushing myself up and crane my neck to spy over the parade of boxes. My eyes fall on an enforcer in a combat jacket and red bandana, his features all too familiar from my time with the gang. I go rigid, my shoulders tight, and then drop back down, lower my head, and fix my gaze on the warehouse wall straight ahead. I sniff the air.

And there it is, that acrid scent, barely detectable above the rotting stink. The prickling heat grows across my skin.

I spin. And my whole body jolts.

A *thing*. Somehow only twenty yards from me, standing in the middle of the alley, in front of the traders and enforcers. A young man in jeans and a hood, plus that undeniable posture – shoulders curled, arms poised, head rotating – its black eyes shining.

I leap to my feet, and with the sudden movement, the familiar enforcer swivels to face me. The *thing* shuffles several steps in my direction and ends up only forty feet away.

The void blooms inside, the darkness so fucking deep now that I can barely breathe. It takes a massive effort not to run, to just tilt my gaze away and keep my feet anchored.

The enforcer eventually loses interest, and the *thing* doesn't approach any closer. It simply stares in that odd way with its head tilted.

I lift one foot and place it behind me. Then another, and back away slowly down the alley toward the stalls at my back, ignoring the faint soreness in my ankles. The *thing* mirrors my movements and approaches me with that awful crab-like motion. And *damn,* it's tough. The void expands as it gets incrementally nearer, my body gripped by a growing urge to flee. I tense my arms and legs and continue, one shaky step after another.

Finally, I arrive at the end of the alley, the extensive area of market stalls behind me, seventy yards square with warehouse buildings on three of its sides and a maze of narrow passages in between. The sense of constriction's already squeezing my chest, and I force myself back into the first passageway. It's only a few feet wide and fifty feet long with rows of empty stalls on both sides. Each has a table and metal frame, while a patchwork canvas roof hangs between them, inches above my head.

I breathe and keep going, slow and steady, making sure to keep the *thing* in sight. A strange timelessness pervades my senses as I retreat, as if the entire space is empty, silent, traders gone for miles around.

My gaze remains locked on the *thing*, and it shuffles forward again till it reaches the start of the square space, the maze. And there it stops and watches me with its tilting head but comes no further.

My feet reach the end of the first passageway, and still the *thing* doesn't move. It glances to the side, down the wider corridor that runs around the edge of the maze – an easy escape.

"Hey!" I yell without thinking.

I go to rattle the frame of the nearest stall, but its head whips back around to face me even before my arm extends, its black eyes boring into mine.

The sight freezes the air in my lungs.

Then the *thing* scampers toward me down the passageway, covering twenty feet in a matter of moments. The void floods my body as memories invade my mind. I see my mother die, and a part of me longs for the rage, for flames to pluck me from the darkness. The image comes of me darting forward, smashing the *thing* in the chest—

I scrunch my eyes shut and stagger backward, gripping a stall to my side and hauling myself around the corner. Out of fucking sight of the creature.

My feet continue to stumble rearward, my gaze fixed on the passage end, and my mind conjures images of the *thing* careening around it.

I hear a shuffling sound behind me, and I whirl.

Another trader stands right in the centre of the thin passageway, packing up vegetables into plastic bins on the stall table in front of him. He's only fifteen feet away and in full view of the corner.

Shit, shit.

I scramble toward him. The trader looks up, and I can't help glancing over my shoulder. The guy starts to follow my gaze.

And there it is – the *thing* – appearing around the end of the passage.

Squeezing past the trader, I throw out an elbow and shove one of his vegetable bins, sending its contents of onions tumbling to the ground inside the stall. The guy swivels toward me and opens his mouth to yell, but he doesn't bloody budge.

"My bad!" I shout back.

The trader continues to glare as I dash past his stall and across a junction, keeping the two figures fixed in my peripheral vision. The guy turns toward his spilled produce with his hands on his hips. The *thing* closes in fast and low from behind, almost upon him.

I hold my breath. Finally, the guy sighs and steps out of the passageway to pick up his stuff, just as the *thing* scuttles past, its eyes burning into mine.

Reaching the next corner, I barrel around it and then force myself to calm, to slow my retreat. After ten more yards down the new alleyway, I stop and wait.

I see no sign of the creature.

A chill slinks into the sensation of prickling heat. The void's just as fathomless inside me, the memories still stabbing at my mind. I spin around and try to pick out the *thing* through the canvas sheets at the rear of the stalls, but they're too thick. My brain projects visions of the creature stalking along neighbouring passageways, only feet away.

Shit, shit, shit …

I drive myself on, stalking past junction after junction, rehearsing my planned turns through the maze. The sense of timelessness increases with each step I take, yet there's still no sign of the *thing*. The void's deepening further now, though, and familiar images ravage my mind – my mother dead, then Natasha, too.

The sunlight grows ever weaker through the ripped tarpaulin above, time advancing, and my doubts chatter louder. I turn the penultimate corner.

And there it is, poised in the middle of the final junction only thirty feet away, blocking my damn path.

I take a breath and step slowly toward the *thing*. The darkness yawns wider, and the abyss plunges deeper, the fire simmering just above the surface. The figure doesn't move but remains right in my way, continuing to stare.

I swallow, my hands shaking and my heart hammering in my chest. The *thing* tilts its head as if curious. I whirl to the side, plant my foot, and leap over a stall table and through the canvas curtain at its back, aiming for a parallel passageway. The sheeting wraps around me and breaks my fall, but I end up smothered by it, struggling to squeeze under the next table.

The strange jabbering starts up louder in my mind. My pulse fires, and I lurch blindly into the neighbouring passageway. I scramble along it, parallel to the one with the *thing*, clattering into tables and frames while making a dumb racket. I finally manage to shake off the remaining sheeting and careen around the corner at the far end and past several more stalls. I thrust aside the canvas of the fifth stall and dive through it, barely clearing the table.

After a forward roll, I arrive back in the final passageway. It's a dead end, the rear stall thirty feet away, and I've cut out the *thing's* junction entirely.

I swivel to face it but then stumble back, off-balance. The creature's only ten fucking feet from me, grinning inanely, the smell of sulphur almost overpowering. The void yawns even wider inside, the temptation to give myself over to the fire immense.

I try to face the darkness as I did with my mother, but I can't. Her presence isn't here to buffer me, and the darkness feels all-consuming. My body jerks away, and I end up more off-balance, my arms windmilling, unable to right myself.

The *thing* scuttles toward me, and I scrabble backward, my momentum the only thing keeping me on my feet. We become locked in this awful dance, me stumbling back, the creature scuttling forward. The layers of tarpaulin grow thicker above our heads as we travel, the corridor darker with every scrambled step.

The *thing's* black eyes gleam brighter, and the jabbering intensifies in my mind, the memories swirling faster. I focus hard on containing the raging fire.

Then the last stall arrives, the rubbish piles bigger to my sides, a canvas wall behind – dead end. The *thing* darts forward another few steps and ends up directly under the final tarpaulin only feet from me. The void grips my core, black waters filling my insides, the heat burning my face. And the creature opens its mouth wide.

I launch myself backward at the canvas sheet and shout, "Now!"

Just as the *thing* shrieks.

The stall collapses around me, pulled apart from the outside. I end up flat on my back as the walls and ceiling fall away, opening the area at the rear of the passageway to the sky and revealing Natasha and Father Thomas standing on opposite sides.

The remaining sunlight pours down, reflected off the glass-like panes they each hold, which they angle at the *thing,* trapping the creature with the daylight.

My crazy idea.

The *thing* spins around, its eyes wide, frantic, and I scramble back to my feet, breathing hard. The creature shifts its gaze between the three of us – Natasha on one side, the priest on the other, and me straight on – an empty passageway behind it.

I fling my arms out to make myself look wider. Yet instead of running the way it came, it bolts for the space between Natasha and me and heads for the maze of stalls at our backs.

"No!" I scream.

The *thing* barrels forward, only feet from Natasha. The darkness plunges away inside me, and I let the river of flame flow wild. The fire catapults me beyond the veil, time slows, and energy careens through my body, the void forgotten.

I leap to cut the *thing* off. But it's so fucking quick. It stops running and shoots out a hand at my chest, the movement a blur. I raise a forearm to deflect it, and the blow strikes me on the shoulder. The impact's like a whip crack and sends me tumbling to the ground again. Pain flashes down my arm.

"Jake!"

Natasha's yell sounds warped in the slowed time.

Father Thomas flings his pane. The *thing* simply smashes it back. It's made of some composite material – reflective, light, and immensely strong – stolen from a building site, and it doesn't shatter. It slams back into the priest, who staggers but somehow keeps his feet.

Lying on my stomach, the *thing* only feet away, the fire burns hotter inside me, energy crashing through my body. I tense every muscle and concentrate hard on maintaining control, yet the flames grow ever higher, too much to hold. An overwhelming desire seizes me to move, to act, while whispers echo sweetly in my ear – *attack, maim, fight …* Black spots creep in from the sides of my vision, my mind about to shut me down.

I scramble toward the *thing* and bellow, putting all my energy into it. The sound comes from the very tips of my hands, my feet, and it feels like I'm hurling it across the market, the city, the entire world.

My eardrums vibrate like they do after one of the *thing's* shrieks, and the creature freezes with the sound, flinching as if struck by an invisible force. It stares at me, and again our eyes meet. I recognise the same look of curiosity, of intrigue. Then it spins and careens back the way we came, back down the corridor of stalls.

And runs straight into the janitor.

27

The Orisha's hidden further along the passageway of stalls, just where we agreed. The *thing* makes it several lolloping strides before the janitor steps into its path while ripping down the canvas sheeting from the neighbouring stalls in the process, opening the space to the sky.

The janitor towers over the *thing*, like a blue wall in his overalls and coloured bangles. And he grips it with one arm while his other one hangs limply down his side – injured from his fight with Gabriel in the incinerator room.

The *thing* lashes out, hands and feet, incredibly quickly. The Orisha pins both its arms, his massive forearm across its chest, and I feel the familiar sense of timelessness growing around us.

My eyes dart to the huge composite panes. The priest's already grabbed his from the ground, and he's sprinting toward the janitor, the pane angled to reflect the little remaining sunlight on the *thing*, while Natasha's crouched down at my side.

"You okay?" she asks.

I swallow and croak, "Fine," barely able to get the word out. "But the other pane." I jab a shaking finger at the discarded sheet behind her. "We need it *now*."

Though doubts churn, my crazy idea, that the black creatures, the puppeteers, can only enter or leave their hosts when they're away from the sun. Everything points to it – the creature fleeing Gemma's body in the dark tunnels, the *things* throwing themselves at external doors when chased in the daylight.

Natasha swivels to locate the pane behind her. And the *thing* continues to buck and thrash in the janitor's grip, hissing, spitting, jabbering the strange language. It seems about to choke, spittle flying from its mouth.

"Go, go, go!" I yell and shove at Natasha's shoulder.

She grabs up the other pane. I clamber to my feet and run down the passageway in her wake.

She takes up position in the centre of the now open passageway, opposite the priest, with the possessed man in between them. Both panes reflect the dying light from above onto his body.

I slow my steps and stop ten feet away. The void's cavernous at my core, and it expands the closer I get.

The *thing* stops struggling against the janitor and fixes its gaze on me. It starts to jabber and, as before, the strange language conjures images from the darkness, the memories so fucking real. My mother's last moments, her beaming smile, her hand on my chest. The creature leers at me, and the image forms of the *thing* lifting her up and then smashing her head into the worktop.

The flames build, and I let them burn, the river of fire surging through me. Such fucking relief. Every muscle itches to act, to fight—

"It's okay."

The priest's voice. He's standing, holding the pane, his eyes on mine.

"We're with you," he says.

I blink, the fire lessening inside, the darkness a fraction easier to hold. Staring into his eyes, somehow I get a sense of his own pain – abdicating his role, refusing to take an apprentice, pursuing Gabriel, and so turning his back on his mentor, his lineage, and everything he'd ever known.

Father Thomas smiles, and a new warmth blooms in my chest.

I nod back at him. "I got this."

And focusing on his soothing presence, I grit my teeth and open my heart to as much of the void as I can. With legs shaking, I step toward the *thing*.

"What are you doing? Why are you following me?" I cough, my voice so hoarse.

The *thing* burbles on, rasping unintelligibly. More images come – countless memories of the gang in my childhood home – the void growing with every moment, the river of flame a heartbeat away. I force a deep breath, root my feet, and keep my heart open to the darkness.

"I know you can talk," I say.

It says nothing in reply, simply continues its strange jabbering as spittle dribbles down its chin.

"Tell me!" I yell, embers flaring.

The *thing's* whole body shudders with raking coughs, the janitor's arm still around its chest. It looks delirious.

Then the realisation hits.

It's not coughs. The *thing's* laughing.

"Loosen your grip!" yells Natasha. "He could choke!"

The janitor shifts his arm a fraction and the coughing eases.

I go to speak. But the *thing* twists its body impossibly around and directs its gaze on the janitor.

"You've fallen low, ancient one." Its voice is a strange screech, the words barely comprehensible. "Human company?" It spits at the janitor's feet. "No power. So far from home. On borrowed time. I can see your end!"

The laughing coughs begin again, its whole body shaking. The Orisha maintains his quiet. Just as he did when we found him in the morgue this second time, sitting there like he was waiting for us. A Yoruba god of the oppressed – that's what the priest said – disguised as a janitor. He simply nodded when I asked for his help, and then he smiled.

The *thing* laughs on. And the flames blaze inside. The energy flares down my arms, and I find myself marching forward a couple of steps, getting even closer.

"Speak to *me!"* I hiss, and the urge seizes me to slam this man into the ground and destroy everything, everyone …

The priest presses a hand down on my shoulder, and the relief comes again. Then Natasha steps forward, too, on my other side. From behind the *thing*, the janitor gazes deep into my eyes, the sense of timelessness palpable all around us.

Again, the flames recede, and the darkness blooms in its place, but again it's easier to hold. Staring at Natasha, I feel her care for me just as I feel my care for her. In fact, I feel care from all of them, my heart somehow bigger, a vastness familiar from so many years before.

And my mother's final words return … *Only by knowing pain can we truly know love.*

I grip the priest's arm and squeeze. Then I approach the *thing* till we're only a couple of feet apart. The void swells again, and somehow I can sense not only my pain but that of the entire world, of populations manipulated and terrorised by demons and angels for thousands of years. The fire burns hot at my core.

"You're going to tell me what you know," I say, my voice trembling.

The *thing* swivels to face me. "Or what?" An awful growl, barely understandable through the bubbling saliva.

My fingers tighten like claws. The sky continues to darken above, less light reflected onto the *thing* from Natasha and the priest's panes. Time ticking down.

And while the void's easier to hold, the river of fire still calls to me. I let more of it flood my body as I grab at my belt, unbuckle it, and yank it from the loops of my jeans.

The *thing* laughs again, descending into a coughing fit.

"Jake!" Natasha says. "There's a real person in there!"

I whirl on her. "This is our only chance!"

She glances across at the priest. But he's gazing intently at the *thing*, adjusting the angle of his pane to maximise the dying light.

I grip my belt and raise it up toward the *thing's* chin.

"You think we fear pain?" it gabbles before giving a lurid smile.

"Who said anything about pain?" I say, my jaw like rock. "I'm simply going to kill you."

I lift the belt and snap it around the *thing's* throat. The creature thrashes and strains against the janitor's grip. I step even closer, the darkness plunges again, and the fire burns somehow hotter. It rampages up my chest, down into my arms, into my hands. I focus my attention on the sensation of the priest's fingers on my shoulder, on Natasha's calming presence at my side, and yank on the belt, pulling it tight.

"How many thousands of years have you existed?" I bark. "How many people have you tormented?"

Images from my recurring dream revolve around my head – my mother's dead body, Natasha's, the image of the knife in my hand. The river of fire surges ever faster through me, and I focus on opening my heart to the pain again, on maintaining control.

"It's all going to end now," I say.

The *thing* thrashes even harder. It reaches for the strap, and the janitor strains to hold it tight. His massive arm shakes.

"Reducing your numbers," I go on. "I'll be a fucking saint."

I pull tighter on the strap as the shadows continue to lengthen around me.

"What's your plan? What are you *doing?*" I demand.

"You have no idea," the *thing* splutters, its features twisting. "You cannot stop this. You have no idea at all."

"Oh, I do," I say, nodding. The fire drives me on, the words like fiery sparks shot from my lips. "The devil, your master, is back. We've seen the three slashes. We want to know *why*."

The *thing* cackles again. More spit drips from its chin. "You think the three slashes is the mark of the devil?" it says before convulsing in a laughing fit.

I pull even tighter on the belt to strangle the *thing's* grating sound.

Natasha grips my arm, her nails digging in. But the pain just adds to the wildfire in my chest. Black spots appear at the corners of my vision, my awareness shutting down. I hang on tight to the belt strap and maintain the tension.

"The slashes," the *thing* splutters, the words barely discernible, "they represent not the devil, but his weapon, the trident."

I hoist the belt strap and spear the underside of the *thing's* chin with the buckle. All the while, my vision hazes further, and I feel myself starting to float up out of my body.

"It has great power," the *thing* babbles as I squeeze. "The ability to control the earth, the air, and the sea, along with the vastness of his army. It was bound with its master."

"Bound by whom?" the priest asks.

"By some of the oldest angels," the *thing* says.

"*Who?*" the priest shouts.

The *thing* turns on me instead and shakes its head madly. "You can do nothing to stop it," it says. "The world will be changed forever!" Such frenzy lives in its black eyes, such glee.

I sense myself floating higher above my body. And again, I try to face the darkness, to control the fire, to hold on. It's like trying to contain a volcanic eruption.

"*Who?*" the priest booms. The voice echoes around us as the light continues to fade. Shadows creep up the reflected panes.

I watch my hands yank the belt ever tighter from above.

"Binding angels," chokes the *thing*. "Six of them." It

speaks hurriedly, spewing words along with saliva. "One leader and five others, but no longer."

I can't speak any more. Disembodied thoughts float through my mind.

Six, but no longer ... Binding angels dying ...

"Who was the leader?" demands the priest. "*Who?*"

The answer's so obvious.

The river of fire encompasses my entire being, the darkness a memory, my heart scorched raw. Unconsciousness yawns. I'm going to black out.

The *thing's* answer is barely a whisper. "Gabriel."

And then a shadow falls across the marketplace, the sun disappears behind a building, and the man collapses. A wave of exhaustion grips me, my awareness plunged back into my body. At the same time, I glimpse a flash of black limbs scampering beyond the janitor and away.

Night has come.

28

First thing in the morning, the day after black-market town, we hurry back to the church Capell sent us to – All Saints in Stepney Green – with its same veneer of stained-glass windows and destroyed statues. The grey sea of Puritans is much deeper, though; frothing more intently, too.

A few at the rear stare at me, but I ignore the attention and wade into the midst of the throng, past annoyed glances, past veiled whispers. Father Thomas stumbles along at my back while Natasha traipses several feet behind, still keeping her distance despite everything we've just learned.

"We've got to warn them, Nat," I mutter, the embers smouldering in my chest. "We've got to warn the angels."

The crowd grows denser, obstructing my way, and I channel the flames, pushing myself on. The more heat I embody, the more the surrounding Puritans stumble rearward, as if singed by burning cinders. And quickly, we're at the entrance.

The interior's even fuller than last time – every pew and aisle rammed. A preacher stands shouting some fire-and-brimstone sermon from the pulpit, and his audience sways back and forth, their mumbled prayers rising in my ears.

I spin to face the packed rear aisle and use my elbows to

shove through, driving my way toward the corner and its drainage pools. Murmurs of annoyance grow louder as Puritans press back at me. Nevertheless, I keep going and burst out of the crowd before the square recess.

And there, my feet come to an abrupt halt.

It's packed with worshippers. Some lie prostrate on the stone ground; others stand hunched over in silent prayer. All surround the drainage pools, blocking them off.

With my chest cramping, my gaze darts toward the front. The preacher's tone is still building, his sermon nowhere near over. The embers burn hotter.

"Hey!" I yell at the packed corner.

A few of the nearer Puritans raise their heads and glare, yet make no move to leave. The flames suddenly flash down my arms – escalating power – and the image comes of me storming in among the Puritans, scattering them like twigs.

The priest shuffles right past me before squeezing his way between prostrate worshippers. With exaggerated difficulty, he leans down and speaks to two of the elder Puritans kneeling toward the back. His breathing is laboured, his knees popping. They give no reaction, but he keeps going, whispering incessantly, like a wasp buzzing around their ears. Still the Puritans ignore him.

My toes tap a rhythm on the stone floor, the fire continuing to simmer. A few more of the nearby Puritans shoot me suspicious glances. Their eyes rake my ordinary clothes.

I tense my neck and force myself away. Right into Natasha. She's standing with her back to the church wall, her hands pressed together and her eyes shut – just like last time. But now she's mouthing some kind of silent prayer, that single line creasing her brow.

Beneath the flames, I can't ignore the cavernous void. It pulls just staring at her. She's hardly said a word to me since we left the market the night before.

I find my mouth opening. "Nat, *please* …" I say. "Isn't this what you wanted?"

She doesn't reply but simply continues to murmur some silent prayer, the crucifix on her necklace held between her pressed palms.

"We're *doing* something—" I start.

"It's not the what. It's the how, Jake. The *how*," she whispers. "I do not think you understand the risks."

"Risks?" I hiss, the heat tightening my throat. "Gabriel … becoming the devil again … unleashed on the world. You don't think that's a *risk?"*

With my outburst, several sets of eyes turn to stare at us from the rear pews. I thrust down the fire, lower my head, and keep my arms pinned to my side. The sermon continues to echo from the front of the church. And from the corner, I hear raised voices – a Puritan snapping at the priest, followed by another.

"Evil. You have to remember that evil begets evil," Natasha goes on.

"Because we engaged one of those *things*?" I demand, trying to keep my voice low.

She sighs. "You don't think it's odd that it talked to you?"

I can feel my forehead knit while images from the marketplace come back to me. The *thing* thrashing with the belt around its neck. Flailing more wildly the tighter the leather squeezed.

"Self-preservation," I say with a nod. "It must fear annihilation. I saw one of them try to fight its way into buildings as I chased it. If it didn't fear death, why run?"

Natasha opens her eyes and stares toward the front of the church.

"I don't know," she says, "but you cannot use the tools of evil without propagating it. It corrupts everything."

I whirl on her. "That's so simplistic!" I say, and my fingers squeeze together.

A dozen sets of eyes swivel now. And this time, I glare back with my jaw clenched. Gradually, the Puritans turn away and begin whispering among each other.

"It's some kind of *demon*," Natasha says. "How can you believe what it—"

"Because of what it told us!" I interrupt. "Gabriel, the lead binding angel? It's exactly what we thought. We know he's the master architect, the ultimate conman, and this is the perfect ruse. Him pretending to bind himself as some kind of pact with the other binding angels, probably swearing them to secrecy. If they're even aware of what happened. Perhaps he bound himself and then escaped, took Gabriel's place. And now he's been the archangel for so long, no one would believe what he was before."

Natasha just stares back at me while my pulse beats faster.

"And now we know what he's after," I say. "The three slashes represent the devil's weapon, *not* the devil himself. *That's* why we're seeing them. It's the *weapon* he wants – one he bound when he pretended to bind himself, and one he can use to command his entire fucking army, not just the rogue ones he's sending after me. And now he's close to getting it." I grip her arm and lean in closer. "We have no idea how many binding angels are left, how many more he needs to get rid of."

Still Natasha holds my gaze. A sadness lingers in her expression, and the sense of hollowness deepens in my chest.

"Jake, you are moving so fast," she says. "Don't you think you should stop … reflect?" Tears glisten in the corners of her eyes. "You've just lost your mother, and you were apart for so long. You must have so much pain." Her voice softens. "You need to face it."

"*Face it?*" I stammer. The darkness swells, the flames crackling on top. "After all that pressure you heaped on me, you think *I'm* moving too fast?"

She purses her lips.

"Nat, we're finally making *progress*—"

Disgruntled noises echo from the square recess. I spin.

The Puritans are moving, the entire group scrambling to their feet. The priest's behind them, still whispering in the ears of the rearmost worshippers. The group paces off in the direction of the front of the church, their expressions fixed in various stages of outrage. And one of their leaders is gesturing angrily toward the altar, calling for someone's attention. I glance back at Father Thomas.

"We won't have long," he mouths.

I nod and hurry into the now empty corner of the church to the border of the first drainage pool. Then I stare down into the water and rotate my head to get the angle right. The reflection of the stained-glass window, and *there* … the blue sky to its side.

The heavenly realm … with the emissary, Nakir, intent on killing us there, and the angels even more bloody dangerous. My heart beats faster, and my mouth becomes suddenly very dry.

Natasha steps to the edge of the water, and I meet her gaze, the sadness still so obvious in her eyes.

I swallow. "It will be okay," I whisper.

Raised voices emanate from the front of the church, and my head turns. The leader's now speaking with some kind of official and pointing over the crowd toward us.

I shoot my gaze back to the drainage pool, set myself, and jump for the water.

29

Leaping into the pool again, I relive the incredible experience of floating, the sensation of falling upward and downward simultaneously while a myriad of colours swirls before my eyes. Eventually, the smells of freshness and cordite pique my nose again, and the soft ground cushions my body like a pillow.

I jump to my feet and stare around. The shimmering landscape settles much more quickly than before, and I find myself standing on the same gentle slope around an oval pool of water, staring at the familiar features of the heavenly realm beyond the crest.

The green landscape rises and falls in lush hills, winding rivers, and shining waterfalls, all interspersed by the same square islands of stone with their sublime fountains and arches. And all of this extends forever, forward and back, on one narrow strip of land a couple of hundred yards across. And my strip's just one among many, the others veering off in all directions, vertical and horizontal, spanning the crystalline blue expanse. The flitting butterflies seem more numerous in the sky.

And there's no sign of emissaries or angels that I can see.

My gaze shoots over the pool, over the reflection of the church we came from, and I scan the far bank. There they are – Father Thomas already ascending the grassy rise on the other side of the water, while Natasha's several paces behind him, climbing to her feet, staring out across the vastness ... avoiding my eye.

And still the relief comes, my chest relaxing.

This new warmth bleeds into the sensation of bliss, of timelessness, I remember from the last time. The ache in my heart is nearly gone, the void, the wild anger a memory. Instead, I feel a sense of joy, of peace, deep in my core.

I gaze around at the heavenly realm – perfect from every tuft of grass to the snowy peaks in the distance. Beyond erosion, beyond decay. The same for thousands of years. The grassy bank under my feet calls to me, and in that moment, the pain I've carried feels like a great weight. A voice whispers from the back of my mind. *Stay. Let it all go.*

Yet, eyeing the place, more thoughts nag at me; it's a haven of bliss but also one of forgetfulness. Enjoyed by angels whose power has been built on the beliefs and fears of millions while the masses live in hardship.

My jaw tightens. I take a long breath and sense down under the bliss, to the vaster darkness my mother opened inside me. And the river of fire stirs. I pace to the top of the bank, my gaze fixed on the slope beyond Natasha and the priest. The same stone island lies at its bottom, entirely complete now with no sign of the destruction, no dead angel. As if it never happened.

I close my eyes and dive into the very depths of the void. I picture Gabriel on the incinerator chute, smashing the vials with which he intended to kill millions ... billions. Just his latest crime in a multitude. And deep in the darkness, I focus on the flames. Feel them growing, carrying me out of the void, the river of fire flowing faster ... up my chest, into my throat. I tense my shoulders, fix my gaze upward at the crystalline blue, and let out a bellowing cry. The sound reverberates through every inch of my body and out into the ground, the stone, the sky. The entire landscape throbs with it.

And then, from absolute stillness, the wind picks up. It begins to howl, to scream, even louder than last time. My ribs vibrate, my gut twists, and my gaze darts to Natasha. She's staring at me, her eyes wide, from atop the crest on the opposite side of the pool.

Fucking idiot.

I throw myself into a sprint along the crest of the grassy bank. My legs windmill, my feet hardly touching the ground. Natasha edges toward Father Thomas, both of them scanning the sky, searching the geometric maze around us. The howling sound becomes a single wail. I keep running, pushing myself on faster.

I'm still a fair distance away when I hear a tremendous explosion, and several figures crash down from the sky. The noise resembles cannons firing, and the ground heaves like a rolling sea. I shift my balance to flow with the movement and barely keep my feet as I run. The smell of cordite stings my nose.

The figures unravel to their full heights at the bottom of the grassy slope – four of them poised in a line before the stone island, forty yards away from us. I recognise the two emissaries, Eleth and Nakir, along with two others I've never seen before. Both are blond, both male, both massive. Their chiselled features are so similar they must be twins.

All four of them wear mixtures of golden armour and flowing robes. The twins stand with muscled breastplates and protectors on opposite arms. Nakir is bare-chested with curving plates over both shoulders and his lower legs. And Eleth wears knee-high boots, along with twin bands that cross her chest and a circlet around her forehead. They all have cloaks joined by the same symbolled clasp.

Even from that distance, I can make out Nakir's blazing eyes, his taut muscles. His rage vibrates the air and pitches the butterflies into crazed spins. Sensing the heat growing inside me, I throw myself on faster and reach Natasha and the priest just as Nakir draws his sword. He levels it in our direction, and the twins do the same.

My gaze finds Eleth. She's staring back at me, the same curiosity and intensity in her bright eyes. She also draws her blade, hefting it in front of her.

And with escape to the church beckoning down the slope at my back, I face all four emissaries. I take a deep breath and hold my arms out.

"You must listen!" I start.

"We need not listen to anything you say, child!" Nakir booms.

His thunderous tone shakes my chest and squeezes my throat. And when I open my mouth, I'm unable to speak.

Nakir strides up the slope toward me, Eleth just a few paces behind, her sword still held out before her. The twins move to either side and fan out across the grass, preparing to flank us.

Gradually, Nakir's echoing tones die away. I swallow and wrest the words out.

"Angels are being killed. Aren't they?" I say and fix my gaze on Eleth's expression. "Not just the one we found here."

Not a hint of surprise crosses her face. And none of the emissaries pause in their movements.

Nakir's only twenty yards from us now and approaching fast. "You do not get to speak here!" he shouts, his voice even louder. Its resonance shakes my body.

I clench my chest, keeping all my focus on Eleth. "But do you know *why?*" I spit, the words barely audible. "Do you know why they're marked with three slashes?" I jab my finger toward the stone island behind her. "Because that wasn't the first time you've seen them. *Right?*"

Her eyes narrow for an instant, though she says nothing. She just continues her advance.

"This is nonsense!" Nakir yells, the sound pulsating every bone in my body, my lungs barely able to suck in breath.

Still I keep going. "The devil is real. Isn't he?" I rasp. "Was bound two thousand years ago. It's all in the book of Revelation. *Isn't it?"*

Nakir is drawing nearer, the tip of his blade even closer.

"Jake!" Natasha shouts.

She and the priest begin to retreat down the grassy bank toward the pool at our backs. I follow just after, my gaze still focused on Eleth.

"But do you know *how* he was bound?" I manage to get out.

"Silence!" Nakir clamours, now only a few feet from the top of the crest. He raises his sword behind his shoulder, and the muscles in his neck stand out like the rigging on a ship. However, he doesn't strike.

I rotate my head. Both twins have reached the crest on either side of us. They jog down the other side, ready to block off our exit to the pool. The perfect reason for Nakir's delay.

The void starts to grip me, but I shove it away and dive back into the river of fire, keeping the words coming.

"The devil was bound by six angels, in secret," I shout at Eleth. "Five and one leader. *These* are the angels now being killed."

The twins have reached their destination. They remain poised directly at our backs, between us and the pool, while Nakir towers above us at the top of the slope.

I lift my hand toward Eleth. "And you know who's doing it, don't you?" I say, forcing the words out. "You know who the leader of the binding angels was."

Nakir clenches his jaw before roaring at me. "I said, *silence!"*

His anger's like a hot wind in my chest. It drives the river of fire inside me faster, wilder, the energy climbing my throat.

"Don't you?" I holler, still reaching for Eleth. "I must speak to the angels!"

"You will be *quiet*!" Nakir bellows, louder than ever.

He leaps down the slope and throws himself at me. I feel the flames roar in him as they roar in my chest. I'm thrust beyond the veil, and my mind stills automatically. The world shimmers, and the sensation comes of being connected with everything – the grassy slope, the pool behind, even the surrounding air – while power pulses in my veins. I set my feet.

Nakir swings his sword downward.

Eleth yells, "Nakir, wait!" while Natasha shouts, "No!" Both voices distorted in slowed time.

Nakir's blade careens diagonally down toward me in a vicious arc.

I channel the power into my legs, kick off the ground, and drive myself away from Nakir. I sail backward down the slope and away from the flying sword as the blade screeches through the air. The same smell of burning metal bites at my nose, and I fling my hands forward and my body away from the sword's screaming tip. It misses my navel by a hair's breadth.

I land twenty feet from the pool, both twins behind me, and then throw myself to the side just as Nakir crashes his blade into the ground. It cleaves a two-foot tear through the earth. I roll away from Natasha and the priest to scramble further along the grassy bank, maintaining my distance from the twins.

Nakir keeps coming. Holding his sword in one hand, he slashes, and I dodge. Beyond the veil, I concentrate on the telltale signs of his neck muscles, his shifts of weight. Nakir jabs again, swift as flame, and then grabs at me with his free hand. I spin backward, and massive fingers brush my shoulder as my head rotates out of the way.

"Nakir!" Eleth yells.

Her command is like fingers holding me in place, and I end up poised, mid-movement, breathing hard, my heartbeat thrumming. Nakir stops also, his sword levelled at me. He turns his head to stare up at his fellow emissary, his brow furrowed. She stands further up the slope and fixes her gaze on me, her green eyes shining.

"Stranger," she says, "you cannot see the Malakh." And the next words echo inside my mind. *"It is forbidden."*

Still the river of fire burns in my chest, the void cavernous underneath. My jaw tightens. "After thousands of years of tyranny," I say, my thoughts starting up and the veil slipping back into place, "they won't face us?"

She stares at me with features sharp as flint. Yet her eyes soften, just a fraction, and the tip of her blade drops an inch.

Nakir grips his sword in both hands and levels it at me again. And again, I can *feel* his burning anger. A wind gusts across the landscape and pulls at my arms, my legs. The fire rages at my core. White-hot.

"I will see the angels if I have to tear you to pieces," I growl, channelling the growing power into my limbs.

I throw myself at Nakir.

In an instant of shock, his sculpted features fall slack. Then he places a foot behind him in defence and lifts his weapon above his head to strike. But his sword's so long, he's too late.

I smash into him and crash my elbow into his bare chest. It's as solid as rock, and my forearm vibrates in agony. But I push down the pain and let the river of fire carry me, the veil peeling fully back in an instant.

Landing, I bring my knee up hard into Nakir's groin. He rotates and fends off my knee with his thigh. Then he tenses his arms above him and grips his sword hilt tighter. With time slowed, I fix my attention on the contraction in his shoulders as well as the twist of his pelvis. So when he crashes the hilt of his sword down toward the crown of my head, I'm already throwing my neck backward. The hilt flies just in front of my face.

Then I clench my jaw and slam both hands forward and up, palms out, toward the sword. A fucking stupid idea. Yet somehow, I smack the flat of the emissary's blade as it shoots past my nose, driving it into his forehead.

A huge clanging sound rings out, like metal against stone, but that's it. The guy hardly flinches. He simply takes one hand off the sword, whips his arm from inside to out, and backhands me across my torso while bellowing a roar.

I fly head over heels as pain howls in my chest. The heavenly planes careen through my vision, my sense of direction scrambled. I force my eyes closed for an instant and feel the shimmering world, the connection to the distant strips of land and the grassy slope that was right beneath me. I concentrate on it as I channel my fire and focus hard on the meadow below. Eventually, the ground slams into my feet.

I'm off-balance, stumbling, and fall to my knees. And with the flames diminishing, the pain rises to take their place – my chest and forearm screaming, my ankles throbbing.

The winds gust ever faster as I push myself back to my feet and glance around, the veil slipping before my senses again.

Thirty feet to the oval pool, the twins still blocking it off. Natasha's hurrying to my side, the priest just behind. Eleth remains up the slope from us, her sword held diagonally away from her.

While Nakir ….

He takes another step down the bank toward me and points his sword directly at my heart. Then he nods to the twins at my back, who direct their swords at me also while forming attack positions. Nakir's burning eyes narrow, his breathing rate increases, and he raises his sword above his head.

Crazily, I steel myself and plumb the void once more, driving my fire and building my power. And as it grows, I start to peel the veil away again …

When I feel a sudden change.

Everything stops around me. *Everything*. The wind, the

butterflies flitting. They just hang motionlessly in the air. All four emissaries drop to their knees and prostrate themselves, arms out in front of them.

My gut twists again, and I whirl around, my pulse thumping as I scan the clear blue sky.

30

For an instant, everything is plunged into darkness as if the light from the entire heavenly realm has coalesced into a single spot – the eye of a storm. I ready myself. A shock wave careens outward and sweeps me off my feet. I sense the realm being reorganised, the planes re-forming around us as if mountains are becoming valleys, bridges becoming streams, sky becoming land …

My eyes open, and I push myself up on my knees. The strips of land seem to head in new directions through the sky. Where once were dips on our strip, now are rises, but I'm not entirely sure. All the features remain the same. Natasha and Father Thomas still stand twenty feet to my side along the grassy bank, the pool at our backs, the blue sky above and below us. All seemingly identical.

Except a new sun hovers beyond the crest of the rise, thirty yards away, and the smell of cordite's strong in my nose. I rip my gaze from the fierce glow, my retinas burning as a fresh chill fills my insides. Plus, an undeniable knowing of who or what stands there. Slowly, I swivel my gaze to face him.

The fierce glare abates, as if Michael has turned down his luminescence. Peace envelops my heart, a brimming warmth in my chest, the pain almost forgotten. The archangel's radiance extends well beyond him. Michael, the head of God's armies – I remember Natasha's lectures. And in the air, the butterflies stir. They coalesce behind him – millions, billions – forming themselves into iridescent arcs of yellow, into wings. Enormous wings, each one fifteen feet across. Dozens of the butterflies make up every individual feather.

Michael raises each massive arm out to the side at shoulder level. Here in an angelic realm, he stands as the colossus – three feet taller than a normal man – and blinding too, like he's made up entirely of light. The emissaries keep their foreheads pressed to the ground before him, two behind me and two in front, though the muscles in Nakir's body and jaw remain taut with rage.

I narrow my eyes and peer up at the archangel, trying to make out features. Different faces appear and disappear in the brightness: male, female, young, old. He wears no distinguishable clothes, either; it's like his body has been carved out of marble with shining colours of white and pearl morphing and shifting.

My mouth drops open. His posture – the arms held out at right angles to his torso, the massive wings that arc behind. It's the symbol – the tattoo I glimpsed on the pursuer's chest all those months ago, the clasp the emissaries wear around their necks, the crucifix with a crescent moon.

Natasha's on her knees at my side, her hands pressed together and body shaking, all her attention fixed on the archangel. The sense of calm still feels like a quilt that swathes me.

I grit my teeth and rise to my feet, searching again for the fire within and fuelling it with memories of my mother's death, Qetesh's. I open my mouth and drive whatever energy's left up my throat. Yet as soon as the flames spark, they die again as if the fire in my chest has been starved of air.

Michael lowers his arms and stares directly at me. "Respect where you are," the archangel says, his voice soft, the tone multilayered as it echoes from all directions. And here in this realm, his words are clearly understandable, not discordant at all. "We want no more violence … no more of your ire in this place." Michael makes a dismissive gesture, his faces continuing to shift.

"*My* ire?" Again, I try to conjure the flames. The angels' rule, a thousand-year con. God as the greatest manipulation. And still the serenity reigns at my core.

"Whatever you intend, you're misguided," he says. "Go."

With this last word, Michael beats his mighty wings, just once. And the movement brings forth a tremendous rush of wind. It shoves against me and drives me down the bank toward the pool. My chest and arm throb again, and I have to focus hard on keeping my balance, my feet slipping further backward.

"The angel!" I shout into the biting winds, my voice barely a croak. I throw a hand toward Michael. "The one who died. I know who killed her!"

Michael ignores me. He beats his wings again, and the wind continues to push at my limbs, my torso.

"Don't you want to know?" I ask, my voice even weaker.

Eleth raises her head and gazes at me, the same softness in her expression, the look of curiosity back in her eyes. Michael turns to her and lowers his wings. The wind settles, though the remaining butterflies continue to flit around me in wild spirals. I find myself able to stand upright again.

"Gabriel—" I cough out, my throat raw.

"You will not find him here," Michael says. "He is exiled. We do not speak of him."

The archangel's features continue to change, unreadable, and his radiance cools a fraction, as if he's sad.

My mind flits to Gabriel being the devil, to the likelihood that Michael has no bloody idea.

I clear my throat. "Why?"

Silence. Michael continues to gaze at me, the female emissary also, while her colleagues remain prostrate on the ground, foreheads pressed to the grassy floor.

The priest steps forward. "Why was Gabriel exiled?" he says.

More silence. Then Michael's voice echoes as a distant sound on the wind. "You do not understand."

The faintest sparks form at my core. "So tell us!" I yell.

"You could not comprehend." Michael's disembodied voice grows louder, his body shining brighter. "A flower has no concept of the sun that sustains it. Just as you could not grasp the role of the pantheon." The archangel's wings extend further out to his sides.

"We are purity, the light," he continues, and his gaze shifts to Eleth again. "Untainted by fetters of feeling. An example to humanity. The source to which the flower will ceaselessly align."

My fingers tremble. I clench them hard, my forearm aching. "You've not answered my question."

The archangel turns to me, and his radiance changes again. A fraction redder … hotter. And his features resolve a little. I glimpse dark skin, silver armour, a shining breastplate, muscles like sculpted boulders, legs like aged trees, and an unchanging face … as beautiful and as awful as that first time I saw Gabriel's.

"Your arrogance," Michael says, his tone remaining completely level.

"You were human once!" I say.

His wings flex, and the wind blows again, this time like a massive sigh.

"That was a very long time ago," he says.

And for a good while, he says nothing. I shift my weight.

"We were chosen," he says eventually.

The sparks grow inside me. "You've kept humanity in bondage—" I start.

Michael's radiance burns, and he beats his wings harder. A blast of wind hits me like a fist to the torso, spearing my upper chest with pain. The words die on my lips, my body tenses, and then he cools again.

"Have you any notion of what the world was back then?" Michael asks, his voice still level. "What it would be like without our example?"

A stream of images bombards my mind … Gabriel's blazing eyes. The victims of his plague. Qetesh's slain body again, my mother's. Society's countless homeless, parents scrambling for food, their children recruited by gangs as thieves. The fire smoulders inside, and I ball my fists.

The female emissary rises to her knees, still gazing at me. Michael turns in her direction.

"Eleth?" he says, his voice rumbling.

She doesn't meet his gaze but just lowers herself back down. The archangel turns slowly toward us again, any hint of features in his brightness gone.

"You wish me to answer your question, why Gabriel was exiled?" he says. The surrounding colours intensify – the green of the grassy slope before us, the blue sky above. "You and Gabriel are more alike than you imagine."

The embers flare, and the words are out of my mouth before I can stop them. "I am nothing like—"

"The rage that burns, that reigns over your actions, that twists your conceptions. It is created by some past pain, by some unfulfilled want. Am I right?" he says.

More memories come … my childhood home, the gang, my mother, the drugs, me leaving … And I sense Michael riffling through my brain. Just as Gabriel did.

I breathe and focus on calming the fire, on stilling my thoughts, on shutting down my mind.

Michael shrugs. "This rage is the same affliction that besets my brother," he says.

Then the archangel steps forward, and I'm seized by a sudden compulsion to prostrate myself before him. I need to concentrate hard to remain standing.

"He believed fiercely in man's potential, in your pursuit of the sacred," Michael says, his radiance burning so brightly again that I need to shield my eyes. "And with the scriptures, he has given humanity the greatest gift." He pauses, and then his voice softens. "And therefore, he becomes ever more frustrated when you consistently fail."

I sense Nakir's eyes burning into me, but I keep my attention fixed on Michael.

"Gabriel is an archangel," Michael continues. "He is exiled because his rage is deluded and dangerous. Just as yours is." He nods toward me. "Emotions have great potency. They can shape our beliefs, drive us beyond all doubts, beyond all limitations. You *know* this."

Again, the thoughts come unbidden. *Yes*. The wild fury. The immense power.

"But they also confuse and confound," says Michael, his voice quieter still. "It's a choice. For all of us."

He stares down at the emissaries, and the revelation comes. *Fuck*. My eyes widen. This is a bloody lecture, aimed at his minions, not at us. We're simply props, which means I have no hope of convincing him and never did. The flames blaze again, and my insides tighten.

"Angels must remain the sun," Michael says, continuing to gaze over his emissaries. "We hold the purest expression of feeling – compassion – transcendent and immutable. Impersonal and eternal love. *This* is the way we serve humankind."

"By hoarding the light, you keep humanity enslaved," the priest says.

Michael turns toward him. "Humanity is full of sin," he says, his glow blazing no hotter. "Your appetites, your aspirations, your ambitions. You need guidance, examples to strive for. Without the teachings, the scriptures, without our acts of wonder, humanity's pursuits would be entirely hollow."

His words are so similar to Gabriel's. I shake my head.

"You yourself know the corrupt fruits of humanity's labours," Michael says to the priest, his voice so calm, his glow so serene.

And my mind conjures images of gated mansions, towering skyscrapers, the luxury yachts of the rich. My sparks of anger start to fade.

Michael turns his shining eyes on mine, and I force the energy up my throat.

"But … there's something else, something worse," I say, my voice shaky. "Gabriel – he's recreating an older order, a world of battling forces, becoming his prior self."

The wind dies, and all four emissaries lift their heads. Michael's radiance intensifies. And sweat trickles down my neck.

I push myself on. "The devil," I say. "Gabriel is becoming the devil again. He'll free his weapon, his trident, his army to rule—"

"You see?" Michael says, and his brightness spears my retinas. I shut my eyes, but still the light presses through my closed lids. "More delusion. Anger confounds. The devil is a memory."

And then there's calm again. Cooling gusts. I open my eyes.

Michael glows peaceably once more from the crest of the rise. "He was bound," he continues. "It paved the way for this age, a world of peace. No sign of him has been seen for two thousand years now. *Two thousand years.*" And the first hint of severity creeps into his tone. "The devil is *not* coming back."

Michael begins to swivel away. And still each emissary stares at me. I take a faltering step forward.

"And the dead angel?" I ask.

The archangel shakes his head and continues to rotate.

"And the symbol left behind?" I continue. "The three slashes carved into her back?"

Michael stops moving. Nakir spins to face him, and the silence feels thick in the surrounding air. Eleth keeps her eyes on me.

"Whoever it was, it is a sick joke," Michael says.

"You're wrong," I say and shake my head vigorously. "You've got to investigate, to confront this ... to do *something*."

Michael gazes off to the side, as if contemplating the heavenly landscape around him. "You do not understand," he says. "I have told you already. Engaging with such plots means abasement." He ripples his wings and another breath of wind issues forth like a sigh. "It would mean sullying ourselves with low emotions – desire, anger, fear. We would risk a quagmire, the relinquishment of clarity. Anything we did would risk perpetuating that which we might wish to change."

Then he swivels his gaze back to me. "We would become like Gabriel," he says. "Like the brother you accuse, like the billions of humans who trample each other every day in the hope of attaining this craving or that."

And Michael raises his arms again into the cross-like shape, beats his massive wings, and rises majestically into the air. The resulting blasts of wind slap my cheeks, and I focus hard on remaining still.

"You are misguided," he says, and his voice rings out. "We cannot help you. We must stand removed, above, an inspiration. *That* is our role. We have played it for thousands of years and we will play it for thousands more." He rises higher. "So be gone!"

The fierce gust from a beat of his wings sends me stumbling backward down the slope again, toward the pool behind. The twins back away along its edge, making room for our escape.

"Wait! Stop!" I yell into the wind, the throbbing in my chest worse, my feet skidding on the slick grass.

Michael continues to beat his wings, to rise into the air. And the gusts blow stronger, sending the remaining butterflies rolling and reeling. A few come much closer than before. They flit in front of my face and then collide with my shoulders and torso, bringing jabs of pain.

Nakir and Eleth have also jumped up, both by the ridge. The male emissary brandishes his sword again and aims its point at my stomach. Even so, I focus on anchoring my feet, the pool only twenty feet behind me.

"How many angels have already been killed?" I bellow at Michael.

But he ignores me. Just drifts further away. I dive deep into the void, searching for fire, for power. But I find nothing, the wind pressing hard against my body, my emotions.

"How many thousands of years old were they?" I yell. "Could they have been with Gabriel at the binding?"

Still, Michael doesn't turn, and the wind pushes ever more powerfully. It's like being thrust backward by a concrete wall. I try to hold my ground but can't. The butterflies continue to swarm and attack. More and more of them rain down on me, stinging my skin ever harder.

"Yes, go!" Eleth says.

She's striding down the hill in our direction, Michael at her back, her sword raised up high. Her body acts as some kind of break to the wind, and the pressure on my limbs eases a fraction.

"There's nothing for you here!" she yells and stretches her other hand toward me, her fingers spread. The softness returns to her expression, her green eyes blazing.

The butterflies swirl faster. I have to turn my body against them as they slam against my shoulders, legs, arms, and back … And then one of them darts into my hand. It remains there, warm and light against my palm. Then, in an instant, it grows heavy.

I'm about to glance down at my hand when her voice speaks insistently in my head.

"Don't," she says.

I keep my chin up and gaze straight back at her while feeling the shape in my palm. A few inches long, elongated, made of metal, and cool against my skin … the butterfly somehow transformed.

"May it bring you light where you venture," Eleth says, a half smile on her lips, the words again spoken for me alone.

I peer more closely. Something changed about her appearance … I take a sudden breath. The clasp from her cloak … *gone*. Now sitting in my palm.

My fingers squeeze tightly around it while Michael's butterflies continue to bombard me from all sides. With the archangel drifting away, Nakir closes in on us. He grips his sword two-handed above his head, the fire still burning in his eyes.

"Go!" he bellows.

I spin with Natasha and the priest, and we dart between the twins for the pool.

31

BACK UNDER-FUCKING-GROUND, the thin finger of my flashlight beam sweeps along yet another set of branching tunnel walls, illuminating slivers of curved brick and looping cable all choked with grime, the darkness squeezing in around me.

The final junction looms up ahead. I hurry on, counting my steps, a crowbar gripped in one hand. And though my upper chest and forearm continue to ache, I'm leading now, pushing faster, the priest padding at my shoulder while Natasha walks several paces behind.

Father Thomas reaches the junction and peers around the corner with his flashlight. Capell's entrance lies beyond.

"All clear," the priest whispers.

I nod, though my eyes dart back down the tunnel, probing the blackness. We've seen no sign of the *things*, no scent of sulphur. Yet a shiver still passes through me.

"Come on," the priest says, and motions us forward.

I follow him down the fusty tunnel, and still Natasha remains a few feet behind us. The void's ever present at my core. My fingers find Eleth's clasp in my pocket, and I squeeze it tightly. *She believed.*

The priest stops walking. "This is it," he says and traces

the line of the door in the tunnel wall with his flashlight beam.

Our eyes meet, and he shrugs. I step forward, crowbar in my other hand, and kick hard at the middle of the door. The impact sends juddering pain up my leg into my chest. And, unsurprisingly, the door doesn't move an inch.

Locked.

I heave a sigh and knock with the crowbar, keeping it light. No response. This time, I bring up the crowbar and begin working at the edge between the door and the tunnel, trying to squeeze the metal claw between them. But the gap's too tight, the seal too perfect, all the way around the edge. I step back, sweat forming down my sides. My ribs tighten.

"Capell!" I yell at the door, my voice booming in the narrow passageway. "It's us! Jake, Natasha, and Father Thomas. Our efforts came to a bit of a dead end. We need to talk!"

The sound echoes away down the tunnel, and I can't help glancing into the darkness again, sniffing the air. Still no sign of a *thing*. Still only silence. I clear my throat. Set my feet.

"We know you lied!" I yell.

Natasha and the priest turn to stare at me. I keep my eyes on the door.

"Well ... we know you didn't tell the whole truth," I continue. "You said you didn't know much about the devil, but that wasn't any ordinary angel you pointed us to. Was it?"

I hold my breath, listening hard. No response from beyond the door.

"It was a binding angel," I shout, heat rising in my chest. "One of those involved in the devil's incarceration. You knew about Revelation. Didn't you? The devil being cast into a fiery pit, two thousand years back. You were aware that it's not just some story, that it's all supposedly true! We learned that for ourselves." I pause for breath, my heart thumping in my ribs. "We learned a lot more as well."

With a dull metal click, the door in the tunnel opens inward an inch. I blink at it and then glance up and scan the ceiling of the passageway for some kind of camera or microphone. Nothing obvious. Still, I gently put down the crowbar and push open the curving section of the tunnel wall. The door's ajar at the end. I pad across the wooden slats of the dimly lit entranceway.

And there he is. Capell. Sitting at the head of the glass table, in the middle of his immaculate rooms, breathing his purified air, exactly where we left him. Same upright posture, same pristine outfit – an embroidered dressing gown over a starched white shirt. And he's staring directly at me.

I move to stand by the table; the priest strides to the same chair he sat in last time, to my right, while Natasha pads further over. She goes to stand on the priest's far side, and with her distance, I feel a stab of pain amid the deep void inside me. And I have to breathe it down, every emotion so bloody intense now.

None of us sit, and Capell doesn't invite us to. He surveys us evenly, his posture somehow more upright than before.

"Did you tell?" he demands, his voice low but firm.

And his final words come back to me.

"Well, did you?" he says.

"We said nothing," Natasha says quickly. "Told no one about you."

He relaxes a fraction, his shoulders descending a quarter inch. Then he fixes me with a glare.

"So what did you learn?" he asks.

"From the binding angel?" I retort.

He nods.

"Nothing." I shrug. "She was dead."

He goes quiet, rigid, his lips a fraction apart, hardly breathing.

"Dead?" he asks simply.

I find myself nodding. "When we arrived. Murdered. With three slashes carved into her back."

His skin seems to grow somehow paler than before, his body as still as a pillar of salt. Is that guilt in his eyes? I place my hands on the chair in front.

"So, why d'you not tell us?" I demand. "Why weren't you honest about what you knew?"

His gaze eventually focuses on me, and a flash of hurt crosses his face.

"I *was* honest," he says. And then the haughty look re-forms – thin lips, lifted chin. "The scriptures say nothing about binding angels." He wags a finger and continues in his superior tone. "That rumour hailed from someone who truly conversed with the angel you saw. I couldn't prove it myself, however. And the more I revealed, the greater the risk that you'd compromise me, that you'd compromise my source. You *must* see that." He sits taller. "However, I shared enough for you to find the information you needed. I could have done nothing more."

And with that, he goes silent.

"Well, clearly the rumour is true," I say. "There are six of them. Six binding angels, with Gabriel as their leader, and they're dying. Being killed. But what do we do?" I lift my hands. "Michael refuses to help—"

"You saw the Archangel Michael?" Capell asks and leans forward now, his air of haughtiness slipping again. He gazes at me in shock, his eyes wide.

I nod. "He's powerful, no doubt, but wouldn't engage. D'you think we could persuade him?"

Capell says nothing. Just gapes.

Father Thomas shrugs at my side. "Perhaps," he says. "But we'd need some kind of evidence."

"And we don't have that," I say. "But could we find the binding angels still alive and warn them?"

I eye Capell, and he shakes himself. Then, eventually, he meets my gaze.

"If you are asking if I'm aware of their location? I am not," he says, his tone abrupt. "I'd heard nothing more than rumour that they were even real until a few moments ago."

"They are likely to have gone to ground, anyway," Natasha says. "No one will be able to find them."

"Except Gabriel," I say.

Capell tenses in his chair and begins to fidget, his fingers clenching.

"And we don't know how many of them are still alive," the priest says.

"Yeah," I agree. "How many Gabriel has already—"

"The gates," Capell says.

"What?" I ask.

"The gates," he repeats. "Again, I cannot verify this, for nothing is documented about it in the scriptures. But the rumour indicated that each binding angel erected a gate." His tone grows more excited. "And apparently each gate can only be opened by the corresponding angel – in life, or at their death. That's how you gain your evidence. You ascertain how many are still closed."

A sinking sensation starts in my gut.

"And these gates will be in hell?" Father Thomas says.

For a while Capell says nothing. Then he nods.

"And does hell's entrance have a physical location?" the priest says.

"There are many references in the texts, but yes," Capell says. "We may find some agreement." He places his hands flat on the table as if smoothing out some kind of manuscript. "It will be complex to interpret and will require a little conjecture—"

"Wait!" Natasha says and grips the chair before her. She leans forward over the table and glances from me to the priest and back again. "Just think about what you're saying. You are talking about going into *hell!*"

The priest gives a half smile. "We must," he says softly. "It's our path. What other option is there?"

She purses her lips but doesn't reply. And I feel split

between the sense of momentum in my chest, the fire, the drive … and a growing reticence, countless internal voices yelling at me.

Natasha shakes her head. "If the entrance is real, it has been hidden for two thousand years," she says. "How would we even find it?"

Capell stands bolt upright.

We all turn. He remains there, blinking, and then gazes down at his feet as if as surprised by his sudden movement.

He clears his throat. "You would need my help."

32

"LADIES AND GENTLEMEN, we're starting our descent to Istanbul airport," the steward drawls over the loudspeaker.

The engines roar, the plane drops, and new glimpses of the Turkish landscape flash past the window – rolling hills, river valleys, and roads that cross them like scars – all so damn far below.

Again, I press the back of my head into the seat and curse Ben. He was all smiles at Natasha when she asked him. Came through with money, passports, and tickets leaving the next day. My chest tightens just thinking about it, the constriction adding to the growing nausea in my gut.

My eyes find Natasha. She's sitting in the aisle seat next to me, Father Thomas on my other side, and her eyes rest on a well-worn copy of the Bible on her lap, opened to the book of Revelation. Somehow, she's able to read it as we bump about, her fingers continuously playing with her crucifix necklace.

Capell's sitting across the aisle with his own satchel of papers, but he never looks inside. He simply holds it tightly to his immaculate jacket and waistcoat, perched upright in his seat, a full two inches off the stained backrest. I glance up at his lifted nose and chin. *Why* did *he come?*

The plane lurches as it drops faster, the wing tips wobbling, and the cabin vibrates more intensely. A lady in front of us prays, and my stomach climbs somewhere up my throat.

I grab a magazine from the seat pocket and begin flipping through the pages. I find the map of Turkey, and there it is, the town of Pergamon – Capell's recommended location – and a six-hour drive from Istanbul.

Natasha turns to me. "You coming up with a plan?" she asks with bite. "To find hell, discover how many gates have been opened, how many binding angels are still alive, and then somehow get the evidence to Michael?"

I blink up at her. She's gazing at me with those large hazel eyes. I find myself nodding. "Yeah, and all before Gabriel bloody kills them all."

She scoffs.

I lean in. "Nat, you heard Capell's warnings," I say, the void still lurking deep inside, the fire just simmering atop the surface. "The devil being without equal, waging a war outnumbered ten to one, angels versus his demon allies. Humanity the victim."

"But even if we can prove it, what makes you think Michael will act?" she demands.

My mouth opens, but nothing comes out, the archangel's words flitting through my mind … *Emotions are powerful, Gabriel's rage dangerous, just as yours is.*

Natasha continues to stare.

Evil begets evil, after all.

"We have to try," a voice says suddenly.

I swivel. The priest's reclining at my side, his eyes closed and a tranquil expression on his face. So comfortable and calm. "What else can we do?" he says.

I shift in my seat as the plane descends, the engines roaring louder. Natasha goes back to reading, and my hands clasp the armrests all the way down till the wheels land with a massive bump.

Finally, the plane comes to a stop, and I'm the first to stand, my bag slung across my shoulder. The sky's already a deepening blue above. Dusk approaching fast.

Passengers trudge the aisle. And we follow on behind, Natasha, Capell and the priest ahead of me. The old man shuffles forward without his stick. I step out of the plane door after them, onto the top of a set of steps.

And stop dead.

My fingers grip the edge of the open hatch. It's as if I've been punched in the gut. Besides the scorching heat, the burnt rubber, it's the void, but *different*. Not just anguish, but a despair too – a flatness, a hollowness at my core – like nothing I've ever experienced. I have to focus hard to keep breathing. My legs wobble.

Natasha pivots on the stairs. "Jake, you okay?" Her brow is pinched. "You look deathly pale."

I swallow. It's like every surface is paper-thin, the darkness skulking just behind. My eyes flit to the bottom of the steps, and images come of the void as a reservoir of oil seeping up through the tarmac, ready to devour me whole.

Several people behind mutter at me. Then someone prods me in the back. Fire flashes through me, and before I know it, I'm spinning, the muscles in my arm bunching—

A hand grips my other arm. Natasha holds me fast, and I focus on the cool touch of her fingers. The flames calm, and I'm able to slow my breathing.

"Come with me," she says and tugs me by the arm.

I manage to nod, and she helps me down onto the tarmac. But it's tough. My body shakes, the darkness eating me from my core. All I can do is concentrate on her hand on my arm, on putting one foot in front of the other. And eventually, she leads us through a set of doors into the terminal building.

It's a grey panel-lined hall, a hundred feet in width and much longer, with large windowed walls and a ceiling that's fifty feet above our heads. Six passport booths line the rear of the space with three lengthy queues in front of them. I'm breathing hard, the air red-hot in my throat.

Father Thomas shuffles into the middle queue, and I traipse along at his back. He glances up at me with a grim expression.

"Well, we know we're in the right place," he says.

"Too true," I whisper, almost doubled up. The void's incredible, inside and out, like a blackness lies behind the walls and floor, creeping its way toward me.

The priest eyes the passport booths. "We just need to navigate security and get out of the airport," he says. "Then we'll find a hotel for the night."

I nod, my legs trembling. The lines are moving so damn slowly, security taking an age with each passenger. There's a heavy military presence too. A dozen soldiers line the hall, machine guns in hand, each one surveying the crowd with suspicious eyes. Occasionally, they grab a random passenger and march them to a seventh passport booth at the end of the row, staffed by military personnel.

I keep my breathing steady, the call of the fire still so intense, and focus on Natasha and the priest, on their calming presence at my side. They continue to talk in hushed voices, Capell poised silently behind.

The thin bar of daylight ebbs toward the base of the large plexiglass windows, the occasional star peeking out among the deepening blue. My insides tighten, and I scan the queues for the *things*. There's nothing obvious. Yet my gut twists, my internal alarm.

I crane my neck and peer beyond the lines toward the passport booths and the sides of the hall beyond the soldiers. Still no sign of the hunched posture.

My gaze falls on three of the guys in full military gear, one with a sidearm and two with machine guns, all staring at me. The sidearm soldier – probably some kind of captain – leans in to speak to the others. I yank my head down and squeeze my fingers, the void swelling like the oil's permeating my legs from the floor.

The shout doesn't come. The line continues to inch forward. And I'm forced to shuffle along with it, my eyes to the floor, while my internal alarm rings on.

Two-thirds of the way to the front of the queue, a strange hissing starts up in my ears, and painful memories seize my mind. So fucking vivid. Still, I keep going, my jaw clenched and fingers gripped around Eleth's clasp in my pocket.

Finally, I reach the front of the line. The border officer in one of the two booths calls me forward.

Natasha squeezes my arm and whispers, "We're almost through."

I nod and step forward when someone barks from the side. I spin. It's the captain from before, and he's standing by the seventh passport booth, his eyes fixed on me.

No, no, no. The heat flares inside.

Natasha's called forward to an empty booth, and she touches my shoulder as she goes. "It will be okay."

The captain snaps at me again and points insistently at a spot before the final booth. I bow my head and shuffle over, the void deepening with every step away from the priest and Natasha.

I go to stand in the allotted space while the captain hovers a dozen feet to the side, watching me.

Some senior officer mans the seventh booth. Grand moustache, greying black hair, and numerous stripes on his shoulders, more than the captain. He's barking at the passenger before him while another soldier stands poised in the middle of the exit channel.

And there I wait, my heel bouncing and hands shaking. The darkness continues to fill my insides, like the oil's clogging my lungs.

The moustached colonel gives a flick of his hand, and the soldier in the channel hauls the passenger away. Another soldier replaces him, and the colonel calls me forward. My gut twists further, my internal alarm clamouring. I take a breath and take a step when an acrid scent hits my nose.

My head whips around, my heart thumping, and there it is. In a shadowy corner beyond the captain, beyond the booths, right at the side of the hall. A hunched figure with contorted features, dressed in a policeman's uniform and invisible to a soldier only a few feet in front. The *thing's* gazing directly at me, and the hissing sound roughens into the strange jabbered language while the memories flash faster through my mind.

"Hey!" A barked command.

I turn, blinking. The captain's staring with hard features. The colonel bangs a clenched fist on the counter. My legs quake, and the void continues to deepen while the embers smoulder atop the darkness with whispers of sweet relief echoing at the back of my brain.

"You!" the colonel yells this time and jabs a finger at me.

My eyes find the exit channel, Natasha, the priest, and freedom beyond with one of the many soldiers standing in the way. His hand tightens around his machine gun, and my eyes track back to the colonel. I tense my neck and force myself on toward him, offering my passport while working hard not to glance to my side.

The colonel takes a fucking age examining it. The heat scorches my insides, and I glare back at him, the jabbering sound intensifying. My vision blurs, and I see myself grabbing the guy's decorated collar and smashing his head into the counter, those sweet whispers calling louder … *let go, rage, fight.*

I clench every muscle, hold myself still, and breathe, the fire burning inside.

Eventually, the colonel tosses my passport on the counter, shakes his head, and opens his mouth. My gaze darts to the soldier in the channel, the guy's hand already raised to come and seize me.

But he doesn't move. The colonel's expression has

morphed – his tight features fallen slack, his eyes wide, his mouth fully open. And he's staring pale-faced at something over my shoulder and to the side.

But not in the direction of the *thing* at the end of the line of booths. He's staring toward the *other* side.

33

Muted gasps sound from the lines behind me. My insides wring tight, my internal alarm clamours, and my eyes dart to the exit channel. The soldier in it and the colonel are both gaping to the side now, mouths wide. Distracted.

Yet with the smell of sulphur stinging my nose, I find my head inching around.

The passengers in the three passport lines are all scrabbling backward to get away from someone – a woman in a charcoal business suit, hunched over, with arms hanging down and that same awful stare. She's lurching along the front of the queues in my direction, only twenty feet from me.

My pulse hammers in my veins, and I can't avert my gaze, as if my eyes are hooked by invisible threads. Meanwhile my mind conjures images of the police officer *thing* at my back, on the opposite end of the row of booths. The two of them stand ready to flank me.

The crowd continues to retreat. No one yells. No one screams. The female *thing* gazes straight at me. Her lips jabber, and the strange language fills my head, agonising memories whirling ever faster. The sweet whispers intensify. *Fight … tear … slash …* And the river of fire rages. My mind is gripped by the vision of me tearing her to pieces.

Again, I steel myself and try to face the darkness, to open my heart to it. But it's too much, *too much*. My entire body feels flooded, the pain like claws raking my heart. My fists clench, and the fire surges higher inside. Anything for release.

No, no, no!

The female *thing* opens her mouth wide. I grit my teeth and focus every ounce of energy on wrenching my gaze away. I barely manage it, my eyes burning with the effort.

My gaze seizes upon the exit channel – my escape route – and the soldier standing in my way. My legs tense, and I'm about to bolt.

Then I stop.

The soldier's still staring at the female *thing*, his eyes wide and unmoving as if hooked by those same threads. And his hands … they're shaking, one still gripping the handle of his machine gun while the other releases the safety catch. He's lowering the barrel toward the woman, and toward the hundreds of passengers behind her.

I throw myself down the channel and at the soldier. Just as the *thing* screams. Bulbs explode above my head, and my teeth jangle with the sound.

The soldier grips the gun tighter, the barrel almost horizontal now, his finger almost on the trigger. I careen into him from the side, slam his body back against a booth, and thrust his gun flat against his chest with both hands, the barrel pointing upward.

The soldier's eyes are still fixed on the *thing*, and he struggles to bring the gun back down. I grip his bulletproof vest and, while cannoning off him, yank him around, breaking the guy's gaze. I end up stumbling away from the booths, my feet tripping over each other. And with gawking passengers all around me, I grab at a nearby suited guy to right myself, miss, and crash into someone on my other side.

I'm sent sprawling, the impact like rock, and my sight hazes completely. Grey corridors and lacquer floors vanish, and instead, I glimpse a wasteland of craggy stone, billowing clouds, and a red sky. The void grips my insides while a fire burns not only under my skin but within my very bones. The breath seizes in my lungs.

A moment later, my vision returns, and the ground slams into my back. Pain shoots up my spine. I skid to a halt on the slick floor, my ribs throbbing, and end up gazing up at the figure I smashed into.

They hardly budged at all.

An elderly woman. Wearing a long skirt, a draped shawl, and a hijab. And she's hunched over, her arms hanging downward, and her eyes … completely black and staring down at me, transfixed.

I scramble upward, my feet slipping. The heat's still raging at my core, the jabbering intensifying in my ears again – faster, angrier. I force my shaking legs down the corridor, poised for the grip of bony fingers on my shoulders as hordes of passengers flee the passport area with me.

Some run. Others simply hurry along, encumbered by wheelie cases. And the whispering has started, people chattering in numerous languages, the fear obvious in everyone.

I scan the corridor ahead and spot more soldiers running toward us. Several glance at me, and I hide myself among the front of the hastening crowd. My eyes search the throng left and right. No sign of Natasha or the priest, both of them undoubtedly well ahead. Nor do I see any sign of the *things*. Even so, my body shakes, the flames simmering just under my skin. I pass quivering hands over my arms and chest. My heartbeat calms a fraction, and the fire diminishes the further I run, the void that bit more distant.

The blue exit signs lead me to the baggage area. It's massive with a towering ceiling, a cavernous width, and eight belts full of luggage, crowds surrounding them all. A few passengers drift away, craning to spy down the corridor behind me, their eyes taking in the crowd hurrying forward at my sides, and the soldiers and security guards hastening in the opposite direction.

I keep my pace steady through the space when an announcement blares on the PA system. The voice is Turkish, the concern obvious in her sharp words. Then another announcement. Faster. Louder. And in English.

"We will close the exit!" it bellows. "Please remain in baggage claim!"

Orange lights flash to either side of a passageway in the far wall. The only way out of the room, and well over a hundred yards away.

I hurry my steps, the confusion spreading fast. More people around the belts stare up at the speakers, a mixture of shock and unease on their features, while those already near the exit hasten faster between the flashing lights.

An alarm sounds and plexiglass doors begin to close the passageway, swinging inward on both sides. I press on faster among the scrambling passengers, their squawks intensifying, with snatches of Turkish and English phrases echoing in my ears. I hear the word *terrorist* multiple times.

Then, suddenly, I stumble to a stop. The throng's bunched in front, blocking my path, many of them standing and gawping at the closing doors, the exit still thirty bloody yards away. And at least three *things* stand behind me.

I glance around one more time for Natasha and the priest. No sign. And the doors begin to shut faster.

I focus on the void inside, on the blazing fire. I channel it up my throat, dip my head, and bellow as loudly as I can, "Look out!" I jab my finger randomly over my shoulder. *"Bomb!"*

There's an instant of quiet, but then cries of concern ring out. Dozens more passengers flee for the passageway, some taking their bags, others abandoning them, which prompts more to do the same.

I press on with the growing horde, and while the doors continue to close, more of the panicked crowd pours through every moment, showing no sign of stopping despite the increasing chance of being crushed. In the next instant, the operator abandons the attempt, and the doors swing back open.

Eventually, I reach the opening of the passageway. It's ten feet wide, thirty feet long, and crammed with passengers hardly moving into the main body of the airport. I peer forward, and my torso goes rigid.

Police cordon. Just beyond the end of the passageway. Several officers stand across the exit, stopping passengers from going any further. And behind them, hundreds of onlookers – families, friends – howl angry accusations, a few officers yelling back.

I push forward with my hands and elbows, driving myself through the crowd. A door opens to my side in the middle of the channel, and police officers appear. They bark at people to herd them fast through the new opening. Passengers surge in all directions now, making it bloody difficult to keep moving. I strain and shove my way between people, working ever harder, with sweat seeping down my neck.

Ten feet from the cordon, the smell of sulphur assails my nose again.

My insides twist even more, the void like a dark mouth below me, and the river of fire its tongue. The energy surges around my ribs, and my arms vibrate with power. Images come of me towering above the shouting crowds, cutting through them like a fucking scythe.

I tense my chest and swivel on the spot, desperately scanning for the *things*. My vision hazes again, absolute silence descends, and the scene before me morphs entirely …

The people … suddenly they're dead, scattered across the ground, eyes vacant, limbs flung over each other. And beyond them, the airport is now made of crumbling stone, with huge holes in the walls and ceiling, revealing angry clouds visible through the gaps. A raw heat scorches my skin.

Just like my dreams.

I blink hard, and finally my vision returns. The bedlam erupts in my ears again, and my fellow passengers jostle me left and right, people pressing in even tighter on all sides. I try to thrust my way in every direction, but there's nowhere to go.

Once more, the abyss plunges deeper, the fire calling louder. I focus everything on keeping the void and rage at bay, almost stumbling over the passengers in front of me. My fingers squeeze Eleth's clasp in my pocket.

A big shove sends me rearward, and I clock a police officer a couple of feet before me, part of the cordon, with one arm spread and the other wielding an electric baton. His face is flushed, his hands shaking. A passenger just before me gets too close. The officer clenches his jaw, and I hear a crackling sound as he jabs the passenger with the baton. The guy screeches and topples to his knees while a caustic smell assails my nose.

I focus on keeping my feet as more of the crowd ahead tries to scramble away. The officer snarls at them all, his baton lifted high. The growing chaos builds the energy in my chest. The scent of sulphur's even stronger. My head whirls, and suddenly I'm seeing a hundred *things* around me, every one with that same hunched posture, those black eyes all burning into mine. Again, the river of fire rages wild, the desire now immense to let it flow, to use the veil, to smash through the cordon, to get the *fuck* out of here.

But the same images come from my dreams – scenes of destruction, bodies strewn.

The crowd behind thrusts us in the direction of the cordon. The shove sends me and a few others floundering toward the officer. I'm about to lose my balance. Yet this time I don't even try to regain it. Instead, as the policeman shocks another passenger to my side, I rotate around the guy as he falls and use his body as a screen to hide myself. Off-balance, I throw myself under the policeman's raised arm an instant before the fucker notices me.

He spins and stabs his baton down like he's spearing a fish on the ground. I scramble away – and then again as he keeps stabbing, stalking me with teeth gritted and eyes burning, creating an ever larger hole in the cordon.

Several other passengers burst past him, the other officers unable to keep them back. This creates a flood of movement. The guy pivots, but too late, and gets knocked down. He finds himself trampled by passengers swarming through the cordon.

I stumble to my feet, almost get felled myself, and lurch on toward the main exit from the terminal building. Finally, I shove through the doors and out into the open air.

I take a massive breath.

And find myself on the edge of a sprawling concourse, full of scrub grass, low trees, and intersecting paths. I try to breathe deeper to settle my heartbeat. I'm trembling all over, like the void's in the very air. There's chaos all around. People pour out of the building behind me. Others run down the paths while cars rev at the taxi rank and in the four-storey car park beyond.

A hand grips my shoulder, and I whirl.

The priest's warm eyes are staring into mine. "It's okay," he says as his fingers squeeze.

I blink. Then gradually my breathing calms. Natasha's standing just behind him, Capell behind her. The man's still got his satchel in one hand while the other straightens out his rumpled clothes.

"What …" I start, my throat like sandpaper.

"We were right behind you," Father Thomas says with a smile. "Tried to keep as close as we could." Then his smile fades. "But we do need to get out of here." He glances around the concourse, his expression tight. "Now."

"Wait," Natasha says. She's at my side again, staring into my eyes. "You need to sit down, Jake. You look terrible."

My legs wobble, and she grips my hand to keep me upright.

"I'll be fine," I say, tensing my calves and keeping my attention on the calming presence of Natasha and the priest.

"We need to hire a car," Father Thomas says, swivelling to face the terminal building.

I shake my head. "There's no time."

Then I take another deep breath and turn my gaze toward the car parks as several horns blare at the taxi rank below. "I'll get us one."

34

After twenty minutes of pitifully slow thievery – finding a guy I could steal a fob from – I'm hunkering down in the back of his stolen car, watching the outskirts of night-time Istanbul slip by past my window: barrelling traffic, neon shop fronts, and towering minarets.

The city is so alive, while I'm almost dead inside. As the fire fades, the flatness and hollowness take its place, my limbs losing energy and my body sinking further into the seat beneath me.

We pass a large highway sign, and Natasha bolts upright at my side. "Wait, that was the exit to the city centre," she says, pointing. "You missed it!"

Father Thomas keeps his eyes fixed on the road ahead. "We're continuing on," he says, steering our stolen Mercedes out of the way of more hurtling cars. It's like being in a stampede. Cars gun past on both sides and swap lanes before us.

"All the way to *Pergamon*?" she says with incredulity, and her gaze falls on Capell.

The man says nothing – just sits there in the front passenger seat, his satchel pressed to his chest.

The priest nods. "It's still our best-guess location."

"But that's a six-hour drive," Natasha says.

"Probably nearer eight," the priest says. "We'll take brief stops overnight. Share the driving."

"We can't," Natasha says and turns her nurse's eye on me, that single line creasing her forehead. "We need to sleep. Jake needs to recover."

Father Thomas shakes his head. "There's no way," he says. "It's too dangerous."

"But—" she starts.

"I'm the danger," I croak, and then pause. "The *things* are attracted to me. And anywhere we stayed, I'd bring them down on us."

Natasha glances at the priest, whose jaw remains tight. He doesn't contradict me but simply continues to direct the car around the larger coaches and lorries. Eventually, Natasha sits back at my side, takes my hand, and squeezes. With her touch, the void diminishes a fraction.

Awareness slams into me. I take a choking breath and grip something soft by my legs, an immense weight pressing down on my chest. I squint. Spots of red and white play before my eyes, creeping across a black background.

The car. We're in the stolen car. In the middle of the night. The spots are headlights on the highway ahead. I try to ease my breathing, but it's hard. Memories of my dream dart around my mind, all too familiar and more intense than ever.

Something touches my wrist.

"Jacob, are you okay?"

The priest sits driving alongside me, Capell and Natasha silent in the back, asleep. My eyes find the clock. Four in the morning. With quick stops for fuel and a map, we must have been driving for seven solid hours. Natasha and I once each. Capell refused. And this is the priest's second stint. He insisted.

I rub my hands down my face. The images won't go away.

"Another dream?" the priest asks in a hushed voice. "What did you see?"

The same wasteland of fire and ash. A roaring wind on the horizon. Approaching fast. And bodies everywhere. So fucking real. Plus that familiar image – the three slashes – hovering over everything, as if the symbol's been carved into my pupils. It still hangs over the windscreen as I gaze out at the night.

"Death," I say. And the sense of void doesn't leave me, the hollowness so deep at my core.

The priest drives on, barely blinking. The Turkish countryside slinks by, bathed in blackness, the outline of the occasional hill visible beyond the shoulder of the highway.

"I'm not sure I can do this," I breathe eventually.

He glances across, and his eyes hold mine without their customary sparkle, duller than I've ever seen.

"The darkness," I say. "I can't face it. It's too much."

"I'll be there with you," he says with a faint smile, and his gaze returns to the road. "We all will."

I sigh. "That's the trouble," I say. "What if I lose control? I barely kept it together back there."

Father Thomas takes a long breath. "Your powerful feelings, your emotions – they're not the problem," he says, eventually. "You understand that. Don't you?"

The memory slips in. I can't help it. My mother. That dark room. Her intense stare. Her hand on my chest. The immense love and pain that flooded my heart.

"For me, it's compassion. My love for humankind," the priest goes on, his eyes finding some of their old shine in the darkness. "It's what drives me, keeps me going."

An outline of the three slashes continues to hover over the windscreen. Then it morphs. And the image of Gabriel blazes through my mind. The archangel framed in blackness. His weapon, his trident held in hand. Those same crazed eyes burning into mine. And I hear Michael's words – *You and Gabriel are more alike than you imagine.*

"Father, what if this is a giant mistake?" I ask, turning to him again. "Us coming here. What if Gabriel already has his weapon? What if there *is* no hope?"

"Jacob, if there was no hope, if there was nothing we could do, we would not be here. It's that simple," he says, his hands gripping the wheel. "We are all fated to play our roles, all part of a bigger weaving. This is about humanity's liberation, reclaiming our birthright, a war that's been waged over thousands of years." He glances at me. "The darkness *exists* to help us find the light. Never forget that. And when the time is right, you will know what to do." He nods. "*Believe.*"

I heave a breath in my chair, the weight a fraction lighter in my chest.

I hear a moan from behind me and turn. Natasha's twitching in her sleep, her eyes closed and brow furrowed again, her lips forming unintelligible words.

"Soon, you'll need to be there for her," the priest says, his voice soft, "but she'll be there for you before the end."

I swivel back to face him, my heartbeat quickening. "The end?"

The priest leans forward and peers at a sign at the side of the highway. "I'm going to pull over so we can swap," he says, and yawns. "I must get a little sleep."

He glances at the odometer on the dashboard. I blink down at it as well.

"We're almost there," he says.

35

THE SUN'S already a good couple of inches above the horizon when Bergama – the nearest town to Pergamon – appears over the top of a ridge. I'm driving, the priest next to me, with Natasha and Capell awake in the back seat. In fact, the scholar's passivity has shifted in the last few miles. He still clings to his satchel, but now he's peering intently out of his window, staring at the arid, hilly landscape with fields laid out between areas of brush, his nose almost touching the glass.

I drive us past the city limits, the sight as different to the bustling streets of Istanbul as it's possible to imagine. The place is a ghost town. We pass houses, shops, and a square, finding them all deserted. There are no visible pedestrians or animals, not even birds or insects. Nothing moves at all, and up above, the sky shines blue. Yet somehow, it's darkening.

In the early morning.

I keep us weaving through the narrow streets, sensing myself increasingly pressed down into my seat, the sense of darkness so heavy in my bones. I follow tourist signs toward Pergamon, and soon we're heading out of town again, the desolate buildings falling away. We end up driving across scrubland with low trees planted on either side of the road.

We pass open areas for parking and a few refreshment stands but still no cars, no people.

A part of my brain's urging me to drive faster, images of the *things* appearing by every building and outcropping. Yet I can't help slowing us down, a growing unease gripping my insides.

The road turns from tarmac to gravel and ends up arcing around the middle of one of the steeper hills in the area. Its surface is covered in rocks and parched yellow shrubs with a few clumps of trees dotted about. Two hundred yards down the slope lies a sprawling lake, and up near the summit sit the remains of an amphitheatre cut into the hill. By the time we reach the end of the gravel track, I have us barely crawling along.

"Stop here," Father Thomas says.

I bring the car to a halt but keep the engine running, following the priest's gaze.

He's staring up at the top of the hill, at the ruins of an ancient city. According to Capell, all laid waste many hundreds of years ago with only broken plinths, half walls, and strewn blocks of stone remaining. Thousands of them cover a wide area. Cracked columns rise in rows from the hard earth, the remnants of an acropolis.

The priest opens his door and climbs out while I stare through the windscreen at the edges of the barren hill and baked ground that extends around us. No movement. No army of *things* comes scrabbling for me. Capell steps out as well and eyes our surroundings – the stones atop the hill, the lake at the bottom.

"Come on," the priest says. "Let's search."

He hikes up the hill toward the ruins, Capell right behind him.

Natasha and I climb slowly out of the car. The dry heat hits me like a slap; there's a total lack of wind. I take a shallow breath and gaze up at the sky. Still no birds or insects, though there is something else.

Inch-long flecks of grey float in the blue, like ash. I lift a hand to touch one, and the flakes swirl around me, keeping their distance. They coast up and down in invisible air currents. Just like the butterflies in the angelic realm. But these flecks are blocking out the light rather than radiating it. They cast strange, mottled shadows on the ground.

The priest's already exploring the edge of the ruins, and though there's no doddering persona, he's moving sluggishly, his boundless zeal gone. I take a deep breath and try to summon my energy, but the void's massive here. The darkness lurks inside me and behind every surface – the rocks, the bushes, the ground – like the entire place has been poisoned. My legs feel so weak.

The priest and Capell hunt amid the stones and columns while I traipse among the lower ruins, focusing only on keeping upright and going through the motions. Natasha remains by the car, her arms tight around her.

After thirty minutes, we have found nothing.

The priest hunts on, his head down, with sweat pooling at his temples. And I sit on an old stone block, gaze out over the ruins, and try to imagine some kind of entrance.

The flakes of grey hang in the air. I have a sulphuric taste in my mouth, plus the acrid scent – stronger than before. The entire place feels possessed. And oddly, there's still no sign of the *things*.

Capell's stopped searching as well. He stands totally erect despite the burning heat, and he's no longer gazing around him. Instead, he's staring at the bottom of the hill … or at something just beyond it.

The lake.

The day remains completely still. A row of trees lines the far side like sentries, the liquid surface as flat as glass. In its reflection, the sky stretches out, not a single cloud visible, and at the edge, groups of shrubs cluster beyond.

I blink at the water, and the realisation clicks an instant before the priest gives the order.

It takes a full two hours to circumnavigate the lake. The four of us walk in silence, seeing no sign of animal or man. The sun rises higher in the sky, yet the strange gloom still persists, the flecks just as numerous in the surrounding air, always just out of reach. I plod on at the back of the group, my feet heavy, the sense of void and desolation so acute it's like tendrils of black are reaching up from the earth, pulling me downward. The priest strides staunchly out in front, leading us on.

Finally, we arrive at the far side of the lake to several feet of coarse sand beach. The air remains entirely still, the water flat with not a ripple or curve. The reflected images are impossibly crisp. The priest paces up and down the shore, tilts his head, and peers at the ruined city's reflection from different angles, searching for some kind of portal.

I just stand there, my own gaze drawn to the lake. Nothing seems unusual, only the reflection of the ruins. Yet I sense the image drawing me in, like it's pulling at my eyes. Plus, a subtle hum starts up in my chest, as if my ribs are vibrating.

Father Thomas continues to search, crouches down, and then straightens back up again, constantly moving his head. With every passing moment, the pull on my eyes becomes a fraction stronger.

I shuffle closer to Natasha, and we stand there on the beach, side by side. Being nearer her, I feel a sliver of relief, and new thoughts come. *Hell's entrance. Successfully hidden for two thousand years. Maybe we won't be able to find it.*

Capell steps forward, pads to the water's edge, and does the strangest thing. He leans down, rolls up his trouser legs, and tucks his satchel inside his jacket – all an exercise in precision. Then he steps lightly into the shallow water, and the surface of the water remains perfect, glass-like. Not a single ripple.

My heartbeat quickens, and gooseflesh rises across my neck.

Capell swivels to face us, his back to the ruins, all traces of haughtiness in his features gone. He simply stares at each of us, his expression so hard to read. Then he bends all the way forward till he's looking through his own legs, facing the main body of the lake. He places both hands in the shallow water, and somehow, his feet fall upward into a perfect handstand, as if gravity's reversed. He ends up upside down, facing the ruins on the other side of the water.

My throat constricts, and my mouth gapes open.

In the next instant, ripples form around his arms before reaching up to devour his entire body – shoulders, head, waist, knees, feet. And then the water falls away, and it's as flat as it ever was.

Capell's gone.

36

I STARE DUMBLY at the lake. There's not a sound, not a stir. Capell is nothing more than a memory. The pull's still there, the tug on my eyes. And my body leans to the side, my head tilting. I find myself inching toward looking at the reflection upside down. The further I go, the more the world spins and the more my stomach cramps. My neck's just beyond the horizontal when the reflection in the water transforms, and the sight hits me like an iron fist.

While the ruins remain atop the summit, a gigantic cleft severs the hillside from top to bottom, somehow blacker than night. The colour … It's more than an absence of light. It's as if the darkness itself is alive, seeping out of the cavern, invading the world. Nausea grips my stomach, and tempests rage inside my head. Screaming voices, howling winds, all carving out the insides of my skull.

Staggering backward, I lurch straight again.

The sounds die in an instant, sensations too, and the cleft vanishes from the reflection. I'm left breathing fast on the beach, Natasha a few feet away.

"How did he know?" Natasha demands, whirling on Father Thomas. "Was it in his books, his scriptures?"

"I'm not sure," the priest says and paces toward us. "But we have to follow him."

My body tenses, and a part of my brain screams at me to run, to never come back. Yet I remain staring at the lake, the tug on my eyes stronger than ever.

"We *must* go," the priest says, urgency in his voice. "Hell's clearly been opened, but Gabriel may not have his weapon yet. We still have time. If we can find out how many binding angels are still alive, Michael won't be able to ignore us."

He glances between us, and the darkness continues to swell inside – fucking immense – while the world starts to tip as if in anticipation. The strange hum builds in my chest.

My hand reaches out, and I grasp Natasha's fingers. She doesn't shake me off, and with her touch, the void abates a little, the abyss that bit more distant. Natasha's got her eyes fixed on the water.

"We cannot leave him there," Natasha repeats, her voice barely audible.

She finds my gaze, and I let out a slow breath as I squeeze her hand. Then we pad down to the water's edge.

Reaching the lake, my vision lists, and I sway. Natasha grasps my fingers and holds on tightly. We step into the shallows and swivel back toward the bank. The priest looks at both of us and nods with furrowed brow and shining eyes.

Then, facing away from the ruins, I lean forward like I'm touching my toes. The world pitches and the nausea seizes my stomach again. I quickly place both hands into the water as Capell did, and immediately everything stops spinning. Peering between my legs, the reflection morphs, the hill opposite transformed …

The sky's no longer blue but bitter grey, awash with frothing shapes of clouds – angry faces, taloned fingers – just like in my visions. And running down the centre of the hill is the same cleft, the vertical fissure of black, as if the entire world's been cleaved open.

The knowing comes …

This is the origination point, the source of the darkness behind every surface, and of the void, the hollowness at the core of me. No fucking doubt.

I find my gaze drawn to the cleft's edges. The grey rock shifts and morphs, outlines appearing of writhing bodies – men and women – limbs flailing, mouths open in silent screams.

I try to yank back my hands, but they're stuck in the water, the cleft pulling more strongly at me, the darkness magnetic. And then, without even trying, my legs kick up into a handstand, my feet tumbling toward the sky like Natasha's at my side.

And the cleft moves. From hovering across the expanse of water, it now hangs directly beneath me like a gigantic mouth, and the blackness sucks at my limbs. I sense myself starting to fall, the ground gone.

My fingers reach, and I grab Natasha's hand again as she grasps mine. We tumble downward, the lake swallowing us whole. Darkness swamps me as I cling tighter to Natasha. I feel myself being hauled away, my body buffeted by roaring winds, my fingers slipping, slipping ...

And she's gone. I stretch out wildly in the absolute dark as I'm tossed around, and the air grows ever hotter. The pressure increases against every inch of my skin, as if the cleft is biting down on my limbs, my ribs, crushing me and leaving all my nerve endings on fire. I open my mouth to scream, but nothing comes out, the air squeezed from my chest.

It's like I'm falling for an eternity.

Then the ground slams into my side. Pain explodes in my hip and back. I tumble onto my front and lie there, my eyes closed, drawing air into empty lungs. My whole body throbs, and the pain doesn't settle. The ground's uneven, the ridges razor fucking sharp. A dozen furrows dig into me, bringing more agony with every movement. The sounds of screams echo in the distance.

My eyes fly open. The ground's covered in crests of black

rock, the peaks five to ten feet high. The valleys between them fall to ground level, like waves of sculpted glass. It resembles the fallout from some kind of volcanic eruption. Winds howl and the grey clouds boil above.

Pushing to my feet, I stare around. No scrubland. No lake. Just the black craggy landscape as far as the horizon, the hill before me, the ruins of Pergamon perched on its summit. And carved into the hillside below hovers the dark cleft in the rock, only a hundred feet away. I can still feel its call.

From the cleft the wind howls, increasing in strength. It pushes against my chest, my stomach, against every part of me. It brings the screams and the foulest of smells – a sickly sweet scent of rotting or singed flesh plus the acrid smell of cordite underneath.

I lean into the wind just to keep still, but it shoves me back like a physical opponent, more strongly with each second. My feet slip, and I have to strain against the gale to remain stationary. The strange hum is still present in my torso, in my gut – but louder, stronger.

"This way!" Capell yells.

The scholar's there, thirty feet to my side. He's trying to haul himself forward between the crests, fighting the strengthening wind, with his satchel still fastened inside his jacket. But he keeps losing his footing and scrabbles behind a nearby rock to stop himself tumbling backward. The fierce gusts whip the flakes of ash ever faster around him.

I swivel, scanning the crests and valleys for Natasha and the priest, when a flake slices at my cheek. Then another. And another. The barrage increases with every moment. I hunch down behind the nearest peak while continuing to search, but all too quickly I'm forced to turn my head away. The ash flakes hit me from all directions, striking against my legs, my side, my face. No position gives me cover; there's no angle from which I'm protected.

The fire burns deep down in the darkness, the embers sparking as if blown by the screaming wind. With each ash strike, the void grows, and a part of me is desperate to lose myself, to give myself over to the flames, to feel the power and fury. My jaw clenches, my fingers tighten—

"Jake!"

A voice … Natasha's. Barely audible in the roaring wind. I spin toward the sound, finally able to spot her. She's on her hands and knees, twenty feet to my side, scarcely visible behind one of the smaller wavelike crests. It's hardly any cover from the swirling wind and ash, and she's already slipping. The priest's struggling toward her from the far side but getting nowhere in the raging gusts.

I stagger out from behind my crest. The flakes bombard me, and the gale blows even more strongly from the fissure. It's like a million hands shoving, pressing, pushing me backward. I grab for a peak and recoil, the edges as sharp as knives. My soles skid on the uneven ground. The screams in the wind become laughs, the fire burns hotter inside, and taunting voices urge me to let go while the flakes of ash attack me like angry insects.

I grit my teeth and tense my chest, focusing everything on maintaining control. My feet slide backward, faster now, and I try to face the darkness, to open my heart to it. But again, it's fucking impossible. The void's all-encompassing. My entire body trembles with it. And with every step I take toward Natasha, I'm being pushed back ten more by the wind, about to lose my footing.

Gripping Eleth's clasp, I fling myself behind a larger wavelike peak and manage to get out of the howling wind. My eyes find Natasha again. She's further away now, thirty feet ahead and twenty off to the side. Plus, she's cowering even lower by her rock, the strengthening gusts yanking at her body about to throw her backward. And the image comes of her being shredded by the razor-sharp rocks behind.

Still crouched, I swivel to face the cleft, and just facing its source, the void plunges deeper, the sense of despair colossal inside me. Yet I don't turn away. Instead, I straighten my knees, push myself up beyond the top of my glassy crest, and wait for the fire to claim me.

The wind smashes into my head, my shoulders, my chest, the laughter ringing louder in my ears. Flames rage again within, the river of fire boiling hot, and I let it. The power courses up my throat.

I tense my arms and yell, "Get behind me!"

And I push myself toward the cleft, every inch of me alight. Power flows through my veins, and I drive one foot in front of the other, my body cutting through the wind.

The ash flakes strike me ever harder, and I picture Gabriel building this place. His architecture of pain. The archangel sustaining a tyranny. Humankind suffering for thousands of years. The fire burns like an engine at my core, the river of flame propelling me onward. The wind roars while I blaze hotter and thrust my way between the rocky crests as Natasha, Capell, and Father Thomas scramble across to get into my wake and shelter behind me.

Yet already, black spots are appearing at the corner of my vision. I sense myself floating up and out of my body, my mind starting to shut me down.

No, no, no. I'm only halfway to the cleft. And the gusts push ever harder against me. I'm slowing down, every foot of progress a fucking battle, and I can feel Natasha and the priest at my back. The same words howl in the wind as whisper sweetly in my mind … *Kill … maim … rage.*

My limbs vibrate with the frenzied power, my vision darkening more with each moment, and I risk diving even deeper into the fury. I conjure the images that haunt my dreams: my mother dying, her head smashed against the counter, Qetesh's slain body, her throat cut in front of me.

The river of flame flows quicker, and I sense myself growing, the anger like an eruption. The spots grow bigger across my eyes, and memories meld with the present. I glimpse the strewn bodies from my visions – my delivery contact, my mother, Natasha, the priest. And with the fire so high, the desire to lash out is almost overwhelming, to ravage and destroy, with Natasha and the priest pressing ever closer behind me.

I roar into the screaming wind, forcing myself to move faster, to run. My feet grind at the uneven ground, all my attention fixed on the cleft ahead. The flakes of ash dive at me and rake my skin. I turn every hurt into fuel for the fire, letting it burn bigger, wider. I push myself harder while squeezing Eleth's clasp so tightly it spears my palm. Still my awareness floats higher above my body, my consciousness shutting down as the fissure looms up before me.

I aim one last yell at the hillside ahead, tense my arms and legs, and hurl myself at the yawning cleft.

And then there's only darkness.

37

FROM RAGING wind and boiling sky comes absolute stillness, absolute darkness … I try to sense my hands, my body, to open my eyes. But there's nothing. Only blackness. Inside and out – an unfathomable vastness all around me, as if I'm a mere pinprick in the expanse. I shrink away from it while the sensation grips me of being horribly alone.

Then I notice a vibration. The notion coalesces in my consciousness, and my mind scrambles to make sense of it. It's a sound, and it comes again …

"Jake?"

Again, I try to open my eyes, to listen, to feel. I'm lying on my back, some kind of ground beneath me. There's still no light, no observable features. Just a flat, hard surface that's cool through my clothes. And the sensation of cold grabs me for the first time, not as a temperature, but as something possessing my core. A sense of pointlessness … a feeling of absolute insignificance. It seems futile to even breathe.

I have to force my lungs to work, my diaphragm up and down, my ribs in and out.

Then the smell hits me – the same stench of sulphur, of burnt flesh, from outside but stronger, the scent of cordite barely noticeable underneath. I try to gag, to move, to tense my muscles, to push myself up. But my body won't obey. I'm spent, my energy gone. The rage, the fire, a distant memory.

I see movement and drag my gaze upward. The flecks of ash float all around, grey and luminescent. I blink. Unlike the butterflies, they don't cast a glow on anything. Everything else is still absolute black.

A hand touches my side. Another, my shoulder. Warm pressure.

"Sit up." Natasha's voice. And her figure forms out of the blackness, kneeling before me.

I try to comply, to contract my stomach muscles. The air's thicker than normal in my lungs, and again, it requires concentration to breathe.

Outlines of the priest and Capell appear, standing behind Natasha. The sight brings a lightness and then a great weight.

We made it … We're all in hell.

Capell and Father Thomas remain rooted to the spot, staring in my direction … or just above me. I swivel my neck to follow their gaze.

And for a moment, the image drives my thoughts into screaming insanities.

It's a gate of incomprehensible dimensions. A deep knowing strikes me that to truly fathom its size would mean giving myself over to madness. So I blink repeatedly and keep my gaze level, focusing only on the lower parts that rear out of the black before us.

A massive frame of wrought iron, inconceivably vast, it has bars and railings the size of towers. Seemingly a mile away, at least as wide, and miles and miles high. Again, I have to force my eyes downward. Any attempt to glimpse the top makes my head spin.

"The first gate," Capell says, his voice trembling.

And the thing's been torn apart – iron scythed through like paper, the mountainous pickets peeled back as if they were grass stems, revealing open darkness in between.

"So it's true. At least one binding angel's dead," the priest says softly, hands on his hips.

Natasha shivers at my side, her gaze still on the massive gate. "What did they work so hard to contain?" she breathes.

In that instant, the three slashes flare before my eyes. And the *thing's* garbled words come back to me.

"The trident," I say, the sounds barely rasps in my throat. "With the power to control the earth, the air, and the sea, along with the vastness of his army. Remember?"

Natasha pushes herself up to face the priest. "We can leave now, surely? We have what we came for. Gabriel is opening the gates. We have the proof. We can get out of here. Go tell Michael."

Hope sparks in her eyes, yet not even a glimmer forms inside me. My gaze finds the priest. The old man's already shaking his head.

"It won't work, beautiful child," he says, glancing back at her, such sadness in his expression. "Without Michael seeing it himself, this is not proof. And a simple tale of one gate open will not be enough to overturn his vow of disengagement. For him, the devil is long gone, a force no one would conceive of releasing."

Summoning my remaining energy, I clamber to my feet and sway. The same strange hum's back inside my ribs – a scratchy sensation in my chest – but amplified. I feel as if a note's been struck somewhere, a bell resonating somewhere in the darkness.

Father Thomas swivels to face the gate. "No, we must somehow find evidence he will believe and also discover how many gates have been opened. So if Michael does refuse to act, we will know how many binding angels remain and may find a way of alerting them."

I take a long breath. "How many will there be?"

"According to the rumours, six gates in total," Capell says, staring reverently at the split gate. "One for each binding angel."

Again, the vast opening calls to me. The darkness pulls at my eyes as I step over to stand by Natasha and grip her hand.

Capell and the priest pad off toward the gate, and I trudge on at their back, keeping Natasha close. Capell walks with a frantic energy, while the priest pads hesitantly forward, even though the gate's still miles away.

"Be careful," he says. "The laws of nature may not apply normally here."

I slow my steps as well, hobbling on gingerly. And then, after only a minute, I stagger to a stop, my lungs seizing.

The open gate's suddenly right there, the four of us only ten feet from the threshold. Its torn edges veer up on both sides, the splintered vertical bars many dozens of yards wide, and even staring at the bottom of them makes my head reel.

I tense my neck, keeping my gaze straight. And peering into the darkness, the pull's stronger again.

"I am not sure how this works," Capell says, his brow deeply furrowed. He edges his foot forward to test the ground before him. "I find it difficult to believe that these gates are laid out in a horizontal arrangement. Many of the writings describe the hell realm as being unfathomably deep."

I turn to the priest, who motions us closer to him.

"We stick together," he says.

Capell and Natasha take up positions on either side of him, the scholar with his arms squeezed across his chest, his satchel still tucked into his jacket. And I stand on the far side of Natasha.

"And go slowly," the priest adds.

We shuffle forward in line and pass through the smashed gate. Nothing happens. After a few glances at each other, we keep going, a few halting steps at a time.

Twenty feet on, I breathe a little easier. And after the ninth glance toward the side of the gate, the change hits me. The splintered edges are no longer directly in line with us. They're half a mile bloody back.

"Wait!" the priest yells and comes to an immediate halt.

The rest of us are a fraction slower. I'm in the middle of a step, my arms windmilling as I desperately try to throw my weight backward, but the world's already tilting.

The ground swings away under my feet like a trapdoor, and the darkness ahead pulls even harder, gravity shifting. I start to tumble forward as if over a cliff face while nausea clasps my insides.

"Hold on to me!" the priest yells.

Lightning fast, he grabs Capell with one arm and Natasha with the other as I fling myself toward the old man and grasp his shoulder, hooking my arm under his.

And we're in free fall, plunging downward through the thick air, swallowed by the dark. My free arm flails, and my stomach slams up into my throat, throttling me.

"Remember, float!" Father Thomas yells.

His exact command from up on the rooftops. And for an instant, I'm transported to our endless practices, the old man spurring us to challenge gravity and defy the very fabric of accepted belief, the highest accomplishment of his order.

"Have faith!" he shouts, slowing our fall and tugging us upward. "*Believe.*"

In that instant, I begin the count, still my mind, and reach out to feel the solidity of the air, just as he trained us—

But the moment the veil peels back, every sensation gets magnified a hundred times. The darkness is so immense it's like I'm plummeting directly into the void. The pain becomes me, like it did at my mother's side, and the strange language jabbers inside my skull, conjuring images from the black. Memories, visions. My past … or future. Natasha and the priest dying in new ways. New tortures. Every one of them so real. The fire blazes wildly at my core, that potential of sweet oblivion. And the whispers start up – *fight … rage … lose yourself* – with Natasha falling only inches away.

I scrunch my eyes shut, tensing every muscle while driving my thoughts again to abandon the veil, and grip the priest's upper arm instead. I hold on to it with all my strength, and with my other hand, I squeeze Eleth's clasp in my pocket, focusing hard on keeping down the fire.

And there I hold myself for what seems like an age.

"Get ready!" the priest yells, his voice shaky.

My eyes fly open. The next gate rushes upward out of the darkness below, dazzlingly bright. It's not vertical but laid out flat, as if we'll plunge straight into it. Father Thomas continues to slow our fall, his brow furrowed, jaw set, his expression gripped in a look of absolute concentration. Even so, we're approaching all too quickly.

My jaw clenches, my thoughts still, the veil starting to peel back again, the desire to help fucking huge. But in that instant, the void seizes me, overwhelming, and I channel all my focus back into shutting out the voices, quelling the burning fire, and keeping the veil in place while my fingers squeeze Eleth's clasp ever tighter.

The gate careens up to meet us, and when we're almost upon it, the world lists again, and gravity pulls from the side instead of down – the reverse of the earlier shift. The dazzlingly bright gate now rises vertically to one side of us, absolute blackness underneath. And then the ground slams into my feet. My knees buckle, pain flashes up my legs, and I crumple onto the invisible floor.

38

I LIE ON MY SIDE, panting, my intense focus scattered and my mind drained. Then my memory kicks back in, and I shoot my head up.

Another gigantic cavern, the next gate towering upward before us. And not iron-grey and made of bars like the last one, but solid white. The monstrosity's equally mind-bending and stretches up toward infinity.

And open, too – exploded down the middle.

Capell's on his feet close by while Natasha and the priest stagger upright at my sides. My core relaxes a fraction, and then the darkness swallows the moment's relief, the sense of pointlessness weighing more heavily than before.

I take a strained breath and force myself up on aching legs, the strange humming still there within me, the scratchy sensation in my ribs.

The priest stands hunched over and breathing hard, his fingers gripping shaking knees. I've never seen him so depleted.

The stench grows fouler – sulphur and burnt flesh – the flecks of ash more numerous. They hover silently around us, keeping their distance.

Natasha trudges to the priest's side and places a hand on his shoulder. "How will we get back?" she asks and glances up into the endless dark above.

"We'll find a way," he says.

He straightens slowly and stretches every muscle in his back and shoulders, his expression contorted. Then his eyes clear as he gazes down at her.

"There's always a way," he says and forces a smile. "Navigating one gate isn't necessarily easier than six."

My eyes find the splintered gate again. Four more. This one made of gigantic mounds of white crystals.

"Salt," breathes Capell.

And the obviousness of the idea leaves my head spinning.

"*This* is our proof," I say, my heartbeat speeding up.

Father Thomas meets my eye.

"Most likely, each gate will be made of a different material," I say. "And I can't imagine they're recorded anywhere in the scriptures?" I spin to face Capell.

He blinks back at me and then shakes his head. "They are not," he says.

"So, this is what we tell Michael," I say, the void a fraction lighter, the tiniest ray of hope gleaming within. "No insect will have seen them." I gesture toward the gate of salt. "And so travelling through these open gates will be the only way we could know."

The priest nods back. "There's always a way," he says, and the smile widens on his lips.

We head for the salt gate and use the same process – step carefully through the gap, prepare ourselves for gravity's shift, and then the priest slows our fall.

We also use it for the next gate.

And the one after that.

Because each one we discover – ice, stone, and fire – has also been ripped open, and more of the tiny hope I feel fizzles out.

The priest ends up having to support us as we fall for miles, the sky so far removed above. And the stink grows ever stronger, the descents deeper, like we're journeying down into the fucking Earth's core.

By the time of the fourth jump, it's like we've been down there for years, for decades … for our entire lives, the sense of pointlessness a constant background.

And with each fall, the darkness swells inside me, like a dial's being turned up. The jabbering grows louder and the memories intensify. And somehow not just mine. I relive times from my mother's life, her treatment by the gang members. And then Natasha's. And others' as well. Experiences of humanity's suffering since time began. Sights, sounds, smells, and tastes, each of my senses screaming.

And while my mother's words about the anguish revolve around my head – *it's your gift* – the void is all-encompassing, every part of me desperate to turn away, to give in to the burning fire. And so as we plummet I'm forced to do nothing but grip Eleth's clasp, tense my body, and concentrate everything on keeping control, while the priest has to slow our descents all on his own. He grows more exhausted every time.

After each fall, he picks himself up and stumbles toward the next open gate, breathing more heavily, sweating more profusely, his legs trembling. I stumble behind him, my body and mind almost as wrecked from the intense focus.

We reach the fifth gate. I haul myself to my feet – it's harder every time – and stare at the pillars of fire. The blazing doors have been peeled open, while immense flames still burn on either side. And a bit more of the hope dies in my chest. I swivel and spy Father Thomas lying on the floor. He remains there, barely moving, Natasha crouched by his shoulder.

"We cannot do this any more," she says, her voice breaking.

I stumble toward her and then stop. The flecks of ash are

far more numerous here and floating more animatedly around us, like they're being stirred by an invisible wind. Many of them drift toward the open gate while the air's a furnace, sweat coating my skin. And the strange hum continues on in my chest.

Capell's standing, staring at the open gate also, arms clenched over his jacket and satchel again.

"Are we already too late?" I find myself whispering.

The priest sits up with a groan and then takes a deep breath. And another. The old man grasps Natasha's hand, and she helps haul him to his feet.

"Father—" Natasha starts.

"There's no going back now," he says, his voice so weak. "If the final gate's open, we must warn the angels. They *have* to know."

I watch him shuffle ahead of us toward the open gate, the burning pillars, his body stripped of all youthfulness and his limp more pronounced than ever. My heart wrenches, and the darkness yanks me down like weights.

"Father, I'm so sorry," I say.

The priest stops shuffling and edges around to face me. The faintest glint forms in his eyes.

"It's meant to be this way, Jacob," he says. "There's always a reason. Trust in that … Never forget."

And the old man reaches out a hand toward me. I take a faltering step, and together we pad for the gate. Flames crackle on each side of us, and I try to shut out the sensation of the growing heat.

We all pass through the opening, and Father Thomas inches forward and back till he's found the threshold. And then we all line up before it for the fifth time. The darkness continues to pull me on.

"Remember, sometimes God only shows us the next step," the priest says, and his eyes find mine. Then he turns to face the black once more. "Get ready!"

Again, Natasha and I grip the old man's arm, my other

hand in my pocket, my fingers clenched around Eleth's clasp. One final breath. The priest nods.

"Now!" he yells.

And we leap.

39

It's like nothing I could have imagined. The fall ... longer, deeper. The jabbering becomes even more intense as if the strange voices are within my head, and the resulting memories slash at my mind, my heart. In the blackness, it's as if I become suffering itself – no limit between inside and outside. I *am* the void. All of it. The river stirs, the fire so fucking tempting. Nevertheless, I push it down. Scrunch my eyes shut, tense every muscle, and hold on to Eleth's clasp. I squeeze it so tightly it feels as if my fingers might break.

The fall takes an age.

Natasha yells a warning. Yet I don't let up my concentration as we fall. My focus becomes everything, my entire existence – like a bit gripped between my teeth. I hold my breath for what seems like minutes, hours, my chest ready to burst.

Light squeezes through my closed eyelids. The wind buffets my body, and finally I open my eyes to find the last gate dazzling in the darkness. From a point of light to a flickering star. So bright it's almost impossible to look at.

"Hold on!" the priest yells, his voice so hoarse.

I squeeze his arm tighter. The old man's features contort, his whole being alive with the struggle through the viscous air.

The world lurches, gravity rotates by ninety degrees once more, and the new gate shoots from below us to towering up to one side.

Then my feet crash down into the ground. My knees give way and slam up into my stomach. I topple over backward, and the back of my head thwacks against the hard ground.

Pain. Though it hardly makes a dent against the pressing void. I take a breath and stare upward, the flecks of ash far fewer here.

Eventually, I roll over and push myself back up. I almost don't make it, my arms shaking with the effort. Plus, I feel the same scratching discomfort between my ribs, the hum now a full ringing sound and louder than ever.

Father Thomas lies sprawled on the ground, unmoving, one arm folded under his stomach. I shove aside the strange sensation, strain against the flatness, and struggle toward him. My heart beats hard. And my eyes scan his body for some form of movement.

Natasha pulls at his shoulder. "Father?" she says.

No response. She checks his pulse, and I kneel next to her, putting my hand on the old man's chest. I feel the subtlest tremor, the faintest of movements.

Natasha stiffens and grabs my wrist. "*Jake*," she says in a trembling whisper.

She's staring over the priest's body, her eyes wide. I follow her gaze and stumble backward.

The gate. Obsidian black. Its glass surface comprises the contours of a thousand writhing figures, all frozen in time and shining in some invisible light. A vertical line runs up the centre, stretching high above us. Unbroken. The gate stands complete. Closed.

The lightness kindles again at my core, a tiny flickering amid the darkness.

The priest groans. The old man retracts an arm and pushes himself up onto his knees.

"Father!" I say and grab his shoulder to steady him.

His whole body's shaking. Natasha grasps his other arm, and together we help him to stand, both of us propping him up. Then all of us stare wide-eyed at the unopened gate.

Something hovers behind the join, a few feet from the ground – long, thin, and painfully bright – on the far side of the black glass. The trident. The devil's weapon. Imprisoned there at the centre. As yet unclaimed.

"One of the binding angels is still alive," Natasha breathes.

While the lightness persists inside me, again I feel the strange hum in my bones, the ringing sound intensifying. The vibrations are strongest in my lower torso, prompting a deep sense of unease.

My eyes find Capell. He's facing away from the weapon, from the gate, peering intently into the blackness. He removes his satchel from under his jacket and holds it tightly in one hand.

While I feel the trident calling to me …

I swivel back to face it, only twenty yards away. It's frozen in an ocean of glass and probably unlooked upon for millennia. It is made up of three rods that wind around each other to form the central shaft before diverting near the top into three spikes, though they're difficult to make out. The weapon seems alive behind the curved glass. Its shape twists with every breath I take, as if desperate to escape its prison.

My palms itch, and my fingers tremble with the weapon's draw. Suddenly, I see myself wielding it. Me. Weapon in hand. With power raging through my veins.

I swallow, my throat parched, and my eyes flick to the side. The priest's staring at me.

Still, I find myself stepping toward the trident, and in an instant I'm before the gate, right in front of the join. My pulse speeds up. The triad of spikes continues to coil and weave behind the glass while deep currents move within the void at my core. The image of the three slashes appears before me, superimposed on the shining surface.

I reach up, touch the join, and then whip my hand away. *Fuck*. The glass burns, so cold it scorches hot. A caramel-sweet smell fills my nostrils, and I press my scalded fingertips with my thumb.

The trident remains where it is. Just inches from my nose and unreachable. Worlds away.

I touch the glass through my shirt and then punch it to crack the join. The gate remains intact while the trident continues to dance behind its undulating surface. My heart sinks more. And, all the while, I sense my attention drawn back to the discomfort in my lower torso. The feeling changes again, and the humming becomes a twisting deep in my gut. So familiar. I drop my hands from the glass, and gooseflesh rises across my back.

How the fuck did I not recognise it before?

My internal alarm. It clamours inside me while my body temperature descends by degrees.

I spin around.

A thunderclap explodes out of the silence and reverberates throughout the space so loudly it leaves my skull ringing. Like Capell, I peer out into the blackness. The clap comes again, and while the trident's draw becomes ever more powerful, I thrust myself away from it, toward Natasha and the priest, scrambling to eat up the distance between us.

They stumble toward me as well. Natasha supports the old man, her arm under his. And I throw myself faster on, my heart like a drumroll in my chest while my eyes continue to search the space.

There, a hundred yards away, a figure steps out of the dark.

40

Gabriel. Undeniable. His outline resolves itself steadily out of the blackness, rippling and burning before my eyes. His aura shines as brilliantly as his archangel brother, and despite being a good distance away, it's still too bright to make out. The flakes of ash, conspicuously absent before, have coalesced into millions of grey feathers, into enormous wings that spread up above his shoulders.

My mouth gapes, my thoughts still, the veil peels back, and the smell of cordite's stronger in my nose. He stops clapping, and the echoing thunderclaps gradually cease.

"Welcome," he says, his brightness ebbing. The multiple tones of his voice weave in perfect harmony.

And with the glare abating, I'm able to see so much more. Gabriel's golden armour – arms, legs, and chest bracers. His skin shines so brightly, as if he's been hewn from white stone, and while his face doesn't morph as Michael's does, it still glows with the same painful perfection. And as with all angels, when behind the veil or in an angelic realm, I see him as the colossus – a couple of feet larger than a normal man.

"I wondered if you'd come," he says.

And then I notice he's staring not at me, nor the priest or

Natasha. But at Capell, who's standing ten yards away to my side.

I follow his gaze, and the sight sends me stumbling. The scholar isn't hovering there. Behind the veil, Capell stands as a giant, too. His tailored suit has changed into glowing plate mail armour, and the remaining flakes of ash have coalesced into wings behind his shoulders as well. Elements of Capell's angular features remain, but they've morphed into the same caustic beauty as Gabriel.

An angel.

We brought a fucking angel into hell. All the way from his underground lair.

I just stare on, my thoughts continuing to ramble. And the veil slips back into place.

"So why *are* you here, Cassiel?" Gabriel says.

"I have come here to see this madness for myself," Cassiel says, his layered voice full of emotion. "I could not comprehend that you would do such a thing after all we went through together." He grips the air before him with a giant hand. "And to reason with you, brother ... *please*."

Cassiel steps forward, his grey wings beating once and then twice. A part of me wants to dash in front of him, to haul him somehow away. But I remain totally rigid.

"If you follow through with this, the world will be changed forever," Cassiel says. "There will be no undoing it, no going back. After everything you've accomplished, that you've strived so hard for, it cannot be worth giving it all up."

"*Accomplished?*" Gabriel seethes, bitterness overtaking his tone. "For *far* too long, we have been idle. *I* have been idle." He jabs a finger at his wall-like chest. "Depravity has engulfed mankind like pestilence. Never have their efforts been so profane, with their endless shrines of towering glass, their slew of hollow pursuits. Remember the wonders they created, Cassiel, the marvels we inspired in them!" And for a moment, joy sparkles in his eyes. "The art, the music, the basilicas, the cathedrals – entire populations dedicated to the effort." And then his lip curls. "Now all they forge is meaningless on an unparalleled scale."

Cassiel takes a deep breath and straightens. "Yet still, we must not go back," he says.

"You're blind, brother," Gabriel says, the bite growing in his tone, his radiance burning brighter. "You think the pantheon will survive if we do not act? My efforts have been the only reason we still exist!"

Standing there, Ben's and the priest's words return to me – all the dark ages Gabriel's created since his Gospels, all the suffering, and all aimed at undermining humanity's growth.

"You oppose me now, yet every one of you stood by," Gabriel says and sweeps an accusing finger around him, as if pointing to others unseen. "The countless times I laboured for the pantheon, excised the corrupt, purified humanity, strengthened devotion, you profited." Now he stabs his finger at Cassiel. "All of you benefited, yet you maligned my endeavours, you exiled me." And now he smiles a sly smirk. "Me … the dirty little secret."

And then Gabriel beats his enormous wings and leaps in our direction. My shoulders tighten, and I dart toward Natasha and the priest once more. The archangel covers a huge distance in a single jump and ends up only fifty yards away from us and half that from Cassiel. Just as I reach Natasha's side.

"You know what I intend," Gabriel growls at Cassiel. "So, I ask you again – *why are you here?"*

Cassiel doesn't move a muscle. "Because I had to speak," he says. "I had to attempt to sway you."

Gabriel says nothing but simply stares back at him.

"And I knew you would find me eventually," Cassiel continues, anger creeping into his tone. "I will not be exterminated like the others, stabbed in the back."

And while the last revelation's inevitable, it still spears me.

The final binding angel. My body wobbles, all hope gone,

the weight of an entire world pressing down on my shoulders.

Cassiel holds his satchel out before him. "We forged this place together, brother," he says. "Here, you have no advantage."

Then he reaches inside the satchel with his free hand and hauls something out. The hilt of a weapon. And he keeps pulling till a sword of gleaming silver, two metres long, appears from the small bag.

"You became the best of us, brother. Our visionary, our champion … *our saviour*," Cassiel continues, and his voice cracks with emotion.

He holds his sword out straight, entirely still.

"But this … this is madness," he says. "I cannot let you do it."

Again, Gabriel remains silent. He simply reaches up an enormous hand and grabs something from behind his shoulders – a sword of his own, this one black and immense.

"Merely the boldest, my friend," Gabriel says, his tone almost sad.

Cassiel's voice shakes. "I fight for my brothers and sisters," he says, taking up a defensive stance. He grips his sword in both hands by his ear, its tip aimed at Gabriel while his wings enfold the sides of his body. "But I fight for you just as much, brother. Know that."

Gabriel nods gravely and stands there, his eyes down, his larger sword held loosely at his side. He takes another deep breath.

The angels face each other in front of us, entirely still, while I feel the tension growing as a building pressure in my lungs. I find myself scanning the darkness behind them, searching for a way to sneak past.

Yet I don't move. The priest's so weak, and the towering angels are only yards from us, their swords gargantuan. We'd get squashed in an instant. Plus, my gaze finds Cassiel, and I hold my breath, unable to deny the faintest glimmer in my chest, a lightness growing once more. *Could he win?* The angel keeps his blade pointed at Gabriel. It doesn't waver an inch.

The archangel stands taller. And hurls himself at Cassiel.

41

In a blur Gabriel throws himself fifteen yards in a heartbeat. Cassiel leaps away from us and directly toward the careening archangel, his sword arcing around.

Rooted to the spot, my mind stops, my thoughts suspended as the veil peels back again and time slows. I glimpse a fraction of the last movement – their swords colliding. The sound's so deafening, it makes Gabriel's handclaps seem like snapping twigs. I hunch over and grab my ears.

Both angels remain thirty yards before us, feet anchored, heaving the blades against each other with incredible force. Gabriel leans incrementally over Cassiel, his beautiful features twisted with fury. Cassiel strains back. His legs quiver, about to buckle against the immense weight, as lines appear across his perfect forehead.

My gut twists again.

Gabriel thrusts even harder while Cassiel rotates his body and rolls out of the way. He whips one of his wingtips at Gabriel and catches him in the face, slicing his cheek.

Cassiel leaps toward the side of the cavern, and Gabriel roars in anger, the sound quaking the ground beneath our feet. I grip Natasha's wrist to keep us steady as Gabriel swings his sword at Cassiel's retreating form. The blade passes harmlessly through the angel's other wing. The feathers of ash part to let it through and re-form themselves immediately after.

Cassiel lands gracefully a fair distance away across the cavern and turns. A sheen of sweat glows across his face as the two giants face each other once more. Gabriel's blade is held out before him, both angels still too fucking close for comfort. I yank Natasha and the priest back toward the closed gate behind.

Again, Cassiel forms his defensive stance – sword gripped by his ear, pointed at Gabriel, and both knees bent. The archangel paces back and forth on the opposite side, staring fiercely at Cassiel, his eyes burning. Then he takes up his own fighting stance – one leg forward, his sword raised above his head, his other hand stretched out.

And there they stay. Swords levelled, wings spread, and gazes fixed on each other. I squeeze Natasha's arm. Time stretches, yet neither angel moves a muscle. Absolute silence descends.

Then there's an explosion of movement. Even in slowed time, it's almost impossible to make out. They pounce toward each other, their wings lashing at the air, propelling them forward. Their swords swing and clash repeatedly in front of us – silver on black with sparks flying.

My head aches with the intensity of the fighting. The angels wield their immense swords like toothpicks, whipping them through the air at great speeds, only to be deflected by either sword or feathers of ash. Both of them use their wings simultaneously as shield and propulsion, beating to thrust the angel into an attack or to retreat beyond the reach of the other's sword.

Cassiel battles as if inspired. I can't help picturing him fighting for the entire pantheon – every one of them lined up behind him. He darts forward and back, thrusts with his blade, and draws quick parries before unleashing a swipe at

Gabriel's shoulder. His courage shines like a beacon in the darkness.

However, my gut squeezes tighter.

Gabriel's a different ilk, the art he weaves palpably distinct. Quick, yes. Agile. But so much fucking stronger. And his weapon … Gabriel wields it as spear and sword simultaneously. He stabs with the spear to toy with Cassiel at a distance before spinning the hilt to draw him in. His wings, as well, are longer, broader. Their razor edges slash out every time Cassiel tries to retreat. And with Gabriel's reach, there's nowhere to go.

Gabriel swings with a hard arcing blow, crashes his sword into Cassiel's, and nearly rips the angel's weapon from his grip. Cassiel darts underneath and parries the follow-up with a wing jab at Gabriel's heart. But the archangel beats his wings to close the remaining distance between them instead of extending it. He catches Cassiel in a snare and pulls him into its jaws.

Almost chest to chest, Gabriel blocks one thrust with the middle of his massive blade, the next with his hilt. Then he swings his sword back across Cassiel's side with a cutting arc. Light flares with the spilling of divine blood, and the angel cries out in pain. My lungs seize.

Natasha yells, "No!" at my side.

Gabriel whips his sword up and aims a stabbing blow at Cassiel's chest. The angel beats his wings frantically, only just avoiding being speared through the heart. He careens backward, his ash wings falter in mid-air, and he falls. Natasha darts toward him, and I grip her wrist to hold her tight.

Cassiel scrambles to his feet, and his wings re-form behind him. A gash yawns across his side, dark stains growing around the plates of his armour, and his huge legs tremble for an instant. Natasha grasps my hand with both of hers, and I squeeze hers back.

Cassiel shakes himself, his lips mumbling silent words. Then he takes a massive breath and expands in size again. He yells his fight, beats his wings like crackling fire, and careens back across the cavern toward Gabriel.

The archangel doesn't flinch. He merely springs forward at the very last second and deflects Cassiel's jab with the tip of his sword. He brings both wings together in curving arcs to crush the angel from both sides.

Cassiel flies on with so much momentum, straight into Gabriel's embrace. The swords clash and spring apart, Cassiel's face momentarily unprotected, and Gabriel smashes his shining forehead down upon it.

The impact's like a boulder splintering. Cassiel's head rebounds backward, his nose broken. His legs quake, and his sword arm trembles as he tries to raise it. But Gabriel's already pivoting. With one wing tip, he blocks Cassiel's vain thrust while the other supports Cassiel's head as if cradling it. The archangel brings his sword back behind his shoulder, spins as quick as wind, and cleaves his blade through Cassiel's neck.

The severed head hangs in space for a moment and then falls to the ground.

Gabriel's spin slows and stops. He remains still, his back to us and the gate, facing the darkness with his sword still stretched out. Then he lowers its tip, and blood trickles down its edge.

Cassiel's body collapses. His wings disintegrate, and the flecks of ash scatter into the space. Many of them flit to above Gabriel's shoulders, enlarging his wingspan yet more.

Then there's a rumbling detonation, and the ground shakes violently beneath our feet. I flinch and throw out my free hand as the ground jerks wildly, the sound like glass cracking – the gate opening behind us. And my mind conjures images of Gabriel's army of demons just beyond it.

Nevertheless, I keep my gaze on the archangel, my pulse thumping fast. He's turning ever so slowly back around. Natasha steps before Father Thomas, the old man still so weak, while I dart in front of her to shield them both.

Gabriel swivels all the way around to face us, forty yards away, his massive sword still clasped in one hand as blood continues to drop from its tip.

"No, no, no!" I stammer as more images come, visions from my dreams – Natasha and the priest dead, eyes blank, mouths gaping. The void coats my insides, and my legs shake.

Gabriel's revenge. This is finally it.

"Back!" I scream and press Natasha rearward.

My thoughts babble as the veil slips into place before my senses again, and I force her and the priest toward the gate behind.

The archangel takes a giant step toward us. Tottering backward, my vision hazes, and the three slashes blaze before my eyes. Before I can stop myself, I'm glancing over my shoulder, my heart stampeding.

The gate's split right down the middle. And there it is: the trident. Floating free in the dark gap, only fifteen feet away. Ready to scorch me, to freeze me, to turn me into an angel or a demon. I don't fucking know.

Natasha grips my arm, and heat flares against the side of my neck. I whirl my head back around. Gabriel's closer, his sword extended.

My pulse thunders as I retreat. The tug's still there, even stronger from behind, and the three slashes flare brighter across my vision. Gabriel takes a larger step as Natasha squeezes my forearm tighter.

"Get away!" I yell and break her grip before spinning right the way around.

The heat bursts against my back, and I throw myself toward the trident.

Memories seize me of Gabriel in the hospital – the archangel crossing the space in an instant, his burning fingers clasping my throat. I sprint faster, my arms windmilling and my feet pounding at the rock-hard floor. My eyes remain fixed on the weapon – pristine white against the black background. Its three twisted vines are solid and steady, no longer dancing outside its glass prison. And now dropping as gently as a feather, only five feet above the ground.

I stretch out a hand for the shaft right under the split, where the three vines become points. My body stiffens, and I grab it with quivering fingers. Ready myself …

Nothing happens.

I feel no pain, hardly any sensation at all. The trident doesn't weigh a thing and is neither hot nor cold. It's like holding air.

I tense my legs, shove aside the barrelling thoughts, and swing the weapon around to face Gabriel.

42

THE SIGHT of the archangel sends me scrabbling backward. Only twenty yards away now, his height towers over me, and his radiance presses into my eyes like burning fingers.

My gaze shoots to Natasha and the priest. They're five yards nearer, Natasha yanking Father Thomas in my direction. Her eyes are fixed on Gabriel's fiery image, on the massive sword still gripped in his hand. My heart's like an avalanche in my chest.

"Stop!" I croak at Gabriel, my throat raked raw. I tighten my fingers around the spiralling vines of the trident and stab it toward him with one hand.

Again, nothing fucking happens.

The archangel continues to sweep forward, approaching steadily and taking his time with us.

The void plunges as deep as ever inside me – a crippling sense of impotence and despair. My arms shake, and I clench my free hand around the trident to stop it from trembling.

And with the weapon held in both hands, something clicks.

Instead of the darkness only growing at my core, it begins to *move*. A circular flow starts from my navel to the top of my chest and down my back. The current's slow at first but becomes steadily faster. It spreads across my shoulders, surges down my arms, and glides out … into the trident.

And with the movement comes *relief*. The weight eases in my chest at the same time as the weapon grows fractionally heavier in my hands. Black forms flash across its surface, wisps of smoke pumping down the vines toward the three spikes at the end. And with the darkness churning inside me, I sense my energy and power rising.

All the while Gabriel continues to advance, his wings stretched out and his glowing outline reaching ever higher into the darkness. I channel the building energy up my throat and thrust the trident toward him.

"Stop!" I bellow with a force that stuns me. The ground vibrates with it, the power projected through the weapon far more than from my mouth. And the few remaining flecks of ash swirl between us.

Incredibly, Gabriel halts. He waits, his radiance dimming a fraction, his eyes two shining points of light, while Natasha and the priest lurch to my side.

"What are you doing, little one?" Gabriel asks, his tone as lyrical as it is mocking.

His voice sets off a chain of memories … The archangel crushing those vials to unleash a plague on humanity. Qetesh's immense beauty erased as Gabriel's minion cut her throat. And Gabriel's *things* continuously stalking me, making my life a living hell. The void churns, the fire flaring hot, my chest like a cauldron. Energies whip around ever faster, flowing down my arms, being pulled into the trident. The weapon grows ever heavier. The vines writhe as they did behind their glass cage.

Gabriel goes to take another step.

I stab the trident more powerfully toward him. "I said, *wait!*" I cry, hurling the words out.

Again, the archangel stops. He pauses, his eyes now glowing black in the darkness.

My vision morphs, and I see similar shining eyes, twisted

features surrounding them … The *thing* that killed my mother. And in that instant, I'm back in her kitchen, watching the creature smash her head into the counter. And down in the darkness, the river of flame surges, now flashing around my entire body and out through my hands. The weapon grows hotter as my fire builds. The black shapes flash faster across its white surface, and I sense my hands glued to the shifting vines. I couldn't take my hands off if I wanted to.

And I don't want to.

My eyes find Gabriel – the being who's enslaved humankind for millennia. My body brims with the swirling fire, but no spots appear in my vision. I'm not losing consciousness. Holding the trident, it's as if a circuit's been completed. It's amplifying the feelings and drawing them out of me at the same time, ever faster. And for the first time, it's enlivening instead of depleting. Excitement drives my heart-beat. I lick my lips and grip the trident tighter as images swirl of Gabriel dead, of scenes of destruction, of scattering the fucking *things* before me.

A smile pulls at my mouth, and I fix my gaze on Gabriel. A grin splits his features as well.

Then Michael's words echo in my head … *You and Gabriel are more alike than you imagine.* The thought sends me reeling. And automatically, I go to remove my hands from the trident.

They're stuck fast.

I stare down at the weapon. It's vibrating more violently than ever, the energy rushing faster around my body, the fire building ever hotter, ready to erupt.

And now Natasha's words come back to me … *Evil begets evil.* And still I can't move my fucking hands.

I grit my teeth and force my attention from the wildfire. Instead, I dive deep into the void and bring back the memory of being with my mother that last time. But this time, I don't let the anger carry me away. Instead, I force myself to remember her death. Every horrible moment of it. Once again, the abyss opens inside me, so immense, and while feeling Natasha and the priest at my side, I try to face the darkness, to open myself to it more than I've ever done.

My teeth chatter. The vines cease writhing as much beneath my fingers. Nevertheless, I can't take my hands off the shaft.

So I force my mind back further. To leaving my mother on the doorstep, to the sense of aloneness that crushed me, to the revelation that I deserted her for all the time since, abandoned her with no security, no way to find me. I bare my heart to as much as I can.

Finally, with trembling breaths, the vines stop writhing entirely, the wildfire gone. And I'm able to shift my fingers across the surface of the trident.

"Are you finished playing, child?" Gabriel asks, his expression somewhere between curiosity and contempt.

"Almost," I find myself replying.

And though my brain screams at me, I tense my shoulders and remove one hand from the weapon, letting its spikes drop to the floor. With the connection broken, the darkness veers massively inside me. It takes my breath away and plunges me to my knees.

"Jake!" Natasha shouts at my side.

I shut my eyes, and as low as the void plummets, the river of flame spurts high, calling to me and promising sweet respite. And while every fibre of my being longs for it, I clench my teeth and focus everything on keeping my second hand free of the trident, on holding myself open to the pain. I kneel there, barely able to breathe.

Natasha's hand grips my shoulder, Father Thomas just behind, and the contact brings relief. The love I feel for them and from them is like a light in the darkness. I'm able to stumble back to my feet. To face Gabriel again.

"You *should* kneel," he says, his fingers tightening around the hilt of his sword. Then he raises his blade. "You will *all* kneel!" His voice shakes, and fury burns in his gaze.

Michael's words shoot through my head again – *you and*

Gabriel, more alike than you imagine – and I scrunch my eyes shut. I cast my mind back to the rest of what he said ... *The rage that controls your actions. Created by some past pain, some unfulfilled want. The same rage that afflicts my brother.*

My eyes go wide.

Gabriel sweeps his blade back to his side.

I force energy up my throat. "They abandoned you. Didn't they?"

His beautiful features warp, and he narrows his eyes at me.

"Your brethren, your fellow angels," I say and swallow. "After all you did for them, the scriptures you created, all the efforts you made. They still abandoned you, exiled you."

His radiance flares, and the heat scorches my cheeks and neck.

My hands tremble. "I know the abandonment," I spit out. "But only over a decade, while you've lived it for *thousands* of years."

"I am no insect!" he bellows, and the sound leaves my ears ringing. He levels his massive sword at me. Natasha shifts at my side.

"No, but you used to be," I say. "You were human once. You feel as we feel." I press a hand to my chest. "And like me, you push away those you care about." I raise a finger toward Cassiel's inert body, still hearing the sadness in Gabriel's voice before they fought. "You relish your exile from the pantheon, you interfere with the world just as your brothers and sisters deplore, and you try to force humanity to love you despite knowing we'll always disappoint." I shake my head and continue more softly. "It is never going to work."

This time he says nothing. His lips form a thin line, his eyes burn, and he twists his sword in mid-air.

"Please," I say and lift up the trident. "You don't have to go through with this. Here ..." I fish out Eleth's clasp and offer it to him with my other hand. "This was freely given. For you."

Gabriel glances from the clasp back to my face, the sword still gripped in both hands. I peer closer at his expression, at the slope of his cheeks. Is that a hint of gentleness?

But his outline fades as he pulls the darkness in around him like a cloak. From blazing brightly, his features become shadowed entirely.

"Take it," I say and extend Eleth's clasp further toward him. *"Please."*

Still, Gabriel remains enshrouded in black, ten yards away. Immobile. Unreadable. The flecks of ash hang motionless in the surrounding air. I hold the silence.

Finally, he issues a ringing sigh and raises an arm toward me in the darkness, his fingers extended. My eyes flick to the clasp.

Something is ripped from my other hand instead.

The trident.

It flies across the space toward Gabriel, growing in size, the vines weaving and dancing, before slamming into the archangel's massive hand. He grins, his outline brightening, his armour gleaming. He holds his sword in one hand, the trident held vertically in the other. And while the weapon was under two metres in my hands, now it stretches way over his head.

"You are right, child of man," he says, his voice so low, its tone reverberates my ribs. "You *do* always disappoint. And hence, this cycle will be your last."

I can only stare as Gabriel takes a deep breath and slips his sword into its sheath across his back. The remaining flecks of ash churn in the surrounding air.

"There will be no more chances," he continues, and with each word, his body glows brighter, his voice grows in volume, and the shaking in my chest increases. "No more space for your vanity, your ignorance, and your conceit." He spits the final words, and my pulse gallops in my neck, my stomach clenching to the size of a tennis ball.

Then he lifts and rotates the trident, holding it in front of him with both hands. I can't help fixating on it. The strands are alive to his touch. They wrap around each other as if caressed by a lover. I hold my breath.

The archangel raises a knee and brings the weapon crashing down upon it. The trident splinters with a cracking sound like a million shattered panes of glass. An inhuman shriek emanates from it but is immediately cut off.

My legs stagger. My head spins.

"I created this era, and I can end it just as easily," he says and hurls the fractured halves of the trident out into the darkness. Then he stalks toward us, toward the broken gate behind.

I can barely move. Natasha grabs my arm and hauls the priest and me out of the way. My body tenses as we flounder sideways, just waiting to be cleaved in half by Gabriel's blade as he passes.

But he simply strides beyond us, steps through the open gate, and then turns.

"You find me merciful, however," he says after a moment. He glances over our heads toward Cassiel's body, his massive wings folded behind his shoulders. "You brought me Cassiel." Then his gaze seizes on us again, the heat shimmering from his outline in the dark. "And so, I gift you your lives." He motions toward the blackness behind us, the way we came. "You may leave, if you like."

43

Gabriel strides away from us through the open gate. The darkness deepens, gravity doesn't flip, and his form shrinks a fraction with every second that passes.

Natasha steps to my side. "Do we go?" she asks.

My head tilts toward the archangel and the gaping black around him. "Imagine the horrors beyond," I say, images of countless *things*, of Gabriel's army, rotating through my mind.

"But he destroyed his own weapon," she says.

I nod, my eyes still glued to Gabriel's retreating form while something niggles at the back of my brain. "Yes, why?" I murmur.

"Cassiel believed in us," Natasha goes on, her gaze on Gabriel as well. "That is why he came."

I shake my head. "We were his perfect marks. First, he tries to use us to warn his fellow binding angel. And then he shadows us to Turkey as an opportunity to stay in human form, in case we discovered it was all nothing. That way, he wouldn't give up his disguise."

Gabriel stops far ahead and stands side-on in the darkness. "Decide now," he calls.

I swivel. Natasha's gaze is fixed on mine, her lips pressed together, and tears stain the corners of her eyes. The void is immense in my chest, the pain and guilt a crushing weight as damning thoughts squawk on at me.

"This is all my fault," I whisper.

And while my body yearns to turn and run, I take a breath and hold her gaze as I extend my hand.

"But I'm not sure I could live with myself," I say, "if I didn't try."

Her lips form the weakest smile, and her fingers entwine with mine. "I am just as responsible as you," she says.

I squeeze her fingers and smile back. "Together," I say and pull gently.

She offers no resistance. And we pad forward, hand in hand, through the open gate. Toward Gabriel. Toward failure and death. An almighty shiver rolls through me.

My eyes find the priest. He hobbles at our side. No walking stick, his body still hunched over, his face so pale. I search his features for any sign of hope, but his expression is unreadable.

Gabriel strides ahead of us, his wings now half-open, increasingly haloed in a strange glowing red. I can't help picturing the dead binding angels, the three slashes carved into their skin – the ideal bait to drive Cassiel out of hiding. And we played our part fucking perfectly. My jaw clenches, the darkness inside me so thick it chokes my lungs. Masterful manipulation – Gabriel's very essence. I ball the fingers of my free hand and try to push the thoughts out of my head, to focus on our surroundings as we walk.

Reds infiltrate the blackness on every side, as if the horizon's been sliced open and is bleeding slowly upward into a dark sky. A growing heat prickles my back and neck while the smell of sulphur and burning bodies becomes even fouler. So strong that the scent of cordite's barely noticeable now.

My gaze flicks to Gabriel, who ceases striding ahead. We stop also, thirty yards away.

The gloom continues to lighten in all directions. First diffuse reds, oranges, and yellows above the horizon, and deep grey below it. And then the new world appears out of the haze.

A desert of black rock under our feet, broken by pits of bubbling lava that throw up gases into the air. This craggy wasteland continues in a strip, two hundred yards wide, far ahead of us into the distance, ending at the base of a volcano that spews fire and smoke into a red sky full of billowing dark clouds.

I glance around me, eyes wide. Not only does the realm resemble my vision in the airport, but the shape of our strip's all too familiar from the heavenly realm.

Stepping over knolls and ridges, I pad toward the edge of our band of jagged rock, just far enough to peer over the side. And, of course, mirrored strips of black rock continue off in all orientations and directions. But instead of a radiant blue between the strips, here it's red sky and dark clouds, forming wrathful shapes like hungry mouths. And with the link clear in my mind, I gaze around till my eyes find Gabriel. Or rather, what he's standing on.

A kind of stone island. The remnants of shattered walls sit atop a crumbling foundation. The grapevines of heaven have become dark cracks in the stone surfaces which bleed a black tar-like substance. Gnarled branches leach the flecks of ash to the wind while the same tar bubbles from a broken fountain, falling through the fissures in windows, in the floor, and plummeting down into eternity below, parallel to some other narrow strip.

The entire realm is a monstrous reflection of its shining counterpart.

My eyes search for the nearby lava lakes, my mind fixed on the pool of the heavenly realm, our potential method of escape. I clamber toward the nearest one, Natasha hastening in my wake, and I gape over the side.

The breath congeals in my lungs.

Writhing bodies, just beneath a flaming yellow surface,

hands reaching for me, tortured expressions, eyes and mouths open in desperate pleading.

I lurch backward and away from it, almost falling over the ridges in the ground. My gut starts to twist, and I swivel around. Natasha's gazing over my shoulder toward the lake.

"What—" she starts.

I shake my head violently and raise my hands to block her off, trying to usher her back in the direction of the priest.

Eventually, she comes. But the visions of the lava lake won't leave me – the writhing bodies, the pleading expressions. And scrunching my eyes shut, I bring back the priest's words from the heavenly world ... *These realms are more pliable than you know, the power of belief is augmented here.* And so I tell myself the images aren't real, over and over, while stumbling to Father Thomas's side.

"I have to concede to being pleased you refused my clemency," Gabriel says. He's facing along the length of our rocky strip of land and staring off into the distance as if waiting for something.

A sudden sound draws my attention, a strange chattering from the side. I whip my head around.

Beyond a nearby ridge, I spy a flash of black. Then another. My eyes try to follow them, flicking from crest to crest, but each time I'm an instant behind the darting movements.

"Two thousand years," Gabriel says, still facing away from us. "Two thousand years since I stood here last."

I keep staring between the grey clefts, only able to catch the dark flashes in my peripheral vision. And memories swirl – images, voices – the jabbering language making them brighter, louder.

"What did you see?" Natasha asks, her voice low. She moves to my shoulder and follows my gaze.

"I'm not sure," I say, though my gut continues to constrict.

I wait for a pause between the movements and then dart a couple of steps to peer behind one of the larger crests.

There. A black body three feet high, bent over in a crouch, its four limbs poised mid-movement. I've pictured them so many times, yet the sight still freezes my insides. A bulbous head, shining dark eyes, and a yawning mouth. Here with no host, it scrambles toward us between the valleys and ridges.

Now, having seen one of them, I spot two. Then four. Six. All coming from nowhere, like they're popping out of the ground.

And all of them advance closer. But not to Gabriel. To *me*.

Instinctively, I push in front of Natasha and Father Thomas to shield them from one side. But more creatures approach from the other flank as well. And the front.

Plus, the nearer they get, the deeper the void plunges inside me. And again, I find myself craving the sweet anger, the escape, with Natasha and the priest right by me.

I grit my teeth and tense my stomach.

The creatures halt ten yards away, the fuckers surrounding us on three sides in a semicircle. Natasha and I take up position on either side of the priest and in front of him. The old man's staring not at the creatures but beyond them, out across the wasteland, a dullness in his eyes. And all the while, the heat continues to intensify. My head aches and sweat streams down my back.

Still Gabriel does nothing. He just stands erect, chin up, on the far side of the half ring of black creatures, undoubtedly enjoying our punishment. And with the creatures' jabbering and the damn memories they spark, I can't help the embers flaring within.

"So, what now?" I find myself yelling at Gabriel. "You have your domain, your army—"

The archangel turns on me with an eyebrow raised.

"My army?" he repeats and shakes his head. "No, no, no." His beautiful face splits into a grin and his voice grows more excited. "The army is not *mine*. I have always been the craftsman, the architect." He lifts his enormous arms wide as if to encompass his extraordinary accomplishment.

I blink and shake my head. And then I notice my internal alarm clamouring louder as a skulking dread forms at the base of my spine.

Gabriel paces back and forth across the strip of land in front of us. "After thousands of years of fighting, we won the greatest of battles," he says, speaking with a new nervous energy. "The dark forces were brought to heel."

The black creatures jump up and down in the growing circle before us, their movements increasingly frenzied. And I find my gaze drawn over Gabriel's shoulder toward something in the distance. A dark speck. Barely visible against the grey rock. Natasha's staring at it as well.

Despite the heat, a chill climbs my spine, like claws piercing each vertebra, while new winds gust around us.

"We offered a bargain," Gabriel says. "That he would be bound. His army also, in a space beyond time, and that he might live. You see? I am no monster."

The comments are addressed to us, though he doesn't turn. In fact, he's staring at the same dark speck, which grows into a black outline, into something that's approaching along the rocky strip of land.

I feel my gaze transfixed, my thoughts entirely scrambled now.

"You see, I can be merciful," Gabriel says.

And the dark form continues to grow. Humanoid in shape, it approaches steadily while the winds howl greedily around us.

44

THE GUSTS COME from all directions now, pulling me one way and then the other. And the nearer the dark figure draws along the rocky strip, the more my gut constricts as if it's being turned inside out. I can hardly breathe in the growing heat.

Gabriel turns back to me. "Never again will mortals scorn our divinity," he says, his voice shaking. "Two thousand years of grace are at an end. You were given the chance at redemption, to show yourselves worthy, but that is gone." He waves a hand in a dismissive gesture as the wind continues to strengthen. He yells louder into the rumbling gusts. "An older time will be renewed. An enduring war with every human heart the battleground."

I shake myself, barely able to focus on the words as part of me desperately tries to kick-start my planning mind. The dark figure's still a fair distance away. Maybe two hundred yards. Natasha and the priest stand to my side, the old man exhausted.

I swivel toward them, and Natasha stares back at me, her eyes wide. My mouth opens, but the words won't come. The void's growing so fast at my core, and each of my thoughts stutters and dies, my brain unable or unwilling to comprehend what's happening. And all the while, this new figure continues its advance as I just hold Natasha's gaze.

In the next moment, he's here, standing across from Gabriel only twenty yards away, having crossed the final distance almost in an instant. With his presence, the wind dies, a stillness descends, and a tide of despair presses down on me like a thousand physical weights. My legs totter, and the recognition comes that the hollowness and desolation I've felt since arriving in Turkey and even from before flows from *this* figure.

As with the angels, he's larger than a normal man – over a foot taller than me. Yet compared to Gabriel, he's diminutive in height and stature, with a slender build instead of broad.

No blazing gold adorns his outfit, no refined filigree. He wears simple black, but not clothes. It's as if he wears darkness itself, his suit with no crease or detail, like a well of night into which light disappears. He stands barefoot on the rocky ground, his skin deathly pale – face, feet, and hands – and his fingers long and delicate. He has fire-orange hair and mismatched eyes. One emerald green, the other azure blue. A black mask covers one side of his face, framing his single blue eye and sweeping up onto a peak at the top that resembles a devil's horn.

Gabriel takes a step back from him. They both stand beyond our semicircle of excited black creatures, only ten yards from each other.

"Satan," Gabriel says and nods to him, his tone flat.

Satan doesn't face the archangel. He stares directly at us – at Natasha and me. And his attention's like fingers, raking my mind. I turn away, trying to stop my thoughts and shut him out, but my mind's in pieces.

The archangel straightens up, his wings still half-open behind him. "I am—"

"Hush," the devil says, barely breathing the word. "You have brought children." And unlike the angels, his tone isn't multilayered at all. There's simply an awful coldness to it. Devoid of all emotion.

He strolls toward us and sits down on a rock, his head now at the level of mine, and I find myself grabbing Natasha's hand and taking a half step back.

Gabriel frowns, opens his mouth, and closes it. "They have aided me," he says eventually. "You may take them as a gift."

"A gift?" the devil says, still facing us. I feel his gaze like a laser beam.

"Indeed," Gabriel says and nods again. He spreads his grey wings fully, every ash-fleck feather visible. "Two thousand years under the earth, a debt paid … I am here to negotiate your freedom."

"Gabriel," the devil says, his voice low and soft, his expression entirely neutral as he stares at us. "Do you not understand the movement of time in this place?" He speaks with such a strange intonation, without modulation or pause.

The archangel doesn't reply.

"It is not linear," the devil continues. "The day you sealed me in seems both a moment and an eternity ago. Do you know how much strength of mind it requires to retain one's sanity for an eternity?" The merest inflection makes it a question.

Again, Gabriel goes quiet. He just takes a deep breath, his massive chest rising and falling.

"I can be merciful—" he starts.

"Hush," the devil says again and puts a slender finger to his lips, the nail long and sharp. "The children." He sits there, staring at us. "There is great opportunity here, a great symmetry. We must not be hasty." He raises both palms – one facing me, and the other Natasha. "You brought me man … and woman," he intones, as if pondering something, his gaze moving between us.

I swallow, my throat dry as sand.

Gabriel's frown deepens. "They're—"

"Adam and Eve," the devil says with an excited nod, his eyes widening in the first obvious sign of feeling. "*That* is what they are."

My mind flails for meaning while an icy chill grips my heart. I keep hold of Natasha's hand, and my head swivels to scan the nearby ridges for cover. The devil keeps his gaze fixed on me, though, and pins me with his stare.

"What?" Gabriel asks.

"The first people. A new beginning," the devil says. "Their presence represents the next turning of the wheel. They are here to witness the birth of a new age."

My bones vibrate with my beating pulse.

Gabriel tenses his shoulders; his arms and muscles ripple across his gargantuan body. "I will permit you—"

"You won't permit me anything," the devil says and rises slowly to his feet.

He swivels to face Gabriel for the first time, and I'm released from his gaze. My breathing comes a little easier, and I tug at Natasha. Though she remains motionless, her eyes fixed on the archangel.

Gabriel reaches behind his head and pulls out his gigantic black sword. Almost as long as the devil itself. He stands far taller and broader than the pale figure. And the devil has neither weapon nor wings. I stare on at her side.

"I captured you," Gabriel spits at the devil. "Imprisoned—"

"No, no, no," the devil says, padding toward Gabriel, his voice still mellow and smooth. "Please understand. Your ignorance was the greatest of the gifts you gave me. My true torment has been the knowledge that you believed yourself to be my conqueror." He stares softly up into Gabriel's eyes. "But I have used the pain – oh, have I used it," he continues. "It kept me sane, waiting for this moment. For I knew it would come."

Gabriel clenches his massive fists. "You know not why I am here!" he bellows, his eyes burning.

"But I do not need to know," the devil replies, his tone still level. He stops before the archangel. "I knew simply that by removing myself, over the centuries, the angelic pantheon would decline, would eventually tear itself apart." A smile inches up the visible side of his face. "You cannot remove the darkness and expect the light to burn as brightly."

Then the devil places a slender hand on his own chest. "You need me – why?" he says before shrugging. "It matters little."

"Because—"

"Because ultimately you are a fool," the devil says.

I glance from one to the other.

Gabriel's jaw muscles bulge, his aura brightens – red and gold – and he grips his sword hilt tighter while the devil stands impassively facing him, only a few feet away. And though they're twenty yards from us, I feel the pressure building against every inch of my body.

Gabriel retreats ten gigantic strides over a broken stone island and across the width of our strip of land. He keeps his eyes on the devil the whole time. Satan simply folds his hands before him and stares back. Then he breathes in the acrid air, a faint smile on his lips.

"You cannot conceive of how much I have craved this moment, of how much I have bent my entire will upon it," he says.

Gabriel beats his wings and hisses with rage. My heart continues to pound like a rabid animal's, and I squeeze Natasha's hand tighter.

"I knew it would be you," the devil says, and gives another half smile. "None of the others were quite as arrogant. Your anger blinds you."

Gabriel slashes his blade twice through the air, almost too quickly to see. For an instant, the smell of burnt metal overpowers the stench of sulphur and charred skin. Gabriel grips the handle with both hands and points his sword at the devil. He bends his knees and sets himself.

"Fallen one!" he says, his voice vibrating with fury.

I bite my lip and yank Natasha and Father Thomas toward me.

Gabriel leaps high, beats his massive wings, and hurtles through the air toward the devil. Satan doesn't dodge or take up a defensive stance. He merely clenches his fist, and the archangel's wings vanish in mid-air, the flecks of ash flying apart. With the sudden lack of buoyancy, Gabriel plummets forward and hits the ground hard, smashing into one of the stone island's crumbling walls.

My gaze darts to the devil. He does the strangest thing. Thirty yards from Gabriel, he turns side-on from the archangel and faces us. Then he lowers himself and sits down cross-legged on the rocky floor.

"You think you can best *me?"* he says, the first hint of steel in his tone. His visible cheek blazes red for an instant. "*I* am master here."

Gabriel staggers to his feet, his sword clenched in one hand. The devil takes a slow breath and closes his eyes. And there he waits. Undefended.

Silence reigns. And the faintest thrill chimes in my chest.

Gabriel lifts his sword slowly above his head and trains it on Satan's back. Then he takes a careful step toward him, his movement entirely quiet.

I hold my breath, and my eyes find a rock a couple of feet away. My hands shake, and adrenaline pumps around my veins, my mind conjuring images of me grabbing and hurling it, providing Gabriel with a momentary distraction. I take half a step toward it, and my feet crunch on the craggy ground, the sound like boulders scraping in the silence.

Natasha grabs my arm, and I freeze. My gaze flies back to the devil. He remains seated, hardly breathing, with his eyes closed, and Gabriel maintains his noiseless advance. I don't move a muscle, don't breathe. Just pray.

The devil sighs, his voice soft again. "I have always been your master," he says.

Gabriel takes another silent step forward but then stumbles. He strains to lift his leg while vines of shadow entwine themselves around his calf. He glances down, his brow furrowed. The shadows morph into the multiple limbs and misshapen heads of two of the black creatures. They scale one boulder-like thigh while two more climb his other leg. And more come. They crawl out of cracks in the stone floor. Many leave the semicircle around us. And all throng toward the archangel.

"From two thousand years ago, this moment was inevitable," the devil says. "It has all transpired as I meant it to."

Gabriel grabs the creatures from his legs and sends them flying. Then more swarm in and advance on him from all directions – from underneath and up high – climbing down the broken walls of the stone island.

For a while he's able to keep them at bay, slashing with his sword at enormous speeds and kicking at the ones that get close enough. But they continue coming like a flood. More of them stream up his legs, his hips, and the closer they get, the more pointless his sword becomes. It's too long, and he ends up swinging it in vain arcs at those approaching from afar, his legs anchored to the ground with the weight of the grappling creatures.

All too soon, their combined strength becomes too much. The mass of them topple him over onto the stony ground.

The devil remains still the entire time.

Gabriel roars with anger and immediately scrambles back to his feet. He drops his sword and begins clubbing the black creatures with his enormous fists, smashing them away.

More come, always more. Several perch atop the higher walls of the stone island and begin tipping the broken stones onto Gabriel while others pin his legs and arms. Rocks crash down from all angles and detonate against his shoulders, his chest, his head, leaving him staggering.

Two dozen creatures climb up the side of Gabriel's body

and push him into the path of a toppling giant arch. It crashes into his legs, bending them backward, and he topples to the ground, screaming.

The black creatures swarm all over him and pull his limbs into the raining stones. Then they pile rocks over him, and it's like watching something being consumed by a legion of ants. I almost retch while Natasha's hand goes to her mouth.

Then all's quiet again. Rocks cover every inch of Gabriel's unmoving body before several of the black creatures withdraw.

45

The devil takes a deep breath, keeping his eyes closed, and the air of hell remains entirely still. The dark clouds billow in the background on all sides while the grey strip of rock extends into the distance behind him.

"I know what you wish for, but I will not grant it," the devil says, his voice raised for Gabriel though he continues to face us.

My eyes find the huge mound of rocks, the archangel somewhere underneath. And there's no movement. No sign of life. The horde of creatures squat on top.

I edge backward, ignoring the scraping sound of my feet, my hand across Natasha's torso. And she pulls Father Thomas with us, though he's still moving slowly, his legs shaking and body hunched with exhaustion.

"Destroyed, you will witness the coming of the next age," the devil calls to Gabriel, still without a hint of anger or enjoyment. "With my long absence, how much weaker are the angelic forces? How many fewer are there?"

The devil maintains his seated position, and I spin around, my pulse firing and my gaze fixed beyond the nearby crags and ridges, focused instead on the dark strips of land criss-crossing the angry sky. But each one's rotating in the billowing clouds. None of them still. Nothing to fucking focus on.

"And so, you will live, entirely broken," the devil continues from behind. "While the pantheon will find me to be as powerful as I ever was. This place is beyond time. Remember?"

I stumble on, my head turning to search the opposite half of the sky, and my gaze falls on the priest. He's lurching at my side, continuing to stare out over the scarred strips, his eyes still unfocused and dim.

A black creature scrambles in front of me, and my feet stagger to a halt. Another comes, and I dart to the side to find a third blocking our path. Then I swivel all the way around. And jump backward.

The devil's still seated cross-legged, but he's even closer than before. Somehow, only fifteen feet away. And he's staring directly at me, eyes wide open.

"I told you," he says, and his mismatched eyes gleam. "We must not be hasty."

More of the black creatures leave Gabriel's pile of stones and scuttle toward us, forming a semicircle behind the devil while a few others remain on our other side. I force a slow breath, my heart thumping.

"Now, Adam and Eve," he says, and his eyes flick between us, his voice soft again. "What are we to do? We mustn't rush into things." He shakes his head. "It is too important."

The creatures continue to stare on at me, that same reverent gaze I remember so well. Then my mouth falls open as the revelation leaves me reeling.

"Yes," the devil says, and I can feel his attention combing my mind again. A half smile creeps up his cheek. "Gabriel never sent them. They were never his to send."

I find myself shaking my head, the darkness plunging deeper than ever. And the creatures froth up and down.

"You have been an attractor all on your own," the devil

goes on. "Gabriel shattering the initial gates meant the timelessness bled into your world. They were drawn to you for the role you were *going* to play."

Nausea grips my stomach, and my voice trembles. "No," I say, the void so great, the heat building inside.

The devil nods. "Yes, indeed," he says.

The creatures bounce wildly. And memories whirl around my head at breakneck speed. The *things* stalking us, stalking me, killing my mother. And deep down in the darkness, the river of fire flows faster. Plumes of flame fill my chest and arms. The sweet voices whisper ... *Just let go, fight, rage, maul ...*

I grit my teeth, squeeze my fingers together, and focus hard on keeping down the fury.

The devil stares intently at me, a sharpening glow in his eyes. "You are an interesting one," he says, his voice almost a purr.

He shifts his gaze to Natasha at my side. He rises to his feet, and his left hand vanishes into white smoke before reappearing stretching out toward her. The black creatures jump higher, their jabbering so loud as he leans forward. His slender fingers move to tilt up her chin as if he's examining some kind of showpiece.

Natasha shudders and edges away from him while the flames burn fiercer inside me. Energy flashes up my legs and into my chest. I see myself jumping at the devil, snapping his arm from his shoulder. And still the whispers continue ... *Just let go ...*

I tense my calves, my shoulders, and reach into my pocket for Eleth's clasp. Grasping it tightly, I barely maintain control.

"I know what we have," the devil says, stepping back. He retracts his hands and folds them in front of him. "A new epoch coming, a new original sin."

"A new *what?*" I say, the words spilling out.

"While Eve's birth from Adam's rib marked the beginning of the first age," the devil says, looking from Natasha to me, "her death at his hand will mark the dawn of the second."

Natasha goes ashen white, and I can only stare back at the devil. The black creatures around us bounce higher, and the memories become visions. The image forms of Natasha as it has so many times … her body sprawled out, three slashes carved into her back, with me standing over her, knife in hand.

I take a breath and shut my eyes for an instant. The devil speaks again, and I try to focus hard on the words.

"Yes, a perfect symmetry," he says, a tinge of excitement in his tone. "Consider the story we will create, the new scripture we will write."

"What do you mean?" I splutter.

He simply nods, and the smile widens across his lips. "You will live," he says, his voice so soft. Then he turns to Natasha. "And she will die."

Natasha clasps my fingers and grips them tightly.

I try desperately to kick-start my floundering brain. "A new scripture, a new Gospel?"

The devil tilts his head with a slight frown.

"But there's no one here to witness it," I manage to get out. "No one will know it happened—"

"*You* will know," he says, staring intently at me, his voice raised for the first time. The hint of redness returns to his cheek.

And then it's gone again.

"Besides," he goes on, his tone flat once more. "My covert escape is more important. And while witnesses would be useful, they are unnecessary. With your help, the other angels will know soon enough." He almost grins. "I am sure they will believe you."

The void plunges, memories coming of Michael's disapproval of me. And the river of fire flares once more. Again, I take a breath to cool it.

But the devil steps toward us, only twelve feet away now,

his creatures scrambling closer in his wake. And the flames erupt even higher, the sweet whispers becoming shouts in my head. My biceps clench, every muscle ablaze. And I find myself leaning toward the devil, teeth gritted, with Natasha still just to my side. With the raging fire, I can hardly feel her fingers in mine.

I yank myself out of Natasha's grip and spring away from her.

The sharp glow is back in the devil's eyes, a full smile on his lips, and he pivots to the side and starts to pace in an arc around me. He saunters along the inside of his semicircle of black creatures to keep me between him and Natasha, to prevent me from further distancing myself.

I dart a few steps further to the side, away from the black creatures, away from the devil, so he can't push me back onto Natasha, can't squeeze us together. Hence, we continue like this, the devil padding around me in a twelve-foot circle while I arc around Natasha and the priest in a smaller ring, always keeping a couple of paces away from Natasha and a couple ahead of him.

The devil taps his long white fingers against his leg. "I tell you what," he says, his tone easy. "I will give you a chance." He raises a finger. "A single chance to save her. Come, strike me down. My army will not intervene."

And it's as if the creatures understand. The few that were behind us scuttle to join the semicircle on the opposite side, and the entire mass retreats several yards, bouncing off each other.

I continue my small circle around Natasha and the priest, and the devil continues to circle me, his eyes still glued to mine. We're both on the other side of his line of black creatures now, and he's on his own, a slender figure, much smaller than Gabriel, slighter than Nakir … Crazy ideas flash through my brain.

My shoulders tense, the growing heat tightening my ribs.

"Jake, don't—" Natasha chokes out.

The devil's voice cuts through hers with more excitement than I've heard before. "What other choice do you have? There will be no escape from this place," he says to me. "And here I am, unarmed." He raises his open hands and creeps a little closer with every step, tightening the circle. "I *know* you have it in you. I can *feel* it."

His words slink into my ears like smoke. The sweet whispers start up again, urging me to let go – Qetesh's voice, my mother's, Natasha's – some bizarre chorus. The fire continues to build. Flames rush through my chest, my arms. And the fantasy comes of me destroying the devil, pulling him limb from limb.

I gnash my teeth and focus on damming the sounds, the images. But they begin to run together – the memories, the visions, flashes of the scarred landscape – while more thoughts whirl through my mind.

This could be it … my one shot.

Yet with the fire raging, I lurch further away from him and back toward the black creatures, continuing in my circle around the priest and Natasha. I maintain my focus on her, on her calming presence.

The devil continues his circle also and soon reaches his army, the beginning of his arc of creatures behind. And he's still spiralling ever closer. I scramble onward to keep a few steps ahead.

He issues a hissed sigh. "That was your last opportunity, Adam," he says.

His creatures scuttle forward once more, cross the ground they'd given up, and press even tighter around us. The void grows yet more intense at my core, the flames rising ever higher. So damn hard to resist. And I'm forced to stumble back alongside Natasha and the priest again, to focus intently on their presence, on trying to open my heart to the slice of darkness that I can. My fingers grip Eleth's clasp so tightly.

The devil comes to a halt directly between us and his arc of demons. He leans closer, only ten feet away.

"The new scripture *will* be written," he says.

And suddenly I feel cold metal in my hand. Not Eleth's clasp, but the sensation of holding a knife. So fucking real. And again, I tense every muscle in my body, concentrate everything on damming the wildfire. My limbs shake, my thoughts coming in spurts. I'm going to lose control at any moment.

Fingers grip my shoulder, and I spin to the side and raise my hands, my pulse thumping.

It's the priest, staring at me, his face so gaunt. However, aliveness shines in his eyes again. He squeezes my shoulder, and some of the fire diminishes inside me, a sense of coolness among the flames, the imprint of the knife gone from my hand. I reach up and grip his fingers.

Father Thomas spins to face the landscape again, a frenetic energy in his movements. "I see it now," the old man says, gazing around in all directions.

I peer more closely at him, a strange prickling sensation climbing my chest.

"I see it!" the priest says more loudly.

The devil edges back a fraction and cocks his head. "You see what, old man?" he says.

"The perfect symmetry you speak of," the priest says. He reaches over and grasps Natasha's arm. He yanks her around from the devil to face the tortured scene.

"Look, look!" he says in a frenzy, his eyes wide, every muscle taut.

I fix my gaze on his face. Saliva trickles from one edge of his mouth.

"What do you see?" the priest asks Natasha, pointing a shaking finger at the scarred landscape.

Natasha narrows her eyes and then follows his gaze. I do the same, glancing out at the lakes of lava, the shattered walls of the island, the charred trees, the racing clouds, and the angry volcanoes that spew ash even higher into the air. And all the while, a wind builds around us. It comes in gusts and spurts, bringing sulphuric smells and whipping the flecks of ash around our faces.

The priest is still staring fixedly at Natasha. He opens his mouth and then closes it before grabbing her hand. "You must see it yourself!" he cries.

I stare again at the surrounding hellscape, trying to imagine what he's seeing. The prickles climb the back of my neck.

"Remember the tapestry," the priest says, his eyes shining at Natasha, his voice rising against the growing wind. "Stories weaved together. Greater than all of us. We're part of them, just as they're part of us. *Never forget their power*."

I shake my head and find my gaze drawn back to the creatures. They're pressing ever tighter in their semicircle around us, so close now, only twenty feet away. And the wind's coming in rabid gusts and individual shrieks.

The devil towers higher into the air above our heads. "This spectacle has gone on long enough," he says.

The priest doesn't face him. He grips both of Natasha's shoulders and keeps her gaze on the surrounding landscape.

"Think of who and what surrounds you," he says and starts to shake her while the wind tears at his words. "Do you not *see?*"

I raise an arm and step in to separate them, to save her from his madness.

Then Natasha glances at the devil and quickly back at the rocky scene. And her eyes go wide.

46

Natasha whirls back from the landscape of twisted rock and bubbling lava to stare at the priest, her mouth gaping. "The garden," she breathes.

The priest nods, a feverish look in his eyes. "Genesis," he says.

I blink across at the devil. The black-suited figure's mild amusement has morphed into a frown. And his army of dark creatures froth up and down in the semicircle behind him.

The priest squeezes Natasha's hand. "Have faith, my child," he says, a tear following the network of lines down his cheek. "Whatever happens … have faith."

And then the old man pushes forward to stare up at the devil, still poised only ten feet away.

"Oh, great serpent, we see you now!" Father Thomas shouts into the wind.

Peering at the devil, my thoughts splutter. He looks identical standing there. I shake my head. Adam, Eve … the devil as the serpent. Is this place supposed to be a new Eden?

The priest and Natasha glance intently at each other. And I search their faces for signs of madness. They're poised side-on from the devil, Satan's eyes narrowing and his lips tightening. The priest is easily in striking distance, and Natasha spins to scan the landscape, her face suddenly aglow.

And idiotically, I turn away from the devil also and follow her gaze, my stomach taut. Despite Natasha's many lectures, I know pretty much jack shit about Genesis, the garden, the tree of knowledge, the apple …

The tree.

My mouth falls open, and a shiver coils up my entire body.

There it is … The ground behind us descends into a massive basin of dark rock, and in the centre, many hundreds of yards away, stretching up toward the billowing sky … stands the biggest tree I've ever seen.

Enormous. As wide as our strip of land. And shaped like the explosion of a nuclear bomb. Its trunk is formed of countless massive roots, all weaved together like a colossal rope, and from the top of the trunk, they spread up and out to form a crown of twisting branches – thousands of them – reaching out like talons to rake the sky.

My gaze is drawn into the middle. And there, behind all the crisscrossing branches, amid its wooden prison, hangs a large apple. So red, it's visible from this far away.

I can only stare, random thoughts firing. Was the tree always there? Or did it appear because of Natasha's realisation … Eve's realisation … called by some ancient power of myth?

Natasha whirls back to face the priest, awe in her eyes. And my thoughts jabber on.

Father Thomas grips Natasha's wrist. "You know the story. You know what happens next!" he says.

"What happens next?" I yell at him.

But he keeps his gaze fixed on Natasha. "Go!" he yells and shoves her away from him toward the tree.

She hesitates, caught in mid-movement, and the black creatures behind the devil leap up and down with excitement, like a pack of hounds waiting for their master's release.

The devil's voice rings out at our backs. "Yes, go," he says, anticipation in his tone.

My gaze cuts back to Natasha. She's standing there, chewing her lip, the strengthening gusts pulling at her hair.

With shaking hands, the priest thrusts harder at her. "Go, Eve, *now!*" he yells.

And this time she spins and sprints away from the devil, from the creatures, toward the tree, her feet beating out against the uneven ground. I swivel to face the creatures and crouch down, extending my arms, ready to leap and block them off.

But they don't scramble after her.

A few jump forward before rearing back, thrashing and biting at her shadow. And the devil's staring at me, not her, that gleam of excitement in his eyes.

The shiver descends my spine this time, and my gaze darts back to Natasha, still running toward the tree. Such a long way away. And then the realisation hits …

The more the devil delays, the better for him. His creatures can travel faster. I'll need the raging fire to keep up. And the more rage I use, the more likely I'll end up killing her.

The devil smiles at me. The creatures inch closer, clambering over each other, their hunger for her scouring at my insides. And again, the flames surge up my torso, the river of fire so fucking hot. I grit my teeth and try desperately to keep my focus. But my sight blurs, images from my dreams flooding my vision … Strewn figures. My mother, Natasha. Their bodies broken and bleeding. Father Thomas lying dead among the ridges of stone.

My vision clears, and the devil's still staring down at me, his eyes shining. And the flames burn even hotter, even faster, mad currents of fire cavorting inside me irresistibly. I clench my jaw, ball my fists, and tense my legs, again concentrating everything on clamping down the rage.

I feel a hand on my shoulder again. The priest. He's

gazing into my eyes, his fingers trembling. "You have to let go," he says. "Trust this!"

And the devil's taunting words ring inside my head. *"Yes, do."*

And while the void plummets deeper, I tense every muscle to control the fire.

Father Thomas squeezes my shoulder tighter and leans closer. There's such determination in his face, yet his eyes glow softly. "I'm here for you," he says, his voice hardly a whisper. "Always remember that." And he smiles.

I spy movement in my peripheral vision. My ribs tighten, and I shoot my head around. Satan's stepping forward, only ten feet from me now. And his circle of black creatures scrambles closer behind him, many of them poised to leap.

The priest swivels back to face the devil and anchors his stance, one hand still on my shoulder. He takes a deep breath and then stamps his foot hard on the ground.

And the entire world lurches.

Gravity flips by ninety degrees, our strip of land tilting upright, and for an instant, I find myself standing on a vertical cliff face, the devil above me.

My insides turn over and my hands flail. Father Thomas keeps his shaking hand on my shoulder, pressing my feet hard into the cliff. And somehow, like both the priest and the devil, I remain anchored to the cliff face. Gravity doesn't yank me down.

"Hold here!" the priest yells.

And the memory comes of flipping gravity in the angelic realm. Scrunching my eyes shut, I focus fiercely on the cliff being horizontal beneath my feet again, channelling the power streaming through me into the memory and concentrating hard. And when my eyes fly open, the flip's reversed. The ground is horizontal, the devil and his scuttling demons before me once more. I find my head turning. And the sight almost scrambles my concentration …

Natasha's no longer sprinting toward the tree but falling,

gravity still flipped for her. And while her descent's not as quick as it'd be in the real world, it's much faster than running. Plus, she's flying over the basin that slopes downward to the base of the tree. Which means she's heading for the branches, not the trunk, plummeting toward them as if they're a massive net of razor-sharp threads.

"Ezelk!" The devil yells the strange command, his voice high and strained.

A chorus of shrieks fills the air, and I spin back around. The devil's expression is contorted in rage, and half a dozen of the black creatures scurry to either side of him, ready to leap after Natasha.

"Jacob, you must!" the priest shouts and whips his hand from my shoulder.

Again, the world lurches for an instant, and I have to focus intently to keep the ground horizontal beneath me.

The creatures launch themselves down the cliff face, and Father Thomas jumps toward them, blocking them off.

He's a blur, and with his lightning movements, I bite down hard on my thoughts – it's automatic – and the veil starts to peel back from my senses. The shimmering world balloons around me, bringing extra power and making it easier to keep gravity flipped. However, without the buffering of the veil, the void tears through my insides and leaves my body shaking, my teeth chattering.

Even so, I keep my attention focused on Father Thomas, on slowing time. The blur resolves itself, and I watch him grab the first tumbling creature by one of its limbs. He lands back down on the cliff face and then hurls the creature at the others that jumped, slamming them apart like bowling pins.

And with that, they stop targeting Natasha and turn on Father Thomas instead. One springs at him, and he kicks back, sending it careening into space. Then more creatures fling themselves at him, clawing and biting, and as they fight, I narrow my eyes and focus harder on the priest's darting form, on keeping the overwhelming sense of powerlessness, of darkness, at bay. All the while, the fire threatens to spark, to obliterate my control.

The priest ducks and dives, striking when he can and evading when he can't. Then more creatures attack, and more again. From three at a time, to six, to nine … They inundate him – an island engulfed by a black flood. All the while, the devil's gaze flicks between the priest and me, his eyes shining brighter than before, and he inserts the priest's words directly into my head.

"Trust this … let go …"

Still I stand there with fingers like claws, my body shuddering. And with each creature that swamps the old man, the wider the abyss opens inside me. With the veil peeled back, it's immeasurable. And without the priest and Natasha, there's no way I can hold it. The fire ends up burning wild, like a volcano rumbling in the dark depths, its fiery mantle pushing up my torso, ready to explode. The pressure, so fucking immense.

Natasha's yell of shock rings out from below. She's reached the tree. While the creatures continue to swamp the priest – his face barely visible – black limbs scrabbling all over his body.

The devil leans closer to me, his mouth stretched wide in a grin, his voice still echoing inside my brain. *"It'll soon be too late."*

The fire surges higher. I tense my arms, legs, and chest to contain it, but it's not enough. The power's proportional to the immensity of the darkness. My entire body quakes with it, my muscles tightening randomly.

So I ignore every screaming warning of my mind, clench my jaw, and plunge into the cavernous void inside me – so fucking terrifying. I try to face it, knowing I can't. My body convulses, and I wait for the sweet relief …

Flames explode from the depths. Rage as power catapults me out of the void, and I find myself leaping at the pile of creatures, my fire burning with every colour – orange, yellow, red, white – within every inch of my body. Heat beyond understanding.

I reach the first creature and grab it by its arms. The skin burns – so cold. I just grip harder and haul it backward, sending it skimming across the landscape. Another leaps at me, and with the veil peeled back, sensing its movements in advance, I club it with both fists in mid-air.

More creatures attack, and I glimpse my own hands flying, the creatures being hurled left and right. Some climb my calves and my knees, and I kick them off. Others claw and scratch, but the pain only fuels my fire.

All the while, I keep the image of Natasha in my mind – her clambering through razor-sharp branches, heading for the damn apple for whatever fucking reason … Though an instant later, the question is scorched in the heat of my single-minded determination, and I concentrate on her image as a lifeline, a tether to sanity. I continue to yank and swing, sending creatures tumbling this way and that, the priest buried somewhere in the middle of them all.

Suddenly, there is no middle, no beginning, no end. All my perspective is gone. The fire is simply too fucking vast. The void barely a memory. My awareness starts to float out of my body as I watch myself fighting and flailing in all directions – fists, fingers, feet. I grab, smash, throw … whoever, whatever. Creature, human – it's all just flotsam flung about in the uncontrollable eruption. Such elation, such release. The anchors of Natasha, of the priest, of Eleth's clasp, all almost impossible to hold on to. I glimpse only flashes of cloud, of fire, of rock, of red … my hands raw and bloodied.

And here in the depths of hell, there's no way for my mind to shut me down.

Then fingers grip my wrist with a sudden sensation of coolness, and I come to a rest. My vision clears, and the veil slips back before my senses. I shake my head, my breath coming shallow and fast in my chest, and gaze around me. The creatures have been scattered and are currently regrouping in a wide circle, scuttling toward me again, crouching to attack.

And before me ... a face. Familiarity chimes. Creased cheeks lined with many cuts and bruises. Nose broken. And his chest heaves with a sickening wheeze. Multiple cracked ribs. I remember striking at the creatures, at him ... And a plunging weight adds to the void inside.

"It's okay, Jacob," the priest says, his voice barely audible. His soft eyes stare back at me. "It's okay."

His fingers tighten around my wrist, and gradually, the fire keeps diminishing, and my vision continues to clear. The old man glances toward the tree behind us. I follow his gaze.

Natasha's crawling through the web of branches, moving laterally against the altered gravity, and so bloody slowly. The apple is still a good distance away, and now, the devil's not focused on me but on her, his knees bending.

The priest leans in to whisper in my ear. "Trust this," he says.

The void's like grappling hooks around my insides, and I freeze, entirely stuck.

The devil glances down at me. "Let us go and see your friend. Shall we?" he says and nods toward Natasha.

Then his image hazes and lightens as he morphs into white smoke. His body elongates above our heads, dissipating into the raging wind. The devil flips gravity for himself and starts to fall toward the tree.

The priest lets go of my wrist. "I'm always there," he says.

I reach across to grab him. But the darkness holds me fast. And the priest moves like a shot to fling himself at the devil. The images run in slow motion, flashes blurring together while currents of cold roll up from the depths.

Father Thomas rockets into the devil's thinning white shape and diverts its fall, wrapping himself around it. The smoke becomes a ball and then coalesces back into a humanoid shape. And the next instant, the devil's there, his white hands gripping the priest's chest.

He hangs in mid-air with his visible cheek flushed red, his teeth bared, and his eyes blazing blue and green. Then he crashes back downward – ten feet away – and drives Father Thomas's body into the rocky ground, over and over, like a child smashing a hated toy.

My legs go weak. I stumble forward, my eyes fixed, unable to breathe. The horror wraps itself around every inch of me, squeezes …

The devil straightens up, his face a lake of placid calm once more. He pins me with a gaze and gives a wide smile while the priest's body lies broken at his feet.

Entirely still.

47

I JUST STARE at Father Thomas's prone form smashed on the jagged ground before me. The fire's fled, and it's like I've been hollowed out, my body a wasteland of ash and ruin. The darkness fills every pore, hell magnifying the pain more than I could ever have imagined.

The devil stares over my shoulder at the tree behind me. "Shall we?" he says again with that same satisfied grin.

Then he leaps toward Natasha, his figure thinning out again to become the liquid smoke. And he keeps his eyes on me the entire time.

I roar. The darkness is too much. The fire blazes, and I let it reclaim me, my body itching to jump and fight. The devil's form elongates over my head, and the wind howls like a massive set of bellows to the flames inside. Every muscle tightens, every tendon, the river of fire churning through my whole body. Immense power. The sweet whispers start again, and I feel a desperate hunger to do their work.

The devil speeds toward the tree behind me, and I spring after him, my attention trained on the ground becoming a cliff face. With the energy running through me, the world lurches in an instant, gravity shifting easily, and I plummet head first toward the gargantuan tree below, toward Natasha.

The creatures' jabbering voices fade behind. And the air's so viscous, the wind so strong. It's like hands pressing at the top of my head, my shoulders, incrementally slowing my fall.

I tilt my neck back and glimpse Natasha scrambling between the branches. She's getting closer to the centre of the crown, to the apple. Maybe fifty feet away. However, the tree is growing before my eyes, the branches slowly extending, the apple moving ever further away from her. While the devil falls toward it, unencumbered by the wind, pulling away from me, and homing in on Natasha ever faster. He'll be on her in moments.

Again, the fire explodes inside me. And images from the past and present run together – my beatings as a child, fights in the gangs, the priest's bloodied face in my hands, the old man being smashed into the ground by the devil – repeated over and over. Consumed by burning flames, I stretch my arms in the direction of the devil, my fingers reaching to get hold of him, to tear the fucker apart as I fall toward the tree and Natasha below me.

And the obvious thought comes next … that this is exactly what the devil wants.

Alongside the wild fury, I get hit by the inevitability of it all – the darkness of my fate looming wide while the memories churn one after another …

Me helping to stop Gabriel from unleashing a plague and ultimately prompting him to release the devil. Qetesh – that beautiful being – aiding us and dying for it. Me abandoning my mother before leading a *thing* to her door. Then forcing Cassiel out of hiding and bringing him here to die. Even killing my delivery contact by ushering a *thing* right to him. And now I see the priest. Injured at my own hands and then killed by the devil.

Ultimately, his release is my fault, and I can't banish the image of his creatures staring at me with that reverent gaze, at their saviour who's been doomed all along.

In the face of it all, I drag my chin up and force myself to stare right at Natasha again, at my next victim. Because it's fucking inevitable. All the devil has to do is fuel my wild rage, and I'll end up killing her. Unable to stop myself.

Falling toward him, my body stretched out, arms reaching, the fire inside becomes consumed in absolute darkness. It's as if I've been speared by it. And for the first time, I have no desire to keep it at bay. Ultimately, I can't. There's no escaping the void, the pain. It's too huge. And too inevitable. It just *is*. To deny it would be pointless.

And so I close my eyes, stop stretching out, and finally let my body relax. I turn toward the darkness without a plan, without an anchor, without hope. I bare my heart to it with no effort to hold on to the priest's faith or Eleth's.

No longer reaching, my body tilts in the fall, my arms drop, and the wind presses against my torso, legs, head, shoulders ... I let it pound every part of me while the void devours every inch of my insides – every bone, every pore, every cell. For the first time, I let *all* the darkness in. Just waiting to be destroyed by the immensity.

After a few moments, my eyes spring open.

I'm still here.

It seems like years have passed and only an instant. I'm still plummeting toward the tree, my limbs flailing, the monstrous crown of branches a couple of hundred yards away. And the devil's dropping ever faster, twenty feet ahead of me.

Watching him, I'm no longer gripped by the flames inside. Instead, it's as if I'm a part of the darkness and the darkness is part of me. Inseparable. Unavoidable.

And in remembering the priest's death, I'm not consumed by fury. Instead, amid the hurt, I feel a huge appreciation for him – for his warmth, his humour, and his undying faith in me. The pain I feel is an indication of the depth of my care – a bittersweet ache in my chest – and glimpsing Natasha struggling below me, my heart brims with such tenderness and love. She's been a beacon in my life from the first moment we met.

I centre my gaze on the devil, on his accelerating form, and while the pain grips me of potentially losing Natasha, I don't turn away from it. I don't close my heart as I've done for so much of my life. Instead, I keep my eyes fixed on them, my body relaxed. And a new fire burns at my core. But it's not anger. And it's not all-consuming because I'm no longer resistant to the darkness underneath, no longer trying to bear the pain, to get out of it. No longer using the anger as relief. For I know I can't. I'm not in control of what will happen and never will be.

Instead, the fire burns as part of the darkness, indivisible from it. It's no longer about feeling more of one or the other. With my attention on Natasha, I can simultaneously feel the pain of potentially losing her along with the burning desire to do what I can to stop it.

And the revelation comes that one reason I'm not destroyed by the void's immensity is that a huge amount of my pain came from resisting it in the first place.

With the growing flames, the flowing power, I don't turn my back on the darkness. Instead, I feel its weight and pull my arms to my chest, my knees upward, and imagine myself as a rock, as a ball of lead. Anything to channel my belief. And I will myself faster toward the devil through the billowing air.

In an instant, the devil's no longer ahead of me. We're falling together, our bodies parallel, only a foot from each other. My body starts to uncoil, and his face of black and white leers into mine. Then his features morph ... He becomes Gabriel; Father Thomas, broken and battered; then Don and Twist; then gang members from my childhood home. We plummet almost nose to nose, but hardly moving, frozen in space, in time.

And with every image, with every torment, still I don't turn away from the pain, the void. There's no need to. The fire burns inseparably from it. I simply focus on my care for the priest, for Natasha, and for the world itself. And the more I do, the more intense the flames become, and the more power flows through me.

I shoot my hands up to shove the devil off course. He smiles and his arms vanish from his sides, white smoke forming in their place. Then, from nothing, pain detonates behind my ribs. I glance at my torso. His fingers hover there, coated in mist and buried up to the first knuckle in my chest. I scream, my mouth open wide. It feels like a furnace is burning beneath my skin.

And while my mind yells warnings, I grab at the white mist with both hands. I squeeze with my fingers, and the mist grows hard, his skin like porcelain. The contact burns with a fire that eclipses mere sensation. It has smell, sound, and taste as well as touch. Still I don't let go. I don't even try to wrench his fingers from my ribs. Instead, I use his grip as leverage to bring my feet all the way up to his chest while summoning every ounce of the burning power. Then I kick out with everything I have.

First my feet hit fog and then the solid matter of his torso. The impact sends him careening off through the gusting wind. We start to fall again, and he flies away from the tree, away from the entire crown of branches, as I dive toward its core.

Hope glimmers for a moment.

Then the devil's windmilling arms become smoke, and his dark shape slows its drift away from me before swooping back in my direction, elongating above me.

I peer downward. The tree's only fifty yards away as Natasha clambers deep within the razor-sharp branches, her cheeks cut and bloodied. And the devil zeroes in on her, more of his body morphing into white smoke, plummeting ever faster.

I reach out and grab for his leg. He kicks out, and the blow hits me square on the shoulder, sending me spinning while the impact thrusts him quicker toward the tree. The branches approach me fast now, like a thousand pointed knives.

Thirty yards away.

Twenty.

I still my thoughts and use the burning power to peel back the veil. I concentrate on feeling the air as solid around me, on swimming instead of falling.

My dive slows a fraction, and I smash into the branches, plunging straight through dozens of them with my eyes clamped shut. Their splintered ends slice at me, and pain flares across my cheeks and down my back as I tumble into their midst.

Finally, my fall stops. My eyes fly open, and I try to breathe, to turn my body, to gain some kind of orientation while the broken points stab at me with every movement.

The branches are everywhere, in all directions. The smaller ones fork off larger branches before curving over to meet each other with razor-sharp barbs at each end, like the fingers of a clawed hand. Pockets of space exist in between, some of them large enough to crawl through, and the sensation's like being trapped in a giant wasp nest.

Voices jabber in my ears, growing steadily louder, and more memories thrust and bite at my mind. My eyes shoot up, and I spy dozens of the black creatures falling down the cliff face toward me, only fifty yards away.

I force my gaze back down to get my bearings and spot the tree trunk. With our narrow strip of rock still vertical, it juts out horizontally, twenty feet below me and eighty feet to one side, an unfathomable drop into nothingness below.

I spin and stare in the opposite direction, spying Natasha fifty feet away from me and still scrambling from pocket to pocket, all her attention on the shining red apple ahead. She's moving so slowly, the branches like a maze in between. And the devil's closer, his body smoke-like, travelling easily through the tight spaces, just over thirty feet behind.

Gripping a branch near my head, the contact's like

touching splintered glass. I let the pain drive the fire and haul myself through the maze, though I'm so far behind. And the wind's gusting harder, shoving at my body, pushing me toward each stinging branch.

I wriggle more quickly through the spaces, contorting, writhing, and twisting my body. The jabbering grows louder, the creatures scurrying through the branches at my back and closing in on me.

I fix my eyes on Natasha and keep going. She's still twenty feet away from the apple, the devil the same distance from her, and he's moving faster. The void clutches at me again, and I just continue gripping the razor-sharp branches and thrusting myself on, the pain and care still burning together in my chest.

The creatures grasp at my feet, my calves, tugging me backward. And visions play in my head – the priest dead, Natasha sprawled before me. I kick at the creatures and send some tumbling away while more skip through the branches above and below to surround my struggling form. With well over forty feet between me and Natasha, the devil continues to close in on her, only fifteen feet away now.

There's no way I'm going to make it.

I tense my neck. "I'm here!" I yell at him. "Come and get me!"

The devil doesn't turn, doesn't slow his approach at all. Still, I strain toward her, pushing even harder as I wrestle forward through a tight gap. And then suddenly, my waist's caught. I focus harder on the pain, the fire, and jerk my body to free it. But I can't move. I'm totally stuck between two branches.

Glancing down, the sight's a hammer blow.

One of the branches is clamped tightly around my waist, around something in my pocket. I grab at my hip and fumble desperately to free myself as my head shoots up.

Natasha's balanced at the end of a branch, her body swaying wildly in the wind. The apple is on the far side of an impossibly large gap in front of her … and the distance is getting ever wider. Plus, all her attention's trained forward while the devil's drawing steadily nearer from behind.

My chest seizes, and the word's out of my mouth before I can stop myself. "Nat!"

She whips her head around and sees the devil, the white shape slipping toward her.

And freezes.

The creatures climb my legs, claws reaching for my waist. And while every part of me longs to look away from Natasha, to avoid watching her die, I keep my eyes fixed. My fingers still fumble at my pocket to free myself from the vice-like branches.

"Jump!" I yell at her, putting every ounce of power into it.

She spins to face the open space, the apple, just as the devil coalesces back into human form. His dark torso, the fiery red hair, the porcelain-white hands are only five feet away from her. He reaches for her branch.

The hand that's been fumbling in my pocket comes free. And there, sitting in my palm, is the object that was stuck behind the branch, that was holding me back, metal and jagged.

Eleth's clasp.

I gaze back up at Natasha, at the devil, and at the myriad of branches in between us – a fucking labyrinth.

In the narrow space, I draw my arm back and bring the clasp to my ear. The creatures grip my legs and jabber louder while new memories flash through my mind … the numerous plans I've messed up, the countless times I've let people down.

Natasha bends her knees, whips her arms back, and leaps. My mind stills in an instant. The veil peels back. The darkness intensifies, but I hold fast. Time slows. She flies, strangely suspended in mid-air. The devil jumps onto her branch, his blade-like fingers stretching. The anguish flares inside me as the fire burns, and power sparks in my core.

While focusing on Natasha, on the devil, I hurl Eleth's clasp as hard as I can.

It soars between the branches, through the pockets of space … two of them, four, eight … faster and faster. I keep expecting it to be blocked, to be knocked aside.

The creatures scrabble over my back, their touch freezing cold. And still I stare forward, focusing everything on willing the clasp through the maze.

The devil reaches effortlessly for Natasha. His arm turns to smoke as it elongates across the gap toward her jumping form, his hand like a hook, sweeping for her unprotected neck.

I can only watch, the breath stopped in my throat. And still the clasp hurtles on. It doubles in size and doubles again as it flies faster and closer to the devil's grasping fingers. They're only inches from her.

And the symbol smashes into his hand.

He gives a shrill cry of pain, of anger. The creatures' claws tighten around my neck. And Natasha grabs the apple. Still in mid-air, beginning to fall, she brings it to her mouth, bites down, and a blinding flash erupts around us.

48

My body shifts, and I feel pain. Everywhere. Yet it's dulled, all sensation muted. I feel myself lying on my back, uneven ground beneath me, my mind scrambled. I raise a knee to turn onto my side, and the pain intensifies, layered on a foundation of bone-crushing exhaustion. It's like a thousand weights are pressing me into the craggy rock.

And memories come. The last moments – the devil reaching for Natasha, the clasp flying, Natasha biting the apple ...

I take a sharp intake of breath, my ribs screaming, and strain to prop myself up.

A broken landscape comes into focus – red sky, billowing cloud, and grey rock. My vision remains blurry, and a bright light blazes from one direction, the outline of the gargantuan tree towering above it, many hundreds of yards away. I swivel, and sure enough, I'm back where we entered the realm, the limp figure of the priest fifteen yards away with Natasha crouched by his side.

The void's still alive in my chest as I stumble to my feet and almost fall. My eyes find the familiar heap of rocks just beyond them, Gabriel's massive hand visible between two boulders. Cuts crisscross his skin, and though it still shines, it's nowhere near as bright.

I scan the surrounding crests and ridges; not a single black creature visible anywhere. Instead, a peaceful glow radiates over everything. Fewer flecks of ash hover in the air, and the smell of sulphur's weaker in my nose, the scent of cordite steadily replacing it. Plus, there's no sign of the devil.

Hope shimmers in my heart.

Then a new heat itches the back of my neck. And I spin around to shield my eyes.

The light's even brighter than it was, and closer, its source halfway between the tree and where I'm standing. I peer into the brilliance. It resolves into several sources of luminosity, spread out in a horizontal line. Two gigantic wings extend out from either side of the central figure whose brightness dims first.

Michael.

Colours and features shift across his marble body as the colossus approaches up the rocky basin. Eventually, the brightness ebbs to either side of him, and six other angels come into view.

They walk in a V shape at his back, three per side, each possessing the same glowing magnificence, the same grey wings of ash. And at either side of the V stalk the two emissaries – Nakir and Eleth.

Eleth is staring directly back at me, her perfect features etched with that same curious expression. My heart beats faster while my fingers search for her clasp in my pocket. But of course, it's gone.

"Who summons us?" Michael says, an edge in his multi-layered tone.

"Summons?" The word tumbles out of my mouth.

"And to where?" he says, ignoring me, and gazing around at a seemingly unfamiliar landscape.

My eyes dart back to Natasha, more of her Bible lectures

sparking in my brain … Genesis … Eve ate the fruit … which summoned the angels to throw them from the garden.

I shake my head, my gaze falling on the priest. How could he have known?

There's a sudden yell from the angels, the sound like the blast from a hundred trumpets. One of the female angels beats her wings and careens at us.

I hurl myself toward Natasha. And Michael yells, "Uriel!" his transcendent calm slipping further. His features resolve, and his glow flares redder, hotter.

The female angel Uriel ignores him and leaps over our heads. She lands by the pile of rocks carpeting Gabriel and kneels to start removing stones from the heap, slowly uncovering the archangel's body.

"Brothers, sisters," Michael says and raises his massive arms at his sides. His glow is cool again, his mask of equanimity back in place. His features subtly morph across their marble surface. "We are the light. We must remain calm."

He gradually lowers his arms, and the remaining angels form up the V shape behind him, twenty yards from us. Eleth and Nakir go down on their knees on each side. My eyes find Eleth, whose attention is now on her master.

"What has happened?" Michael asks, still ignoring me. He sweeps his gaze around him as if demanding answers from the hell realm itself.

No one replies; the only sound is Uriel gently removing the stones from Gabriel's body.

I draw a deep breath. "The devil," I say, my voice barely a croak. "He was here …"

My throat constricts. Michael's peering down at me now, the archangel's glow darker, having morphed from shifting marble to a fiery gold. His flint-like features appear, his eyes burning into mine, and the memory hits me of the other maimed angel he found us with.

I swallow and then focus on what little energy remains in me, channelling it up my throat. "Gabriel—"

"Gabriel was a great help," a voice says, its emotionless tone echoing from somewhere behind me.

My heart thumps hard, and I whirl away from the angels, from the tree, a new sense of cold invading my spine.

"But you all played your part," the devil says.

And I find myself staring at his slender figure, striding evenly toward us from the other end of the craggy strip. His army of black creatures scamper along in his wake, and their strange voices jabber again in my ears.

I hear cries of shock from the angels at our back, and the emissaries spring forward to either side. They draw their swords and take up defensive positions while Michael's form resolves completely into his huge muscled frame with rippling silver armour. His wings extend high above him.

I stare in all directions. Natasha and I are right in the middle of it all. Michael and his angels stand behind us, with the devil and his army in front, Nakir to the left and Eleth to the right. Uriel remains crouched over Gabriel's broken body, in between us and the devil, only twenty feet away.

"Dear Michael, how high a perch have you erected in my absence?" the devil asks and halts thirty yards before us, his voice remaining soft and level. "How righteous a role have you created for yourself? How abstract have you become?" His tone lilts a fraction, showing the faintest hint of pleasure.

Michael doesn't reply but simply stands there, his gaze fixed on the devil while a new tautness infiltrates his brittle calm as if he's waking from a thousand-year-old dream.

I hold my breath as Natasha gazes up at the angels from my side.

"You are ... bound," Michael says.

The devil barks a laugh, his tone horribly shrill, and then shakes his head with a slow ease.

"No, no, no," he says and places a white hand over the absolute darkness at his chest. "I *conceived* this moment, two thousand years ago. I *chose* to be bound then, and there is no reason to choose it again." He performs a tiny mocking bow. "The gates stand open, and while it is unfortunate that you should witness my return, you cannot prevent it. It is heartening to see you brought so low." With a sweep of his hand, he motions to Natasha and me. "You are no more of a match for me than these children."

There's almost affection in his tone, and his creatures jump excitedly up and down behind him, many of them staring directly at me. Several of the angels swivel in my direction as well, and as the weight of their stares builds, I force my gaze away.

The devil grins, and for the first time his voice rings out, full of passion. "Barachiel, Raphael, Ariel, Netzach, Jeremiel, Uriel, I give you one last chance!" he calls and lifts his pale hands high toward the angels. "Brothers, sisters, join me. Your leader's power is spent. And while the pantheon has slumbered, I remain as strong as ever."

He steps forward, his words reverberating with power, echoing from every corner of the realm. "Your reign is at an end! A new dawn approaches, a *red* dawn. The world *will* burn, and it *will* know my name!"

None of the angels move. My gaze flicks to Michael, and two of the angels glance at him as well. The archangel doesn't react. He anchors himself more keenly in his serenity, and his dark features disappear behind the shifting marble veneer once more. His warm glow blunts the jagged edge of every rock, every crest.

"You can either help me set the kindling," the devil says and glances from one angel to the next. "Or burn with it."

From crouching at Gabriel's side, Uriel leaps to her feet and, in one swift motion, pulls her sword and points it at the devil. She stands directly between her fellow angels and Satan, only twenty-five yards away from him.

The creatures jerk up and down, biting and thrashing at the air. A few of them leap toward her before retreating. The angels behind Michael all draw their swords in unison while I leap between the devil and Natasha, who is still crouched by Father Thomas's body.

Satan smiles and fixes each angel with a stare. His eyes shine green and blue. "So be it," he says.

And then he swivels in my direction and pierces me with that awful gaze. I try to look away but can't.

"Until next time," he says and grins.

Then he spreads his arms and tilts his face up. His form elongates up into the sky, his legs dissipating into a plume of white smoke.

"Stop him!" Uriel yells and bends her knees to leap, her wings extended.

"No, wait!" I shout and throw my hands toward the angels.

The devil's form continues to lengthen, a silver dart lifting above my head. Every angel except for Michael springs forward, beats their wings hard, and soars into the sky in pursuit. I spin away from the angels and launch myself on top of Natasha, though I can't help glancing up.

Rising higher, the devil claps his hands together, and the crash echoes like thunder. The grey wings of the angels disintegrate, and they flounder, fifty or sixty feet in the air.

I yank Natasha closer, and the angels plummet back down. All six of them smash into the craggy ground, one of them barely missing us. Michael stands there, watching impassively as the devil shoots away, disappearing toward the broken gates and freedom.

49

KEEPING low in the driver's seat, I bring the car to a gradual halt in the darkness and edge it under a spindly tree.

A block of fenced-off wasteland stretches down one side of the street while a row of three-storey apartments lines the other. There are no garages, no overhangs, no obvious places to hide. And all's quiet, the streets deserted.

I turn off the engine and glance at the dashboard clock. Eleven thirty-nine p.m. Natasha stirs in the passenger seat at my side and gradually opens her eyes.

"Where are we?" she asks, blinking, her voice so weak.

"Istanbul," I say, keeping my voice hushed.

"The centre?" she says, gazing around.

I shake my head. "Too risky. I almost got chased out of the last station forecourt."

The fourteen-hour journey from Pergamon was a nightmare. It took four stops to find someone willing to serve us just petrol, food, and a newspaper.

I glance over my shoulder at it on the back seat, the front page showing images of the multiple mosques reduced to rubble, enraged crowds shouting before them, still looking for perpetrators to blame. And, *there*, the date clearly marked in the top right-hand corner – a whole week later than we left

Istanbul. A whole bloody week. I shut my eyes and grip the wheel.

"So, what is the plan?" Natasha says.

I glance back. She looks a mess, her face peppered in cuts and bruises, her clothes covered in rips and ash. And she's sagging in her seat, her eyes distant. My mind flashes back to the day before.

Eleth helped us carry Father Thomas out of hell, and then Natasha and I buried him under a solitary tree by Pergamon's ruins, Natasha almost breaking down at the graveside.

I swallow down the weight in my throat. "We need a place to stay, to clean up, to eat."

"Around here?" she asks, her brow furrowed.

"The suburbs are our only chance," I say. "We can't go to tourist areas looking like this, especially in a stolen car. We'll be arrested on sight and probably blamed for the religious attacks."

I nudge open the door. "Come on." I haul myself out of the car, the weight so heavy in my limbs. And the same sensations hit me as I've noticed since leaving hell.

I feel a new thrumming charge in the air, a stirring energy. It speeds my heartbeat, tightens my chest. And images come of the drivers and station attendants I've seen – their coiled muscles staring at me, the frenzy in their eyes. It all sets my teeth on edge.

I check the street. Still empty. And pretty much every light's off in the apartment buildings, all curtains drawn.

Natasha's climbing out of the car also, moving so slowly, and I wave her away from it. The car's a high-end Mercedes. S-Class. Quite a contrast to the beaten-up minivans and scratched pickups around it.

I pad down the road to the next junction, moving as quietly as possible. Then I press the lock button on the stolen key fob before hastening around the corner and away from the car's winking lights.

And I find myself staring down another empty street of

faded apartment blocks with open dumpsters and vacant yards in between.

I lumber on, heading roughly toward Istanbul city centre, and I can't help scanning the skies for the angels or devil as my mind spirals around why they left us alive.

Then my thoughts flash to Ben. He promised to get us a ticket back home, and he'd want to know what's happened fast. But the weight builds so quickly in my chest.

I shove the thoughts aside and focus on the streets beyond. We reach another junction, a cluster of shops a hundred yards ahead. All closed. And still there's no sign of a hotel or any place to stay. Natasha's head droops lower at my side, her shoulders increasingly hunched and her feet starting to drag. I urge us on faster, my eyes scanning every building.

At the next corner, my gaze finds a group of guys striding across a junction fifty yards away. I freeze and then yank Natasha back and out of sight, my heart pounding.

She stares at me, her eyes so hollow, and I gaze behind her. Our street is still empty. After counting to five, I check the corner again. The group's passed, so we keep plodding on.

Six more blocks. Twice more we're forced to hide from late-night wanderers. And Natasha's moving more sluggishly with every minute. I begin searching garages and private doorways, but everything's locked up tight. And when finally we pass a house with an open front door, my feet stumble to a halt, and my eyes blink at it.

I take a step forward at the same time as a woman comes bustling through the doorway, a broom in hand. She sees me, opens her mouth, and starts yelling. She spits Turkish words at us like hailstones. Her fingers wring tight around the broom handle, and the same frenzy shines black in her eyes.

Spinning away, I grab Natasha and haul her on down the road, keeping to shadows and moving as fast as she allows. The yelling continues, and after another couple of blocks, I glance behind.

Sure enough, a group of people are giving chase – five of

them. They're striding steadily on, getting ever closer. I hurry beyond the next corner onto a smaller road. Its low apartment blocks choke off the night sky. Scanning the fenced-off garages, my mind conjures images of us heaving ourselves over the rusty bars—

I stop and peer forward down the narrow street, just able to make out a faint light shining in the distance. The pavements are lined by apartments and houses with vacant lots in between. No pedestrians, no shops. So, no way it's a hotel. Still, I hasten us faster toward the glow, making sure to approach on the opposite side of the road.

The place is a bar, the light coming from a couple of old neon signs – adverts for a Western beer and a soft drink, their colours fading. The entrance is a set of steps down from street level, two bouncers poised at the top. Both are well dressed, decked out in tailored jackets with pressed white shirts. At a bar, with burned-out signs, in the middle of fucking nowhere.

I sigh, my insides tightening, while Natasha's leaning on my arm now, barely able to walk.

With a bite of my cheek, I grip her around the waist and steer her between parked cars and across the road.

"Follow close," I say, keeping my voice low. "But keep behind."

The two bouncers are joined by a third man who climbs the stairs. He's more casually dressed, in a shirt and trousers. They're all smoking. I step onto the nearby pavement, thirty yards away, and the nearest guy swivels to face me. Then they all do, and silence descends.

I shove my free hand into my pocket and stride up to the first bouncer, my fingers raking the little money that remains. The guy looks me up and down with narrowed eyes, and I grab out a couple of Turkish notes to extend toward him. On automatic, he lifts a hand to take them, and I grip his fingers in a handshake, squeezing the money between his palm and mine.

"Can we come in?" I ask in English, my voice shaking. A

wave of tiredness passes through me, and my legs sway. I force myself to hold the bouncer's gaze.

Eventually, he nods, and I withdraw my hand, leaving the notes in his palm. The guy slinks aside, his eyes on Natasha with a thin smile on his lips. I lead her down the steps into darkness, the smells of damp and stale cigarettes merging in my nostrils, and the glow from the neon signs fades above.

50

AT THE BOTTOM of the steps, I push through a curtain and step into a large, low-lit basement room, the air oppressive with smoke. Natasha presses in closely at my back.

The space is fifty feet wide and almost as deep. Wood panelling covers the walls, and two fans hang from the ceiling, neither working. Three alcoves with chairs and tables have been cut into the side wall while a bar stretches most of the way across the end of the room, a couple of shelves behind it with only a few liquor bottles and no decorations. Another curtained door stands midway along, the only other visible exit.

Stepping forward, I keep my gaze firmly fixed on the four guys standing at one end of the bar. They're all staring directly at us, but no one's speaking. There's no movement aside from a flickering TV that's playing on silent on the far wall.

Three of the guys are young and trim – two in shirts and one in a jacket – and each one holds himself ready. The fourth guy is older, must be in his sixties. His hair is slicked and balding on top, and he's wearing a beaten leather jacket with the sleeves rolled up and a black vest underneath. The guy's well built with powerful arms and shoulders, only some of his bulk gone to seed. He simply gazes back at me, his face impassive.

I stride straight toward him and concentrate on matching his expression. The guy doesn't move a muscle but remains leaning behind the bar. The faded tattoos on his forearms come into focus along with numerous scars and tracts of calloused skin around his knuckles.

Again, I fish out a few bills from my pocket and shove them down on the bar by his arm.

"Can we speak a moment?" I ask, trying to steady my voice.

The barman holds my gaze but gives no indication of whether he's understood my English. While my neck prickles from the three guys staring from Natasha to me, I don't fidget or look away, my old training from years spent in the gang kicking in.

Though, standing there among these people, the void blooms again at my core because I'm back where I fucking started. But now I'm bringing Natasha into it all.

I push against the growing weight and force myself to stand erect. "Please?" I ask and slide the bills toward him across the bar. "Just to talk."

And still, I don't let my gaze waver an inch.

Eventually, the barman turns his head – takes an age over it – and shares a few words in Turkish with his group of guys. They all laugh in response as my toes tap the ground.

"Come," the barman says, his voice gravelly.

He ambles along the bar, keeping it slow and leaving the money where it is. He passes the TV, and my eyes flick to the screen.

Twenty-four-hour news. The sound's off, but the image is clear enough: Paul Hawcross, British prime ministerial candidate and Ben's boss, shaking hands with a leader on the steps of some foreign building while warring crowds scream support and outrage outside the building.

The barman reaches the end of the bar, flips up a section of the wood, and ambles toward an alcove set into the side of the room. I hurry to catch up. There he hefts himself down, his back to the panelled wall, and his arm stretches along the top of a battered leather sofa, leaving us with our back to his minions.

Nevertheless, I pull a couple of stools opposite and sit down.

The barman keeps his eyes on me. He doesn't even glance at Natasha. "So?" he says.

"We need somewhere to sleep," I say. "To clean up."

The barman frowns, the expression hardly visible on his lined face. "This is no hotel," he says, his English heavily accented.

"That's why we're here," I say. "A man with your ... connections. I'm sure you can organise it."

Again, the barman simply stares at me, the grimace all too obvious.

"Just a place to sleep, to clean up," I say again and lift my hands.

Then my thoughts dart to Ben, the weight building inside once more.

"Oh, and a phone call," I find myself adding.

The barman sneers. "So, what do you have for me?"

I slip my hand into my pocket and bring out the key fob for the Mercedes. "An S-Class. Brand new. Parked somewhere safe. Thirty minutes away. I can draw you a map."

The barman stares at the keys, his eyes a fraction wider in the low light. Then a smile pulls at one side of his mouth.

I take a heavy breath and offer the fob. He takes it, not asking where we got the car, not saying a thing. He can probably make most identifiers disappear easily enough.

I retract my hand, the weight continuing to grow.

The barman rises to his feet in the narrow alcove and pockets the fob inside his leather jacket. "I will need to check it out," he says. "Someone will come and get your directions. Then we will see about the room."

The smile remains etched across his lips, its meaning clear enough. The fucker doesn't need to give me anything. He can get the car and throw us out immediately after.

The barman moves to push past me, and I stand and turn sideways, not making much space in the alcove. He's forced to squeeze by me. I raise my hands at the level of his chest, palms toward him, as if to get them out of the way, which means the lapels of his jacket brush my hands as he passes.

Almost beyond me, the barman quickens his step. I dart my fingers into the inside pocket of his jacket, feeling for the fob, and manage to pull it out just as the guy gets out of reach.

He strides back toward the bar while I spin away, the fob enclosed in my palm, and slip the key into my pocket.

The barman shares a joke with his crew, and a few of them laugh. I retreat slowly into the middle of the room and plaster a confused look on my face. Then I swivel. The barman's got his back to me, reaching for a bottle of beer on the bar.

"Excuse me," I say, forcing strength into my tone.

The barman spins back, any levity in his expression gone.

I clear my throat, reach into my pocket, and pull out the key fob, lifting it up. "D'you not need this?"

The barman stares from me to the fob. Then he pats his jacket as his entire crew stares at him.

My heartbeat thumps in my ears while sweat breaks out down my sides. Again, I hold the guy's gaze.

Eventually, the barman leans back and barks a laugh at the ceiling before slapping his hand on the wood, a genuine smile on his lips now.

A slow breath leaks from my lungs.

The barman shakes his head. "You will have to show me how you do that," he says in his stilted English. Then his stare grows intense again. "We will get you your room and Emir can find your car."

———

THIRTY MINUTES LATER, a middle-aged woman is marshalling Natasha and me through another basement door into an underground apartment. She's speaking a near constant stream of Turkish, as she's been doing ever since emerging from the curtained door behind the bar. Standing on the threshold, she offers me a plastic bag filled with packages of wrapped food, the smell of fried meat filling my nose. And she points to a corded phone on a cheap laminate kitchen table.

My phone call.

I take the bag, and she retreats outside, still babbling what might be instructions or warnings. Then she shuts the door behind her, plunging me into silence.

After a moment, I pad back over to the front door. It's solid wood and sturdy with three locks and a chain. Two of them I'm able to fasten from the inside.

Satisfied, I turn and survey the apartment. It's compact with combined kitchen and diner, and a small room with camp beds beyond. Like the bar, it has hardly any decorations, only bare whitewashed walls and brown kitchen cupboards plus a table and four chairs.

Natasha's already shuffling toward the beds while I remain still, just waiting to feel the relief, the calm. It doesn't come, the void still gripping my insides. My eyes find the phone, my thoughts whirling again.

Ben has to know, has to be warned, but what the fuck would we say? We released the devil. The situation is now much worse than it was before, and we're probably tainted, damned.

A wheezy breath comes, the weight as heavy as ever in my bones. Would we risk him by getting in touch?

I stare at the phone and then lumber past it and into the tiny bedroom. Natasha's lying on her side, her legs curled up, with her back to me. She's not moving but not asleep, her breathing shallow, the tension so obvious in her shoulders and neck.

The priest's words in the car return to me – that I'd soon need to be there for her. Is this what he meant?

I sit down on the side of the bed and begin to stroke her arm. Then I brush a strand of hair from her wet cheeks.

"It's okay," I whisper, my voice barely audible. "It'll be okay."

However, my doubting thoughts whirl faster, the abyss dropping further away inside.

Gradually, Natasha's breathing deepens. Her body settles, and her eyelids flutter as she drifts into dreams. I unfold a blanket from the neighbouring camp bed and drape it over her before clicking off the light in the room. And I just stand there. Alone.

For the first time, Father Thomas's death presses in at me. My heart aches like it's been stripped raw. I drop my head, tears welling at the corners of my eyes. With Natasha asleep, I finally let them come.

The priest's warm smile, his faith in me, in our path. All gone. Silent tears trace paths down my cheeks, reach my chin, and fall onto the blanket at my side.

At the end of things, Father Thomas still chose to believe. The bigger picture, the broader story. *Trust this.* Yet in that moment, it couldn't feel further from the truth. And as Natasha sleeps on, I take a shuddering breath. The old man's gone. No longer here to help us make sense of it all.

So, I just sit here ... on my own ... with the shadows deepening all around.

THE FAITH TRILOGY reaches its gripping conclusion in book three – **Death** – which is currently available on Amazon. If you've not grabbed your free ebook – **Faction** – join my reader list today and get a bonus deleted scene from Wrath as well as updates on the series:

https://www.thefaithtrilogy.com/wrath

SPREADING THE FAITH?

Thanks so much for joining Natasha and Jake on their second adventure. If you've enjoyed the trilogy so far and have a moment to spare, I would greatly appreciate a short review on Amazon. Even just a sentence is wonderful, and reviews make a big difference in helping new readers find the series. Thank you!

FACTION - YOUR FREE EBOOK IS WAITING

Destroying Gabriel's disease was just the beginning. Now Natasha and Jake are on the run, hiding from an irate archangel, and being urged by Father Thomas to develop the abilities they'll need for the coming fight. Natasha's desperate to discover Gabriel's plan, to identify angelic activity, while Jake's working hard just to keep them safe.

Yet perhaps he's looking in the wrong place.

When the gang that enslaved him for six years re-emerge, they aren't merely seeking their best thief; it turns out a growing Mandem army want Jake for a specific job, and one that bears all the hallmarks of the angelic activity he's trying so desperately to avoid.

Jake soon realises that what's at stake isn't just his own freedom and Natasha's safety, but the freedom and safety of a growing army of the downtrodden – young grunts just like him. And as Mandem's plan unfolds, it becomes clear that there won't be a corner of London unaffected.

In this heart-pounding tale of survival and rebellion, Jake must confront his past, harness his powers, and lead a revolution against forces both human and divine. The fate of a city hangs in the balance.

If you have not already received it, get a free ebook copy of this short story between Faith and Wrath – **Faction** – along with updates on the series and a bonus deleted scene from Wrath, by visiting:

https://www.thefaithtrilogy.com/wrath

ABOUT NICK NIELSEN

Nick loves reading clever, fast-paced, and engaging fantasy stories which say something about the real world we live in. So much so that he decided to write them. Professionally, he's an award-winning entrepreneur, the director of the social change agency Osca, and the founder of Envision – a Guardian Charity Award winner. He's also a winner of the Shackleton Leadership Award. In his fantasy stories he leans heavily not only on his professional background working in the area of behavioural psychology, but on his twenty-year experience learning from real magicians – practitioners of the mystical arts – from Eastern, Western, and African lineages. Nick lives in London with his wife, two overly chilled teenage children, and one neurotic bunny rabbit.

ACKNOWLEDGMENTS

First to you, the reader, for not only investing your valuable time in this book but also for continuing through the scrubland of the back matter to find out who I might be humbly thanking. And first of all ... this is you. Your care and attention are the reason we authors write – to entertain, enliven, and bring you joy. But this is only possible because of your curiosity and commitment, without which there would be fewer stories, and the world would be a considerably poorer place.

So thank you. I sincerely hope you found the investment worthwhile.

Continuing on, there are a great many people to thank. Foremost is Leslie Watts, this trilogy's amazing editor. When I first came to her five years ago with the story idea, she showed nothing but enthusiasm for the project, despite the roughness of my writing. I am so thankful for her kindness and enduring patience in helping me to improve my craft over the innumerable drafts, for her dedication to the project over the five years it took to complete, and her absolute commitment to the craft in not letting me run ahead and publish before the books were as good as we could make them.

In finishing the final versions, thank you so much to Amanda Brown for her love of the words, and to Alison Birch for her eagle eye. Thank you also to Stuart Bache for the wonderful cover designs.

And then there's my amazing tribe. Thank you Eva and Luke for your love, patience, and impatience with this project, and for understanding the stupid thing their dad does every single morning at five am. Thank you, Beth for always being there, for being my biggest supporter and most demanding critic, and for more than I can ever say. Thank you to a mother whose heart and home are always open, and to a father for whom it all became too much in the end. We miss you, we honour your choice, and we thank you for everything you gave us. Thank you, brothers and sisters – Thomas, Trine, Sach, and last but definitely not least, Steph. Thank you, fellow story craft lover, both for the ongoing support with this project and for walking alongside me on this crazy journey.

Thank you to my own Father Thomas – Colin, Saniel, and Krishna. My debt of gratitude to you, your care, and your work is also more than I can express.

Thank you to my readers over the years – to Ian, Mark, Chris, Thomas, Debs, Ray, and Dave – and to my teachers of the craft, Danielle and Rachel and the many others. Thank you also to Shawn Coyne without whom these books would have been published five years ago, and yet so much of the richness in both them and me would have been lacking.

Thank you to Ian Craig, who was there near the beginning. And thank you to Jean who encouraged me right from the start. It's almost fifteen years ago now, and I don't know if I'd have gotten here without you.

Thank you all.

www.thefaithtrilogy.com

For any enquiries regarding this book, please email: nick@thefaithtrilogy.com

British English spellings have been used.

Book Cover by Stuart Bache.

Printed in Great Britain
by Amazon

39454795R00202